J.D. Astra

With

J.A. Hunter

Viridian Gate Online:

FIREBRAND

ELDGARD

SVARTALFHEIM
STONE REACH
GLOME CORRIE
THE BARREN SANDS
THE BLEAK SEA
ANKARA
ELDGARD
HARROWICK
WYRDTIDE
NEW VIRIDIA
TANGLEWOOD
ROWANHEATH
WEST VIRIDIA
SHINING PLAINS
N
STORME MARSHES
ALAUNHYLLES
YUNNAIR
RAE HAIM

ONE

Apocalypse Hacking

THE CLICKS AND CLACKS OF MY KEYSTROKES reverberating off the empty chairs and standing desks at Osmark Tech were the only sounds, aside from the hammering of my heart. I'd been afraid before, working for Osmark, but never *this* scared. If I was right, they would do much worse than kill me for what I was about to commit.

My cursor lingered over the "deploy to prod" button. Under normal working hours, my fresh lines of code would've been peer-reviewed, sent through the sanity checker, unit tested, then deployed to staging. But eight months straight of crunch coupled with the impending doom of the planet left everyone eager to get to their capsules when Osmark dismissed us not an hour before.

I glanced around the large open space one more time to ensure everyone had in fact gone, my heart still jackhammering away. My finger trembled as I pressed and held the left-click down. I could still back out, forget what I'd read, forget I had seen what Osmark had planned.

"No one else is going to stop him. You *must* figure out what these 'scrolls of allegiance' are, and why so many high-rolling wretches paid out the wazoo for them," I reminded myself, then inhaled deeply.

"Plus, you spent your entire overtime bonus check sending Jack that capsule. You're gonna need something more than just the end of the world to break the ice when you meet up again, and you know how much Jack loves a good dungeon crawl. If that's what this is. Who knows what billionaire drug dealers pay millions for in a virtual world? It could be full of godmode codes that somehow subvert our anti-cheating protocols."

My hand curled to a ball as I retracted my finger, doing the undoable. The screen read, "Committing new code to production. Estimated Completion —> 280 seconds."

The building trembled at the sound of a muffled crash, accompanied by terrified shouts, and my gaze shot past the screen to the fading light outside. It had been a while since I took more than a fleeting glance out a window, a few days at least. Most of us had elected to stay indefinitely at Osmark Tech since the global announcement of 213 Astraea weeks ago, as it was just safer here.

I walked to the massive UV-protected glass framed by columns of wide-leafed plants that hadn't been watered in weeks and looked down the eight stories to the streets below.

Chaos. That was the only word to describe it. Someone had driven a truck through the screaming mob, trying to ram down the doors of Osmark Technologies, but they had failed. A fiery, smoking wreck lay at the foot of our building, and civilians scrambled to get out of blast range.

When Osmark ordered security improvements for the front desk a few months ago, reinforcing the walls and windows of the bottom floors, I thought it was just because of the recent mass shootings, to protect us from something like that. Not something like this. Not trying to protect us from desperate cries for salvation.

213 Astraea, nine miles of pure destruction, was what they were terrified of. A mass of rock and ice carving a path through space on a collision course with our little speck of paradise: Earth. I was scared too, but less so. I knew I had a chamber waiting in the basement where I would hopefully transition into the game I'd been helping develop for the last four years. A lifeboat for humanity. Viridian Gate Online.

A lifeboat that had cost me six precious months with my father and being there for his dying breath. *It's critical*, Osmark had said, *life altering*. I wish he'd told us all the truth sooner—it would make resenting him for missing my father's funeral a little harder. But no. Osmark was a deplorable man and a terrifying boss. He'd known about Astraea for months and refused to tell us until he realized DevOps wouldn't complete until it was too late. He told us a few weeks before the global announcement, some kind of incentive to work harder.

Still, I chose to trade the last minutes of my father's life for work. Osmark had needed me, but if I had left, even for one day to see my father into the ground, he would've made sure no one needed me. I would've been blacklisted to the tech industry, my career and sole source of income destroyed.

If I'd known then there wouldn't be any other sources of income today, I would've gone to see him, at least one last time. To hell with Osmark, he would've taken me back. We had been desperate for Senior Systems Architects for months since the last three abandoned the game at the news of Astraea. The excuses didn't make me feel much better, but now that we all had somewhere safe at the end of the world, I was less upset about my choice.

Plus, I had another choice now and a new purpose. I was going to discover Osmark's plan with these in-game "scrolls_of_allegiance" and end his reign here, before it could transfer into the game. He would never control anyone like he did at Osmark Tech, never again.

I took one last glance below and mourned the loss of so much life. They wouldn't get in, not until I and the other employees transitioned into the game, and even then, there were only four hundred capsules they could use. In a day or two, a security team would run a raffle and bring in one thousand two hundred people from the screaming mob. With the transition taking up to seventy-two hours, a little under twelve days left until Astraea hit, and a one in six chance of dying instead of transitioning, we could only save about twelve hundred lives by reusing our capsules. A few less, if we counted the technicians who had the gut-churning job of removing the corpses from the capsules and cleaning them for another occupant.

My watch buzzed, and I turned the face toward me. "Deploy Complete" read the email title. I jogged past the desks full of half-drank coffee cups, plates with pizza crusts, and empty packets of Skittles. My computer screen came to life at my touch, and I checked the full deploy log. "Warning: error in (NullObjectReference-CaCoCa_Scroll) - Line 241."

The pounding in my chest dropped to the pit of my stomach.

"You have got to be shitting me."

I pulled up the console, fingers dancing across the keyboard like a drunkard's ballet; violent and clumsy. No, no, no. This can't be happening. Not *now*! I checked my watch again: 5:28. I had approximately thirty minutes to get to the Integration Room: our *mass grave*. I needed to watch this push through to completion. There was no way I would go into V.G.O. not knowing if the code was actually delivered.

Line 241… the line referencing the in-game object [Aleixo_Carrera-Scroll_of_Allegiance.OBJ]. How is that possible? The object doesn't exist yet? I traced the lines of code backwards through mentions and discovered the culprit.

Tricky son of a bitch. Osmark had the game data committed, but the .OBJ for the actual scroll wasn't in there. He was going to run a patch in approximately eleven hours that would remove the <inactive> flag and deploy the scroll .OBJs automatically.

I could just create my own scroll .OBJ from any random asset lying around and copy the data… but that might not work. There could be something else at play here and—

"Attention, all employees," the PA system rang out, and I jumped, my train of thought derailed. "The Integration Room will be locked for your safety in approximately thirty minutes. If you have elected to participate in Osmark Technology's V.G.O. integration, please wrap up your personal affairs and proceed to sub-level three to claim your capsule. Thank you."

The synthetic voice was more than enough to raise hairs. Osmark and his core team were at the pinnacle of AI creation, making things so close to real, they'd pass a Turing Test some humans couldn't. So, why they had gone with a cold and jagged, easily distinguished AI voice for the office PA, I guess I'd never know.

I turned my attention back to the problem at hand, pushing and prodding at Osmark's security systems, praying not to set off any alarms. Blocked, rigged, protected… damn it. There was simply not enough time to do this hack. I'd have to get creative, quick. I pulled the desk into standing mode, and my back straightened as my fingers gained their last purpose.

Selentium was from the days of old, it was automation script for the web, but I knew how to make it sing for any task. I cranked away, script after script, lacing together a fragile plan. Coroutines within subroutines emerged until finally I had it. My automated script would open the console and run command line to deploy my filesync to prod exactly five minutes after Osmark's. Meaning I would be delivered a copy of that Scroll of Allegiance five minutes after he was and know exactly what he was up to with that secret area. Or that was my hope.

I'd have to pick my username carefully, as that was the only thing binding this code to my in-game persona. A few keystrokes, a username, that's all that stood between Osmark and the likely tyranny of what remained of the human race.

The overhead PA system sprang to life again. "All employees, please be aware the Integration Room will be locked for your safety in fifteen minutes."

Just enough time for a test run. I set the timer on the automated script to the current time and drummed my fingers, *rat-a-tap, rat-a-tap*, as it executed. Command prompts opened, filled with lines of code, and closed. I sighed as the deployment screen read, "Committing new code to production. Estimated Completion —> 280 seconds."

I chewed on my bottom lip, watching the seconds tick down and not allowing other thoughts, self-defeating thoughts, to enter my mind. The server came back with the same error on line 241. Perfect. I changed the time back, set the computer to stay awake, and unplugged the monitor, just in case someone wandered through and felt like turning it off to save a few watts of power at the end of the world.

"All employees, please be aware the Integration Room will be locked for your safety in ten minutes."

"I know!" I roared at the ceiling.

My heart thumped again as I imagined missing the deadline. I grabbed my backpack and jacket… then stopped. I wouldn't need them where I was going. The straps slipped from my shoulders, and I reached for the picture of my mom and dad on my desk.

"I'm so sorry I wasn't there. I'll make you proud, I promise."

I returned the picture to its place on the desk and jogged from the empty room. The typically bustling halls were devoid of life. Everyone had either gone home to accept their fate or run to the Integration Room for their final transition. I pressed the button for the elevator and imagined what it would be like to live life out in a video game. Not even live it out, but live *forever*.

I loved RPGs just as much as the next nerd, but to never grow old, never raise a family—unless Osmark had another team working on a secret fertility project—it would be life without progress. Well, not so true. We would have our character levels, stats, the talent tree, gear, and plenty of dungeons to raid as long as the ever-present, godlike Overminds did their jobs. Maybe it wouldn't be so bad.

Ping! My eyes shot forward as the elevator doors opened, and a familiar face stared back at me. "Hi, Leon," I said without much gusto. Leon was a technical artist. He had spent his last few days making sure noses could scale appropriately to face dimensions.

"Hey, Abby. Headed to the Integration Room?" He placed his hand against the door for me.

I nodded. "Yeah. Just wrapped up the last call with my mom," I lied. I called my mom three days ago and begged her, for the very last time, to accept Osmark's offer for family of the V.G.O. team to transition into the game for free. She refused. *I miss him. I want to see him soon.* She believed in an afterlife. Believed that my father was waiting for her in heaven. I hoped she would find peace at the end, no matter what happened after death.

"Yeah, it's nice to have some family to confide in at the end of the world." He shrugged his shoulders, gaze dropping to his shoes. Poor guy, he probably didn't have anyone.

The elevator doors tried to close again, and I hurried in next to him.

"So, have it all planned out?" he asked with a plastic grin as I pressed B3.

"Have what planned?" My voice peaked a little too high, my heart pounding as I thought of the code waiting to deploy on my machine.

He elbowed me casually. "I assumed Abby the Architect would know exactly what race you were going with, what city you'd make your home, what class you'd pick." He laughed. "You're such a planner, I figured you would have everything worked out by now."

I gave him a curt smile. I had some of it planned, sure, but it's not like I couldn't roll with the punches. That was the point of Viridian Gate Online: as soon as you felt you had your bearings, Sophia or Enyo would throw a curveball.

The Overminds, computer AI game-masters, were always ready to increase the difficulty or create a new challenge. Strife was the point of Enyo's existence, and Sophia sought *balance*, though it was a vague term. It sought to ensure the player had *just* enough difficulty to remain entertained, but not so much they wanted to ragequit.

Three months ago, ragequit would've meant a loss of revenue for Osmark Tech, but now, ragequit meant something entirely different. How would someone quit the game? Suicide, was it even possible? Could you end your simulation voluntarily? The questions turned my gut.

"Anyway, I hope you make it." He gave me a nudge as the doors to B3 opened, and he walked away.

"You too," I called after him, my short legs unable to keep up with his *please get me out of this situation* pace.

I did hope Leon made it. I wanted to make it, too.

The white concrete walls amplified the sound of Leon's hasty retreat from me, and I felt more alone than ever. I was going to die. Perhaps my consciousness would be copied into the game simulation, but perhaps not. There was a near 17% chance that I would die for real and never make it into the game permanently.

The unending thump of my heart faltered as I thought of my whole life. Was it a life I was proud to lead? Maybe. My thoughts fell on my father, my mother, how I wasn't *there*. Sure, I would call, and I would video chat, but it wasn't the same as being *there*. Was I a good person?

"Attention, employees, the Integration Room is now closing."

My breath caught in my throat and I ran. The doors were sliding shut, but I slipped through with a sigh.

I took in the tomb: short ceiling, maybe eight feet, fresh concrete everywhere, organized, methodical, and sterile. Osmark had bought and renovated this space months ago for a "storage center." What could we possibly store as a tech company, other than servers?

Coffins. Or their equivalent. We would die in the capsules. Either by transitioning from our bodies into the game or by being incompatible with the code and wasting away into cardiac arrest after three days. Then our bodies would be removed, and the capsules reused for some of the dying mob outside the gates of salvation.

My eyes roved over the claustrophobia-inducing landscape, and the memory of the first death, the first disappearance into the game, replayed in my mind. I recalled Osmark and his right hand, Sandra, standing on the stage in front of employees and investors, describing the incident.

They'd downplayed the death like it was just another failed prototype, wrote off the loss of human life like a dysfunctional server. What they didn't explain was how they'd *lost* the human consciousness into the code. It was processed and digitized, then vanished into the trillions of functions executing every second.

"Abigail Hollander!"

UGH! Abigail is not *my name!* I wanted to say, but I turned to Tristen, my manager-who-wished-he-wasn't-my-manager, with a terse smile.

"What's up, Tristen?" I hoped he wasn't going to go on about, "Now that I'm not your manager anymore, could we like, go out for pizza some time?" Or would it be roasted chicken now? I didn't think pizza made it into V.G.O.

He eyed me with teeth clenched. "You were cutting it close. What were you doing?"

My stomach fluttered at the thought of what I was *actually* doing for the last hour. Hacking into Osmark's private code, inspecting his future commits, writing automated code to copy them, and more.

"I had to call my mom. She didn't want to transition, so I had to say goodbye for good." I entwined my fingers, not wanting them to wiggle and look suspicious.

"Oh." Tristen looked down, then placed an awkward hand on my shoulder. "I'm really sorry."

"It's fine. We said what we had to say, and I'm ready." I filled my chest with air in an attempt to shake his hand from my body, but he held tighter.

"That's good. We need people like you in the new world."

The New World, Osmark's world. My resolve returned. I wouldn't let him dominate the people who put their faith in him, in Osmark Tech. Sure, they may "survive," but would they be saved? No. They were entering into a dictatorship they couldn't have imagined. Not on my watch.

"Yeah, totally. I hope it's just as awesome as we coded it." I smiled again, trying to get out from under his grasp, but his grip was strong as he pulled me into an embrace.

"It's going to be okay."

I gritted my teeth and pulled away. "Yeah, it's going to be fine." I offered him a punch to the shoulder, and his cheeks flushed red.

"What's your username? Maybe we could meet up?"

I bit my lip. "I haven't picked mine yet. I haven't had a chance to play at all." I shrugged to mask the lie about not picking my name, and he laughed.

"Yeah, cool. Great. Well, maybe I'll just see you around."

My lips pursed. "Yeah, definitely."

He shuffled his feet, and as I turned away, he grabbed my hand.

"Abby…" His voice was soft.

"What's up, Tristen?" I didn't want to hear it again. I wanted to get into the game. I wanted to start leveling. I *needed* to get a head start on Osmark, because his people definitely had a head start on me.

"I just wanted to say… you're awesome."

I stopped short. It wasn't the same old rhetoric of *why aren't we dating*. He was just being nice.

"You're awesome too, Tristen." I smiled.

He nodded. "It was nice being your manager. I hope these last eight months weren't absolute torture."

It was perhaps my last human interaction ever. I had to make it count. I had to try my best.

"Yeah, you did a great job. I hope you make it."

He gave me a thumbs-up, classic Tristen. "I'll see you in there. My tag is Triskiller."

I groaned under my breath. What a terrible name to be stuck with for the rest of your life. But whatever.

I walked the rows, looking for "H." So many D's, what the heck? Ah, "H." I walked in a few capsules to find pod 8. It was open and ready to receive me.

Unlike in Star Trek, the pod next to me didn't have a glass cover. I couldn't see the person inside, couldn't watch them decay as their body died in the transition.

"Ms. Hollander. Please remove your clothing down to your underwear," the pod said in the same artificial PA voice.

"Why?" I asked, though when I looked down, the clothes of those near to me littered the floor.

"The transition can be difficult on the body, and heat regulation is important. Removing some items of clothing can help us do that at a lower cost."

There Osmark goes with the costs. Of course, do it fast, do it well, do it cheap. He wanted every point on the iron triangle, and he got it. Not by noble means, but he got it. This game would be amazing, a technical wonder, completed by slave labor and crime. Who would oppose him at the end of the world, though?

I unbuttoned my shirt, removed my flats, then my slacks, and hopped up into the tanning bed gone

VRMMORPG simulator. I took my last breath in this world and closed the lid with the touch of a button.

It was dark for a moment, and as the machined whirred to life, so did the white loading screen. "Hello, I'm the CEO of Osmark Technologies, Robert Osmark, and I'd like to personally welcome you to Viridian Gate Online, the most advanced full-immersion video game in the world." Osmark's voice was unmistakable.

I blinked hard, and his face came into view. Such a retro, Steve Jobs look. Thin-rimmed, round glasses, dark turtleneck, and shaggy hair about his face.

He went on. "Viridian Gate Online is truly the first of its kind. And that's not the typical hyperbolic language so cavalierly tossed around in tech circles. No, I can assure you, I truly mean this is the first of its kind."

Yeah, yeah, yeah. Get me into the game!

"Our revolutionary work with massive memristive neuromorphic computing systems has created a paradigm shift in AI technologies, and the result is an experience second to none. Moreover, through Osmark's patented NexGenVR capsule you will experience a whole new world as though you were there in the flesh. Even the pain is real."

The system stuttered, Osmark froze on screen, and the robotic voice of the AI took over. "Patch 1.3_e announcement update: Employees of Osmark Tech."

Osmark's face resumed its idle movements. "Hello, employees of Osmark Technologies, or close friends and family of the employee." I was tired of hearing his nasally, droning voice, mostly because I'd heard it so many times in the last few months.

"You have done us, no, humanity, a great service. Either you contributed to the game, Viridian Gate Online, or you supported a technician working day and night to complete this new world. For that, we all owe you our lives. This couldn't have been possible without you and the contributions of our benefactors."

Benefactors. Right. He meant the politicians and criminals. Those able to give worldly support for virtual compensation when the end came.

"In the next seventy-two hours, you may experience some discomfort, and at the end of it, one in six will not be able to survive the transition to the game. Allow me to explain how it works."

Osmark's recording went into the layman's version of the nano-tech copying the brain's patterns line for line into a digital form over the next three days.

"Truthfully, that's far more candid than I ever expected to be about how the process works, but this is the end of the world." Osmark offered a genuine, yet exhausted, smile. I appreciated that. He was a dick and a whip cracker, but he could be real sometimes.

He went on to further explain that the nanobots now coursing through my veins would be copying my *essence* and uploading it to the servers deep underground, protected from the catastrophic EMP 213 Astraea would discharge on entering our atmosphere.

"We installed neural inhibitors into all the capsules which automatically logged players out after six hours of gameplay, but Patch 1.3 has changed all that. The neural inhibitors have all been disabled, and after twenty-four hours of in-game time, the logout button will permanently disappear, leaving you stranded in the game."

No skin off my back, I didn't plan on logging out.

"If you choose to upload yourself to Viridian Gate Online, you have a chance at surviving Astraea, at least in a digital form. Now, let me take a moment to address some of the concerns circulating around the internet rumor mill. First, I can personally assure everyone listening to this message that Patch 1.3 is our last major update—the game is locked, and all essential functions are now being administered by the AI controllers."

The *Overminds*. I knew them all pretty well, understood their roles. I had to. My code needed to know who to call to complete a function, so I'd had to learn them all, though I only created code for two of them: Enyo, the Overmind of Chaos, and Sophia, the Overmind of Balance.

Osmark went on to discuss the fears of hacking, which we "secured" against. We certainly did our best, but someone with time and a lot of dedication could hack what we did. It would be hard, nearly impossible with the time the world had left, but they could do it.

"By watching this warning, you hereby remove all liability of damages from Osmark Technologies, its corporate owners, and its subsidiary entities. Would you still like to proceed?"

I knew what needed to be done, and I was the one to do it. Even if I only had three days until my heart stopped, perhaps stopped for good, I would make them count. I would make Osmark pay.

I cherished my last moment as a living, breathing, fleshy being, then answered. "Yes."

TWO

DEV DIVE

THE SENSATION OF PLUMMETING ON A RAGING rollercoaster sent shivers up my spine as an imaginary world of wonder rushed up to meet my feet. Or was I falling? Mountainous peaks, sprawling fields of green, huge shimmering lakes, and the pockmarks of civilization came into view on the brilliant globe I was steadily approaching.

"Traveler"—the booming voice of an announcer, the same one from our commercials, added to my gut-clenching nerves as I soared—"prepare to enter Viridian Gate Online!"

Icy wind nipped at my exposed skin as the virtual "floor" drew ever nearer. I was certain the very first experience after the loading screen wouldn't be painful, but for a moment, I wondered if this was Osmark's last brutal act on the employees. A character screen created just for us in the 1.3_e patch designed to hurt us on entry.

I closed my eyes when the ground was a few yards away, but the rushing of air slowed, and the queasiness in my gut subsided. A gentle vibration shook my legs as I touched down, and I peeled my eyes open.

It was breathtaking. Snowcapped peaks loomed in the distance, with one spitting gouts of liquid red: an active volcano. Flowers on the grassy knolls below blew in a gentle wind that smelled of pollen and pine. My senses were alive with the outputs of the virtual world, and *damn*, it was hard to tell the difference.

The pine scent was less woody than I remembered, but pleasant all the same. The slight chill to the wind raised hairs on my arms. *My arms*. I inspected my body to find it all looked just like me, but cleaner somehow. The fifteen-year-old scars on my arms from my hellacious cat were gone, and the skin was unbelievably smooth to the touch.

I ran my left hand up my forearm, and suddenly, it was sensory overload. I gasped for air, bending at the waist and placing my hands on my knees. It took a moment, but a few steady breaths later, my racing heart was calm. *Wow*. So, this is what I helped create.

Thunder crackled overhead, and dark storm clouds moved in from over the mountain peaks. Tiny droplets speckled my body, and I turned my face up to the sky. It felt absolutely indistinguishable from the real thing. I opened my mouth and caught a few of the sweet, slightly sulfurous drops in my mouth.

"Volcano water." I gripped my throat and hummed, feeling the vibration of my vocal cords. It sounded like me, too.

As if sensing my discovery moment was over, the game prompted me with a character creation pop-up. The view filled my forward vision with a transparent overlay, and my body was the subject matter of the window. It had me in little more than a bikini, but I guess it was necessary to see nearly all the parts of my forever-body.

Short, shorter than I'd really liked growing up, dark skin that shimmered from the rain, brown eyes, a teardrop face made even more so by the auto smoothing of the game simulation, a mess of brown curls down to my chest, and generously curved hips… though quite a bit less pudge on my tummy. Eight months of Osmark-mandated crunch with takeout every day, candy whenever stressed—which was always—copious amounts of sugary coffee, and very little exercise had left me chubby. I was relieved to see the game ignored my recently added pounds.

It was fantastic to have my pre-hell-year body back and better than ever in the snap of a nano-synapse. But this was no time to admire myself. It was time to get down to business.

The interface running along the left side gave way to all the options I could engage with: Race, Build, Gender, Face, and Name. I eyed the Name tab, my heart thumping in worry. If I got this wrong, everything I'd done in the other life to discover Osmark's plan would be moot.

First, the body I would use for however long the game simulation ran. I scrolled through the races, though I'd already settled on Wode weeks ago. I wanted to look human, like I had in the real world, so I could keep a bit of my mother and father with me. *But* it never hurt to see what I'd look like with wings!

I scrolled to Accipiter and selected it. With a pop, my human form shifted, growing massive dark-feathered wings laced with hints of gold, just like my hair. My skin took on an almond hue, growing a little lighter, and my eyes became a piercing yellow to match the highlights of my wings. The teardrop shape to my face became hawklike, my nose growing narrower along with my cheeks. My body leaned out as well, the curvy hips sculpted into longer legs, with pointed feet that hovered just above an invisible ground as my massive wings pumped.

Beautiful! A pop-up appeared at the bottom of the semitranslucent window.

Accipiters

Though war-torn and isolated to the Burning Sands, this gregarious race thrives in the deserts of the far west. While most make their homes in the grand shimmering city of Ankara, known for its crystal spires, some still take to the mountainous wastes beyond. The Accipiters' nimble shape and lightweight bones give them a +10% Dexterity bonus at all levels; however, they are restricted from wearing heavier weight armor, such as plate mail. Accipiters excel at classes requiring speed and keen eyes, such as rangers.

Ugh, but so impractical. Accipiters had a sweet dexterity bonus, but that's not at all what I needed for my class. Wodes didn't have any bonuses like the Accipiter, but it didn't have any restrictions, either. I could be whatever class I wanted, with features that matched my IRL body.

I idly scanned past a few of the other options. Imperials, very Anglo looking. Risi, massive, terrifying, positively *disgusting* looking seven-foot beef slabs with skin ranging from a gray-green to a puke-inducing lime green. Hvitalfar, also known as Dawn Elves, were tall, delicate looking things that served well as caster classes due to their Spirit bonus. I was tempted to pick a Hvitalfar, but I didn't want to look like a Barbie doll for the rest of my life. Dokkalfar, the Murk Elves, were similarly tall, with pointed ears, but that's where the similarities stopped. The Dokkalfar were dark-haired, dark-skinned, dark-eyed, with athletic builds. They looked cool, but their poison resistance bonus was fairly useless to me.

Okay, enough messing around. I inhaled, holding my breath at the top, and switched over to Wode as I sighed. My form shifted back to regular Abby, and I was a little disappointed to see her. Another pop-up appeared at the bottom of my screen.

Wodes (Human)

The most numerous of Eldgard's races, the Wodes are a flexible and resilient people known for their impressive stature and steadfast nature. Though Wodes are not blessed with any particular affinity for one class or another, they can assume any profession or nonrestricted class without penalty. This adaptability has allowed the Wodes to spread far and wide, making them as at home in the mountains as in the forests or plains.

Yep, that was my boring pick. I fiddled with my height a little, just a little, and my face structure before looking on the Abby I'd live in for the rest of my life with mild satisfaction. It was Abby 1.5, not quite a 2.0 shift. She looked fierce, strong, beautiful—taller—but still me. I selected the "create" button, and a new prompt appeared.

Time for my name. Why oh why had I decided to go with Abby Hollander as my username? Because I was rushed and panicked? I'd planned out several other awesome names a week ago, but when the moment came to code in where I would direct the scroll copy, I choked, forgot, and typed in my name. I rolled my eyes. Too late now.

"Abby Hollander," I said aloud, though I was certain I didn't need to.

The guy from the commercial was back again. "Are you sure you would like to create Abby Hollander, the Wode? Once you create a character, you will not be able to change your racial identity or name. Please confirm."

"I confirm."

The character screen disappeared, and the full view of the mountains was restored. The storm clouds swirled over the active volcano, and steam billowed up where the rain fell on the rivers of lava coursing their way down the obsidian mountainside.

Nothing was happening.

"Hello?"

I turned and looked over each shoulder, suddenly paranoid that Osmark had found me out and had stopped my character creation process. If he figured it out before I transitioned, he could kill me in the tube out IRL, where I was helpless and unaware.

Trumpets blared, and I screamed, holding my chest to keep my pounding heart from escaping.

"The year is 1095 A.I.C.—*Anno Imperium Conditae*," the disembodied announcer bellowed over the music, and I swallowed back the knot of fear in my throat. It was just standard loading lag. No one knew what I'd done or what I was about to do.

"Dark power and the stirrings of war ride upon the winds of Eldgard, the provincial outpost of the Great Viridian Empire."

The view before me became murky, waving and bubbling like I was looking through a stream.

"Imperial legions," the announcer continued, "allied with the forces of light, march from the east, bringing the natives of Eldgard to their knees through flame, magic, and steel."

My vision filled with the scene of a massive battlefield. All manner of dark-aligned creatures, ogre-like Risi, the dark-skinned Dokkalfar, Wodes, and more charged across a field made bare from so much combat in a disorganized horde. The battle formations of Imperials stood unmoving on the opposing side, their plate armor gleaming under the smoke-streaked sun, and war banners whipping with a crack in the wind.

"Bringing progress. Building roads. Cities. A kingdom. Civilizing the dark-natured Wodes, the swamp-dwelling Dokkalfar, and the Accipiter of the far-western deserts, enlightening them in the ways of the Ever-victorious Empire."

Silhouetted by the setting sun, a grand white castle surrounded by innumerable hills littered with homes faded in as the forces on the battlefield collided. Sprays of blood and spurts of elemental magic sparkled at the impact points, and the cries of the combat filled my ears.

"But the natives of Eldgard are not so quick to give up the old ways—to heel for foreign masters. Though the rebellion is yet small, they fight on. Hour by hour, day by day…"

The ground dropped away, leaving the storm clouds above as I soared over a marshy swamp filled with gnarled deciduous trees and murky water. Another overlay, two dark-skinned Dokkalfar, appeared before me. They stood tall, the male clad in oiled leathers with a wicked bow at his side and fletched arrows at his back, the female in a crudely stitched robe with a short sword affixed to a belt at her side.

Light exploded from behind me, washing away the forest and Murk elves as a flock of Accipiters flew over me, curved right, and loosed nocked arrows from steel bows. The enemy below cowered in the rain of arrows and—

The vision rippled, faded out, and Germanic Wodes working away in a forge overtook the space before me. The furnace blazed, heating my face. I touched my cheek in surprise as the cutscene affected me. The sound of metal on metal rang as a blacksmith hammered down on a red-hot sword.

"But in the far-flung North," the narrator's voice boomed again, startling me, "another threat looms." The working Wodes waved away into frigid mountain peaks topped with pure white snow.

"The reclusive, mountain-dwelling Svartalfar have unwittingly burrowed into the prison of a dusty and long-forgotten god. A monstrous being of true dark, eager to return to the land of mortals once more."

The scene rushed forward, through the mountainside and deep into the smoldering caverns below. I passed through stout dwarf creatures as they mined away at precious metals and jewels, coming to a rest in front of a crack etched into a rocky mining surface. The wall trembled, and the crack widened, purple-blue light spilling through the opening. A piercing green eye peered through the gap, sending shocks of electricity through my limbs.

"The breach is small, but large enough for Serth-Rog, Daemon Prince of Morsheim, to call acolytes to his cause… Imperial. Rebel. Light. Dark. Living. Dead. Which side will you choose?"

There was a tugging in my gut, and the scene rushed away from me as if I were being flung from the mountain. I passed through the walls harmlessly and sailed backwards through the air away from the frosty peak. My stomach dropped as I soared over the chain of rocky spires, and I resisted the primal urge to close my eyes as I imagined splatting hard against the ground.

The mountain range gave way to smaller hills and green valleys, and my backwards death-flight slowed. My whipping hair changed to a soft flutter, and my feet touched down on solid ground. I fell to my knees, gasping for precious air after holding my breath.

What. A. *Rush!*

The emotions, the feelings, the sensations, everything was so spot-on to the real thing. I'd never flown backwards through the air over a mountain range at 100 miles per hour IRL, but I assumed it would've felt just like that.

I gained my feet, brushing gravel from my roughly sewn robes… *those* would have to go, soon. The garment was long sleeved, but baggy, brown, and the texture of a potato sack. I felt around and found a string at the waist, which I pulled tighter, and two pockets at the hips. Great.

The air was chilled, sun just reaching the tops of the peaks not far off from the valley I'd landed in, and the wind carried the scent of a campfire. I hummed and closed my eyes. I hadn't been camping in years. Oh, it was glorious, the smell better than I remembered. But there was something else on the wind, too. The clashing of steel, children screaming, and a host of cackles sounding like the Witch of the West.

My eyes shot open, focusing on the town not far down the barren slope in front of me. Without a doubt, my NPC, non-player character, companion would be there. That entity was the key to success in the game. They would guard me, guide me, and help me with every request I had. Every player started with one, and if they used them right, could be on top of the game in no time.

I scanned the distance between me and the town. It looked as though there'd been a rockslide here not long before, and the base of the hill gave proof of that. A rushing stream carved between the hill I stood on, and the town was full of boulders. I glanced to the left and right, searching for a way off the hilltop. There didn't seem to be an easy path, so I hiked up my ankle-length brown robes and started down the decline. My clumsy feet slipped, and my palms moistened with fear.

Fear of pain. I knew the Sensory Dev team had worked tirelessly on figuring out a way to lessen pain, or make it less traumatic, but in the end, everything they tried dampened *all* sensations. It wasn't the optimal choice, but with time running out, Osmark had to allow the features to proceed as they were.

My right foot came out from under me, and I slid on my butt down to the next large rock, holding it with trembling fingers. I inhaled slowly through my nose and steadied myself. A deep grinding rumbled from my tailbone up to my shoulders, and I spread my hands out from the boulder, reaching for anything. There was nothing else to hold onto as the ground gave way.

Sand and grit kicked into my eyes as the huge stone rolled forward, pulling the dirt around me, *and me*, with it. My left arm came up to shield my face instinctively, and I tumbled forward. I rolled onto my back, trying to stay on top of the tiny stones coursing down the hillside like an avalanche.

Sharp agony stabbed into my mid-back from a buried rock that poked into me, and I was flung forward onto my knees, striking the slow tumbling boulder in front of me elbow first. I cursed as I pulled my throbbing arm into my chest, but thanked the instinct that saved my face from that hit.

The massive rock picked up speed, dragging me and everything else along faster as I did everything I could not to get pulled under it. I fell forward again and struggled to right myself. My skin burned as a thousand tiny rocks whipped against me, into my squinted eyes, and up my nose. I flipped upright for a brief second and gasped as I caught a glimpse of the rushing water below and the cliff face just ahead.

Crack-splash!

The first big stone dropped to the water, and I searched frantically for anything to grab onto. Nothing, not a damned tree branch, bush, or stable rock. I surrendered, trying instead to just stay on top of the moving earth.

Clunk, clunk, splash!

The boulder that started it all rolled off the edge. I kicked my heels into the quick-flowing dirt, but it was fruitless. My feet crossed the edge, and I screamed, arms pinwheeling as I dropped. I pulled myself into a ball, one arm wrapped over my head and the other around my knees.

The icy shock of dropping into the river tightened my muscles. I bumped into the large boulder and released my legs, kicking forward with all my might. I paddled hard and broke the top of the water, sucking in a quick breath. My arms felt like tight rubber bands were pulling them back as I reached out to pull myself from the splash zone.

A microwave-sized rock dropped in next to me, and I forced myself not to stop, not to look up. Just swim. I'd never been a swimmer, and the burlap sack of a robe wasn't making it any easier.

Another large stone fell ahead of me, and I dove under. Breaching the water would slow the rocks down some, hopefully enough to not kill me. I kicked harder, but the stream was pulling me along sideways and turning me around. A muffled splash and sharp pain on the left side of my head let me know the worst had happened.

I was going to die four minutes into the game.

THREE

RISI RUMBLE

SEARING PAIN THROBBED FROM THE LEFT SIDE OF MY skull to the right as I floated to the top of the water. My face breached the surface, and I gasped for air as a notification popped up in the corner of my vision.

Debuff Added:
Concussed: You have sustained a severe head injury! Confusion and disorientation; duration, 1 minute.

Frigid mountain runoff flooded my mouth, and I sputtered. The splashes of boulders all around me were muted as a rushing that overpowered the sounds of flowing water filled my head. Warmth trickled down my ear and onto my neck, coloring the water around me red.

I reached my arms out clumsily as I tried to stay above water. It was hard to see with my eyes clouded and darkness closing in around my periphery. Each kick of my legs, paddle of my hands, and breath in my lungs drove me forward out of danger, and I clung to that hope.

I needed to get ashore, I needed to find my NPC, I needed to collect that scroll and figure out what Osmark had planned for this world.

Though my legs were nearly numb, I kicked harder. As the Concussed debuff timer ticked down to zero, my vision returned to me. A watermill was treading not far down the river, exactly what I needed to get myself out of this mess. The rapids pulled me this way and that as I steered my frozen body toward salvation.

A dip in the river pulled me under, and the cut on my temple ached in anger. Just a few more feet! My arms and legs moved like a marionette's, flailing about as if someone else were pulling the strings haphazardly. My tight fingers groped at the slippery wood of the watermill as it spun with the swiftly coursing river.

All of the edges were soft from water wear, and my hands were too weak to clamp down. I was drifting away from the only handhold possibly for miles. In a fit of desperation, I stuffed my arm into the rotating spokes of the waterwheel, and it caught. My legs drifted along downstream as I held fast to the wood, and it whined in protest at the added weight.

My muscles tensed and convulsed as I painstakingly maneuvered around the wheel and pushed up onto dry land. I rolled over, gazing up at the purple-pink clouds drifting calmly in a deepening blue sky. A new pop-up appeared.

Debuff Added

Hypothermia: Your body temperature has dropped below 95 degrees Fahrenheit, and you are entering hypothermia. Stamina regeneration is reduced by 30%, movement speed is reduced by 50%, and you improve skills 20% slower. Duration, 10 minutes.

Note: Finding dry clothes or warming by a fire will reduce the duration of Hypothermia by 8 minutes.

Dry clothes. Fire. I shivered, rolling to my side and crawling to my feet. There was a cobblestone path leading up the riverbank, and I followed it to the watermill cabin. I grabbed at the rusted metal handle and tugged, but the door was locked. I bashed my shoulder into it once, twice, and finally the frame cracked, gaining me entry.

I toppled to the dark floor, muscles vibrating in desperate attempts to warm themselves.

Someone cried out as I tried to gain my feet. "Rah!"

Pain whipped into my back, and I yelped, crumpling from my knees to my belly.

The voice of a child accompanied the next strike. "Get away!" He was a lot stronger than his voice let on.

"Please stop." My lips quivered, and the words were quiet. "I'm not going to hurt you."

He whacked me again, and I rolled to my side, catching the stick as it came down for a fourth strike.

He whined, "Let go, let go of me!"

I pulled myself up holding the end of the fishing harpoon and glared at the boy. He couldn't have been more than eight.

"Dry clothes," I growled.

He released the harpoon. Dirt streaked his face where tears once carved their way down, and he trembled as he backed away.

"I'm here to he-help." I shook. "I'm freezing."

He backed into the corner.

I didn't have time for this, but I needed to get a weapon, get dry clothes, and find my NPC. A cackle, much like the high-pitched maniacal ones I'd heard on the hill, drifted through the open door and the boy cowered.

"What's your name?" I crouched next to him, holding my hand out as my teeth chattered.

The boy sniffled. "Derik." He wiped his nose on the back of his arm and stood. "If you promise to help my mom, I'll get you the work clothes."

Quest Alert: A Son's Love

Derik's mother has been taken captive at the center of the village. Help a son get his mother free, and you'll earn the favor of the townspeople of Havasil. Accepting the quest will earn you [Worker's Clothes].

Quest Class: Unique, Personal

Quest Difficulty: Moderate

Success: Find and rescue Derik's mother at the center of town.

Failure: Fail to save Derik's mother, or allow Derik to be captured.

Reward: The People's Favor; 1,500 XP.

"I'll help her." I checked under the sack I was wearing to ensure I was still wearing that weird bikini from the character creation screen. Luckily, the devs hadn't made things awkward.

Derik turned to rummage through a pile of nets, and I peeled the heavy robe from my vibrating body.

"Don't t-turn around, just toss the clothes over your shoulder." I covered myself with my arms, just in case. He did as I instructed and kept his eyes on the wall.

I opened my inventory screen and inspected the clothes. They weren't really armor, but they were dry. The black [Twill Work Pants] had a +3 to Fishing skill and the dirt brown [Twill Work Shirt], likely not brown when it was first made, had +1 to Dexterity. Not a good start, but it would have to do. I put them on hastily, and the Hypothermia debuff dropped from 7 minutes to 0, then disappeared. I hugged myself for comfort as the heat returned to my limbs.

Another shrill laugh brought my attention back to the combat outside the cabin and the quest notification blinking away in the corner of my vision. I grabbed the harpoon and snapped off the spear end, discarding it. I'd researched the available classes before entering the game and knew I wanted to be a Sorceress. I couldn't stray too far from my class restrictions or the trainer wouldn't see me as a fit candidate for the role. Picking up a hammer, for example, or grabbing some heavy armor would do me in for sure… but some cloth armor and a makeshift staff should get me on the path to a Sorceress.

I turned to the door and poked my head out.

Derik grabbed at my sleeve and whispered, "Good luck, lady."

"Stay hidden. Don't leave this room. I'll tell your mother where to find you."

He nodded vigorously and pushed the door shut as I walked into the fading light.

The worn dirt path was hard to see in the twilight, but the presence of dancing firelight at the edge of the next building led the way. I held the broken staff firm in both hands, ready to whack anything that came near me, much like Derik had.

A shadow passed by the fire and a short, gangly creature sped through the alley. I froze, but the thing turned back, a manic smile on its long green face. It laughed, pulling a dagger from the belt at its side as it charged me.

I positioned myself for a heavy swing and turned the staff into the path of the [Heckling Goblin].

"Gruh!"

The staff landed solidly against the creature's chest, and the goblin fell to the side.

Skill: Two-handed Staves

Whether you're swinging it around or using it to walk, a Two-handed Staff is a tool of many uses. Two-handed Staves do not have special combat bonuses, but give the wielder the benefit of melee at a distance, decreasing your chances of being struck.

Skill Type/Level: Passive, Level 1

Cost: None

Effect: Decreases the wielder's chance of being struck in melee combat by .5%

"Disable frivolous notifications!" I waved the pop-up away and focused on the filthy creature before me. It wheezed, likely from broken ribs, and came up to its knees. It gurgled and licked its lips. It pulled a dagger from the rough loincloth at its waist, then lunged at me with surprising speed.

I parried the blade with my staff, then whacked its arm away and followed up with a swift kick to its face. If I wasn't careful, I'd put myself on the path to a monk... Too much bo staff use or hand-to-hand combat would start building my skills toward that class kit. Of course, I could just choose to be a monk. No, Sorceress was way too cool to pass up.

The goblin stumbled back, and I swung hard with the staff, landing a hit squarely on its jaw. There was a *snap*, and the creature crumpled to the ground. I stared down at the dead thing, shocked. I'd actually killed it.

I shook off the thought and rolled the body over to inspect its inventory. The dagger was not of good quality, only worth a few copper pieces, but I was broke and my carry capacity was doing fine for now, so I grabbed it. Next, was a necklace of small... ears. Children's ears.

"Help, Mommy!" The cry of a young girl snapped me back from disgust, and I left the body, heading toward the sound. There was a torch at the edge of the crude mud-and-straw building, and maybe fifty feet from there, the center of "town." It was more like a collection of houses and a business or two, probably not even an inn. I peeked around the corner of the building, staying out of the light.

It was difficult to get a bead on the scene at the village center. A huge, forest green Risi man towered above all the rest, slashing low at the goblins as they jabbed at his calves and thighs. The Risi roared, his three-inch, tusk-like lower canines glinting with saliva. Ew.

Every player in V.G.O. was started with an NPC to make sure they didn't get wrecked and could play most of the game solo if they wanted, and that ogre-thing was probably mine. Why, *why* did it have to be a freaking Risi?

"Come on!" the Risi yelled, stomping on a goblin that got too close, ending it in a squelch.

Ugh, it was definitely my NPC. Why had the game's Myers-Briggs analysis paired me up with this *thing*?

I scanned the clearing, struggling to pick out the details. Other races had some cool aided night vision, but not Wodes—they didn't get squat other than no restrictions.

At the far end, there was a mule-drawn cart with a cage on the back, filled with humans, all wailing for freedom. Next to it, a caster-type goblin [Heckling Shaman] glowed green as it sent buffs sailing toward the little fighter goblins.

But there was something else stalking up behind the Risi. What the hell was it? The dim light made it hard to tell, but the nametag flashed above its head in red for a brief second. [Heckling Wolf Rider].

"Look out!" I called, but it was too late. The wolf launched itself at the Risi, jaws chomping down on his sword arm.

The Risi howled and dropped to one knee. If I didn't get in there quick, it could be the end of him. I grabbed the torch and charged forward with my best war cry.

The wolf snarled and turned its shining green eyes on me, then released the Risi's arm. I waved the torch fervently in its face, and the wolf backed away. I turned to the Risi to see two of the Heckling Goblins charge him, burying their small daggers in his chest. He howled in pain as he crushed the first goblin with a meaty punch and tossed the other against the cart.

He stood, stumbled, then straightened. "Stay back," he said, his voice a low grumble. "This isn't a fight for a lady."

"Where would you be now without this *lady*?" I shot back, readying my staff as six glowing green goblins closed in on us.

The Risi grunted. "Fair enough. Let's see what you've got."

FOUR

THE PEOPLE'S FAVOR

"**G**ET THE CASTER!" THE RISI BARKED. I DIDN'T like being told what to do by a few lines of code, but he was right, that shaman was bad news.

"Got it!" I called back and skirted around the six goblins with gazes affixed to the largest target, the Risi. The standard, run-of-the-mill goblin wasn't incredibly smart, but the caster saw me coming and readied himself. That wolf was running around somewhere in the dark, too. I kept my guard up.

The pudgy gray-green shaman was decorated with necklaces of ears, belts of bones, and a crown of blackened feathers. The staff it brandished had a black opalescent stone wedged into the top, and I knew, without a doubt, that was for me.

The caster snorted and cackled, "Stupid girl, you can't fight a shaman of the Heckling clan with a *broomstick!*"

"Fishing harpoon, actually, and watch me." I swiped in low, and the shaman hopped back, exactly what I wanted it to do. Waving the staff around with one hand was incredibly awkward, and not effective in the least, but I wasn't trying to hit the creature, just get it out of range of the others.

The torch was warm in my left hand, and I waved it at the goblin's head. The shaman dove left and tried to circle around me, apparently seeing through my herding tactic. A sharp-toothed smile spread over its face, and its hand shot out, a sickly yellow glowing from its palm.

Debuff Added

Rotting Plague: You have been diseased! You take 1 point per second of disease spell damage. Spirit regen is reduced by 15%. Duration, 20 seconds.

Twenty points? That's like one-fifth of my Health!

If I was going to do real damage to the shaman, I had to drop the torch. The little jerk's hands were waving about in some spell cast, and I shot forward, jabbing into the shaman's stomach with the tip of my staff. It gave a, "Harumph," as I pushed the air from its lungs and interrupted the cast.

I couldn't afford to let it get off any more spells, so I tossed the torch to the ground and gripped my staff with both hands. I glanced up to see the Risi had four goblins left. A glint of green in a dark nook beside a house to the north caught my eyes.

"The wolf is back!" I shouted.

The Risi growled, slicing down through a goblin with his sword. The blood-spray wet the dirt, and the Wodes in the cage cheered, "Ah-toe, ah-toe!"

"Take care of your business, I have mine!" the rude Risi snapped back.

I thrust my staff-end at the shaman again. It dodged with a chuckle, a feature of the Heckling Goblins that was getting old. I wanted to shut its stupid trap.

The shaman stood ten feet from me, flicking its wrists in another spell. I took two steps forward, ready to swing in hard, when the dirt in front of the creature sprouted a spiked vine. Damn it! I pivoted, grabbed the torch, and pressed it against the wriggling plant as it wrapped around my left leg. The vine shriveled and retracted, so I held the torch out to ward it off.

"Stop playing and kill it!" the Risi yelled, the sounds of animalistic snarls informing me the wolf had reengaged with him.

"Yes, girl, let's not play anymore!" The shaman's hands burst with a lime-green light, and a bolt of energy smacked me in the chest.

I gasped for air as I fell back on my butt, watching as my Health dropped below 50%. At least the disease debuff had ended. I gritted my teeth and bounced back upright, swinging the torch and staff in crisscrossing paths in front of me as I made my way to the shaman. If I had any spells this would've been over long ago.

Finally, I was in striking range and the vine had receded back into the earth. I chucked the torch at the goblin's head, and the wide-eyed look let me know it hadn't expected that at all. It dodged, but I already had a good two-handed grip on my staff and was swinging for where it would land.

The shaman ducked, my staff knocking the feather headdress across the town center. I didn't let up, whacking again and again until a hit landed, and another. The shaman tried to back away, but its legs were much shorter than mine and I kept closing the distance. With every hit the creature's Health dropped by 5%. 10% when I critted! But it was slow going, and I wished desperately I had some spells to cast. At least I was interrupting its spellcasting.

The shaman tripped, falling back next to the torch I'd hucked.

"Wait! I can give you gold!"

I stood over it with a glower. "I'll just take it off your corpse."

I whacked down one last time, and the creature gave a death grunt as its life hit zero. I opened its inventory… no gold. Not a silver, *not even a copper*! What a liar! The staff was my real prize anyway, and I snatched it up hastily, along with a [Cart Cage Key].

"Argh!" The Risi cried out, and I remembered the wolf. I grabbed the nearly out torch and ran for the beast. The Risi man's left arm was shredded, flaps of green skin hanging loosely around ripped muscle, and his body was littered with tiny punctures from daggers and dagger-like teeth.

I stuffed the fire into the wolf's face, and it backed away, but only far enough to crouch for a pounce. It leapt, colliding solidly against my chest. We crashed to the ground and panic surged through my veins as I imagined the giant wolf maw clamping down on my head and ripping it off. I jabbed the torch into the wolf's belly as I held my right arm up to guard my face. It bit down on my forearm and a crushing, sharp pressure shot up to my shoulder. My Health dropped to 35%. This wasn't how I wanted things to go on my first adventure.

The bite didn't last long, but the pain remained as the wolf jumped back. My torch set the creature's long black fur ablaze, and the fire ripped around its back, then down its tail in a fury. The Risi, one good arm remaining, chopped down with his oversized sword and beheaded the convulsing, charred wolf.

The Risi spit into the bloodstained dirt and groaned as he grabbed at a red vial on his belt. He popped the cork and downed the liquid. I watched his life shoot up to 75% from 20%. Another interesting thing happened as his health returned: his skin mended, cuts smoothed over, and the mangled arm completely repaired. So. Damn. Cool!

I'd really cut that close, though. I could've been screwed if this *thing* had died on me. He would be my only companion for who knows how long. Hopefully not *too* long. With any luck, Jack got the capsule I sent him and took the plunge.

I knew it was a lot to ask to leave your world behind and join a new one, even if the previous one was about to blow up, but Jack had been my RPG guildmate for a long time, and college friend for a long time before that. Even if he didn't want to help me, it'd be nice to have someone to talk to from the old days.

"Oiy! Come let us out!" the NPCs in the cage shouted, and I remembered the key in my inventory. I trotted to the cart and set the captives free.

"Anyone here Derik's mother?" I asked the crowd as they hopped down into the dirt and charged the Risi, cheering.

"I'm Derik's mother! Where is he?" The brown-haired woman's voice was soft like worn river rocks. She wore a simple gown that strained at the seams from the pressure of her large belly—she was pregnant. She held my hand and shoulder, desperation visible in the creases of her worry-wrinkled forehead. I knew the world had to be populated somehow, and the NPCs would *die* die, whereas the Travelers would respawn… but I guess I figured a new adult NPC would be created by the Overminds when the need arose.

I pointed to the watermill. "Just there. I told him to hide."

She held tightly to my hand as she ran for the watermill. I wasn't really inclined to go waste several minutes out of my precious schedule, but I supposed it was the only way to get my quest reward.

Crickets chirped in the tall grass around the dirt path as we made our way. It sounded as if nothing was awry, nothing had happened. The town center was full of cheers and hearty slaps on the back. Just another evening in Eldgard.

"Derik!" The mother pounded on the door, then pushed against it, but it was barricaded.

A muffled reply came from the other side. "Mom?"

"Yes, sweetie, it's your mom. Open the door, please."

There was some shuffling on the other side, then the door flew open. A huge smile spread over Derik's cheeks, and he jumped up into his mother's embrace. I knew they were just executing predetermined code, but it was pretty cute and heartwarming.

"Thank you so much!" The mother turned to me and shook my hand.

Quest Alert: A Son's Love

You have rescued Derik's mother and kept Derik safe through the Goblin raid. You've earned The People's Favor and 1,500 XP. You may now return to Havasil and receive free accommodations with any resident. Your reputation with the Free People of Havasil has increased from Neutral to Friendly.

Well, that was great. I'd have to loot the goblins for whatever they had so I could feed myself tonight. I patted my grumbling belly. At least I had a free bed somewhere in town, not that I wanted to stay here. Yeah, never mind. That wasn't even an option. I needed to find my class trainer, the NPC who would teach me the ways of sorcery, and they were definitely not here.

Another notification blinked into view:

x2 Level Up!

You have (15) undistributed stat points

You have (2) unassigned proficiency points

Right, all of that. I'd forgotten to insert my first five stat points, not that it would've *really* mattered for falling down a hill and fighting some goblins. I opened up my profile screen and took a look.

Name:	Abby	Race:	Wode	Gender:	Female
Level:	3	Class:	Unassigned	Alignment:	None
Renown:	1,200	Carry Capacity:	260	Undistributed Attribute Points:	15
Health:	130	Spirit:	130	Stamina:	130
H-Regen/sec:	1.3	S-Regen/sec:	3.01875	Stam-Regen/sec:	2.08
Attributes:		Offense:		Defense:	
Strength:	10	Base Melee Weapon Damage:	3	Base Armor:	10
Vitality:	10	Base Ranged Weapon Damage:	0	Armor Rating:	18
Constitution:	10	Attack Strength (AS):	19	Block Amount:	2.5
Dexterity:	10	Ranged Attack Strength (RAS):	16	Block Chance (%):	1.83
Intelligence:	10	Spell Strength (SS):	15	Evade Chance (%):	2.8
Spirit:	10	Critical Hit Chance:	5%	Fire Resist (%):	0.2
Luck:	5	Critical Hit Damage:	5%	Cold Resist (%):	0.2
				Lightning Resist (%):	0.2
				Shadow Resist (%):	0.2
				Holy Resist (%):	0.2
Current XP:	275			Poison Resist (%):	0.2
Next Level:	1,440			Disease Resist (%):	0.2

I was going to be a caster, that was for certain, so I dropped 5 points into Intelligence, 5 into Spirit, and damn it, I was *way* too squishy, so 5 into Vitality as well. My Health jumped by a full 50 points, and I beamed. No plague was going to take me down!

I closed out my character sheet and gave a little wave to Derik, then turned back to the town center, where the Risi was… looting all the bodies without me! *Rude!*

I speed walked and stood in front of him, hands on my hips. He didn't look up.

"Excuse me." I tapped my foot, and he finally glanced my way.

He had a brief expression of embarrassment, then his brow scrunched. "You already looted the Shaman. I did most of the work, so I was getting my spoils."

"I made sure you *could* kill those goblins by keeping the shaman busy, and I did a lot of the work on that wolf. What was on it?"

He stood upright, an attempt to intimidate me. It wasn't going to work. This thing was *my* NPC; he was programmed to work with me, follow my orders when required, and grow an affinity for me, so there was no way he'd hurt me.

I puffed myself up as much as I could, leaning back so I could look at him without turning my head. He rolled his eyes and sighed, then produced a ring from his pocket. He held it out to me.

"There was another one, but it's mine. The rest of it is junk, barely worth a thing."

I accepted the [Simple Silver Ring] and opened my inventory. +2 Constitution and +3 Vitality, not too shabby for first-level mobs. I put it on and closed my character screen.

"So," I said, walking with him as he moved from body to body, "what's your name?"

He raised a brow at me, then said, "It's Otto."

Ah-toe, it made sense now! "I'm Abby. What were you doing here?"

He sighed. "I was hired to protect the village of Havasil from the goblins."

I tutted. "You were doing real great."

He glared, then continued to fish through the dead goblin's inventory.

"Sorry. I mean, you were outnumbered. It was good I came along, yeah?"

"Indeed." Otto stood upright. "And what exactly are *you* doing here?"

I shrugged. "I'm a Traveler, just got here." I knew the NPC would understand what a Traveler was. We'd programmed the Overminds, the gods of V.G.O. essentially, to give the NPCs enough knowledge to understand that we weren't like them, and we would arrive spontaneously sometimes. The NPCs understood that we wouldn't die, not forever at least, and that we were capable of some things that they weren't.

"I see." He went back to rummaging. He didn't seem very interested in me or very apt to help me out. Maybe I was wrong? Maybe Otto wasn't my companion…

I stayed quiet, letting him finish his searching. I was patient enough and knew that if Otto was intended to work with me and was based off my Myers-Briggs profile, he might be processing everything for a little bit. So, I waited.

Finally, amid the occasional pat on the back and thanks from a townsperson, some for me too, Otto turned to me.

"So, I think the people are pretty well off, and we won't be seeing the goblins for a time."

"Maybe," I offered, waiting for him to get to the part where he would say he'd follow me around.

One side of his mouth turned down in a half grimace as he thought. "I guess what I mean to say is, I'm looking for work, if you know of any."

"I want to make my way to the next biggest town. I need to find a trainer. If you'd escort me, I'd pay you."

He put his hand to his chin. "How much?"

I checked my inventory. Not a single copper to my name.

"Well," I stalled, "I will be able to sell some of this junk, and then I can give you whatever I have."

Otto's head jerked back, an incredulous frown spreading down his cheeks.

"I will have some money once we get there and I'm able to sell some of these items. I just got here, remember?"

He looked me over. "I don't think your broomstick handle will go for much."

"I *will* pay you." I tried to think about his weakness, how I could get him to cave to me. He'd called me a lady and seemed to be honor-bound. Perhaps I could be a little bit manipulative and feign being a helpless damsel. Well, that wasn't such a lie at the moment.

I softened my voice. "I don't have a class. I don't have any money. I'm hungry and tired and hurt." I hated myself for what I was about to say. "I need help. Please?"

His eyes narrowed to slits, and his forehead wrinkled. I'd struck the weakness for sure, but would he cave to it?

I gave my best attempt at a pouty face. Otto stared at me a moment longer, then surrendered. "I can take you to Harrowick. It's the largest city near here, has a lot of different things, so I'm sure you'll find a mentor."

"Great!" I beamed, dropping the sad act as fast as I'd picked it up. "Let's be off then. Which way do we go?" I marched in a circle, my hand pointing every which direction.

He had a sour look on his face, like he'd been duped, but it was too late to turn back. I sort of reveled in it, like a game. How far would he bend to my will, I wondered.

"It's a long walk, and we don't have enough money for horses, nor are there any here."

I tried on my pout again. "I really need to get there soon. It's very important."

The muscles in his jaw tensed. "I don't think you understand how far it really is. It's too far to walk in the dark."

My face went stern and serious. "I'll pay you double."

"I have no idea what the base rate is, so that doesn't mean much to me."

"Trust me, Otto, I'm going places and doing things. You'll want to stick with me. I've got a plan."

He crossed his meaty arms. "Does your plan include dying?"

"Definitely not." I waggled my finger.

He mulled it over, but I knew I'd won. His programming couldn't resist my requests.

"Fine. Let's get moving."

FIVE

HARROWICK

HOLY. SHIT.

Otto had not been exaggerating the distance of the walk. We left Havasil at 8 PM game time. It was freaking 11 PM. We weren't taking our sweet time either. My Stamina was low, and the pace we were keeping wouldn't allow it to regenerate. I wasn't playing a helpless damsel anymore. I kinda was one.

It irked me that Otto was so much better off than me, but that was the point. The NPCs started around level 5 to 8 to ensure that the player wouldn't be doomed from the get-go, and they usually already had their class situation figured out.

I'd only heard of a few cases where the NPC started classless and had to go through the same process their player did. Another bug we'd tried to work out, but couldn't manage to find a solution for. Something to do with the player themselves being too undecided in their lives, or uncommitted to any goals, and that carrying through strongly enough in their NPC pairing profile to cause their NPC to be undecided as well.

I panted hard to recuperate a few points of Stamina, swinging my staff like a walking stick to support my weary legs. The [Obsidian War Staff] had been great support, not to mention an awesome addition to my stats. +8 to Intelligence, +3 to Vitality, and +2% to parry. But it was still heavy, and my inventory was pretty loaded with junk, hopefully enough stuff to sell to pay for Otto's company.

He'd told me to keep up a few times, then when he realized I couldn't, offered to carry me on his back. I nearly shot him the bird for that one. He had laughed, not a joyful or belittling thing, but sort of embarrassed, when he realized I was truly incapable of keeping up with him.

It'd made me even more furious, but also more aware of what the game told me about myself. I would feel bad when I overestimated someone's abilities and they fell short... so did Otto. Very interesting.

I pulled over at a downed tree for a quick break. The townspeople of Havasil were nice enough to give us a few torches and a better suited [Robe of Concentration] for me, but it still wasn't enough to make the trek easier.

"We can't camp here, I don't have the proper equipment," Otto said matter-of-factly.

I puffed, "I don't want to camp," and inhaled deeply. "I just need a quick break."

He took a seat on the log as far from me as possible. Did I really do that IRL? How awkward.

"What brought you up to Havasil?" I asked, seeing if the Overminds had provided him with an actual decent reason for being there.

"I needed work," he said stoically.

"You'll walk for hours for a job that pays in dirt and fish bones?"

"It'd be faster if you didn't go so slow," he snapped back, then softened, "and they paid me more than that."

"Yeah?" I asked with skepticism.

He nodded. "Yes. They gave me other valuable things."

I chuckled, my pulse finally slowing. "Like what?"

Otto crossed his arms. His emotions were so terribly obvious to me. He didn't want to answer—he was being totally avoidant because he was ashamed.

"Sorry, didn't know it was a touchy subject." I shrugged, and he shook his head.

"It's fine. They gave me pearls. There's a special freshwater pearl that comes from the oysters in their lake. They're not worth much, but… never mind." He trailed off, and if I knew anything about myself, this wasn't a time to push it. It was time to let it go. So I did, stood, and offered him my hand. He rolled his eyes, then smirked and stood to walk beside me as we went on.

The forest path curved to the left, and I experienced deja vu. There was a walking path near Osmark Tech that curved just like this, the trees the same color and type, but the IRL path had lamps. It was so dark, I could hardly make it out.

That trail would be gone soon. Astraea would wipe it off the face of the earth through fire and force. The blast would rip a hole in the Earth's atmosphere, allowing trillions of radiation particles under our protective shield. Then it would burn up the atmosphere, flash heating the airspace for six thousand square miles in seconds.

The scientists predicted a water landing, but that didn't help anything. The impact would create a tidal wave to cast a shadow on any tsunami, then boil the oceans, killing 99% of all life. The steam would explode out and create an ice belt around the planet that would get sucked back into Earth's orbit. The atmosphere would become unbreathable from the toxic ash, gas, and humidity. Everything on the surface, no matter its location, would die in agony.

"How much farther?" I asked as I rubbed my shoulder, trying to pull myself from morbid thoughts.

Otto glanced about the dark trees, then looked up at the sky. "Not far at all."

The road curved back right, and a wooden gate came into view. There were four torches lining the basic oak-and-bronze opening and two guards. Suddenly, I was nervous. I didn't have any identification, no one knew me. I was nothing. Would they stop us and make us pay some kind of fee?

As we got closer to the gate, I saw the guards' postures move from alert to tense.

"Otto," the woman on the right said, part greeting, part warning. "What are you doing back here?"

"The people of Havasil are safe, for now. I was accompanying Miss... Miss..."

"Abby Hollander," I interjected. I was not good at asserting myself in conversations, but Otto needed some help. "I'm here to meet with the town sorcerer." The guards didn't look convinced. "He sent for me," I added, feeling their eyes scraping over me in judgement.

"I assume you mean Naitee Mungal. *She* doesn't take visitors late at night, nor does she usually send for a, uh"—the man on the left waved his hand through the air—"someone like you."

Heat rose into my cheeks, and I raised my finger to point, but Otto grabbed my hand and put it down. I sucked my lower lip in and bit down as I gave him a sidelong glare.

"Look." Otto stepped up and put his arm around the man. They talked in low voices, but I could still hear them. "She's a paying customer, I'm trying to finish my job. Let us in, yeah?" I heard the tinkling of coins and knew that Otto was bribing the man. It seemed a bit unlike him, well *me*, but I guess in his situation, I might do the same. We weren't doing anything wrong, after all.

"Yeah, okay." The man banged on the door. "Open up, Levari."

There was a creaking and a bang, then the large wooden door swung open. I'd heard a bit of bustling from the other side of the gate, but when the city was revealed to us, it was obvious the whole place was definitely still up.

The inhabitants were walking about, drinking, cheering, strumming musical instruments, playing cards, and dancing. Perhaps the working people who cared about the next day had gone to bed, but everyone else was bright-eyed and bushy-tailed. Hopefully, my trainer would be too.

I sighed as I took in the whole city in its glory. The main thoroughfare was lined with lit oil lamps, giving the buildings a warm glow. Most of the structures were made of wood and not more than two stories tall, but the deeper into town the road went, the taller, more robust, and well-crafted they became. Near the center of town I could see a pair of white stone turrets flanking a modest castle poking up over the roofs of the houses and businesses.

This was what *years* of hundreds of devs had created. Not just this, but dozens of cities just like it, and a handful that were even greater still. This was what endless hours of typing away had earned us: a digital world near indistinguishable from IRL. It was a testament to human tenacity and sheer will.

Otto cleared his throat, and I snapped my awe-opened mouth shut, returning to the moment. I gave a curt nod to the guard who accepted the bribe and took a step through the open door.

"Otto," the woman said, stepping into my path, "no kickin' the beehive this time, right? Your past has a nasty way of messing with our futures."

Wow, the Overminds put a lot more care into the crafting of the player's companion than I imagined. He seemed to have some rich history I'd have to prod him over.

Otto gave a grunt, and the woman returned to her post.

He nudged me as he passed. "C'mon, I know a good, *quiet* inn." The male guard gave a chuckle at Otto's emphasis of the word *quiet*, and the woman rolled her eyes.

Apparently, a *lot* of history.

The door swung shut behind us, and Otto nodded to the person I assumed was Levari, who gave us an exasperated look. Gate duty must be thrilling. My feet ached from the level 1 cloth shoes practically worn through from our trek, and I thought about all of the things I still had to accomplish in such a small window of time: get my class, collect the scroll in seven hours, figure out what it did, then… start a resistance.

No matter what was on the other end of the scroll, it was going to be a *huge* buff to the people getting them. Osmark wouldn't handcraft simple scrolls for people to hide out on "private islands" for billions of IRL donations. No, there was going to be something epic to do with those secret areas.

With the weight of the tasks ahead of me, I asked the next pertinent question, "All right, where's this Sorceress?"

Otto raised a brow. "Do you know what time it is?"

I opened my in-game menu and checked. "11:17 PM."

He rolled his eyes. "It was rhetorical. She's asleep."

"This is important." I stopped, putting my foot down. I was tired of getting pushed around by code I'd helped write.

He turned with arms crossed. "I'm not getting my backside singed for you. I'm going to the inn, getting a hot, roasted chicken, and a good rest."

My stomach growled at the mention of food, and I checked my character screen again. 11:17 PM was a bit late, and I had some lovely debuffs:

Current Debuffs

Tired (Level 2): Skills improve 10% slower; Carry Capacity -15lbs; Attack Damage -5%; Spell Strength reduced by 15%.

Thirsty (Level 3): Health, Stamina, and Spirit regeneration reduced by 35%.

Hungry (Level 3): Carry Capacity -50lbs; Health and Stamina regeneration reduced by 30%; Stealth 25% more difficult.

Unwashed (Level 2): Goods and services cost 10% more; Merchant-craft skills reduced by (2) level(s).

Great. No wonder I felt so heavy.

I was getting sick of this Risi being right. I pursed my lips but nodded my head in agreement.

We followed the main road for a while, then turned off down an alley before reaching the white stone castle. We snaked around through dirt passages, the liveliness growing more and more intense as we went. Loud music, drunken ballads sung to barmaids, brawls over games of dice and cards, and some very inappropriate conduct in some of the darker corners.

I pulled up beside Otto. "I thought we were going somewhere quiet?"

"We are." He stopped at the door to the Boar's Head and gestured for me to enter.

The wooden door was engraved with fire, then painted in brilliant color with a severed pig's head and three figures gathered around it with full tankards. The sign above swung back and forth with a mild creaking, and white smoke curled its way from the brick chimney.

I looked over my shoulder at a disorderly man leaning against a wall, relieving himself, then back to Otto.

"Seriously?" My whisper dripped repugnance.

He shook his head and pushed past me through the door. I didn't have anywhere else to go, didn't have any money, didn't have anywhere to sell my goods, and needed to stick with my NPC, so… to hell with it.

I shoved my way in after him, and when the door swung shut, the rabble of the streets outside was dampened to a mere burbling. The floor and walls of the Boar's Head were solid oak. The scent of smoked meat and sweet honey permeated the room. Saliva pooled on the sides of my tongue at the thought of what those smells emanated from.

I swallowed hard, trying not to think about food. I had no money, and no valuable gems to trade with. I was hoping I could at least sleep on the floor in Otto's room, but even then they might try to charge me.

"Ah, Otto! Take your seat, friend!" the man at the bar yelled with a grin.

Otto seemed well known across Harrowick, or maybe he just took me places where he knew people. That seemed more like something I would do.

My NPC walked across the room with a destination in mind. There was no one else in the tavern, but Otto knew where *his* seat was. I had a place I'd always sit at Osmark Tech for lunch, too.

Otto slid into a booth with a privacy cloth drawn back, and I took the seat across from him. It was cramped. Quite a bit more cramped than I was expecting. Due to his size, Otto had to push the table closer to my side, leaving a small space for me to fit in.

He stared at the table in silence for a while, then finally looked up at me. He opened his mouth when the barmaid appeared beside us.

"Whatsit this time? Usual?" Her long blond hair was in a braid off to the side, and her hands were placed at her hips. The apron she wore was cut down much too far to be useful in protecting her from hot food splatters, but was likely very useful in getting her good tips. I remembered going to Hooters once and seeing a getup just like that.

Otto nodded. "Yes, two usuals."

The barmaid nodded and was gone just as fast.

"Otto, wait. I don't have any money. Call her back!"

He waved a dismissive hand in the air. "You walked far and fought hard. You need to eat." His brow scrunched. "And you already owe me, so it's not much more for a chicken and a bed."

Ah great, so it was going on my tab. My stomach gave a rumble to rival a kraken, and Otto's face broke with a smirk. I hated him being right all the time.

We waited in silence for a few minutes, which was nice. I was relieved to find that Otto didn't try to make small talk. If he had something to say, he'd say it, but he didn't just speak to speak. An excellent quality in a longtime companion.

The barmaid came bustling up, bearing two heaping plates of chicken and potatoes and two mugs full to the brim with the sweet honey smell I'd detected when coming in. My mouth watered at the sight of the crispy spud ends, which looked like they'd been fried in a pot of animal fat, and the browned rotisserie chicken skin.

Chicken was an overstatement. These were more like Cornish game hens. Nonetheless, it was about to be destroyed.

"Anything else?" the middle-aged woman asked, her hand obviously poised for a tip.

Otto shook his head and dropped five silver coins into her palm. She looked down at them for a good three seconds, back up at Otto, then to me. I grimaced and shrugged. The barmaid rolled her eyes and stomped away.

My dry throat called to the mead, so I pulled the mug up to my face for a huge swig. Oh, em, gee, it was amazing. The bubbles hit my tongue first, pushing the sweet notes of honey around my mouth in a wave. Then the tart hit me, packing a punch of alcohol at the end.

I gasped for air, and Otto chuckled. He raised his cup, smacked it into mine, and then downed the liquid in two quick gulps. I pulled my wooden mug up to my mouth and gulped back the last of it, then slammed it down on the table.

That earned me a laugh before Otto turned his attention to the chicken. My gaze dropped to my own, and the hunger overcame manners. I grabbed a potato with my bare fingers, stuffing the salt-crusted carb in my wide-open mouth.

Even better. *So* much better than IRL potatoes. How was the food in V.G.O. so good? If I wasn't careful, all those Hell Year pounds would find me down in the game.

I ripped a leg free of the hen and stuffed it in my mouth. The meat was just as smoky as I'd imagined, with a slight vinegar bite and a salty rosemary finish. Forget fighting Osmark and figuring out what was on that scroll, I just wanted to stay here and eat!

My palm burned as I grabbed another fistful of V.G.O. fries and stuffed them into my mouth, hooing and haaing to let some of the heat out. I looked up, trying not to let the searing oil burn my tongue, and caught Otto's eye. He seemed to be both amused and surprised.

"Whu? Haen't you see' ah hungee perhun behor?" The blazing-hot potatoes hurt my tongue and cheeks, but I didn't care, it tasted so good.

"I have." He picked up a two-pronged utensil and poked it into the chicken.

Oh, mister perfect. Doesn't get tired walking, *ever*, beats up tons of goblins with one totally useless arm, doesn't eat chicken with his hands, he uses a fork. I didn't have the bandwidth for manners, so I rolled my eyes and went back in on the chicken with my hands.

When I'd picked the bones clean and practically licked the salt off the plate, Otto ordered one more chicken for us to share. This one, he grabbed with his hands, which honestly looked a lot more natural than what he'd been doing with the fork and knife. He'd learned really quick I wasn't the kind of girl that needed a show. I needed reliability, I needed honesty, and I needed loyalty. Pretty simple gal.

I leaned back when my belly was full and gave a huge yawn. I checked my character screen one more time. Up to a level 4 Tired, but Hungry and Thirsty were gone. Oh... and unwashed had escalated to level 3. Guess I was a little messy.

Otto stood from the bench and tossed me something small. I fumbled and finally held it tight, my Dexterity seeming to take a hit from the alcohol. I held the object up—a key—then looked to Otto.

"I snore, you'll need your own room."

"More like your own city!" the barmaid chimed in with a grin.

I nodded sleepily. "Thanks, I appreciate this."

"Yeah, I appreciate the fifteen percent interest you'll be paying me."

That snapped me back to consciousness. "I never agreed to any terms!"

He laughed. "Hiring me is accepting my terms."

I squinted my eyes, said nothing, and turned up the stairs for my room. Damn him and his tricks. I suppose I could afford 15%, though, if it meant keeping him around. He was proving useful and intuitive.

The room was modest, but comfortable. It was about the size of a linen closet, with a basin of water on the chest at the foot of the bed. Excellent, there was nowhere to refill the water basin that I could see, so I would have to bathe in my own filth, with a washrag…

But not tonight. I groaned, flopping onto the bed. My feet burned, my back ached, and my muscles thudded from exhaustion. I wanted to stay up and review the forums, see what people were figuring out, but it could wait.

I opened my character sheet and checked the time once more. 12:23 AM. The scroll would be delivered in five hours, forty-two minutes. I set an alarm. I'd wake up just moments before its arrival. With the hard day behind me and a harder one ahead, I closed my eyes and drifted off into a dreamless slumber.

SIX

SCROLL OF ALLEGIANCE

OISE, AS SHARP AS A KNIFE, JABBED IN MY EAR with a constant *Errh errh errh!* I careened out of bed, landing hard on the wood floor. My knees and palms stung, but not nearly as badly as the pain in my head from that stupid sound! I reached up to the nightstand, searching for the alarm clock with furious desperation as the *Errh errh errh* continued, as loud as a train horn. My hand knocked off candles, paper, and unidentifiable metal objects, until the surface was bare. There was nothing.

Realization, gushing like a broken dam, washed over me.

"Alarm off." I spoke aloud, and the noise cut out abruptly.

I spent a good twenty seconds rubbing furiously at both my eyes, taking slow breaths through my nose to calm my pulse. I felt like a battered meat-sack from one of the Rocky films after Sylvester Stallone did his training montage. The *squish squish* of my eyes moving around in their sockets turned my aching stomach, so I cut the rubbing short and got back up on the bed.

I snapped open my character screen and checked the time. 5:58 AM. Two more minutes and Osmark would have his Scrolls of Allegiance. Seven more and I would have my copy of Aleixo Carrera's.

A personal message blinked in the corner. That wasn't right… Seven minutes early? I checked the sender and groaned; it was Osmark Technologies. I knew they had a customer support system to monitor the transition, and I guessed there was some kind of update on my progress there, but I wasn't interested. Either I was going to make it through all three days or I was going to die. I didn't want to know how close I was to doing either, it would only distract me, so I deleted the message.

There was a gentle knock at my door, followed by an older woman's voice. "Ever'thing all right, love?"

"Yes, bad dream."

There was a long pause, and I reached for my staff at the side of the bed. Maybe she was an agent of Osmark, here to expose me or maybe even take me to him. But how could he know? There was no way he could've known what I'd done yet. In a few minutes, however, it could be evident. I didn't know what sort of protections were placed on the scrolls he'd created.

"Sigorsped." The shuffling of her aged steps moved away from my door. I wondered how many different languages Eldgard had, and if I would have to learn them all to understand everyone… I'd just have to assume *sigorsped* meant "okay," for now. I checked the time with a sigh. 6:00 AM. Osmark, or whoever was picking them up, had the scrolls.

I tapped my feet, stood and paced, washed my face in the basin of water on the dresser, then stared out the window and tapped my feet.

6:01 AM.

I inspected my staff, scratched off some blood spots on the wood, laid flat the wrinkles in my robes, and flopped back on the bed.

6:02 AM.

I opened my character screen and checked my stats—just the same as they were when I last looked. I panned over to the standard abilities page and checked on my Two-handed Staves skill. Since I hadn't been doing combat in my sleep, I wasn't surprised to see it hadn't changed, either. I looked at my reserve of ability points, two total. I could sink them into some of the standard stuff, but then I would be a standard caster. I wanted to be exceptional, and that meant I needed my ability points for my class kit, or at least my basic Sorceress skill tree.

6:03 AM.

"Aghhhh!" I rolled off the bed and paced in circles, counting down the time in my head. My feet fell to the beat of my counts, and I bobbed my head to the song of impatience, which sounded oddly like "Night Ride Across the Caucasus."

5.

4.

3.

2.

I popped open my character screen as the time ticked over to 6:05, and my inbox lit up with a little red [1]. The message opened at my command, and I sped to the bottom, where the scroll should be attached.

It wasn't. It was just the message:
You can do this, Abby.

I closed the message and watched the inbox. Maybe the scroll was too big? Maybe it would have to arrive separately? Maybe it would appear in my inventory? I panned over, but it was just full of worthless Heckling Goblin gear.

The despair gnawed on the fringes of my mind as I tried furiously to come up with some other explanation. The "Log Out" button in the upper right corner of my character screen blinked, taunting me. If only I could get out, run the code again, and get back in. The "Log Out" button pulsed and flashed as the game interface noticed my thinking about it. I only had a few hours left, and then it would be disabled forever.

Even if I could get out and back in, what would I do out there? The hack I'd tried failed, and I didn't have the time to craft another attempt, nor the skill. I was a failure. My code was garbage and I sucked. No wonder the game had so many bugs. *I myself* probably programmed in tons of them. I sat back on the bed and clenched my teeth as tears welled in my eyes.

"No. Bullshit, Abby. You don't cry, you problem solve. Get off your ass." I tilted my head back and sniffled away the self-pity, then got up and grabbed my staff.

I pulled open the door and marched down the stairs to the tavern, my mind still cranking away on what could've gone wrong. The code checked out, it ran successfully and did exactly what it was supposed to. So, what had happened?

When I reached the bottom, I was surprised to see Otto already sitting at the table from last night, chowing down on some gloppy substance in a bowl and a plate of thin fried meat, strikingly similar to bacon. At least there was still bacon.

I joined him at the table to see he'd thought of me, too, and there was a place setting similar to his, though with considerably less food. It was fine, I was a third his size and definitely didn't need to eat his portions. I plopped down and leaned my staff against the table.

Otto nodded and returned to his food.

"Thanks," I said, and shoved the spoon into the bowl. The mush turned out to be some kind of barley meal with sprinkles of brown and droplets of yellow. I stirred it vigorously until the scent of cinnamon and honey wafted up through the air on the steam.

I pulled a spoonful to my mouth and blew a few times, ensuring I wouldn't sear the roof of my mouth with gelatinous lava, and took a bite. I wasn't a fan of barley, it reminded me of heavy IPAs, but this was *amazing*. The honey and cinnamon completely masked the taste of beer, and the little barley pearls were a perfect, tender consistency.

The heat followed all the way down to my stomach as I swallowed, and a notification appeared in the corner of my screen:

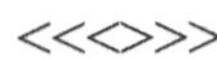

Honey-Cinnamon Barley meal

Restore 20 pts of Stamina per minute. Increase Vitality by 5%. Duration, 30 minutes.

The first bite clued me in to an awareness of my empty stomach, and I shoveled three more spoonfuls into my mouth. Where had all the chicken gone that I ate last night? I picked up the bowl and tilted it against my mouth as I scooped the remnants at the bottom.

Just over the rim of the bowl I caught Otto staring at me, one brow up.

"Should I order more?" His tone asked another question, *Do you always eat like a savage?*

I set the bowl down gingerly and grabbed the crispy pork belly with my fingers, then took a tiny nibble of the edge. Salty, sweet, crunchy edges of fat coated my mouth in a rich, cast-iron flavor, and I resisted the urge to stuff the whole thing in my mouth.

"So," I said as I finished chewing, "you know the guards at the door pretty well?" I took a sip from the cup in front of me. It was just water, but it tasted so fresh, much more so than any of the high-end bottled stuff Osmark would buy for the employees.

Otto cleared his throat. "Yes, I know a lot of people."

"How'd you come by knowing so many important people?"

He rolled his eyes, obviously not impressed by my flattery. "I know the people who can get things done."

"Useful." I nodded and took another, much larger, bite of the pork.

He mirrored my head bob, then his eyes flicked around the room.

This Risi was at least twice as awkward as me. By now, I would've asked what I was doing here or at least asked me *something*. He seemed completely uninterested in who I was or what I wanted to do.

"Uh, so, after we sell the things and you pay me for the escort, the room, and the food, do you," he paused, shrugging, "need anything else?"

Wow. His awkward level was over 9,000. I really hoped I wasn't this bad IRL.

"Yes. I'll probably need help with my class quest. After that, if you still want to hang around me, I've got something a lot bigger going on." And absolutely no idea of *how* I would get on to those bigger things without that damned scroll. I cursed my coding skills, or whatever it was that caused the scroll object not to be copied over to my message.

"My rate is seven silver a day."

Make that awkward level 10,000. No way was I going to get pushed around by *my* NPC.

"How about we split the spoils from the quest, after I pay my fair share for the food and the room?"

He scowled, probably considering how much he could make from the mobs on my quest line.

"Not just the money, but the loot too. I mean, I won't need or be able to carry most of the heavy armor and weapons, so they're yours," I offered.

He bobbed his head, then held his hand out to me. "Deal."

We shook on it and finished our breakfast. The barmaid loitered near the kitchen, her arms crossed and cheeks red. Apparently, we'd scorned her with the poor tip last night, and this morning. As we got up to leave, I pulled one of the rusty daggers, worth ten copper, from my inventory and set it on the table. It wasn't much, but was literally all I could do to compensate her.

Otto stopped me at the door. "Set your bind point here. Don't want you going all the way back up to Havasil."

I nodded, opened my character screen, and selected the "Bindings" tab. I selected the "Set Point" button and a pop-up appeared.

Home Binding

Are you sure you would like to set the Boar's Head in Harrowick as your home binding?

Yes/No

"Yes," I said. Blue light, so bright it looked white, flashed around my body.

Home Binding

You are now bound to the Boar's Head in Harrowick!

I closed my character sheet, and he nodded to me. We pushed through the heavy oaken door, and I was surprised at the quiet. There were birds chirping a happy song, distant sounds of an anvil being hammered on at a rhythmic pace, and the far-off calls of fresh bread, but the roars of drunken ballads and brawls were absent.

Otto led me back through the streets toward the main road. The remnants of last night's activities were strewn about the dirt path, including a few choice-to-avoid puddles, but we finally made it back to the relatively clean stone path.

"Merchant first, my coin is low," Otto grumbled.

"No, Natty Moongal. I want to know what I need for the quest before we go to any merchants."

Otto stopped short, then turned, leaned down, and whispered, "Naitee Mungal. Do not disrespect her. She'll"—he glanced about—"do things to you."

He returned to his upright posture, taking one more furtive look about the mostly deserted street. Great, my trainer was one of *those* types. Full of themselves and ready to punish anyone who didn't notice their greatness. No matter, she would train me.

"Okay, take me to Naitee Mungal first and I'll give you ten silver for yesterday's escort." He didn't look satisfied, so I added, "And I will pay you whatever you had to pay the guard to let us in."

He looked even more upset at the last part, but then his shoulders relaxed, and he rolled his eyes. "Fine, keep up and don't get me in trouble."

Otto turned away before I could say anything else—"Thank you," for instance—and kept a fast pace down the street. We were heading deeper into the city. Wood and straw residences were becoming scarce as brick-and-mortar businesses took over the landscape. Places like "Groffer's Ironworks" and "Twin Sister Bakery" were alive with the sounds of labor and sales as the population on the street became denser.

The crowd bumped me, shoulder to shoulder as we pushed through, until I decided to trail behind Otto, who magically had the ability to part the way. Perhaps it was something to do with his seven-foot-tall, tusk-faced, sword-wielding appearance.

There weren't many things I could see through the crowd, damn me for not making myself a little bit taller, but some fluttering off the path on the left caught my eye. A black spire flying four flags: red, blue, white, and black with a single symbol on each: a burning fire, a drop of water, a snowflake, and a crystal.

"Is that it?" I raised my voice to carry over the noise of the rabble and pointed to the spire.

Otto's gaze followed the direction of my arm, and he gave a gruff, "Yes."

Giddy as a schoolgirl, I pushed my way through the Wodes to the side street on the left. Otto tromped over to me, moving like a shark through a school of fish. For the first time since I entered V.G.O., I was grinning ear to ear, bouncing on my toes, and actually excited. I was going to be a freakin' Sorceress and do *real magic* with my hands!

Otto smirked and motioned for me to lead the way down the side alley to the shop. I hardly worried about the puddles and mounds of debris as we made our way to the tall structure. It stood alone with no other building sharing a wall, looking one part gnarled tree struck by lighting and the other part something like a haunted house.

The roof was all shingled in black, slanted at a greater degree than any other roof in town. The exterior walls were a dark wood, maybe chestnut, and there were intricate symbols drawn in the four colors of the flags. I didn't recognize the language, if that's what it was, but it seemed to create a border around the doors and windows, which were also blacked out with dark curtains.

"Well, are you going to go inside?" Otto broke my trance, and I walked up to the door. The iron knob was warm from the morning sun and turned easily. As the door opened, a wave of heat spilled out onto the doorstep. I was instantly uncomfortable.

The inside was the complete opposite of the outside. White walls decorated sparsely, tan wood floors adorned with fluffy brown and black animal furs, and glass cases, meticulously clean, full of trinkets of all sorts. And gods, was it *hot*. It was like a damned sauna on steroids, at least 30 degrees hotter in here than out on the streets.

I pulled at my robes to fan myself and looked around for signs of life, but the room was still. "Hello?" I asked toward the stairs at the back of the shop.

There was a creaking on the floor above and footsteps, but no reply. I looked to Otto, who seemed perfectly comfortable in the unbearable heat. He shook his head as if to say, "I'm not shouting next."

I took a few more steps into the shop and leaned over one of the glass cases. It was laid out like a jewelry shop, but the displays were a far cry from that standard fair. The cases weren't supported or framed by metal structures, they were formed entirely from glass, with very few to no edges. There were ripples in the glass, like someone dropped a pebble in a gentle pond and froze it in time.

"Like anything?" The strong, accented voice at my back raised hairs on my arms, but I didn't move.

"The glass."

The woman, Naitee I assumed, chuckled. "Thank you, I made it myself."

I turned to see Otto hovering near the door, looking nervous. Red caught my eye, and I turned farther to see a six-foot-tall, pale-skinned, gold-haired Dawn Elf woman dressed in wine-colored robes, with red lips to match, who'd been right behind me. Her haunting blue eyes only intensified her beauty, and she stared down on me with fierce curiosity.

"You're not here to buy anything?" she asked, folding her slender fingers together over her navel.

I shook my head. "I want to become a Sorceress."

She grinned, but didn't speak.

"I want you to teach me." Just in case my intent wasn't clear from the first comment.

Her smile widened into a sinister thing, and her long arm reached out for my shoulder. This NPC was giving me the damn willies, but I wanted to be a caster. I'd already picked the class kit I would get, and most of the spell tree I would follow. One of the benefits of being on the Dev team, I got early access to the content.

Her fingers gripped down on my robes, and she pulled me in. I resisted the urge to retaliate, or make a fuss, knowing this woman was my only chance in many miles to get the class I wanted.

She tilted her blood-red lips down to my ear and whispered, "You would never survive my training."

She released me, and I rocked back on my heels, seething inside. How dare she judge my worth, my gumption, by my appearance. She had no idea what I'd gone through to get here, and no idea how far I'd go to get what I needed.

She waved her hand at me in a shooing motion. "Go run along now and play mercenary with your friend."

I could see Otto fidgeting out of the corner of my eye, and Naitee turned her back, heading for the stairs.

"I will be the greatest Sorceress in Eldgard whether you train me or not. Do you want the honor of being my mentor or the shame of turning me away?" It was a gamble, but I needed to get her attention… and I was pissed off.

She stopped at the first step and looked over her shoulder at Otto. "This one's fiery."

The Dawn Elf cut behind the glass case and moved to a similar style glass shelf on the wall. Her hand fell on many vials, until it stopped at a teardrop shaped container filled with a green pearlescent liquid.

The vial made a tinkling as she set it on the glass countertop in front of me.

"Drink it."

My heart skipped as a new pop-up appeared.

Quest Alert: The Path of a Sorceress

Naitee Mungal has challenged you to become her apprentice. Drink the liquid in the vial before you to prove you're ready to take on what she has in store.

Quest Class: Uncommon, Class-Based

Quest Difficulty: Easy, Gamble

Success: Drink the liquid in the vial before you.

Failure: Refuse the liquid, or die upon drinking it.

Reward: Class Change: Sorceress, Varying Kits; Unique, Scalable Item.

Well, shit, she called my bluff. I grabbed the tiny bottle and popped the crystal stopper out, then glanced at Otto. His face was painted with worry, but he didn't move to stop me.

"Bottoms up." Naitee gave a snarl of a grin.

With the very real fear that this green goop would kill me, I put the crystal to my lips and tilted the vial back.

SEVEN

PATH OF A SORCERESS

BITTER ACIDITY, LIKE SPIRULINA AND LEMON juice, slapped the back of my throat, and I swallowed before I had the reflex to spit it out. I slammed the vial down on the counter and coughed, then gulped a few more times to clear the flavor.

"Brash, determined, a little too trusting, but all things to be honed in time. What's your name, girl?"

Ugh, from lady to girl, what a downgrade. I stifled a burp. "Abby Hollander."

Quest Update: The Path of a Sorceress

You've accepted Naitee's challenge to become her apprentice and survived.

"Well, Abby, it's time to replace the ingredients you just consumed." She corked the vial and put it back on the shelf, then grabbed a piece of parchment and began to scribble.

"Lumalgae, from the Wayward Caverns, at least four ounces. Balrigon soot, from at least ten different Balrigons." I raised a brow, and she shrugged. "I need diversity. You can find all sorts of Balrigons on the mountainside to the north. Let's see…" She continued her scrawling, but I realized she wasn't making me a shopping list. She was drawing intricate runes in a mandala-like pattern.

"Oh yes, Rose Quartz, three or four stones should do it, from anywhere really." She gave me a once-over. "You don't look like a miner."

I held up my arm and flexed, earning a grimace from Naitee. My Strength and Stamina stats were both pretty low. I looked to Otto.

"It's extra," he barked. I rolled my eyes and returned my attention to my new tutor. I wished she'd pick up the pace. Beads of sweat were rolling down my spine, and my Stamina bar was beginning to drop, ever so slowly, from the intense heat.

Naitee finished scribbling and rolled up the scroll, then tied it off and sealed it with wax. "This will get you to the mountains in the north. From there you can walk down into the Wayward Caverns. All the ingredients will be nearby."

"And this one"—she scribbled four quick symbols and repeated the same process in sealing it—"will open your mind to all the magics of Sorcery. The potion you drank unlocked your potential energy, and seeing as you didn't die, it seems you really do have some magic in you."

She extended the rolls of parchment to me, but as I reached out, she jerked them back. "These are expensive. I will not replace them if anything happens," she warned, and I nodded.

Naitee held them out once more, but pulled them back as she started in again, and I bit my lip to stifle an annoyed huff. "You'll have access to the basic abilities from each school for five hours, and not a moment more. I expect you to use all four schools and become proficient. Oh!" She reached under the glass case and grabbed something else. "And here is a return scroll, too—it will take you to your bind point." As she passed them into my hands, a new pop-up appeared on my screen.

Quest Update: The Path of a Sorceress

Naitee needs you to replace the rare ingredients you just consumed and prove your proficiency as a spellslinger. She has provided a scroll to unlock the basic abilities of all four Sorcery magics for 5 hours. Use them wisely.

Quest Class: Uncommon, Class-Based

Quest Difficulty: Moderate

Success: Using all four schools of magic, collect 4 ounces of Lumalgae from the Wayward Caverns, 3 Rose Quartz stones, and 10 soot essences from 10 different Balrigons, then return to Naitee before the night is done.

Failure: Fail to gather all the necessary ingredients in time.

Reward: Class Change: Sorceress, Varying Kits; Unique, Scalable Item.

I accepted the quest and dropped the scrolls into my inventory, out of sight.

"So, for what purpose are you becoming the Greatest Sorceress in Eldgard?" Naitee was oddly more talkative now than when we had first met and definitely warmer.

Did I want to tell her what was going on? Would it be worth risking her blabbing to someone else to earn the right to be her apprentice? There were definitely other sorcerers in Eldgard who could train me, but how far would I have to go to find them?

"Ah, some juicy secret." Naitee grinned and walked around the counter. "Never you mind it for now, child, but," she held my hands in hers and whispered, "I am no friend of the Empire."

This "girl" and "child" stuff was getting on my nerves. I shot a glance at Otto, who seemed not to be paying attention, a thick sheen of sweat visible on his forehead.

"I'm here to take down a tyrant and stop the oppression of every living person in Eldgard."

Naitee squeezed my hands lightly. "Such a noble cause. Though, not many tyrants ruling today. Harrowick is a free city."

I nodded. "He's not come to power yet. We're in a race, of sorts, but he doesn't know."

"I see. Well, girl, best of luck. Off you get!" She pushed me toward the exit, my annoyance peaking at anger.

She held open the door, and I looked back at her from the stoop. "It's Abby Hollander, and I *will* be the greatest Sorceress."

"Of course you will. Hurry up now, those ingredients won't collect themselves." She slammed the door, a gush of hot air slapping me one last time as a countdown appeared in the corner of my vision: 12 hours, 34 minutes, 21 seconds.

I pumped my basic robe, trying to circulate cool air in, and saw Otto do something similar with his pants.

"So, shop?" I asked, finally cool and not so pissed off.

Otto grunted his reply and took off down the alley. The population on the streets had thinned out since the morning sun was delivering a cloudless blast of heat. Though it was far better than the inside of Naitee's shop, it was still uncomfortable.

We stopped in at Portish Goods to sell all the junk, and I was surprised at Otto's bargaining skills. He was able to sell all my ten-copper blades and five-copper worn shirts for fifteen silver. Not enough for me to buy *anything*, but enough to pay Otto back.

After selling, we walked to another nearby shop which didn't seem like the place for Otto at all: Satin and Beech. When I stepped through the door, I was bombarded with smoke from burning incense. The dim light took a moment to adjust to, but when I finally did, I was taken aback by the wondrous things hanging from every wall. Black velvet cloaks embroidered with shimmering crimson thread in the shape of a hummingbird; tall staves topped with massive gemstones, or pulsing spheres of multicolored energy; robes, elegant and flowing with power. This was a shop for *me*. But, I didn't have any money, and I still owed Otto whatever he'd charge me for mining the Rose Quartz.

I turned on my heel and whispered at him. "What are we doing here?"

"You need better robes. You look like…" His brow scrunched. "I don't want to say what you look like, but you don't look like the greatest Sorceress in Eldgard."

"That's because I'm not yet," I said tersely, fully aware of the shopkeeper's approach.

"Hello, welcome in! What can we get started for you?" The man rolled his r's, and it was obvious he wasn't from Harrowick. I turned back to face him and gasped at the flutter of his massive, beautiful black wings. He was an Accipiter.

"I, uh, we made a mistake," I stuttered, pushing Otto with both hands as I kept my eyes on the man.

The shopkeeper grinned. "Nonsense, no mistake. You can look around. You'll find something you want, I know it."

Yeah, that's what I was worried about.

"She needs a new robe," Otto blurted, and I gritted my teeth.

The Accipiter grabbed me and squared my shoulders. "Yes, I see. Of course she does." He put his hand to his narrow chin as his eyes scanned over my body, lingering at my wide hips, and I felt a flare of indignation at his indiscretion.

He snapped his fingers, declaring, "I have just the thing," and pumped his massive wings as he jumped and rocketed himself to the back of the shop.

I shot a glare at Otto, who shrugged in a very innocent way. "How am I going to pay for this? I have *one* silver!" I demanded.

"I'll cover it for now, I know you're good for the coin. I'll just have to stick around until you can pay me back." He slapped me on the shoulder, the gesture sending me off balance, then moved on to pick up a large translucent sphere on an opulent stand.

With the shopkeeper occupied in the back, looking for a robe wide enough for my hips I assumed, I decided to look around. Everything on display was incredibly expensive. If the robe he found for me was anywhere near the prices of the things on the walls, we'd be thrown out for trying to barter.

The whooshing of wings brought my attention back to the shopkeeper as he glided down to the open entrance. "I've found it, the perfect thing." He grinned and held out a blue-and-purple, simply sewn gown.

I took it and inspected the item.

Dignified Robes

Armor Type: Light, Tailored Cloth

Class: Uncommon

Base Defense: 15

Primary Effects:

- +5% Spirit regen

- +3 to Intelligence

We're not all made of money, but we can at least look nice.

"It's great, but—"

Otto cut me off. "How much?"

The Accipiter man shrugged noncommittally. "I could let it go for five gold."

"Two," Otto replied immediately.

The Accipiter looked scorned. "This is a handcrafted garment, not that a brute like you would understand…" He crossed his arms. "Four gold."

Otto shook his head. "Two gold."

I was watching lines of code on a server *barter*. I'd helped build a world where computers could communicate with one another beyond transferring packets and connecting to DNSs. Otto and the Accipiter went back and forth, Otto firm at two gold and the Accipiter trying to weasel a few extra silver out of him. It was a visceral reminder of what The Crunch created, but also, all that was lost to accomplish it. Osmark would pay his dues.

"All right!" The shopkeeper threw his arms up. "Two gold, and you'll bring her back again, she's in dreadful garb."

"Deal." Otto shook his hand. "We'll be back tonight."

They exchanged coin for goods, and Otto beamed as he handed me the gown. I was taken aback. Even my last boyfriend hadn't been this nice. Not that I'd gone out of my way to buy *him* anything amazing, but I'd known Otto about twelve hours, and he was willing to pay two gold, an IRL equivalent of two hundred dollars, for a robe, for me.

I took the gown and held it, staring at the soft fabric. "I don't know what to say," I muttered.

"Say you'll pay me back later." He patted me on the shoulder again, this time softer, and strutted for the exit.

"Thanks," I shouted at him, and he turned back, giving me a huge, tusky grin, then walked out.

I opened my inventory and selected the new robes. The old one popped off into my inventory, and I held it in my hand. Ah… that was a lot easier than taking it off by hand.

"What would you give me for this?" I asked the shopkeeper, and he looked at the old robes in disgust.

He cleared his throat. "I could give you, ah, a few coppers?"

I frowned. "We'll be back later tonight, and I can buy more at full price. Come on, I want to pay him back, at least a little."

The shopkeeper seemed defeated, exhausted. "Fine, five silver." He jabbed a finger at me. "But don't say Hasan never did anything for you!"

I held out the garment to him with a grin, and he groaned, holding it between two fingers as he pulled a coin from the purse at his belt.

"Thank you, Hasan," I said, taking the coin and running for the door.

"You can thank me by coming back to buy my most expensive item!"

The streets were alive again, and the fresh air, sans incense, felt light in my lungs.

"Otto." I punched his arm and instantly regretted it as 10 of my HP leaked away.

He chuckled as I shook out my hand in frustration.

I held out the coin to him. "Here's something for the mining."

"Good," he mumbled, taking the silver with a little less enthusiasm than I expected. He was going on and on about wanting me to pay him, but as soon as I did, he looked upset. What a weirdo.

"All right." I whipped the teleport scroll from my inventory and held it out with a devilish grin, then asked, "Ready to go?"

Otto put the coin away and checked over his body, hand falling on his sword hilt and bandolier. He nodded. "Let's go."

I popped the wax seal on the scroll, and it unfurled on its own, then fizzled in a shower of sparks. The tiny balls of light floated gently, but I could see they were about to burst! Each luminescent sphere vibrated with power, drawing nearer and nearer to one another. The light filled my vision, a rainbow prism of pure magical wonder.

It faded just as quick as it came, leaving behind an ovular window thrumming with a soft beat, beckoning us in. The view on the other side was a calm, green valley blowing gently in a breeze not felt from this side of the portal.

"So freaking cool." I reached toward it, warmth filling my body as my fingers touched the event horizon.

My head swiveled and tilted, but I managed to stay upright as we plopped onto waving fields of grass below crisp white peaks. Blue dots wiggled in my vision, and my head swam as sweet honey-coated bile pushed up my esophagus. I swallowed hard and took a deep breath as a cool wind blew my curly locks.

Portal travel was disorienting, but also the coolest shit since Python. With all the scrolls Naitee gave me, I assumed portal travel was something I was going to need to get used to.

"Check your map." Otto sucked in a breath that closely resembled the type of breath one would inhale when trying not to throw up. I smirked, and he turned away, hands on his hips.

I popped open my interface and sure enough, the map updated with a blinking yellow arrow, and the quest log title of "Path of a Sorceress" blinked yellow along with it. "This way." I pointed north into the trees at the base of the mountain.

"How long do you have?" Otto asked as we headed into the forest.

I pulled the bound scroll from my inventory. "Once I open it, five hours."

Otto stopped us at the first trees, his head turning slowly on his thick neck as he surveyed the land. There was a rustling in the trees and bushes as the wind picked up.

Otto looked me up and down. "You should get some practice shots in first. I don't need you blasting my backside by accident."

I withheld my comments about the size of Otto's backside and how difficult it would be to not hit him. Old gamer culture was creeping back up on me. I nodded my head without a snigger and ran my thumbnail under the seal of the scroll of sorceric knowledge.

All thought shifted, and I didn't remember how I'd ever thought of anything beyond the power surging through my body. I dropped to my knees, hardly aware that I even had knees anymore. Heat swelled in my chest as the colors shifted to red and gold. My hands trembled with a voracious lust for combat. Refreshing blue washed those feelings away, replacing them with devious curiosity. The blue darkened until it was nearly black, and I felt a sense of grounding, stability, and drive.

Before the technicolor smokenado completed, it gave one final thrum of ecstasy-inducing power. My shoulders shook, and I looked at my sweaty palms.

"Well," Otto said, drawing me from the trance, "let's see what you can do."

"Otto, wait!" I demanded as he pushed on into the forest, sword at the ready.

He half turned as he continued his charge toward the bushes. "Don't worry, it'll come to you like breathi—"

A massive black fist smashed through the bush to Otto's left and pummeled him in the face. Otto flew backwards five feet and "oofed" as he broke a fallen branch with his butt.

The fist belonged to some rabid concoction of a gorilla and a bear, with fur like porcupine quills. The [Lowland Balrigon] reared up and beat its chest as it roared. Bits of lava spat from its wide-open jaw, and liquid fire dribbled down its three-inch canines. Oh, shit.

The Balrigon turned to me and raised a massive fist, revealing deadly retractable talons below the spiny fur. The paw swiped down at me, and I jumped back on instinct. I landed hard in the dirt as I groped for the staff at my back. The Balrigon took two ground-trembling steps forward on its hind legs, this time raising both fists.

My fumbling hands couldn't get the war staff free. "Shit!" I thrust my hand forward to block, and in an instant, a thick, gray mass materialized at my palm and rocketed into the beast's face. The object cracked against the creature's skull, and the Balrigon tottered before falling to the side in a heap.

Critical hit!

The Health bar above the thing's head flashed a deep red and dropped to 65%.

"What the hell was that?" I scrambled to my feet and Otto finally found his.

He staggered toward me and then jabbed his sword down hard into the monster's throat once, then twice. It gave a final gurgle as its Health bar hit 0, then went limp.

"That was a Balrigon." Otto wheezed a bit and rubbed his head.

"No," I stammered, "the thing that shot out of my hand?"

Otto grinned. "I told you, it's as easy as breathing."

My eyes widened, and I opened my character sheet with delight.

EIGHT

GRIND FOR GOODS

SORCERY. WAS. *AMAZING*.

I could shoot fireballs out of my hands. *Out of my hands!* And not just fire. I could shoot an ice lance and hurl massive boulders. The passive abilities were just as cool, if not cooler. They were *all* so fantastically useful, too!

I thought before I took the plunge into V.G.O. that I'd picked my class kit. I was going to be a Stonewall, the earth elemental sorcery tree. Now, I wasn't so sure. We killed the second to last Balrigon I needed for the materials, and I held a hand up to request a break to refill my Spirit. There weren't any more Balrigon nearby, so I popped open my character sheet to bask in the greatness one more time.

The scroll Naitee gave me activated all four trees and applied temporary points in the first two abilities for each. In the end, I'd only have access to one class kit, but for the moment, I could see the trees for all four: Hydromancer, Firebrand, Frostlock, and Stonewall. I panned over to the Hydromancer Tree:

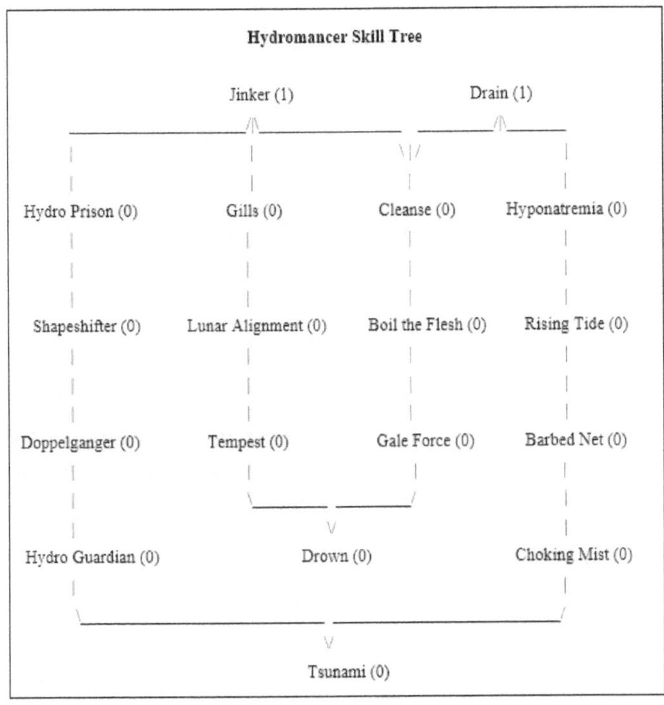

Skill: Jinker

Draw on the agile powers of water! Your body is swift like the coursing river, ready to flow around any obstacle. Increase your Dexterity by 5%, your Luck by 5, and your Evade chance by 10%.

Skill Type/Level: Passive, Level 1

Cost: None

Range: N/A

Cast Time: N/A

Cooldown: N/A

Effect 1: Increase your Dexterity by 5%.

Effect 2: Increase your Luck by 5.

Effect 3: Increase your chance to Evade by 10%.

Pretty cool stuff. But that wasn't all.

Skill: Drain

Suck the very life out of your opponent. Whether it's blood or a blood-like substance, you drain away their fluids, dealing 20-45 damage to the opponent and converting that damage to .5 x the damage done in Spirit.

Skill Type/Level: Spell, Level 1

Cost: 50 Spirit

Range: 10 meters

Cast Time: Instant

Cooldown: 3 seconds

Effect 1: Deal 20-45 points of water damage to an enemy with a liquid regulatory system.

Effect 2: Convert damage dealt x .5 into Spirit.

Now that was wicked. An instant cast spell with a chance to gain back nearly half the casting cost in Spirit, just by casting it! Seemed a little OP to me, but then when I panned over to Frostlock, I understood why:

<<<>>>

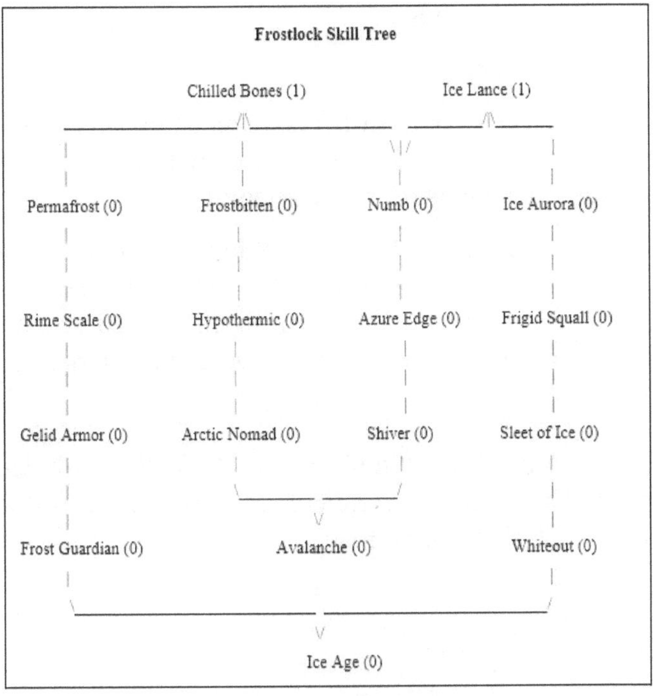

<<<>>>

Skill: Ice Lance

Use the power of frost to create a spear sharp enough to slice through thick leather hide. The spear deals 40 damage with a 5% chance to inflict Numb. If the spear enters and leaves the enemy's body, over-penetrating, deal an additional 10 points of frost damage with a 15% chance to inflict Numb.

Skill Type/Level: Spell, Level 1

Cost: 30 Spirit

Range: 25 meters

Cast Time: 2 seconds

Cooldown: None

Effect 1: Deal 40 points of frost damage to an enemy. If the spear enters and leaves the enemy's body, deal an additional 10 points of frost damage.

Effect 2: 5% chance to inflict Numb, reducing enemy movement and attack speed by 10%, and reducing Health regen rate by 5%. Numb will last 20 seconds. Numb can stack up to three times on any one target.

Three times! Numb would stack, *three freaking times!* That was just ridiculous, and the Frostlock passive, Chilled Bones, made it even cooler.

Skill: Chilled Bones

You've weathered some serious storms. Increase resistance to ice damage and cold conditions by 15%. Increase Spirit regeneration by 10% and ice damage dealt by 5% when the ambient temperature is below 40 degrees. The cold never bothered you anyway.

Skill Type/Level: Passive, Level 1

Cost: None

Range: N/A

Cast Time: N/A

Cooldown: N/A

Effect 1: Increase Cold and ice resistances by 15%.

Effect 2: Increase Spirit regeneration by 10% and ice damage dealt by 5% when the ambient temperature is below 40 degrees.

<<<◇>>>

Some seriously impressive stuff, and I was enjoying every second of it. Stonewall, the class kit I thought I was going to take, was next:

<<<◇>>>

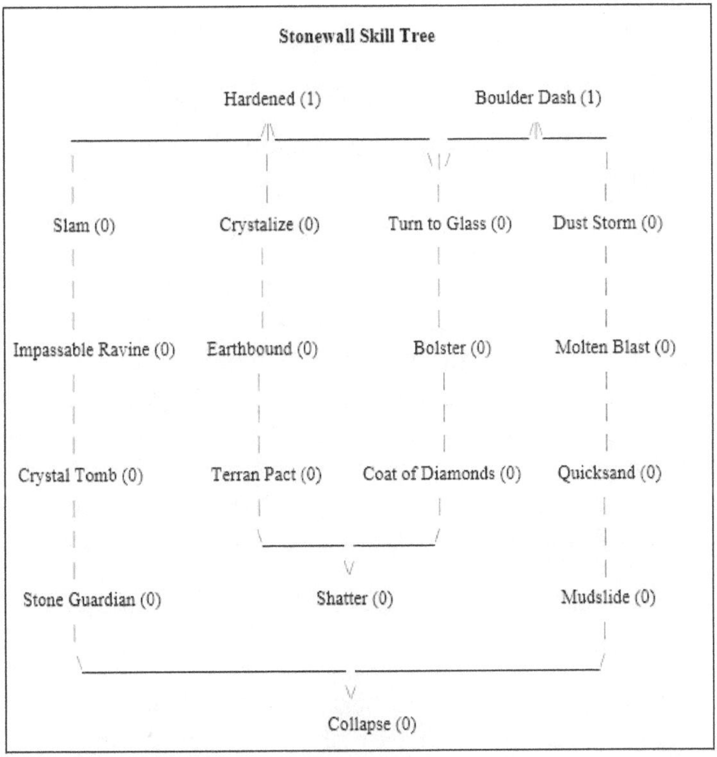

Stonewall Skill Tree

Hardened (1)   Boulder Dash (1)

Slam (0)   Crystalize (0)   Turn to Glass (0)   Dust Storm (0)

Impassable Ravine (0)   Earthbound (0)   Bolster (0)   Molten Blast (0)

Crystal Tomb (0)   Terran Pact (0)   Coat of Diamonds (0)   Quicksand (0)

Stone Guardian (0)   Shatter (0)   Mudslide (0)

Collapse (0)

<<<◇>>>

Skill: Hardened

Your core is strengthened by the essence of earth. Increase your base resistances to all elements by 5%, and increase your base Stamina by 2.5 x character level. No matter your power, be wary of parchment…

Skill Type/Level: Passive, Level 1

Cost: None

Range: N/A

Cast Time: N/A

Cooldown: N/A

Effect 1: Increase all Elemental resistances by 5%.

Effect 2: Increase your base Stamina by 2.5 x character level.

That passive ability *alone* was the reason I'd wanted to be a Stonewall. At a high level, with that maxed out, my Stamina would be increased by 12 times my character level. Which, at level 30, would be like having an extra 30 points of Constitution worth of Stamina. The direct damage ability was still cool, too, and had saved my butt on the first Balrigon, but the passive took the cake, for sure.

Skill: Boulder Dash

Call on your Stamina to hurl a massive boulder at your enemy. Deal 30 points of blunt damage to an enemy within range. If the enemy is out of range, you may still strike them, but inflict less damage. On a successful hit, have a 5% chance to cause disorientation, reducing

Accuracy by 20% for 10 seconds. If struck in the head or brain center, increase the chance to cause disorientation to 30%.

Skill Type/Level: Spell, Level 1

Cost: 20 Stamina and 15 Spirit

Range: .05 x Stamina in meters

Cast Time: Instant

Cooldown: None

Effect 1: Deal 30 points of blunt damage to any target in range. Deal less damage to a target out of range due to Stamina exhaustion.

Effect 2: 5% chance to cause disorientation on a strike to the body, 30% chance on a strike to the head. Disorientation reduces the target's Accuracy by 20% for 10 seconds.

From what I could tell, several of the Stonewall abilities had a dual Stamina/Spirit cost, because a lot of them required feats of strength. Fine by me! With the Hardened ability, that wouldn't be a problem.

Last was Firebrand. I was personally enjoying hucking flaming balls of doom at enemies and watching them catch fire, but I knew in my heart that Firebrand was too damn squishy to solo with—it was a glass cannon. I didn't know how long I'd have Otto for, and I didn't know if Jack, my IRL friend from college, was going to take me up on the offered capsule to transition into V.G.O. I could be completely alone on my trek.

I dismissed the morbid thought and checked out the tree:

<<<◇>>>

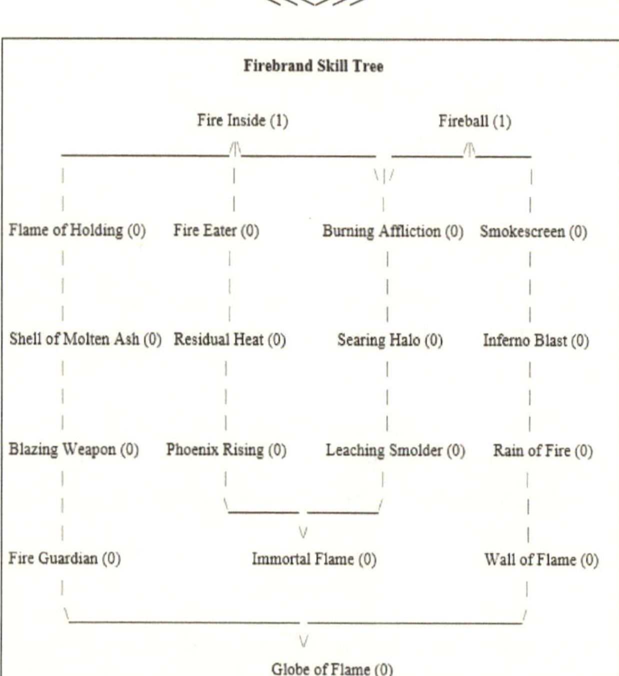

<<<◇>>>

Skill: Fire Inside

You feel the presence of fire in your belly! Fire spells are 5% more potent. When activated, all spells are 50% more potent for 30 seconds. Your Spirit regen is reduced by 25% for 60 seconds upon activation.

Skill Type/Level: Passive and Spell, Level 1

Cost: Spirit regeneration reduced by 25% for 60 seconds

Range: N/A

Cast Time: Instant

Cooldown: 30 minutes

Passive Effect 1: Increase Fire spell damage by 5%.

Active Effect 1: Increase all spell potency by 50% for 30 seconds.

Active Effect 2: Decrease Spirit regeneration by 25% for 60 seconds.

It was the only spell I'd seen in V.G.O., so far, that had a passive and active effect. Not only that, it was the only spell where the price was a Spirit regen hit. I could see further down the tree the Leaching Smolder ability actively stole Spirit from the enemy target based on the number of Burning Afflictions on them. It seemed like the designers had *really* put some effort into creating awesome combos for the Sorc classes.

Then, lastly, there was a standard Fireball.

Skill: Fireball

Channel your fury into a globe of flame! Deal 30 fire damage on hit with a 15% chance to inflict Burning Affliction level 1, causing an additional 30 damage over 10 seconds. Burning Affliction stacks up to 3 times on any one target.

Skill Type/Level: Spell, Level 1

Cost: 30 Spirit

Range: 20 meters

Cast Time: 3 seconds

Cooldown: None

Effect 1: Deal 30 damage to an enemy on hit.

Effect 2: 15% chance to add Burning Affliction to the target, dealing 30 damage over 10 seconds. Stacks up to 3 times on any one target.

Out of all the base abilities, Fireball was far from the coolest, but I could tell further down the tree there was a lot of "synergy," as Osmark would say… Fireball's cast time would be reduced with further upgrades, and the chance to add Burning Affliction would increase. Leveled-up Burning Affliction would increase the chance to land critical hits with fire damage and increase its duration. Leveled-up Leaching Smolder would increase the amount of Spirit stolen from the target per Burning Affliction. They all played off one another.

Lastly, was the General Sorceress tree, and while I thought I would want to save all my points for my class kit, this thing was pretty badass. I'd decided to drop 4 points out of the gate, just to get me a leg up.

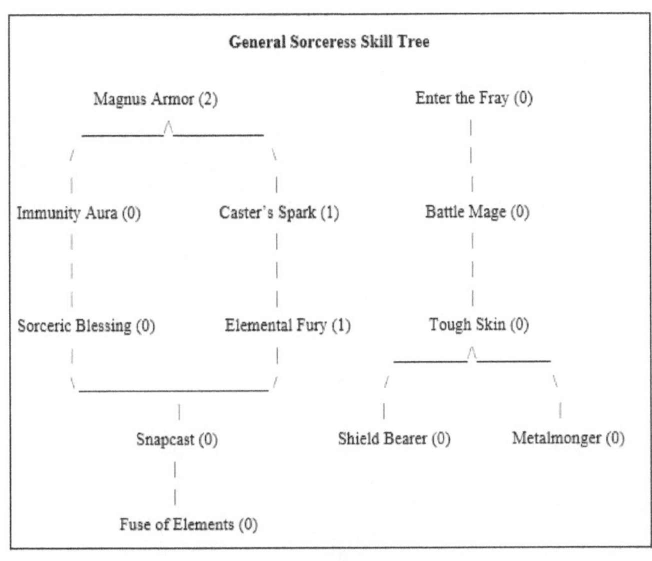

<<<◇>>>

Skill: Magnus Armor

Every good Sorceress wears the best armor and shares with her friends, too! Magnus Armor shields your party members from up to three magical blows, all adding up to or equaling your Spell Strength + your Intelligence.

Skill Type/Level: Party Buff, Level 2

Cost: 20 Spirit per Party Member

Range: 4 meters

Cast Time: Instant

Cooldown: 20 Minutes

Effect 1: Allow party members to absorb up to three magical blows that equal your Spell Strength + your Intelligence.

Skill: Caster's Spark

Your party's spirits may be down, but you've got the spark to light the fire of their inspiration. Caster's Spark will increase your party's Spirit regeneration, including your own.

Skill Type/Level: Passive, Level 1

Cost: None

Range: 10 meters

Cast Time: N/A

Cooldown: N/A

Effect 1: Increase party members' Spirit regeneration by .1 x your character level/second.

 .1 times my character level was a bit weak right now, but it would improve with every level up without me doing a thing, so that was nice. I didn't know what kind of abilities and spells Otto had, but I had to assume he used Spirit, and this would be good for the both of us. Elemental Fury, however, only helped me right now.

Skill: Elemental Fury

Like a tsunami, or raging inferno, the more there is, the stronger it gets. Party elemental damage is increased by 5% when you're within range. When there are multiple party members with the same Element, increase that damage type by another 2.5% per party member who shares the type.

Skill Type/Level: Passive, Level 1

Cost: None

Range: 10 meters

Cast Time: N/A

Cooldown: N/A

Effect 1: Party elemental damage is increased by 5%.

Effect 2: Increase elemental damage of a type that more than one party member shares by 2.5%

"You done fuffling around yet? This is the third time you've stopped to admire yourself," Otto called, and I snapped the character sheet closed, the beautiful mountainside landscape coming back into full view. Pine needles crunched as I marched toward him with a scowl on my face.

"I wasn't *fuffling*," I declared, "I was making sure I know how to use my abilities so I don't accidentally kill you and ruin my chances of finishing this quest. And my Spirit needed to regenerate." I checked the bar to see it was full and probably had been for a little bit.

He laughed. "I don't think you could accidentally kill me with any of your little spells."

I raised a brow at the provocation. The deep roar of a Balrigon echoed through the tall trees and drew our attention. I back-burnered the challenge, focusing on the massive beast who'd taken notice of our presence. The creature lumbered toward us on all fours, looking something like a gorilla crossed with a bear, but instead of fur, the thing was layered thick with ashen soot. The very soot I needed to collect.

Surprise, surprise, Balrigons didn't like having their soot removed from their bodies while they were alive, so it was a painful slog to kill each one and collect a good sample before the corpse blew away in the breeze. That was interesting the first time it happened.

Fortunately, the Balrigons were weak against frost damage, and Ice Lance was very effective in slowing the creature's relentless assault on Otto as he tanked for me.

I conjured a cool spear and shot it toward the Balrigon, which had accelerated from a lumber to a gallop. The spear of ice hit and shattered. A shower of sparkles that clung to the creature's quills informed me the Numb debuff had procced. The creature stumbled and skidded to a halt, eyes locking on me. The mob looked me up and down, then charged, its thick limbs lumbering under the Numb debuff.

"Let me draw aggro, Crazy!" Otto swiped at the creature's legs at it rushed past him, and I smacked it with another Ice Lance.

I grinned. "Try to take it from me if my *little spells* are so weak!"

I shot one more Ice Lance, another Numb proccing and slowing the beast a bit more, but it was still coming for me much faster than I had anticipated. The creature's massive fist barreled toward me, and I yelped, cutting off a fourth spell mid-cast. The wind of its powerful punch blew my long curls as I dove into a roll, evading the blow by the grace of Jinker.

Otto leapt over me, plunging his sword into the Balrigon's back. The thing howled and shook itself, throwing Otto and the sword across the clearing into a bushy pine tree. I heard an "Oof" and a snap, hoping the latter was a broken branch and not Otto's broken neck.

The Balrigon whirled around, eyes flashing in every direction until they found me. It bellowed, meaty fists pounding the ground as it charged again. I needed some distance and time, but had neither. I triggered Boulder Dash over and over, smacking the creature with three good hits, one to the head, which did exactly what I needed.

The creature skidded past me, shaking its head as it wobbled on uncertain legs. I tried to conjure an Ice Lance, but was alerted to a red flashing bar in the corner of my vision. Only 15 Spirit left, though slowly climbing from my decent regeneration rate. The Balrigon had *maybe* 40 HP left—if I could stall long enough to get off one more Ice Lance, I could put it down for good.

I pulled my staff from the handy holster on my back and whapped the Balrigon on the head. My Stamina dropped by 10 points, and the Balrigon took no damage at all.

"Shit."

The creature reacted near instantly, batting me in the gut with a hard backhand. I soared ass-first through the clearing and tumbled as I landed. I gasped to fill my lungs as a notification appeared.

<<<>>>

Debuff Added

Stunning Blow: You have sustained a stunning blow! Attack damage -15%; Stamina regeneration reduced by 30%; movement speed reduced by 35%; duration, 1 minute.

<<<>>>

"Ffff." Air leaked from my mouth as I tried to curse.

My Spirit was back up to 30, but I still needed 10 more to finish this thing off. The Balrigon ate up the distance between us in a rage-filled sprint and flipped me into the air with both fists. My body trembled in agony as it socked me in the gut on the way down, tossing me into a tree. The HP bar in the corner of my vision flashed an angry red, *WARNING! WARNING!* I begged for a few more seconds of Spirit regeneration.

37.

The Balrigon beat its chest, then the ground, preparing to charge.

38.

It dug into the earth, powerful back legs launching it toward me.

39.

The Balrigon wailed in agony and dropped to the dirt, sliding to a hard stop right in front of me. Otto stood thirty feet back, his sword pinned in the beast's back. I dropped to my knees and sighed.

"That was close." I gasped, the effects of Stunning Blow still making it hard to regenerate my depleted Stamina.

Otto tromped across the clearing and jerked his sword free from the dead Balrigon, then leaned down toward me.

"Let me"—he grabbed my hand and pulled me to my feet—"get aggro first."

"I almost had it. Just one more Spirit and I would've lanced the thing."

He shook his head and growled, "One more second and you would've been Wode jelly." He marched off, his shoulders bunched up near his ears with his head hung low. Then he stopped, turned around with his hand up in an accusatory point, and glared at me.

"If you're going to work with me, you have to work *with* me." He spun back around as the Balrigon corpse crumbled and blew away on the wind.

The Stunning Blow debuff finally dropped, and I kicked at the pile of ash, cursing. I'd always been able to solo other RPGs effectively, but V.G.O. was far harder than I'd anticipated, and the debuffs so punishing. If Otto died, and Jack didn't take the leap, I'd be alone forever… and I'd just have to figure out how to solo it. Stonewall would be my only option, everything else was too squishy, easily taken out by a Balrigon backhand, and who knew what else.

"Are you coming?" Otto shouted from the next clearing. "Or are you going to pout all day?"

I gritted my teeth and followed after him. I wasn't *pouting*, just thinking. Not like a big, stupid oaf like him would know anything about that.

"Yeah, yeah. Let's get this over with so I can pay you to get out of my hair. We only have four hours left, you know, so I'd appreciate it if you would stop dallying."

Otto rolled his eyes. "Sure thing, Crazy."

NINE

WAYWARD CAVERNS

W E'D FINISHED OFF A FINAL BALRIGON JUST AS we'd reached the black arch of the entrance to the Wayward Caverns. Right at the entrance had been a rich Rose Quartz vein, supplying me with more than enough for the quest. I told Otto he could keep everything I didn't need to give to Naitee, and he seemed happy with that arrangement. It hadn't even been two hours yet and we'd collected most of the ingredients. All in all, the quest was shaping up to be done in only half the required time.

"So…" Otto hacked down the last Moorkin, a child-shaped, hairless gray monster with needles for teeth and daggers for fingers. "You told Naitee you were going to become the greatest Sorceress in Eldgard to take down a tyrant?"

I shrugged. "Yeah."

We were silent as we picked over the small bodies, collecting bits of gold flakes in corked vials of water or half-eaten fish heads. The loot was pretty slim from these guys, and I was beginning to feel bad that Otto accepted payment in the form of half the earnings.

Otto tossed the bodies into the swiftly flowing underground stream that ran alongside the path we took. He said he was doing it to avoid leaving a trail, but I think he just liked tossing stuff into the water. The cavern walls echoed with the splashes of small bodies, and I looked up through the tiny hole in the ceiling, the only point of light in this area.

It was good I had all the class kits unlocked. Fireball had been most useful as a torch for the last half hour as we wove our way through the maze-like passages of the Wayward Caverns. With a name like that, we should've known it wouldn't be a walk in the park.

"How much farther?" Otto asked as he smacked his hands together in childish joy.

I opened the quest again. When we entered the Wayward Caverns, it had updated with additional information:

Quest: The Path of a Sorceress

Naitee needs you to replace the rare ingredients you just consumed and prove your proficiency as a spellslinger. She has provided a scroll to unlock the basic abilities of all four Sorcery magics for 5 hours. Use them wisely.

Lumalgae will be located at the deepest pool in the Wayward Caverns. The deepest pools will be found where the water's flow ends, to the south.

Quest Class: Uncommon, Class-Based

Quest Difficulty: Moderate

Success: Using all four schools of magic, collect 4 ounces of Lumalgae from the Wayward Caverns, 3 Rose

~~Quartz stones~~, and ~~10 soot essences from 10 different Balrigons~~, then return to Naitee before the night is done.

Failure: Fail to gather all the necessary ingredients in time.

Reward: Class Change: Sorceress, Varying Kits; Unique, Scalable Item.

The collected items were conveniently crossed out for me, and I noticed as I collected each one, a little counter popped up in the corner of my vision, flashing how many I had out of the total needed. The level of care taken for convenience was really nice, though absolutely not necessary for what the game had become.

"Looks like we're on the right path." I shrugged as I closed the quest. "It just says the Lumalgae will be in the deepest pools of the cavern, and the deepest pools will be far to the south where the water flow ends."

Otto glanced to the stream, his face screwed up in frustration, and I had the disgusting realization I was sure he was having. He'd been sending all the bodies along to the deepest pools…

"Great." He grumbled. "At least we have something to follow."

We moved on and the path twisted this way and that, the river an ever-present guide to our destination.

"Who's this to-be-tyrant person you're trying to stop?" Otto asked, and I wondered if it was safe to talk with him about it. Down here in the cavern it was pretty unlikely I would run into other players, and my NPC was supposed to be loyal to me, so maybe it was alright. If

Otto was going to be with me long-term, he'd need to know eventually.

"His name is Osmark. Robert Osmark. He used to order me and many others around before we came here. He's been working with really bad people and has a plan to raise them, and himself, to seats of power. I'm not sure what that plan is yet, but I know he intends to rule over all of Eldgard."

I gritted my teeth at the thought of what he could be scheming, and the fact that I wouldn't know it until it was already happening because of my damn fat-fingered code. If I'd been smart, I would've sanctioned a virtual machine and tested the code there. I should've known better than to trust a potentially false positive from my own machine. Testing in a contaminated environment like my own branch was a second-grade mistake.

The burbling of a Moorkin drew our attention, and Otto waved his sword through the air. The little devils had natural stealth and would pounce at us from the walls, making the start of combat a confusing moment of flame throwing and sword swiping, hoping to land a hit.

It was me this time who struck first, my fireball smacking the Moorkin right in the face. It dropped from the ceiling with a horrible high-pitched cry and splashed into the river. They were effective swimmers, but my fireball had taken most of the thing's Health, and it was carried away by the coursing water.

"He sounds like bad news." Otto sheathed his sword, then stroked his green chin. "The free cities have been fighting Imperial rule for many years. Gaining control of the Imperial cities and their armies would be a good starting point for a bad-news-man like that."

"True." I bobbed my head in agreement. And Osmark would never want to be anything other than human. Stuck up, fancy-pants prick couldn't stand to look less than perfect all the time. Before the crunch, we all had to look our best, too. I mean, come the hell on, we were *developers*; shorts, T-shirts, and flip-flops were our MO, but not at Osmark Tech. It was button-downs and tailored pants or you got a talking to. Well, at least I didn't have to deal with *that* anymore.

Otto continued on. "I think I should stick with you for a while, at least until we get this Osmark character under control."

"Yeah, why's that?" I chuckled. "You gonna take aggro for the whole world?"

He shot a glare over his shoulder. "If I have to, yes."

Interesting, so the Overminds were helping him find reasons to stick around with me from the data I gave him. Were those changes occurring at the core of the NPC's values, or were they just getting weaved into what already existed? There was so much I didn't know about the NPCs. I had worked mainly on the questing systems, which definitely gave me an advantage in power-leveling.

"I care about this place. I care about these people. Not that you would, you just got here, but they mean something to me." Otto walked from the sparse sunlight cast by the hole above us, and around the next corner.

I did care about the people, all three something million of them. I cared what this place might turn into, and I wanted to help shape it into something we would all thrive in. Osmark wanted it under his boot. His creation, his rule, just like with Osmark Technologies.

I conjured a fireball and held it in my hand and double stepped to catch up to Otto. "The reason I want to stop him is because I care what happens here. I arrived a few hours ago, but many of my friends will be arriving or are already here. I care about them, too, and all the other Travelers."

Otto was quiet, following the path of the water, and I couldn't tell if he thought the rushing stream was too loud to talk over or if he didn't want to talk to me. My nagging, anxious gut told me the latter, and I told it back that it didn't matter what an NPC thought of me.

"I don't want anyone to be subjected to Osmark's rule," I added, trying to get anything out of him.

"You want to protect the *Travelers*," Otto snapped. "I want to protect *everyone*."

Otto wasn't real. There was no reason for me to need to protect him, because he wasn't really alive. The millions of people who came here were all alive— thinking, feeling beings. Otto and the other NPCs were just strings of code executing predetermined behaviors on a server.

"I don't want *anyone* to become Osmark's slave, to build his paradise while we rot in the gutters," I added for finality. Having Otto upset with me would make it difficult to work with him. My comment was vague enough that I hoped it would placate him. If not… well, I guess it didn't matter if I lied to a few lines of code.

Otto held his hand up in a "hold" motion, and I stopped and doused the flame. The blackness of the cavern brought a sudden claustrophobia. Slowly, my eyes adjusted, and I noticed a soft green light emanating from up ahead. The stream beside us flowed to a wall with a small gap, just enough for the water to flow under.

Otto motioned for me to come up to where he was, and he squatted down to allow me to see.

The cavern corridor curved once more, and then it opened to a massive cave, lit by glowing green patches on the walls. As I focused on the patches, I saw a tiny descriptor pop up: [Lumalgae]. Ha. I get it.

"Let's go ge—"

Otto clamped his hand over my mouth, and I pulled away, but his hand held me still like a Facehugger. He hushed me, barely making a noise, and then pointed lower into the cavern. There was a drop beyond the path we were following and pools at the bottom. And in those pools, an absolutely gigantic tentacled monster that had no business being in freshwater.

The [Cave-Dwelling Septillian] was curling its twenty-foot tentacles around the dead Moorkin, lazily leaning its head back to drop the bodies into its massive gaping mouth. From what I recalled of sea creatures, squid and octopi had a beak at the center of their bodies, between all the tentacles, but this thing had a very large, very toothy mouth on the ovular abdomen that poked out of the pool.

Knowing I'd seen the threat, Otto released my face. Given its name, it was safe to assume it had seven tentacles, that one large mouth, and… no eyes? There didn't seem to be anything on the part sticking out of the pool other than the mouth, not even ears, but that didn't mean it couldn't hear us.

"What's the plan?" I whispered to Otto. He'd been fairly proficient at tactical planning. He likely knew this creature much better than I did, so I would let him take the first stab.

His eyes narrowed as he evaluated the creature.

"Definitely weak to fire." His gruff voice cracked as he tried to whisper, and so he turned his back away from the opening. "It's distracted now, so getting a few good surprise hits in could be our boon."

A noise I knew well from owning several cats drew my attention. The *hurp, hurp, bleeerrrk* of vomiting echoed at a sickening volume, and we crept to the cave entrance for a better look. The Septillian leaned forward, spewing a rancid smelling mixture of Moorkin chunks and bile into the pool around it.

We watched in wrinkle-nosed horror as the chunks were sucked down into the pool. Shadows of tiny tentacled creatures swimming under the surface zipped past the patches of Lumalgae. Not just a few… dozens.

Otto pulled us back from the edge. "Is this the only place to get Lumalgae?"

I nodded, and Otto mumbled some curse under his breath.

"Let me draw aggro with the first *two* hits, I need two, then you lay into it with fireballs and whatever else will work."

I gave him a thumbs-up. Otto furrowed his brow, and I realized that the NPCs in Eldgard likely wouldn't understand a lot of our gestures and colloquialisms.

"It means 'okay' where I come from."

He bobbed his head and half turned away, then looked back at me, holding up two fingers. I rolled my eyes and shooed him toward the cave mouth. Otto pulled his sword from its sheath and stepped lightly as the massive creature retched again. Hot acid and metallic blood wafted through the opening with the sounds of splashes, and I covered my nose.

I moved to the opening, watching as Otto took the way down very slow and deliberately. Each footfall was purposeful in its placement on the algae-slick rocks, and he remained steady all the way down the twenty-something-foot descent. The pounding waterfall dampened his steps, which were completely inaudible to me, and I hoped to the creature as well.

The Septillian seemed unaware of Otto's presence as he moved within range and raised his sword overhead, his aim to slice down on one of the meaty tentacles. The sword glistened with green moisture as he brought it down into the Septillian. The creature recoiled, its massive mouth giving a high-pitched screech of anguish. Otto moved in for another chop, and I began the cast of my first Fireball.

One of the six remaining tentacles swiped at Otto's legs, and he jumped, narrowly avoiding being swept off his feet. He sliced down on the offending limb and landed another hit. I unleashed my held ball of flame, aiming straight for the creature's wide-open mouth.

The fireball hit with a sizzle, and the monster cried louder. The pool was now alive with movement from the smaller [Cave-Dwelling Septillian Spawn] as the adult thrashed about. The HP bar flashed orange above its head as my next fireball hit and procced Burning Affliction, but it was only missing a mere 5% of its total Health.

A wet *thwap* brought my attention back to Otto as one of the many tentacles smacked him back against the cave wall. I shot two more Fireballs and landed another Burning Affliction hit, but my Spirit was beginning to dip. I needed to pace myself—it would be a long fight.

The monster's many limbs searched the ground and walls as it roared in frustration. Otto, as large as he was, dodged and hopped with practiced ease, making his way back into striking range.

I moved to cast Boulder Dash, but negative buzzing echoed in my ear and a notice of "out of range" appeared in the corner of my vision. I could still cast the spell, but it was very likely I wouldn't land the hit because of the distance. With my poor visual acuity, I judged myself to be about sixty feet away, but didn't really bank on that being accurate. If I came nearly within tentacle range, I should be close enough for all my spells.

Otto grunted as another smack landed him on his ass. His HP bar was at about 50%, and the Septillian… 70%. Okay, it was time to unleash hell. I knew from experience that Fireball would dispel Numb, and similarly, Ice Lance would end Burning Affliction, but disorientation or the Drain spell shouldn't interfere.

I took the way down a little more precariously than Otto had, tripping and slipping twice, but the Septillian was so involved with the tank, it didn't notice me at all.

"Get back up there!" Otto yelled at me as he waved his sword in front of him, landing a few scraping strikes on two offending tentacles.

I tossed a boulder toward the Septillian and cursed when a tentacle batted it away. "I was out of range! I'll be fine!"

My Spirit had recuperated on the climb down, so I hucked a few more fireballs and another boulder, landing a hit to the brain center, which disoriented the creature. Our onslaught was finally having an effect, and the creature bellowed a new war cry as it hit 50%.

Dozens of tiny yips and growls filled the cavern, sounding like an army of angry chihuahuas, as the surface of the pool rippled with the presence of the Septillian Spawn. The squid-beast slapped its tentacles against the cave floor, knocking boulders and stalagmites free as the ground shook below us.

"Go back!" Otto yelled, his Health bar blinking a slow warning at 30%. He retreated a few steps, grabbing a red vial from his bandolier. Before Otto could suck down the liquid, a loose rock fell from the ceiling and slammed into his back just as the Septillian batted him in the gut, sending him and his Health bar reeling.

"Otto!" I screamed, slapping the Septillian with another fireball before running to Otto's aid. I grabbed the vial from the ground—it miraculously hadn't shattered on impact—and tossed it to Otto.

He caught the potion, then pointed the outstretched hand at something behind me and screamed, "Watch out!"

I whirled about, catching a brief flash of tiny tentacles flying toward my face.

TEN

SUCKER PUNCH

I STUMBLED BACK IN DARKNESS AS THE COLD, WET suckers slapped against my cheeks. A notification appeared in my darkened vision:

Debuff Added

Grapple: You are being grappled! Stamina regeneration is reduced by 15% and movement speed is reduced by half until you are freed from the hold.

The Septillian Spawn's tentacles wrapped around my head—or at least tried to. It seemed my mane of hair inhibited the creature from getting a good lock on the back of my skull. I reached up and dug my fingers into the rubbery skin of the monster, tearing the creature from my face.

I gasped for air past bile-soaked lips. I wanted to retch, but I instinctively resisted the urge to do so as I cast Drain on the offending spawn. Red spurted out in every direction as the creature exploded in a shower of blood. The spell critted for 42 damage, killing the little Septillian in one fell swoop and restoring 21 Spirit to my dwindled pool.

Another flying baby tentacle monster was careening my way, and I noticed the adult was *flinging* them at us! What a good, protective parent, sacrificing her babies to save her own skin. Some of the things we'd programmed into the game surprised me still.

Drain seemed effective, so before the flung baby creature came anywhere near making contact, I insta-cast and killed it outright in a puff of red. The little ones only seemed to have about 20 HP, perfect for the Drain spell. I checked my Spirit bar compulsively as I hit the little ones with Drain. The air around us tinted with crimson as baby after baby erupted into red mist from my spells.

Otto was back on his feet, Health bar at a steady 60% up from 20%. Two of the adult Septillian's tentacles had large gashes from Otto's efforts, and I could see a third was well beyond use. With the boss-monster still hovering around 45%—apparently Otto had inflicted some bleed debuff—it was time to get serious. I couldn't be wasting my spells on the infants.

I pulled my staff from its holster and batted the next creature away, only hitting for 10 damage, but leaving the spawn broken on the stone floor. I repeated twice more, letting my low Spirit climb back up. When the bar was nearly full, I ran for the back of the narrow, tall cavern. Here, the thrown babies would splat on the ground before reaching me.

Otto was slicing in at the boss's exposed body near the three damaged limbs while dodging and sometimes getting a nice wet thwack to the gut from the other four. I shot three fireballs in quick succession at the

Septillian, getting a burn off on one of them. The scent of deep-fried calamari and blood filled the room, but the boss held fast to life.

"Just die already!" I screamed at the beast with life hovering around 20%. I had enough Spirit for one more cast, but none of them would do 20% in one hit. I needed a way to inflict serious pain.

The baby squid monsters were beginning to pile onto Otto, and despite his strength, the many little bodies constricting his limbs were having an effect. Otto's Health hit 15%, and a dread I'd been fighting filled my chest. I was going to lose him, my only companion in a world hell-bent on destroying me. I would have to fight Osmark and his court of nobles alone, and I would lose.

Otto roared, his skin seeming to pulse red in the green glow of the Lumalgae, and he tightened his grip on the sword. He dashed in at the Septillian and severed an incoming tentacle… in *one* slash. The boss went down to 10% and I knew I needed to focus on saving Otto, not finishing off the monster.

I hit two little squids one after the other with Drain, and when my Spirit bar was empty, I ran in with my staff. Otto's life was flashing dangerously low at 10%, but I had to trust that he could kill the Spetillian, and I would save him from a thousand baby sucker punches. Each time I swatted a spawn from Otto, I noticed his red aura pulse brighter, like my strike was feeding his fury.

Otto pulled away from me, diving at the Septillian with his sword poised to skewer the creature through its wide-open mouth. The Cave-Dwelling Septillian shrieked a final death cry as the steel pierced through its tongue and stuck out the bottom of its jaw.

Otto slumped into the pool of Moorkin chunks, squid blood, and dead spawn, his life bar flashing a depleted red.

"Otto, no!" I ran to the edge and pulled at his shoulder armor, tugging with all my might. It was no use, he was just too heavy.

The Septillian Spawn lifelessly drifted away from an unconscious Otto, revealing a final potion on his bandolier. With a groan, I reached into the fetid water to grab it. The cork came free easily, and I dumped the liquid in Otto's open mouth, then snapped it closed with my hand as his face went under the water.

"Otto, get up!" I cried, struggling fruitlessly to take off his armor as it pulled me down.

I took a breath before going into the filth, the liquid feeling like molasses as I kicked to stay above water. I tried desperately to lift him out of the pool, pushing, paddling, whatever I could, but we just kept sinking in the depths of the rank Septillian pond.

Something grabbed my waist and I screamed, letting half the air out of my lungs. Otto's massive Risi arms pushed me up to the surface, and I took a breath. His hand continued pushing as he moved us to the edge of the pool.

Otto's head breached the surface, and he gasped for air, then coughed, sounding as if he were trying not to vomit. He gripped the edge and wrenched himself out onto the cavern floor, then lifted me by the back of my robe and yanked me free of the nasty water.

"I thought," I panted, "you were dead."

"Me too." He coughed a few more times, and finally leaned over to wretch, spewing well-digested barley meal on the cavern floor.

He lay back and took several deep breaths. The air was rancid, and the liquid of the pool burned my skin, but we'd freaking done it. I held my hand out to Otto as we lay on the ground, and he looked at it awkwardly.

"Gimme a high five, dude. We rocked it."

Otto held his hand up similarly, and I gave it a wet smack with my own.

"Let's loot this beast, get the Lumalgae, and GTFO."

"Gee tee, eff, oh?" Otto seemed puzzled, and I remembered all my gamer speak wouldn't be understood here.

"It means *let us depart with haste*," I said with a fancy British accent, or my best attempt at one.

Otto sat up, brushing a bit of Moorkin debris from his breastplate, and grunted. "Indeed. Let's geetee effoh."

Before anything else, I wanted to check my notifications. I was sure all this dungeon crawling had awarded me nicely with some level ups. Sure enough, on opening my character screen, I was bombarded with a huge pop-up:

x7 Level Up!

You have (35) undistributed stat points

You have (10) unassigned proficiency points

I quickly dropped 10 stat points in Intelligence, 15 in Spirit, and 10 in Constitution. If I was going to go Stonewall, having hardy Con would be necessary. But, if I didn't, it'd still be nice.

Feeling a bit better from all the stat points, I sat up and moved to a huge pile of the Lumalgae behind the Septillian. I ripped at the slimy mass with my hands, but it wouldn't come free. I scratched at it, shivering as bits of goo collected under my nails. That wasn't going to work…

"Here." Otto came up beside me, pulling a small dagger from his waistband and offering it to me. The hilt was engraved with some text.

"Thanks." I smiled and took the dagger. The words read "Òrdugh an Garda Anam." I wanted to open up the item's info sheet, but felt like that might be prying. It wasn't *my* item, anyway. Then again, he was just an NPC.

"Anything good on it?" I tilted my head toward the massive, now only six-tentacled, monster.

Otto looked down, his lips pursed.

Great… I'd have to thank Naitee for sending us on such a loot-crappy quest later.

The blade was extremely effective in dislodging the algae from its hold on the wall, and soon I had six ounces of it. Better to get more than I needed and sell the excess than lose some and be totally boned.

I turned to walk back to Otto, who was kicking at the Septillian's limbs and mumbling something rude, when a glint caught my eye. I held up a fireball and walked closer to the shimmer. Pure, childlike joy filled my being as I laid eyes on a sturdy, gold-trimmed chest.

"Otto, c'mere!" I walked closer and knelt before the box holding treasures untold, salivating at the thought of what could be inside such a huge, beautiful, high-level looking chest.

Otto whistled at the sight of it, and I could guess what was going through his mind, but I didn't have to as he said, "Looks like this was a good idea after all."

I fingered the latch, worried there might be some kind of curse on the chest. The lock fell away easily, and the lid popped open with a golden shower of sparkles.

"Oh, hell yes." My eyes roved over the contents of the chest with greed. A new breastplate and boots for Otto, and almost a *full set* of gear for me. Boots, rings, bracers, and a belt. It was all awesome.

Soft Tread Boots of Spirit

Armor Type: Light, Woven Cloth

Class: Uncommon

Base Defense: 25

Primary Effects:

- +5% Spirit regen

- +5 to Spirit

Increase Carry Capacity by 15lbs

Ring of Power

Armor Type: Jewelry

Class: Rare

Base Defense: N/A

Primary Effects:

- +2.5% Chance to Spell Critical Hit

- +3 to Intelligence
- +2% Bonus Damage to all Elemental Spells

It's not the only one out there...

Silver Ring of Stamina

Armor Type: Jewelry

Class: Common

Base Defense: N/A

Primary Effects:

- +30 to Stamina

Caster's Cuffs

Armor Type: Light, Cloth

Class: Uncommon

Base Defense: 5

Primary Effects:

- +2 to Intelligence
- +3 to Spirit

Leader's Bandolier

Armor Type: Light, Mixed Cloth/Leather Belt

Class: Rare

Base Defense: 10

Primary Effects:

- +5% Chance to Negotiate

- +5% Chance to Inspire

- +1 to Luck

A leader must be well dressed for any situation.

I'd *never* seen an item with stats like that. Increased chance to negotiate and inspire? So weird. I opened my character sheet and dropped all of the items on my avatar. Rejuvenating power surged through my limbs, and I shivered as I felt myself become stronger. I loved that feeling!

I looked over the avatar with satisfaction. I was a BAMF, and my stats were looking good too!

Name:	Abby	Race:	Wode	Gender:	Female
Level:	10	Class:	Unassigned	Alignment:	None
Renown:	1,200	Carry Capacity:	370	Undistributed Attribute Points:	0
Health:	310	Spirit:	450	Stamina:	350
H-Regen/sec:	8.325	S-Regen/sec:	8.38025	Stam-Regen/sec:	5.42
Attributes:		**Offense:**		**Defense:**	
Strength:	10	Base Melee Weapon Damage:	3	Base Armor:	40
Vitality:	21	Base Ranged Weapon Damage:	0	Armor Rating:	48
Constitution:	22	Attack Strength (AS):	33	Block Amount:	2.5
Dexterity:	10	Ranged Attack Strength (RAS):	30	Block Chance (%):	6.1
Intelligence:	36	Spell Strength (SS):	54	Evade Chance (%):	3
Spirit:	35	Critical Hit Chance:	5%	Fire Resist (%):	3.2
Luck:	6	Critical Hit Damage:	5%	Cold Resist (%):	3.2
				Lightning Resist (%):	3.2
				Shadow Resist (%):	3.2
				Holy Resist (%):	3.2
Current XP:	3,200			Poison Resist (%):	3.2
Next Level:	4,400			Disease Resist (%):	3.2

The chest wasn't done dishing out the goods yet. At the bottom was a hefty pile of silver and a few dozen gold coins. Otto and I split the change, earning me 195 silver and 16 gold. There was one last thing in the bottom of the chest, a simple scroll. I picked it up, and a quest alert appeared. My heart stopped as I read the text.

ELEVEN

A NEW QUEST

Quest Alert: On the Edge of a Blade Hangs Balance

FORCES OF THE VIRIDIAN EMPIRE ARE WORKING TO restore their control over all the lands. With few able to oppose these new would-be masters, it's important to have champions of balance and order who will fight for the freedom of Eldgard. Go to Harrowick and investigate the Drunken Donkey to find clues about who may be plotting to rule the world.

Quest Class: Unique, Personal

Quest Difficulty: Moderate

Success: Go to the Drunken Donkey and discover any details about who is behind the takeover of Eldgard.

Failure: Fail to learn any information, or do not go to the Drunken Donkey.

Reward: Teleportation Scroll, CaCoCa_Scroll; 10,000 XP.

CaCoCa_Scroll was what I'd named my copy of Carrera's Scroll of Allegiance.

"What is it?" Otto placed a hand on my shoulder, and I jumped.

I accepted the quest and turned the rolled-up paper over in my hand, then inspected it.

Simple Scroll

There doesn't seem to be anything magical or interesting about this piece of blank parchment. Maybe you should wait to open it.

I stowed the scroll in my inventory and looked to Otto. I'd talked about Osmark and his gang, their plans to take over Eldgard, and a few other tidbits, but this was different. *This* was Sophia, the Overmind. I knew her well, since I had to work with her codebase a lot. Her primary function was to generate quests to keep the players busy and progressing.

My mind raced to unravel the crazy mess that had just dropped into my lap, until a plausible explanation appeared. Sophia helped with inventory management as well, and so it was possible the scroll delivery in the message I'd sent to myself had been lost in transmission, but the Overmind recognized its destination was me. So, she created a quest to allow the scroll to be delivered.

But why hadn't the Overmind just given it to me in the chest? Why did I have to go to the Drunken Donkey? Otto knew Harrowick well, and he'd know what kind of place the Drunken Donkey was, or more importantly, *who* would be there.

I took a deep breath. "It's a quest." I paused, unsure how to explain what we needed to do without explaining everything that was going on.

"Do you remember when I talked about Osmark wanting to take over Eldgard?"

Otto's fists tightened. "How could I forget?"

"Before we, the Travelers, arrived here, I tried to…" I stopped. That wasn't the right way to go about this. "I tried to get more information about a secret place in Eldgard, but unfortunately, I failed. I was supposed to get a message with a teleport scroll that would allow me"—I faltered at Otto's glare—"allow *us* to investigate."

Otto pointed at the chest. "And that scroll was?"

I pulled it from my inventory. "It's blank, but the quest states that the reward will be the scroll that should allow us into the secret area. Once we know what Osmark is planning with those secret areas, we can stop him."

Otto nodded like all of this was perfectly reasonable. "So, what do we need to do now?"

"Do you know the Drunken Donkey?" I asked.

Otto gave an affirmative grunt. "A sellsword haunt. Some of the best and worst people share drinks under that roof. I avoid it. Not the kind of business I'm usually interested in."

Sellswords. If we needed to learn information about the secret area from hired muscle, it could be some kind of dungeon. I thought back to the stats I pulled on the region. There had been a vertical descent, but the area was completely devoid of NPC's or monsters. It didn't make any sense. All the more reason to see what we could learn from the sellswords.

"Well, are we going or not?" Otto asked.

I remembered what I'd said to him in the clearing, after killing the Balrigons. I wasn't sure he still wanted to group up with me after I told him I wanted him out of my hair, but the question implied otherwise. He was just a series of code designed to be loyal to me, but should I apologize?

"Otto," I started, my voice laden with remorse. He waved me off.

"Don't bother trying to convince me not to come. This Osmark character needs to be *taken care of*," he said, crossing his arms, "and so do you. I wouldn't want the only one who knows a damn thing about this new Imperial threat getting squished into Wode jelly."

I smiled. "That's not what I was going to say."

He cocked an eyebrow.

"Never mind." I shook my head and stood from the empty chest. I wrinkled my nose, the smell of burnt squid and bile reminding me we were standing in a closed chamber full of nasty. "Let's get outta here."

He gave a quick jerk of his head. "Yes, let's geetee effoh."

I grabbed the return scroll and popped it open. A less extravagant, white-edged portal appeared before us, and I stepped through with Otto. White light overtook the dark, green-glowing cavern and with an audible pop, I felt the rocky cave floor below change to something flat and warm. The light dissipated, and Otto appeared next to me at the entry of the Boar's Head.

"Ugh!" The voice of the barmaid from this morning was accosting. "You two *reek*. Get out of here, now!"

I opened my character sheet and checked my debuffs. Sure enough, level 4 Unwashed appeared. It would have to wait. There was serious business to attend to. I gave the barmaid a curt nod, saying, "We'll be back for a bath," and stepped out the door.

We were given a wide berth as Otto and I moved through the streets to Naitee's shop. I knew I smelled bad, but was it really *that* bad? I shrugged it off as we pulled up to the blackened twisted building of my trainer. When I opened the door, the heat from inside mixed with my own putrid smell nauseated me. I choked back a gag and walked in.

"Who brings such filth into my place of business!" A shout of pure hatred boomed through the shop as Naitee stormed down the stairs to meet us.

Her eyes met mine, but they were different. Her whole body was different. The exposed skin on her face, neck, and hands was burnt and cracked, with a fiery red glow pulsing underneath. Her once sky blue eyes were now black as night, with tendrils of smoke rising up through her lashes. Her golden, Dawn Elf hair whipped about in an unseen wind, as did her crimson robes.

Otto backed out the door and closed it behind him. I gritted my teeth and mumbled, "Coward."

Naitee stalked closer. "What are you doing here?" Her once feminine voice was now rich, smoky, and deep, with a hint of fury.

I fumbled to open my inventory and pull out the items she'd asked for, then held them out to her. "I got all the ingredients."

Naitee lifted a glowing hand, the heat of her presence almost too intense to bear. Her fingers singed my palm as she took the collected materials.

"Wait here," she ordered, retreating to the upstairs with the items. The quest didn't update, but she'd taken everything from me. I checked the timer on my spell scroll, 2 more hours, and the timer on the deadline to turn in the quest, 8 hours 29 minutes 43 seconds. I didn't understand, I'd done everything right.

Naitee returned, her skin the flawless pale color it had been when we first met, and her eyes were once again the haunting blue of a wide-open sky. She smiled a wrinkle-nosed grin my way.

"You really need a bath, child, but you did well." Her voice was pinched, as if she wasn't breathing through her nose. The quest update finally appeared on screen.

Quest Update: The Path of a Sorceress

You've successfully gathered all of the necessary ingredients to replenish Naitee's energy potion, but what comes next is no small undertaking.

What comes next? I dismissed the pop-up, and Naitee continued.

"Now, child, you must decide."

I looked at her expectantly, waiting for the rest of the sentence. She stared back.

"Decide?" I prompted her back into action. It was apparent she wanted to speak and breathe as little as possible.

"Sorceric knowledge is powerful. So powerful you cannot survive the undertaking of learning all the schools. Hence the delicious potion you drank this morning."

The flavor of broccoli returned to my mouth at the mention of the potion, and the nausea I'd held at bay nearly overtook me. I covered my mouth, just in case, and Naitee gave a gentle chuckle before her face went stern.

She went on. "You must pick only one, and that is the path you will follow for the rest of your life."

For the rest of my life? That could be forever, technically, and I could never multi-class and never change my class kit. I thought of Otto. We'd worked really well together when I was using the Firebrand and Frostlock abilities, but I would definitely survive better on my own as a Hydromancer or Stonewall. The luck and evasion of Hydromancer would make up where Stonewall was hardy and armor heavy, and still be able to lay down the damage, but it wasn't a group class, for sure.

I didn't know what to do. If Jack joined and wanted to party up, I'd want to be able to work with him effectively. If he was a cleric, Stonewall might be a good pick so I could tank for him. But if he went some other class, Stonewall might be too gimp to help effectively.

Heck. I really wanted more data before making such a huge choice.

"It's a tough decision, child, and you don't need to pick this very moment. Take some time this evening to think it over in a nice hot bath, then visit me in the morning." Naitee waved me off, her other hand coming up to cover her mouth.

Quest Update: The Path of a Sorceress

Return to Naitee tomorrow morning to decide on your class kit.

Quest Class: Uncommon, Class-Based

Quest Difficulty: Easy

Success: Return to Naitee tomorrow morning and tell her which class kit you will pursue.

Failure: Fail to return to Naitee tomorrow morning with a decision.

Reward: Class Change: Sorceress, Varying Kits; Unique, Scalable Item.

I accepted the new leg of the quest, saying, "I'll be back," in my best Terminator voice. Naitee quirked an eyebrow, and I shook my head. "Never mind."

The outside air was a blessing, and I took a moment upon leaving to take several deep breaths. Otto was leaned against the side of the building, his eyes locked on me.

"Well, you're not dead," he remarked as he came to stand next to me.

I nodded. "Thankfully not. I need to come back in the morning, after a bath, and tell her which class I'd like to pursue, *forever*."

"Let's get going, then. The Boar's Head will probably let us back in, once we show them the coin."

I checked my character sheet once more. On top of the level 4 Unwashed, I was also level 2 Hungry and

Thirsty. A relaxing bath would do good to get some clarity and give me time to hunt down more information on the forums. And maybe search for Jack. Food was also welcome, if everything tasted as good as the two meals we'd already had.

Otto walked toward the street, and I followed behind wordlessly. So much still to do, and so little time, but at least now we had a lead, and the scroll would be in hand soon. It was all coming together. Osmark wouldn't get away with this, whatever it was.

TWELVE

THE DRUNKEN DONKEY

IT FELT *SO* GOOD TO BE CLEAN. I SPENT A GOOD portion of the bath scrubbing out my hair, but once I got it clean, and moved to a new tub, I opened up the forums. I prodded around in the sorcerer section but there was very little information to be had aside from unlocking magic, a whole subforum about how awesome that was, and running errands for the trainer. It was still really early, and I was keeping up.

Next, I looked for Jack. I tried a few of the common names he went by, but gave up after the tenth error message. I checked a couple of names from our old raiding guild, The Crimson Alliance, and found a few of them, but they weren't the buck up and take responsibility type. These guys were grinders and raiders. Loot was all they had on their minds, and they couldn't be bothered with clan chores or battle support. No, I'd have to wait for Jack.

I left the bathing area, which was awkwardly at the back end of the kitchen instead of, I don't know, in my room? I supposed it made sense that the bathtubs would be near where the water could be boiled, instead of forcing maids to climb countless stairs with heavy buckets of hot water, all for the water to be cold by the time the bather got in. It was still weird to wash myself next to the turnip shelf.

I met Otto at his favorite seat, and we slammed back a quick meal of roasted boar and turnips, which was the perfect balance of sweet, salty, and gamey. I left the barmaid a decent tip, though not enough to make up for the lack of tip last time, and we took to the street for the Drunken Donkey.

The sun was already on its way down the horizon, and I checked my character screen for the time: 2:25. I noticed the scroll of Sorceric Knowledge had also expired while I'd been bathing or eating, and I sighed as I looked over my completely barren spell list.

"We're here," Otto remarked as I bumped into his backside from blindly following him with my character screen open.

I closed the sheet and looked around the alley. At midday it was deserted, but I could hear the roars from inside. The sounds of an instrument like a piano carried on the hoots of catcalls and growls of "Cheat!" I knew this wasn't a place I wanted to be, but it was a place we *had* to go.

My hand pushed against the thin wooden door, very unlike the Boar's Head, and we were accosted by sound. The piano was amplified by some metal contraption, and the screams of drunken patrons were infinitely louder. Those sitting closest to the door screamed at me to shut it, as the light was blinding them, but the darkness blinded me.

Otto held me close by the arm and pulled me through the masses of sweaty, stinking lushes. Some directed their catcalling my way, at which Otto raised a fist with a grunt that promised much pain, and the patrons returned their attention to the woman on the stage. Not just a woman, but an Accipiter. Her scantily clad form drew the eyes of many, but some maintained attention on the newcomers: us.

Otto pulled me through the roaring crowd to a seat near the bar at the back, where there was at least some candlelight and a bit better acoustics.

"What now?" he asked, and in an instant a quest update appeared in my vision.

Quest Update: On the Edge of a Blade Hangs Balance

Forces of the Viridian Empire are working to restore their control over all the lands. With few able to oppose these new would-be masters, it's important to have champions of balance and order who will fight for the freedom of Eldgard. Go to Harrowick and investigate the Drunken Donkey to find clues about who may be plotting to rule the world.

Some mercenaries have looser tongues than others, and drinks aid the flow of all things, including information. Look for a man who is young in years with a blade that has taken more lives than he could ever live.

Quest Class: Unique, Personal

Quest Difficulty: Moderate

Success: Go to the Drunken Donkey and discover any details about who is behind the takeover of Eldgard. Look for a young man with a well-used blade for more information.

Failure: Fail to learn any information, or do not go to the Drunken Donkey.

Reward: Teleportation Scroll, CaCoCa_Scroll; 10,000 XP.

"We need to find a younger man with..." I struggled to decipher the hidden meaning in the second part of the addition. A blade that has taken more lives than he could ever live. He's done a lot of killing, but how will that be obvious?

"Yes, with what?" Otto asked, and I hadn't realized I'd trailed off.

I shook my head. "I don't understand it. With a blade that has taken more lives than he could ever live. That's all it says."

Otto's eyes narrowed to slits as he looked off in the distance. "It could be the Undying Blade."

"The what?" I asked.

"Not what," Otto said, his stare snapping to me, "who. They're a gang of mercs, deadlier than most. Some say their gifts are the grace of the gods. I wouldn't know which gods would give those abilities... only demons."

I nodded thoughtfully. Otto knew *a lot*, and it seemed like he knew a lot of the stuff I needed to progress on not only my personal endeavors, but my gameplay ones too. Perhaps the Overminds did this sort of tweaking for all players? I had to put it out of mind, for now—I needed to be looking for a young man of the Undying Blade.

We both cast our gazes across the room. Drunks, gamblers, and shady characters abounded, but no one who looked *young* and like they were a lethal assassin. We would just have to wait for them to arrive or reveal themselves.

"Can I get you two sumpthin?" A busty barmaid bustled up to our high top with a wood platter, and I was reminded again of Hooters.

"Mead, two pints." I held up my fingers in case she missed it, and she gave a nod, then hurried away.

Otto leaned over the table, though he was so tall it was not much of an effort for him. "So what now?"

"We wait for the man of the Undying Blade to arrive. We listen. We pretend we're here to drink and enjoy the show." I gestured to the stage where the Accipiter woman was now nearly nude, and the patrons hooted, roared, and some even fainted.

The woman returned with our drinks and I passed her three silver coins. She accepted them, so I assumed a silver a pint was acceptable payment… or maybe over. In fact, I didn't really know what anything cost in Eldgard. Otto had done so much paying and negotiating for me, I didn't know what I was doing.

Hollers brought my attention from my mug to the stage. Otto had already put back the entire cup, and his gaze was affixed to the raised dais next to the makeshift piano. I took a sip and promptly belched. Otto's green skin tone became a deeper, emerald color, and I realized he was *blushing*.

"Have you never been in a strip cl—a dance joint, before?" I asked, correcting my language to be comprehensible to the NPC as I chugged down another few gulps of the sweet, alcoholic elixir.

He looked back at me, the blush deepening. "Yes, of course. I just… just..." He fumbled with the thought.

"I've never been to one with a woman in my company." He looked down. I cackled, unable to contain my sheer joy at his embarrassment.

"You're worried about me?" I jeered and tossed back the rest of my pint, then raised my cup to the barmaid for another. She gave a jerk of her head and hurried to get our order. Apparently, three silver was a nice payment.

Otto sat up straight. "Men here get drunk and look at women. A woman in their presence is inviting calamity."

"Oh." I sat up as well, though I was still two feet shorter than Otto. "So it's *my fault* if something goes poorly here?"

Otto waved his hands over the table, his expression mortified. "No, that's not what I said."

I cackled again, raising my glass as the barmaid returned with a full flagon to fill them up. I cast a glance around the room to see the peering eyes that once followed us were now back on the stage. We'd successfully blended in.

Without my saying so, Otto turned his face toward the stage, but I could see every few moments his eyes would jerk this way and that, getting a good look at the room before us. I did the same, keeping my gaze primarily on my cup or the twin Hvitalfar, Dawn Elf, women who now danced on the dais. Their soft flowing robes moved on an impossible wind, and their voices rose in unison to a slow beating drum.

The women didn't disrobe, but they entranced the room nonetheless. Their sheer shawls of lavender and sapphire whipped around their bodies in a double helix, and then I realized those weren't shawls at all. It was *water*. They were Hydromancers.

I watched more intently as the two women flicked their wrists, bumped their hips, and swirled about the stage in a mirrored duet. It was miraculous and unfathomable.

It was at that moment I realized the entire tavern had fallen silent. Like me, everyone had become enthralled with the two on the stage; even two new arrivals had stopped short with the door ajar. Only the barmaids and the bartender seemed impervious to their snare.

The Dawn Elf women's performance concluded, and they came to rest in a "child's pose" type position. The crowd was stunned, unable to move forward or any way at all. Freed from the Hydromancers' charm, the bartender started to clap. The crowd joined in, including me, and the sounds of heavy coin dropping onto wood roared at the front of the stage.

One loud, male voice rose above the rest as the commotion in the tavern returned. "All right, so what was I saying? Oh yeah, the secret dungeon!"

I found the speaker over the brim of my cup, watched his lips, and did my best to understand what he was saying.

"Dungeon was the best. Never had better haul in me life. Company wasn't great." That was all I captured, despite my best attempts.

Otto nudged my knee under the table and nodded to the same man I'd been scrutinizing.

"I know. Can you get him to come over here?" I asked, and Otto frowned in my direction, then stood.

Otto finished off his second pint of ale, an easy feat for someone his size I was sure, and walked closer to the man at the bar. He leaned against it on the other side of the blond-haired gentleman, and I realized he was a bit younger, maybe in his mid-twenties. I felt like a detective following a lead, watching my partner grab the informant with a bit of bait.

And then he did! Otto grabbed a flagon and cheersed with the younger man in question, then walked back to our table. But the young man didn't follow.

"Just wait," Otto said when his back was to the target.

"Anyway," the young man started back in with the other at the bar, but then cast a furtive look our way. Whether he was checking out me or the flagon of mead, I would never know, but within moments, he was walking our way.

"This seat open?" He pointed to the low-backed stool next to mine.

I gave a welcoming smile. Or tried to. My face was feeling a bit numb. How much mead had I had?

The blond-haired man took the chair next to me and scooted it closer, then sat down.

"What're two like you doin' in a place like this?"

Otto didn't miss a beat. "We're looking for someone to help us with a dungeon crawl. Know anyone like that?"

The man beamed and leaned toward Otto over the table. "I know just the bloke."

He got up from his seat, whipped out a dagger, and twirled it between his fingers. His hand bounced back and forth, but the dagger stayed perfectly in time with his movements. Then his other hand went to work on a small globe of light, rolling it and bouncing it into the air.

He was some kind of caster hybrid. I had no idea what his class kit could be, perhaps some deep dark secret in the realm of the Overminds, or perhaps he went the [Battle Mage] route in the Sorcerer General tree.

The Overminds were generating new class kits all the time, especially at the onset of Global Launch. The dev team just hadn't had time to crank out enough content to keep everyone happy. We all hoped the few we had created could be digested by the Overminds and generated into additional, well-balanced kits. If not, there could be super-players running around out there.

I clapped my hands as he stopped his performance and sat back down. "You're just what we're looking for! Tell me, do you have a lot of experience with difficult dungeons?" I prodded, my words slurred. Oh no, was I getting drunk? I set my third glass of mead aside, assuming a businesslike position.

The young man nodded. "Indeed I am. I just finished a crazy crawl for some high roller. Most of the way was pretty easy, lowbies with decent coinage but not much in the way of other loot. But then"—his eyes widened—"there was the boss."

His offered his cup to Otto as he halted his story. Otto filled the glass and passed it back to him. The man grinned, returning to his story. "The boss! It was a terrible creature of thick hide and all manner of offenses. Acid spit, fire breath, claws as long as short swords! It was at least twelve meters tall to boot."

He took a huge drink, then hiccuped. "So, this beast finally goes down, and there's a chest in the back, but the woman, she doesn't let me see what's inside.

Says it's for her eyes only, whatever that means. She let me have some loot off the boss, then paid me, and here I am, richer than a king and drunk as a skunk."

Otto and I exchanged a glance of *who goes next?* and I relieved him of the burden. "Who didn't let you see what was in the chest?"

He gulped back the rest of his mead. "Her name was Sandra. Some man named Osbark had us take three of these lowbies through a dungeon. She's actually upstairs now grabbin' a bit of shut-eye." He gave me an exaggerated wink. "My performance exhausted her."

Osmark. Sandra. My mind's eye came alive with the image of the two standing side by side in our concert hall, the place the entire company gathered for "State of the Union" meetings. She followed him almost everywhere, but when she wasn't following Osmark, she was doing his dirty work. If Sandra had already gone through one of these dungeons, there was no telling what she had access to now.

"How did you get there?" Otto broke my train of thought.

The mercenary furrowed his brow. "Didn't ask how she came by the scrolls, not my job knowin' that! Though I would like another one for meself to get a peek in that special chest!"

"So, what changed about her after she opened the chest? Was it gear? A quest, maybe?" I probed further, and the man looked a bit put off.

"A merc doesn't kill and tell. You wanna know for yourself, you gotta buy the package." He grinned and leaned in much too close for comfort.

I angled toward Otto, holding onto my coin purse as I did. To my surprise, the quest updated from that little information.

Quest Update: On the Edge of a Blade Hangs Balance

You have discovered a man named Osbark, though you're pretty certain he meant Osmark, and his accomplice Sandra are traversing epic dungeons for some special reward chest at the end. Use your scroll of Teleportation, CaCoCa_Scroll, to enter the realm the Imperials forged for themselves, and uproot their plans.

Tarry not, haste is required. The owner of the secret area could be laying claim to the dungeon at any moment!

Quest Class: Unique, Personal

Quest Difficulty: Infernal

Success: Use the scroll of Teleportation, CaCoCa_Scroll, to discover what's in the chest at the end of the dungeon. Only then will you understand the Imperials' plan.

Failure: Fail to successfully traverse the dungeon, fail to open the reward chest at the end, lose your scroll of Teleportation, CaCoCa_Scroll, or do not begin the dungeon by 3 PM in-game time the day after tomorrow.

Reward: Unknown.

x1 Level Up!

You have (5) undistributed stat points

You have (11) unassigned proficiency points

Otto broke my trance with a nudge, and I swiped away the quest alert. A countdown timer appeared in the corner of my vision: 44 hours.

"If we come across any requiring your level of skill, we'll be sure to return for your services, mister…"

"You can call me Verin." He smiled and reached to shake Otto's hand.

I popped open my inventory and saw the scroll, my copycat scroll, right there. I wanted to fist pump and shout a victory obscenity to the sky. But we were still in dangerous territory. I cast a glance at the soldier looking types at a table near the door, and Verin's gaze followed mine for a fleeting second, and he dropped his outstretched hand.

"Thanks for the information, Verin." Otto gave him a dismissive nod.

Verin smiled, but I could tell he was perturbed. "I'm worth a lot more than juicy details. I'm a powerful man."

Verin had brown stubble on his chin, but couldn't have been much more than twenty-two. I supposed in Eldgard, twenty-two *was* a man. Verin didn't act the part though. He was a cocky child, one that wasn't leaving the table despite his dismissal.

"We're aware of your skills and know where to find you if we need them." I raised my brow and gave him another nod of finality.

Verin looked at us scornfully. He got up from the stool, fluffed out his cloak indignantly, and stomped back to the bar.

"Was that it?" Otto whispered to me with his mug covering his mouth. Otto definitely knew what he was doing, and there was apparently a lot I didn't know about him.

I raised my cup to my lips and gave a quick nod of my head.

"Let's get heading back to the inn," he said, a bit louder than necessary.

I took one more sip of my mead, though I could tell by the warmth in my cheeks that I didn't need to, and staggered up from my stool. Otto put a perfectly stable hand against my side as I tottered and helped guide me toward the door.

"You're drunk," he whispered, accusation thick in his tone.

I shot a glare over my shoulder. "I'm tipsy, thank you." Though one quick glance at my character sheet showed otherwise, I definitely wasn't going to admit that. I stumbled as we reached the door, and Otto's support was jerked away.

I looked back at the sound of an angry voice. "I know you," it said.

The offending man was dressed in the garb of an Imperial soldier, I knew the uniform well from the intro video. One of his hands gripped Otto's wrist tightly, and the other flicked the handle of his sword, popping it loose from its sheath.

"You're that rebel dog, Odo," another man at the table sneered.

THIRTEEN

Imperial Brawl

"It's Otto," he corrected, jerking his huge, Risi arm free of the tiny human grasp that held it. "But I'm no *rebel dog*. You've got the wrong man."

The lead Imperial who'd held Otto's arm stood, but only about a foot taller than me, and a foot shy of Otto's height. His classically blond hair was accompanied by blue eyes, a thick lower lip, and a nose that seemed too large for his tiny moustache.

"I haven't made any mistake. You are the slime from Alaunhylles. I'd recognize your big, ugly, traitorous mug anywhere." The blond man poked at Otto's chest with each accusation.

"Harrowick is a free city. I am no traitor here, just hired muscle." Otto grabbed the poking finger and moved it away from his body.

The Imperial man's cheeks flared red as his free hand pulled the short sword from its sheath.

"Not in 'ere!" the bartender yelled. "Get outside, or I'll end ya meself!"

The Imperial's jaw clenched, and he pointed Otto to the door. "You were just leaving, right?"

Otto didn't look at me, but he shifted so he was squarely between me and the Imperials. "Abby, get back to the inn."

No. Way. Otto wasn't going to get his ass handed to him and die. He was *my* NPC. And if he wasn't going to have his ass handed to him, I sure as hell wasn't going to miss watching him hand these guys their own asses.

"I've paid for this man's services," I said, my words still slurred. "You're not allowed to fight him." I pointed to the lead Imperial.

The mini-moustached man chortled. "I'll let you pay me for services. I promise I'm a far better *swordsman*."

The Imperial men at the table, six in total, all joined their leader in laughter. Sudden realization struck me that we could be in actual trouble. I didn't have any spells. I had a freaking stick. Otto was out of potions, unless he was hiding them somewhere other than on his bandolier.

My Belt of Leadership! I remembered I had bonus percentage to negotiate. Maybe I could word our way out of this. I was never great at speeches, but maybe with the belt's help, I could do this.

"We don't want any trouble, sirs. We just came for a drink and the show, and now we want to get back to our beds for the evening."

One of the sitting goons chuckled. "The show's got her all worked up, and she needs to get back to the bedchamber!" The others hooted.

Well, my belt didn't work…

Otto moved like lightning, his fist slamming into the sitting man's head. His skull bounced off the table, and he rolled back onto the floor, unconscious. The lead Imperial lifted his sword, and Otto caught his wrist, stopping the blade before it made contact with his chest.

The music stalled, and the eyes of the patrons turned to Otto.

"Not in 'ere, for the gods' sake! I will kill ya!" the bartender shouted, his hands glowing with blue light as he pointed.

Otto's gaze narrowed on the leader, and he gestured toward the door. "After you."

"Garret, let it be. We don't need no trouble on leave!" one of the goons implored.

"No, let's take this outside, rebel dog." He spat on Otto's chin. I wanted to *clobber* the dickweed. How dare those lines of code not worth the engineer's fingers who typed them spit on my NPC!

Otto released Garret's arm and pushed through the door. I took a step back and gave a very confident jerk of my head, as if to say, "After you, idiot." Garret stepped through the door, as did the other conscious Imperials, though the brunet goon who'd asked Garret to stop gave a groan on his way out.

I turned to bow to the patrons of the Drunken Donkey. "Sorry for the disturbance." The music kicked back up as the door to the pub swung shut behind me.

Otto's sword was drawn, and his new breastplate on. The golden metal lining of the new chest piece shimmered in the dusk light, adding a touch of regality to Otto's appearance. The six Imperial men encircled him, and I charged down the three steps into the dirt with the action.

"Abby, stay back!" Otto ordered, and I halted at the perimeter the goons had made around Otto and Garret. My rational mind knew I was no match for any of these guys. If I still had my class abilities, maybe, but not when it was just wimp-armed Abby and her cool stick. I'd have to trust that Otto could handle this and come up with a quick plan B that got us both out of here alive.

Garret made the first move, charging in at Otto with a high strike. Otto deflected the blow and planted a heavy foot against Garret's gut. It was clear, in a 1v1 fight, Garret would lose. The Goon Squad realized this just a few seconds after me, and one ran in to flank.

"Otto, left!" I shouted, and he turned at my words, slicing down at the attacker. Their swords pinged, sparks flying away from the point of impact. Otto moved in with a shoulder butt and sent the man sailing to the ground.

Two more charged from behind, and Otto's new breastplate took the brunt of the hits before he spun to meet the new offenders. Garret was climbing to his feet, wheezing, but still ready to fight.

Otto grunted as a sword made contact with his forearm. Red blood trickled down Otto's arm into the dirt. He took a step back, into a defensive stance. I couldn't stand by and do nothing, and plan B wasn't revealing itself in my inebriated state. My staff came free of the Leader's Bandolier easily, and I whipped it around in a close-gripped strike at the man Otto had shoulder butted.

Thirteen points of damage, about 2% of this guy's Health. Shit.

The man rolled away from me, trying to gain his footing. I ran after him, swinging my staff down hard, and whiffing harder. My Obsidian War Staff slammed into dirt, kicking up a plume of brown mist around me and the man.

"Abby, get back to the inn, now!" Otto screamed above the sounds of metal on metal, and flesh.

"I'm not leaving you here to die." I swung down at the man trying to evade me and struck home—this time it was a critical hit for 28 damage and almost 5% of his Health. This was not going well for me, and I spared a quick glance to see how it was going for Otto.

Not great. His HP was already down to 70%, and all five enemies were still standing. Though Garret was only at about 20%. I turned back to my fight. The man I'd been sparring with had bounced back to his feet in the time I took to assess Otto's situation.

"I remember me mum wapping me with something similar. Am I to go to my room next? Or maybe yours?" he taunted.

I didn't care how much more Strength and Stamina this guy had. I had more Luck. He was going down.

I moved in with a low swipe that I put too much effort behind, sending me around a full 360. He laughed and twirled his sword. Cocky bastard. I moved in with a 60-degree-angle strike, but the Imperial parried the blow with his sturdy sword. Fortunately, my staff was dense, and the blade could not penetrate its surface.

I retreated and swung my war staff around my body, going for a hit on his other side. He kicked my weapon away and it jerked from my hands. The wood slid toward the tavern and bumped against the stairs.

"What now, *Abby*?" He leered, and the hairs on my arms stood on end as my gut tightened. We were in real trouble.

The Imperial pulled himself to an offensive stance, then lunged as my heart jumped in my chest. I recalled how real the pain felt when I was struck in the head, bitten by the wolf, and tossed by the Balrigon, and fear surged through my being. I didn't want to hurt like that again, and I certainly didn't have time to die.

The jerk lunged again, and this time my dodge sent me sprawling to the ground. I scurried back, grabbing a handful of dirt in each hand as I did.

"I can be a merciful man"—he lowered his sword as he stood over me—"for a price."

The distant shout of the bartender carried over all other sounds, "I told ya to get the hell out of my place," and the door to the Drunken Donkey slammed open, casting yellow light over us.

The mercenary who told us about the dungeon, Verin, came tumbling out into the dirt. The Imperial turned his head to the door, and I threw both handfuls of gravel in his face. I scrambled to my feet and grabbed my staff then raised it for a high strike.

An angry voice I knew well stayed my hand. "You think you can run your mouth and not face consequences?"

The volume and vehemence in her tone turned all heads to the door of the Drunken Donkey. A tall, slender woman in wicked looking black leathers kicked at Verin's face. He rolled away, holding his nose as he limped and crawled, trying to escape her. *Her.*

It was Sandra.

"What in the seven hells are you all looking at?" she demanded, drawing a curved dagger from a sheath at her hip.

If she saw me, if she knew what I was doing here, it would all be over; she would kill me.

No, she would capture and torture me. Sandra was Osmark's right hand for a reason. She was ruthless and relentless. I had looked up to her for a while, but when I realized she literally did nothing but serve Osmark, the allure dropped away. Still, I did not want to tango with this woman. At least, not *yet*.

I turned away to stand by Otto, when a gauntleted fist smashed into my face. My vision went black, and I felt myself falling. The world went silent, and all I could sense was the wind blowing my beautiful gown as I plummeted.

FOURTEEN

SANDRA

I HIT THE GROUND, AND THE WIND LEFT MY LUNGS. I choked for air and grasped at my chest. My eyes stung every time I tried to open them, but I could see in the darkness as debuff notifications appeared.

Debuff Added

Stunned: You have sustained a stunning blow! Attack damage -15%; Stamina regeneration reduced by 30%; movement speed reduced by 35%; duration, 1 minute.

Broken Nose: Your nose has been broken! Take 1 point of damage per sec and reduce visibility by 25%; duration, 3 minutes or until a potion is consumed.

Damn it! Why did I roll a caster? Why was I so damn squish!

There was more shouting and a swift kick to my ribs, then metal on metal and a deep cry of agony. I rolled to my side and pushed up onto my hands and knees, just barely getting a look at my surroundings through squinted eyes.

Someone grabbed my arm, dragging me backwards until my butt hit something solid. I kicked, scratching at the hand that held me as I tried to pry the fingers away.

"Abby, are you all right?" It was Otto, whispering to me as the clanks and screams of pain and terror went on. I cracked my eyes again to see the dark blur with fair skin and long blond hair dashing through the group of Imperials. When the last Imperial soldier fell, the blur of thick, wicked leathers and long hair stood among them.

"What do you think you're doing getting into a brawl in Harrowick! How dare you disgrace the Ever-victorious Empire in such a way." Her voice cut like the blade of her dagger.

"Sorry, miss. It won't happen again," came garbled words from Garret. It sounded like he was missing a tooth or two, and his mouth was filled with blood.

The tears in my eyes leaked away, and I was finally able to see her. She turned from the Imperials and looked right at me. My body went rigid. What would I say to her? What if she recognized me? Stupid, stupid Abby! Why didn't you make more changes to your avatar!

Sandra smiled as she came to a stop five feet out and crouched on her haunches. "You a Traveler?"

I nodded, unable to get any words out, not only from fear, but damn my face hurt. The Stunned debuff ended, and I took my first deep breath in a minute.

"Your NPC?" She gestured to Otto.

I nodded again. She offered her hand, and I lifted my shaking, sweaty palm to hers. She jerked me up and gave me a glance up and down. The Imperial soldiers gathered themselves and took off down the alley in hushed voices, giving backward glances as they did.

Sandra cocked her head. "Do I know you?"

My heart pounded. My hands shook. *Yes,* my brain screamed. *Yes, and I know you. I know what you and Osmark have done, and I know you're planning something worse.*

I shook my head and looked down.

"Hmm, you seem a little familiar. In any case, don't let your NPC get you into any more trouble. You're lucky I happened to be here." She gave Otto a glare.

I kept my head low and nodded vigorously. "Tha'k you." My voice was so nasally, there was no way she'd recognize it. Likewise, my face was probably so busted she'd never notice who I was. Osmark made a point to memorize his employees, know their families, and know what their passions were. Every employee. He made Sandra do the same. Though it hurt like a sonofabitch, I was really glad my face was broken.

I checked the debuff timer as my life leaked down point by point; 45 more seconds.

She reached in her bag and pulled out a potion, then held it out to me. "Here. It'll stop the bleeding. You should buy a few." She turned away and grabbed Verin, the merc, by the back of the shirt. I held the potion tight as I watched her drag the man away. She stopped and turned back.

"Don't depend on him." She pointed a long finger at Otto. "He'll let you down, he'll fail, he'll die. You're the only one who can save you. Get a move on your class kit." She tugged Verin along the street as she walked away into the fading light.

I looked up to Otto. For once, his expressionless face held very little for me to decipher. What was he thinking? Did her words actually affect him somehow? I wasn't sure if the NPCs were sophisticated enough to react to such a comment from a Traveler.

Otto noticed me staring and finally looked at me. He pulled the cork from the potion and nudged my hand. I gulped it back and was instantly reminded of nighttime cold medicine. It wasn't quite as thick, but still just as sugary and foul as a cough suppressant.

The Broken Nose debuff disappeared and my Health shot up to 100%. Bones cracked and my skin pulled as my nose corrected itself. I yawned a few times, moving my jaw in a circular motion as I massaged the area.

"You clammed up. Who was that?" he asked, his voice standoffish.

I sniffed, my nostrils filled with the salty iron scent of my own blood. "Sandra."

"Osbark's Sandra?" Otto asked, and I contained my chuckle.

"Osmark, yes. That was her." I walked to where the scuffle had been and picked up my staff. There was a new coating of blood on the handle, some of it mine I was sure, and the onyx gemstone was cracked. My finger traced the damage, and I inspected the item card. There was no durability to it, and the stats seemed the same, so maybe I just had to stick it on the magical gear shelf in my room and it would be repaired.

I'd been so glad when taking my bath that the barmaid pointed out the magic wardrobe. Any gear left in it for a few minutes would come out as fresh as hot laundry. I hadn't needed to wash the Moorkin gunk off my gown, and if I had, I may have just paid Otto 2 gold and walked around naked until I could find a new one.

"We should get back to the inn," Otto offered. "The Imperials might come back."

"What was that shop?" I snapped my fingers a few times to remember the name of the Accipiter man in the incense-laden store.

"Satin and Beech," Otto grunted.

"We said we'd come back, and I still need some things if we're going to take on that dungeon."

Otto bobbed his head and turned toward the main road in town without a word. I jogged up beside him as he kept a pace too fast for my shorter legs. His fists were clenched, and his eyes set straight ahead. There was definitely something going on in his artificial synapses that was making him upset.

I wanted to say something, but what? Sandra was right. Otto would die, eventually, and if I wasn't competent on my own, I'd be screwed. Sandra had laid out all six of those guys in *seconds*, and I got my ass handed to me by one fist. I couldn't depend on Otto to save me, and I couldn't depend on Jack or anyone else to, either.

The nighttime affairs were picking up as the sun was coming down. The daily duties of forging, bread making, stone masonry and more were coming to a close as shops locked up their doors and turned wooden signs saying, "Will resume at dawn."

We came to the dimly lit Satin and Beech, and Otto knocked. The door had its own sign up with a similar message of when regular business would resume.

"They're closed for the night, Otto, let's just go back to the inn." There was pity in the tone of my voice, and I hiccupped at the end. The effects of mead lasted even through getting punched in the face and having a potion.

Otto didn't reply, but he knocked again, differently this time. *Rah-ta-tap-ta, rah-ta.* The door creaked open a moment later and the Accipiter man, Hasan, poked his face out.

"Oh, you're back!" The door swung open wide. "Come in, please! I hope your quests were fruitful today."

"They were," Otto grumbled and stepped into the shop, then stood off to the side to allow me through.

The dim lights were difficult to adjust to, and the smoky incense smell burned my eyes as I entered. Without another word, Hasan took my hand and pulled me through the rows of wares to a back room. It was better lit than the rest of the shop, with a desk littered with papers and small trinkets. There was a pile of money right on the table, and I wondered if Hasan trusted Otto and I so much to leave it out, or if he'd forgotten.

"I got a shipment from home!" he proclaimed, his large golden eyes twinkling with joyful mist.

"Great, what was in it?" I asked when he didn't go on.

I suddenly wondered if old Accipiter mothers would send their sons gift packs of dead mice and rabbits, much like how my mother would send me cookies before the post regulations went berserk.

Hasan held his hand up as if asking me to wait and turned to rummage through a large wooden crate on the ground. There were sounds of metal tinkling, small things in some kind of a bag, and some larger things too. He glanced over his shoulder at me, puffing out his wings to block my view.

"This!" He spun around holding a small poncho-type cloak adorned with a pair of sleek cloth shoulder pads. It was beautiful… but a deep crimson. My robes were blue and purple. I withheld my critical statement and put on a huge smile.

"Amazing!" I exclaimed with a bit too much enthusiasm, but Hasan didn't seem to notice.

He held the item out to me, and I touched the soft fabric. It was warm, much more so than the air around us, and I moved to inspect it.

Formel's Mantle of Spirit

Armor Type: Light, Cloth

Class: Rare

Base Defense: 5

Primary Effects:

- +10 to Spirit

- +20% Spirit regen bonus

The dust storms of the Barren Sands are no match for a Formel's mantle.

"It's great," I said, backing away. I knew I couldn't afford it after how much the robes had cost.

"Yes, I think it's for you." He held them out further. "Only eight gold. It's a steal. I will put it out in the front tomorrow for twelve."

That was almost half my gold, and who knew when I'd come across any more of it. The game seemed hell-bent on keeping me broke, until that chest appeared. I'd promised to buy something else, but that was just too much. I opened my mouth to decline and promptly snapped it shut as the old adage my father used to rattle off ran through my mind.

You've gotta invest in yourself if you wanna be something. The sound of his voice in my head was a sweet comfort. I hadn't thought of him, hadn't heard him, in what felt like so long. Maybe it was the mead, or maybe it was the truth nestled deep in me trying to come out.

I had some money, and I needed to be strong and capable. I needed to invest in myself if I wanted to be something. "Okay." I nodded. "I'll take it."

"Excellent!" He clapped his hand against the garment. "I know you'll do great things with it."

He passed me the mantle, and I handed him 8 gold from my satchel.

"Come back again tomorrow!" The business was concluded, and so ended his patient mannerisms. He pushed me out of the back office and through the shop to the front door, where a disappointed Otto shook his head.

Hasan opened the door and motioned for us to leave. Otto rolled his eyes and stomped out to the street. Suddenly, I felt like I'd done something wrong.

Hasan grinned. "See you again tomorrow." He waved his hand through the open door.

I dropped the cloth shoulders onto my character, expecting something strange to happen, but it was just the typical rush of power. I gave Hasan a wave and stepped out. The door slammed shut on my butt and bumped me down into the dirt path.

"You didn't even barter. Now Hasan thinks you're a pushover. You won't get anywhere with him." Otto turned his back and plodded off.

I followed behind as the businesses around us finished closing up, and the distant sounds of music kicked up. We made our way through the alleys, and I realized, though I hadn't been in Harrowick long, we weren't headed for the main road.

"Where are we going?" I asked Otto as we stepped past a pair of youngsters obviously looking for a place to wet their whistles.

"Back way," he grunted.

"Why?" I asked, perturbed.

He turned sharply. "Because I'd rather not run into those Imperials again and have something happen to me while I'm trying to protect you."

Otto grimaced. "And another thing, you've disregarded me, my opinions, and my efforts all day. Yes, you're paying me, but I'm not a *slave*."

Maybe I had, but I'd also saved his ass, and plus, he was only code. That particular reasoning wasn't sitting as well with me as it had when I first entered the game. There were so many secrets about Otto. I knew the Overminds would weave a plot for the NPCs, but Otto's seemed so *real*. Naitee was also a far cry from ones and zeroes. Perhaps I was being—

"Well?" Otto demanded.

"I was thinking." I forced my voice to be steady, even, and low. "I appreciate everything you've done for me."

He raised a brow.

I bit my lip. He was only code but seemed aware enough to want an apology. "I'm sorry you've felt mistreated."

Otto glared at me for a long time, so long I felt like I'd broken him somehow, then his face softened. "Do you believe what she said?"

"Sandra?" I asked, though I knew what he meant.

He gritted his teeth, looked away, and nodded.

"I don't think you'll ever let me down purposefully, and I hope you won't die, especially not for me."

His head kept bobbing along, and he turned back to the alley. We walked without another word back to the inn, stepping inside just as the sun disappeared below the horizon. Otto dropped coin on the counter on his way to the stairs, leaving me in the tavern without even a goodnight.

I took a seat at his table, a heat that didn't feel necessary or justified building in my chest. I'd been honest, and he was upset at me for that? Moreover, he was my NPC, and it shouldn't have been an issue.

The barmaid offered me mead, but I turned it down for some good old-fashioned water and a plate of whatever was hot. Moments later she returned with a cool wooden cup full of the sweetest, most refreshing water I'd ever tasted. I checked the item description to ensure she hadn't brought me some kind of juice by accident.

The cool notes tickled my mind into action. The bottom line was that I needed Otto on my side and loyal to me. If I had to suspend my knowledge of reality and pretend he was just the same as me, then maybe that's what I had to do.

The hot plate was roasted root vegetables and a side of waterfowl, both of which were covered in the bird's fatty grease. It was fantastic, of course, and for a moment, I was sad I didn't have Otto around to watch me scarf it down way too fast.

I dropped some silver on the table when I was done. I wasn't sure how much the meal and the room would be, Otto hadn't told me how much I owed him, but I figured five silver had to be enough given what I'd seen Otto giving the barmaid.

The wooden walls of the staircase were warm with the heat of the fire from the kitchen as I made my way up to the room I'd slept in the night before. Everything was clean, sheets turned down, water basin replenished. I flopped onto the bed and opened my character sheet.

The game was no mystery to me, since I'd helped create it, but I panned through the explanations of this stat and that to take my mind off Otto's strange behavior.

Strength: increasing attack strength (AS) to deal more damage with short-range weapons like clubs, swords, and axes. It also increased the overall base armor rating, which if I went Stonewall, wouldn't be a big deal for me.

Vitality: pretty simple, increased overall hit points and Health regeneration. No additional effects.

Constitution: increases Stamina, Stamina regeneration, and carry capacity. Stamina was the physical "currency" of sorts that was used when engaging in combat, similar to how Spirit was used for spellcraft.

Dexterity: the primary contributor to ranged attack damage, but also increased the chance to evade or block. I was reminded of Jinker, the Hydromancer passive that improved Dexterity, and how it very likely saved my ass with the Balrigons.

Intelligence: much like Dexterity and Strength, it increased spellcasting attack damage. It also improved resistances, poison, disease, and elemental by .01% per point.

Spirit: the stat giving me the most grief recently. Points applied here would increase my Spirit total and would also increase Spirit regeneration.

Luck: the most contentious of the attributes. Players couldn't assign points to it like they could the other stats, leaving it somewhat of a mystery to those who didn't help make the game. I knew Luck would contribute to all sorts of things: loot drops, gold drops, bartering chances, quests presented and quest rewards, and much more I didn't know. Luck was by far the most valuable stat in the game, and the hardest to acquire.

I sighed and panned to the forum as I checked the time, only 8 PM and I wasn't nearly tired enough for sleep. The wiki was alive with excitement as people shared news, tips, tricks, quest locations, and much more. It was nice to see so many people working together after watching them run one another down with trucks trying to get into Osmark Tech.

It was nice to think that maybe the human race could do things differently this time around.

The realization brought sadness as I thought of my mother back IRL, waiting to die. Then my mind fell on Jack, my old gaming friend. I brought up the search friend function and typed away a few of the names I knew he might use. No results. I closed out the menu and pulled the pillow to my chest. I'd have to go Stonewall, no other class could survive solo.

FIFTEEN

BAD CODE

BLUE FLAME WHIPPED ABOUT THE TAIL OF THE comet, 213 Astraea, flowing through an infinite vortex of gravity. The comet spun slowly on its axis, causing the trail of gas and debris to loop in a helix. Astraea rotated in my view, and I passed behind it. My vision blurred as the blue heat battered my face.

How was I still breathing in space?

I looked down to see the V.G.O. capsule I'd gotten into at Osmark Tech. The capsule I was *still in*, at least my living body.

Light brought my attention back to Astraea, and my heart thumped as Earth came into view. Our little spec of paradise, blue mother, cradle of life, was about to be ravaged by millions of tons of iron and stone.

An orange glow started at Astraea's nose. It grew, until the entire rock was enveloped by hot white destruction. The atmosphere ripped open with a green shimmer, like the planet's forcefield going down.

"No! Stop!" I reached out for Astraea as if I could hold it back with my frail arms, but my hands landed against the cold padding of my coffin.

I rushed down toward the flaming asteroid, passing through its wake and into the core. My computer desk stood alone at the center of a dark cavern at the core of Astraea, lines of code dotting the screen. But it wasn't my code. No, I hadn't written *that*. That code could cause problems. There were errors peppered throughout the entire function. No, no… Did I write this?

My body lurched, and my stomach churned as I pulled away from the desk through the back of Astraea. Moisture bubbled up around me as I continued to pull back, farther and farther from Earth as Astraea slammed into the ocean bedrock far slower than seemed possible. The salty seawater clung to my lips and matted my hair as it exploded out into the stratosphere.

The capsule flipped end over end as I plummeted back to Earth, the blinding flash of Astraea's 800 megaton explosion whiting out all other images. The sickening spin slammed to a halt, and my capsule lid burst open.

I clutched my chest and breathed deep. Just a dream. I sat up and felt a wave of familiarity at the back of my mind. Rows upon rows of white coffin-shaped capsules lined the floor, walls, and ceiling of the cavernous underground complex below Osmark Tech.

Oh shit. My capsule broke! I'm trapped here, in this mass grave, and everyone else will transition into V.G.O.! I just needed to get my capsule lid. Maybe I could put it back on and go back to sleep, get back into the game.

When I looked over the edge my breath caught at the sight of the faulty code. It was all over the floor, running up the legs of the capsules and into their computers. One by one, capsule lids popped off with a bang, and resounding cries of terror filled the cavern. My code broke them. My code stranded these people in their physical bodies. My code killed everyone on Earth.

"What have you done?" The unmistakable demand of my boss, Osmark, turned my head. It wasn't Robert standing behind me, but a massive Balrigon, dripping red-hot lava from its open maw.

I yelped as I tried to escape my coffin, but the snaking tubes of sedatives and regulatory fluids tied me down. My skin peeled back as I pulled, trying to rip myself free. The Balrigon advanced.

"Your stupidity and arrogance has damned us all! We trusted you!" His voice morphed from Osmark's to something guttural, omniscient, and powerful.

The Balrigon gripped the edge of my capsule, bending the metal and plastic under its iron fists. Lava dribbled down its chin onto my legs, searing my skin. I squirmed and kicked, but the capsule held me tightly.

The creature grinned. "Now, we'll all die because you failed us."

It leaned in closer, the scorching drool dripping up my legs to my chest. Its breath reeked of sulphur and blood as it whispered, "You failed."

I jerked free of my binds and toppled out of the capsule. The Balrigon laughed behind me as I scrambled to my feet and ran down the alley of open coffins. Everyone writhed and screamed as the capsule tubes constricted around their arms and legs, pinning them into the technology.

"You did this! You did this!" the captives shrieked as I passed, their wide, fearful eyes tracking me as I went. I could feel their judging gazes upon me. I could feel the agony my failure brought.

"You left me to die." My mother's grief-stricken voice boomed through the massive sepulcher, and I skidded to a stop.

The sound of her bare feet padding toward me was wet. *Slap splat, slap, slap, splat.* I could tell by her gait she was struggling to walk.

Her voice returned with an unnatural growl. "You couldn't even take one day off work to see your father into the grave. You're no daughter of mine, you ungrateful, selfish brat."

She spat the words at me. I didn't want to turn and see her face. I knew exactly how it would look. Nose wrinkled, forehead creased, eyes blazing, with her hair in a gravity-defying puff about her face that would be intimidating, instead of comical as it usually was.

I turned despite my instinct. I saw her bare feet first and didn't understand as lines of code wiggled up her legs and around her hips. Her belly button sucked the words in, letter by letter, with a sickening slurp. I didn't want to look up any farther, but my eyes moved of their own accord.

Her transparent rib cage rose and fell with ragged breaths, and the crimson heart in her chest beat like a jackhammer. Glowing green chemicals flowed down her esophagus and blackened as they mixed with the code in her transparent womb. Capsule tubes snaked into her mouth through her cheeks, and blood ran down her throat from the wounds.

My mother's lips pulled down into a feral frown, green liquid spilling out with the words she spoke. "You will never be anyone if you care for no one."

My eyes shot open, dissolving the mortifying image of my mother as I finally woke up from the nightmare.

The black of my room brought little comfort as I sat up in my bed. It felt like an angry rhino was trying to escape my skull, and the sweat-soaked sheets told me this had been going on for a while. My gut turned, and all I could think of was water, ibuprofen, and twelve more hours of sleep… but I had to go to work, or Tristen would shit a brick.

"Lights on."

Darkness…

"Lights on." I called a little more forcefully to my home AI unit.

No reply.

I swung my feet over the edge of the bed and gasped as they touched cold floor. This wasn't my room. Hairs rose on the back of my neck as I felt primal adrenaline surge with my pounding heart. My breathing shallowed.

Then, I remembered. I took a deep breath through my nose and my shoulders relaxed. I was in V.G.O. already, my second day.

I stood from the cloud-like bed and fumbled through the dark for the door, then cracked it. Light from candles lining the hall outside spilled into the room and revealed the medieval tavern inn. My eyes lost focus and drifted over the wood grain. I hadn't noticed before, but texture repeated every fifth board. What a terrible visual flaw… Had I done this?

No, I was being silly. I didn't touch the visual rendering system. I turned back to the bedroom and grabbed the candle from the nightstand and walked out to the hall. I tilted my candle into another and stole a bit of fire. I gazed into the flame, the blue-green of the center was so like the tail of Astraea. So much destruction in one, cosmically small, bit of rock.

"It was just a dream, Abby."

I returned to my room with my lit candle and opened my character sheet. 5:30 AM. I needed to choose my class in a few hours, and I felt like I wasn't closer to a choice. Stonewall would be the only class for solo, but if I ended up in a clan, I'd want to be *really* useful. Frostlock was pretty good crowd control, and Hydromancer was alright. Firebrand was the only one that stuck out as a high-powered DPS, someone who wouldn't get left behind on the big clan dungeon raid. A contributor.

I disabled my morning alarm to prevent it from wrecking my train of thought and panned to the forums again. There had to be information on the four different trees that could help me.

Soft orange light from the rising sun broke through my shuttered window as I scoured the wiki for info on the Sorceress classes. There was less than I was hoping. Each tree had been outlined with the level-one abilities. Most people seemed to still be on the same class choice step as me.

Good. I wasn't behind yet. But the longer I dallied the more of a risk that became.

The clock hit 6:30 AM, and I hopped out of bed and headed to the wardrobe where my fresh-pressed gear hung neatly. It was nice to know that even when my gear was hanging in the wardrobe like that, it was still part of my inventory. It couldn't be stolen, except by a master thief perhaps. But most players were too low level to be doing anything like that, and most NPCs were programmed not to go around thieving from Travelers.

It was a comfort knowing we put a lot of care into ensuring the PvP was fairly safe. Thieves could steal a *lot* of things off my person, but not the gear I had equipped. Being in the wardrobe was an extension of being equipped, so it was still out of reach there.

I washed the sweat off my face and neck before locking eyes with my avatar in the mirror. This was me; now and forever. There was no going back, and no backing down. I had the scroll and knew there was a *dungeon* on the other end of it. I had to know what was down there. I had to stop Osmark.

I donned my clothes and snuffed the candle before leaving the room. The hall outside was bustling with maids. They gave me a smile and a nod as they passed me by, moving from room to room as they prepared for this evening's guests. I made my way down the stairs and was surprised to see two others in the tavern, quiet as mice, chomping away at their meals.

The dream clung at the edges of my mind as I took the seat across from Otto at his table. He gave me a peculiar look, his hands folded in front of him on the table. I took a sip from the cup of water in front of me.

"Did you sleep well?" he asked, his tone accusatory.

I raised a brow. "No. I had nightmares."

His posture changed. He seemed to be expecting me to say yes, to say that everything was fine and I didn't have a hangover. He didn't expect my honesty. He'd need to get used to that because honesty and transparency were two of my highly held values.

"I'm sorry." He looked down, his fingernails scratching into a bit of dried food on the tabletop. "What did you dream?"

The urge to snap at him, to ask him what it mattered, surfaced, and I stuffed it back down. He was my companion, my only friend right now. I needed him.

I *needed* him. I wanted his friendship. Me. Solitary, lone wolf Abby. I *needed* an AI.

"My mother." I took another drink, cooling the lump in my throat.

He frowned. "Thoughts of your mother trouble you?"

I shook my head. "You wouldn't understand."

"Try me."

The barmaid brought two hot plates of fresh bread, eggs, cheese, and apple slices. It smelled divine, but Otto waited. He didn't touch his food, didn't even look at it. His gaze was locked on me.

"I'm a Traveler. You know I came here from far away?"

He nodded.

"My mother did not come with me. Where we were… it was doomed. She'll die soon." I forked the egg up onto the fresh bread and broke the yolk, sending cascades of yellow, fatty deliciousness down the edges, and bit in.

"I'm sorry for your loss." Otto bowed his head, his hands folded in his lap.

The lump in my throat grew and my nose tingled with the threat of tears.

"She chose it." I shrugged and talked through the mouthful of fluffy baguette. "My father is already gone. She didn't want to live here without him, would've rather died than be here with a daughter who didn't go to see her father on his deathbed." I stuffed another huge bite of egg-bread in my mouth and chewed once before swallowing, trying to force down the ache in my chest.

"Why not?" He still hadn't touched his food.

I motioned to his plate. "It'll get cold."

He nodded solemnly, then ate.

When my plate was nearly empty, I pushed it aside. "I had a friend, he might travel here too. He'll be a good ally for us if he does."

"A friend?" Otto grunted as he stuffed the last bit of bread in his mouth.

"His name is Jack. I've known him a long time and told him about how to travel here. If he does, he can help us with this business with Osmark."

The barmaid took our plates, and I dropped some silver in her palm. Still not quite enough silver to make her happy.

"You don't think we can handle this?" Otto asked, his voice defensive.

I seesawed my head. "Maybe. But I'd rather not get you killed."

His eyes widened, and I grinned. He smiled back, and we were quiet again as we watched the other two in the tavern finish their meals and depart.

"You think this Jack will want to help you?" Otto asked.

"Us," I retorted.

Otto's face hardly changed, but I could tell he was happy. His cheeks rounded, and the creases in his forehead smoothed.

I thought on his question. I didn't know. Jack had been my friend, almost my boyfriend. But we were cool.

We'd raided together and had great times in the old Crimson Alliance, the guild a few of us started and took from game to game. He'd never done anything unsavory and was always really kind. I trusted him.

"I hope so."

Otto nodded again as he drank the last of his water.

"I'm going to go Firebrand," I blurted.

Otto pursed his lips. "Is that what's best for you?"

I chewed my lip. No, probably not. Depending. If I was alone, no. Definitely not. But if I was in a clan or if Otto survived or if Jack joined… yes. Firebrand was so cool, too! Seriously, fireballs from my hands. Too cool.

"You don't know." He read me.

I shook my head.

He sighed. "You need to talk to Naitee soon."

I changed my shake to a slow bob.

"Well, I'll follow you while the coin's good, crazy lady." He gave me a wry smile, and I smirked.

I stood and gave a long stretch up, back, and then down to my toes. It felt great. My muscles were still cramped from the nightmare and perhaps a bit from the mead. Otto made a similar motion and yawned a bit, then headed for the door. Apparently he hadn't slept great either.

The streets around the Boar's Head were quiet, filthy, and cool. The morning sun was just breaching the hills outside of town, leaving little etchings of frost on the windows and in the dirt.

"Otto, why is the Boar's Head so quiet in such a rowdy area?" I asked as we snaked our way to the main road.

"It's their reputation. If you want privacy, it's where you go. Prices are a little steeper than most." He shrugged.

I felt there was more to it than that, but decided not to get into it. The population on the streets grew the deeper we moved into the business section, and soon, we were surrounded by people taking on their daily duties. Fortunately, Otto had the power to make others flow around him, so I trailed in his wake.

Butterflies battered against my insides as I saw the four-flagged spire of Naitee's shop. I had to choose. I would have to pick my eternal fate in just a few minutes. Was I going to make the right choice?

Probably not. But any choice would be better than inaction. I needed to keep moving forward, and no matter what class kit I picked, I wouldn't stop until Osmark's plan was revealed, thwarted, and he was ousted. He deserved nothing less than to be banished for his backhanded treachery: selling power and domination over his customers, over the only humans left on Earth, to the scummiest people who ever walked it. Despicable.

"Abby." Otto grabbed my shoulder, and I looked up to see Naitee's shop feet from me. I needed to stop zoning out.

"You all right?" His hand fell away and I nodded.

"Thinking about my class." I sucked in a deep breath and grabbed the handle. The door opened with ease, and for once, I wasn't slapped in the face with unbearable heat.

Naitee sat at the center of the room, her legs crossed and hands held together in prayer. No, not quite. There was a gap between her palms. Little flames licked up her fingers and over her knuckles, dancing with one another, and with Naitee's energy. I could *see* her energy, or at least, I thought I could. Heat waves radiated off her white-blond hair and crimson robes in circles, pushing out toward the walls before disappearing into figments of my imagination.

The door closed behind me, and I turned to see Otto had, once again, left me alone with her. Coward…

"Come here." My mentor's voice was old, weathered, and wise. In this moment of meditation, I felt she knew more than one person should ever know.

I took three steps closer and stopped a few feet short of her radiant energy field. Every inch closer brought more and more heat. The soft furs she sat on glowed red-hot, the warmth from Naitee's body seeping through to the animal hide.

"Sit down," she ordered. I'd come this far following her directions, so I wasn't going to let a bit of bossiness get in the way of me finishing this quest and getting my class. I did as she commanded, kneeling before her.

Her eyes cracked open, their piercing blue a stark contrast to the bright red of her gown.

"You're undecided," she remarked.

I took a deep breath. "No. I've chosen."

Naitee chuckled in a tone that said, "I've been around the block enough times to know when a little babe doesn't know their way."

"Firebrand," I said, cutting her laughter short, and her eyes widened.

Her face drooped from amused to concerned. "Firebrand is not for the reckless. It is not for the weak. It is not for *little girls*."

"I'm none of those things, so Firebrand is for me."

Naitee raised a brow. "You drank a strange vialed liquid from a strange woman just moments after meeting her because some Risi told you the strange woman was a Sorceress."

"I weighed the risks in my mind and calculated the gains. I considered the distance to the next town where I could find a trainer, took my nonexistent coin into account, and then decided, very carefully, to drink the liquid."

Naitee's white brow rose farther toward her hairline, and the flames in her palms grew more wild, erratic. "You can't even mine your own ore. You got your face broken by an Imperial goon and had to be rescued from the fight by a huntress."

The last mention of Sandra raised hairs on my neck and heat in my stomach. Never mind how she found out—Otto probably snitched somehow—I had to defend myself. "I didn't have *any* spells, just my damn staff, and I did a pretty good job with what I had against swords and armor."

"You lack the experience teamwork brings. It is difficult for you to get along with people, which is why your only friend right now is a rebellious Risi outcast."

"At least I have a friend." I clenched my teeth in frustration. Was she going to tell me no? This was *my* damn choice, not hers!

I wasn't weak or reckless. I had tried everything I could to talk us out of that fight. I calculated the future risks on multiple facets of many of my decisions. I took my time in decision-making. I was practiced in making good decisions faster! How could this woman call me a *little girl*? She didn't know anything about me.

Naitee's lips cracked into a smile. "Maybe. Are you sure he isn't following you for the gear and the coin?"

"Yes." My insides felt much softer on this matter than the firm words that escaped my lips with confidence.

"Good, then I think maybe"—she stood and strode to the back of the shop, then grabbed a sheaf of parchment—"maybe you can become the most powerful Sorceress in Eldgard."

SIXTEEN

FIREBRAND

"EXCUSE ME?" IT WAS MORE OF A DEMAND than a question.

"You heard me, child," Naitee scolded as she scribbled furiously on the parchment on the counter. "If you fail this quest in any way, the Firebrand path will be forever out of your reach. If you prove unworthy, the essence of the elemental power will not flow through you."

I opened my quest log again. The pending quest sat at the forefront, and the "Yes" and "No" buttons next to the green "Accept?" text were pulsing on and off, daring me to choose.

Quest Update: The Path of a Sorceress

Naitee needs you to collect one more ingredient, a golden egg from the Basalt Hollows, using only Firebrand abilities. Dying, failing to return with the golden egg, or attacking any way other than with Firebrand abilities or your melee weapon will lock the Firebrand Sorceress kit forever.

Quest Class: Rare, Class-Based

Quest Difficulty: Infernal

Success: Return to Naitee with a golden egg from the Basalt Hollows using only Firebrand magic and your melee weapon to complete the quest.

Failure: Die at any point during the golden egg retrieval, use any items or magic for combat outside of the Firebrand skills and your melee weapon, or fail to retrieve the golden egg and bring it to Naitee.

If you fail, you will never be able to attempt the Firebrand class kit quest again.

Reward: Class Change: Sorceress, Firebrand; Unique, Scalable Item; 15,000 XP.

I took a deep breath and wished Otto was in the room. He was a good sounding board for when my thoughts were disheveled. But this was my choice. If I failed at Firebrand, there were always the other three I could try for… There was only one way I saw myself failing, though. Dying. If I died, Otto likely would too. Then I'd go with the original plan: Stonewall and solo.

"Okay, I'll do it."

I accepted the quest, and Naitee bustled about behind the glass cases. When she turned back, she held a black wooden box in one hand, and in the other, that same lemon-broccoli potion. I grimaced at the sight of the nasty thing, and she rolled her eyes, then slapped it into my outstretched palm. I downed it in a single gulp, trying my best not to let any of the juice touch my tongue.

I shivered, my arms spasming as I plopped the empty vial on the counter. The countdown timer appeared in the corner of my heads-up display, the HUD, this time with twelve hours rather than five. It worried me that I'd have access to the Frostlock, Hydromancer, and Stonewall abilities. Casting those spells had become all too natural in the few hours I'd had access to them the day before. It felt as if the game, this quest, was setting me up to fail. I'd have to take care with every thought, using only the Firebrand abilities.

With that out of the way, it was time for whatever was in the box. Naitee motioned for me to remove to the top and it came away easily. Inside, on a bed of black cloth, sat a red-corked vial of glowing golden liquid. Next to it was a scroll of the same size as the bottle.

"The potion will unlock the Firebrand tree to you further, and the scroll will place temporary points into some of the abilities. You will not be able to add any of your ability points to the tree until Fire accepts you."

I pulled the scroll and vial from their bed. The glass of the potion radiated heat and thrummed like a heart. The beat it pulsed felt similar to how Naitee's energy looked when she meditated.

I was struck dumb. How had I not noticed? "Are you a Firebrand?"

Naitee grinned. "Yes, many long years now."

That would explain the unbearably hot house, the whole turning into living fire when I walked in reeking like death, and the flames that danced in her palms this morning. I felt so stupid for not adding it up.

I lifted the bottle to my chin, and Naitee and I chimed together, "Bottoms up."

The gold liquid oozed into my mouth and coated my tongue. It was hotter than the glass let on. The molasses lava trickled to the back of my throat, and I swallowed hard, using my saliva to move the rest of it along.

The fire intensified as it passed down my esophagus, and I dropped to my knees, holding tight to the glass case in front of me. My eyes squeezed shut to block out the pain, but golden swirls of flame looped behind my lids, reminding me of the hot ache in my chest. My pulse raged and gut roiled. I wasn't sure if I was still breathing, still crouched in Naitee's shop, or even in V.G.O. The pain took me away to a dark place, somewhere far away from life and light.

I lost track of my body, sound, and time.

Then, my eyes were open. Otto and Naitee were looking down at me, Otto with a very unhappy crease in his forehead. Naitee seemed perfectly calm. My ears popped—

"... n't tell me you were going to make her drink it now!" Otto growled.

I sat up. The room was *destroyed*. All of the glass cases lay in piles against the baseboards, the rugs were ash, and the walls blackened. It smelled one part campfire, the other burnt hair.

"What happened?" I looked to Naitee.

"I forgot how"—she cleared her throat—"devastating the effects of magical activation can be."

The tiny scroll had incinerated in my hand, but I could *feel* the knowledge of the spells at the back of my mind. I opened my character sheet, panning to my class tree. Oh mother of fire, it worked. I had unlocked the kit and gained access to five new spells.

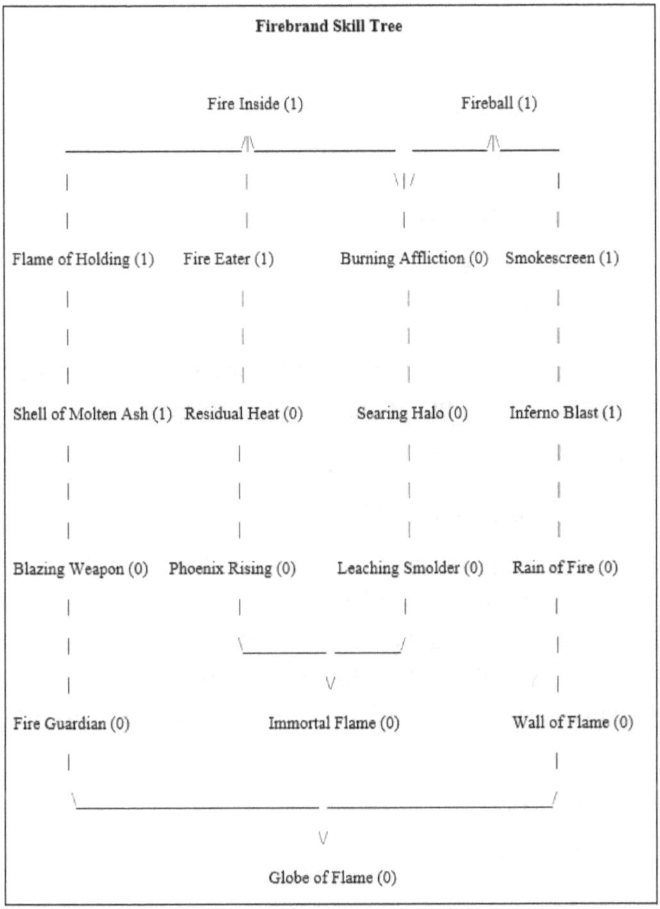

Firebrand Skill Tree

```
          Fire Inside (1)                    Fireball (1)
         ___________/\____________      ________/\________
        |            |          \ | /                |
        |            |            |                   |

 Flame of Holding (1)   Fire Eater (1)    Burning Affliction (0)   Smokescreen (1)
        |            |            |                   |
        |            |            |                   |
        |            |            |                   |

 Shell of Molten Ash (1)  Residual Heat (0)   Searing Halo (0)   Inferno Blast (1)
        |            |            |                   |
        |            |            |                   |
        |            |            |                   |

 Blazing Weapon (0)   Phoenix Rising (0)   Leaching Smolder (0)   Rain of Fire (0)
        |            |            |                   |
        |             \_______  _______/             |
        |                     V                      |

 Fire Guardian (0)          Immortal Flame (0)          Wall of Flame (0)
        |                                                     |
         \_______________________  _______________________/
                                 V

                         Globe of Flame (0)
```

Skill: Flame of Holding

Conjure fiery bonds to detain your enemy. The target is incapable of moving, speaking, or casting spells as long as Flame of Holding persists. You can cancel Flame of

Holding at any time. As long as Flame of Holding is in use, your Spirit regeneration is reduced by 40%.

Skill Type/Level: Cast, Level 1

Cost: 40% Spirit regeneration reduction for duration

Range: 2 meters, single target

Duration: Indefinite, until canceled

Cast Time: 5 seconds

Cooldown: 20 minutes

Effect 1: Bind your enemy with flames, rendering them incapable of moving, speaking or casting spells.

Skill: Shell of Molten Ash

This shield may look cool on the outside, but fire rages within! Protect yourself with a shell of molten ash. Absorb one strike and eject a gout of flame upon impact, dealing 25 points of fire damage to any enemy within a 5-meter, 15-degree cone. Blocks forward visibility until used.

Skill Type/Level: Cast, Level 1

Cost: 30 Spirit

Range: Self

Duration: Indefinite, Until Destroyed

Cast Time: None

Cooldown: 5 minutes

Effect 1: Protect yourself with a shield made of molten ash, absorbing a single strike.

Effect 2: Eject a gout of flame upon shield destruction, dealing 25 fire damage to any enemy within a 5-meter range and a 15-degree cone.

Twenty-five points of damage didn't seem like much, but when I noticed the "Spell Strength" stat read, "Add this value to any spell with a base damage not modified by your character level or another stat," I was relieved. It would do more like 125 points of damage, and only get better over time.

Skill: Fire Eater

The flames are your friends, you welcome the warmth. Increase your resistance to fire damage by 25% and convert 5% of your fire damage dealt into Spirit.

Skill Type/Level: Passive, Level 1

Cost: None

Range: N/A

Cast Time: N/A

Cooldown: N/A

Effect 1: Resist 25% of all fire damage.

Effect 2: Convert 5% fire damage dealt into Spirit.

Skill: Smokescreen

With a raging fire comes choking fumes. Smokescreen fills the air with a cloud of burning smoke! Reduce visibility by 50%, reduce enemy hit chance by 15%, and reduce Stamina regeneration by 15%. Duration, 45 seconds.

Skill Type/Level: Cast, Level 1

Cost: 100 Spirit

Range: 25 meters from caster, 5-meter radius.

Duration: 45 seconds

Cast Time: 2 seconds

Cooldown: 3 minutes

Effect 1: Reduce visibility for those within the smoke cloud by 50%.

Effect 2: Reduce enemy hit chance for those within the smoke cloud by 15%.

Effect 3: Reduce Stamina regeneration for those within the smoke cloud by 15%.

<<<◇>>>

Skill: Inferno Blast

Unleash a blast of flames from both of your hands, 3 meters out with a 10-degree cone from each hand, dealing 3 fire damage per second as long as the target is in range. Spell will continue until canceled or your Spirit is depleted.

Skill Type/Level: Active Cast, Level 1

Cost: 5 Spirit per sec

Range: 3 meters, 10 degrees from the center of your palm

Duration: Until Canceled or Spirit Depletion

Cast Time: Continuous

Cooldown: None

Effect 1: Unleash a cone of fire on your enemies dealing 3 fire damage per sec to enemies in range.

Wow. I was going to own it! Whatever was guarding that golden egg didn't stand a snowball's chance in hell.

"I think she likes it." Naitee chuckled, and I realized my cheeks hurt from smiling. "How about some more?" she asked.

My pulse quickened, and I imagined what I could do with just one more spell. "You can unlock more?"

"Naitee," Otto groaned.

She wagged her finger at him. "Don't you start, Otto. That was an accident. I didn't think Rageweed and Grizzly Talon would react that way, and I did tell you it was an experimental mixture."

She turned her gaze to me. "I have a potion that may allow you to add one of your ability points to the tree."

"Hell yeah, I'm in!" I jumped to my feet, then grabbed Otto's arm as I wobbled.

Naitee looked down.

"What?" I prodded.

"If you fail, the Firebrand tree will be permanently closed to you, and that ability point lost forever." She clasped her hands at her navel and regarded me with pity in the lines of her face.

I was committed to Firebrand, but was I *that* committed? If we died, I'd need every ability point for Stonewall.

Otto whispered to me. "Abby, we can do this without risking your life." He glared at Naitee and said a bit louder, "Or your arm."

Naitee sighed and cocked out a hip as she crossed her arms. "It's not as though healing potions didn't repair the damage. You were fine in a few minutes." She waved of Otto's accusation. Apparently, the two had more history than I knew.

I took a deep breath as I considered the options. Otto believed in me. Moreover, he believed in the power we had *together*. I wanted an edge, but was it worth Osmark getting eight more hours on me if Naitee's potion killed me?

No. We could do this without the cheats. "I think I'll be okay, thanks Naitee."

She bowed her head and pulled two scrolls from an unseen pocket on her robes, then held them out to me. "This will get you to the Basalt Hollows. You'll have a long way down to find the egg. The other is a return scroll. You're lucky I like you."

I took the rolls of parchment and stuffed them into my inventory. That egg was as good as mine. Otto and I didn't need twelve hours, we'd have that thing in four or less.

Naitee grinned and pinched my cheek like an old granny. "You do have fire in you. Be safe, child."

She walked us to the door and showed us out into the warm October morning.

Otto leaned back and stared up at the sky. "We'll need potions."

"I bet you know just the place." I nudged his elbow. He smirked and gave a nod, then marched off down the alley.

At Merrick's Elixirs I learned there were six different tiers of Health and Spirit potions, each restoring more of their respective attributes and getting more expensive. There were some interesting combo potions that restored both, and then some even more interesting "restore over time" ROT and "heal over time" HOT potions. They were all incredibly expensive aside from the first- and second-level potions.

I bought twenty level 1 potions, ten each of Health and Spirit. With Otto's help, I bartered like a boss and got them at a 30% discount. With pockets full of nasty, cold medicine tasting salvation, we left the shop optimistic for the quest ahead.

SEVENTEEN

LAVA PITS

I LOOKED AT THE QUEST AGAIN AND CURSED AS I fanned myself with my hand. Basalt Hollows was apparently fancy shorthand for unbearable inferno mines filled with creatures of fire. Otto and I had already sweated about a bucket in the short thirty minutes we'd been here, and according to the map on the quest update, we still had a good mile down to trek.

The walls were thick black stone, dimpled and pockmarked from air bubbles getting trapped in the once liquid rock. Veins of red-hot magma ran through the walls behind shimmering quartz, which was mineable, but I could only imagine the hot fluids would pour through the second those stones were removed. It did create a beautiful ambiance, though. Without the insane heat, this cavern would be enchanting… romantic, even.

We'd encountered [Flametongue Salamanders], Doberman-sized geckos that breathed fire, and [Leatherwing Heatleachers], bats the size of a basketball whose sole purpose in life was to wrap themselves around anything that gave off heat and suck it out. They usually came in swarms of three or four and moved so fast that only my Fireball could take them out. But Naitee forgot to mention one thing.

All the beasts in the Basalt Hollows were creatures of fire, which had resistance to fire… which meant all my spells, except Smokescreen, did 25% less damage, and Burning Affliction did literally nothing at all. I was completely hamstrung in here, and already down two Health potions and one Spirit.

Otto wiped sweat from his brow and leaned against his sword. "How," he panted, "much farther?"

I got a sense of deja vu, and chuckled. "Not far," I lied. The cavern wound in a downward spiral, like we were traveling the path of an ancient volcanic eruption deep into the heart of the mountain. Every few hundred feet the cavern would open up, giving us a good view of what was above and below, and a break from the heat. The bottom of the pit was a smoking, burbling pit of hot lava, disincentivizing us from trying to climb our way down a bit faster.

The chittering of a new swarm of bats put Otto on his guard, but we had this down to a science now. I popped Fire Inside and followed it up with Smokescreen, increasing the visibility debuff from 50% to 100% just as the squad came into view. The bats shrieked behind the thick black clouds of choking smoke and dropped to the ground, stunned. Otto chopped down through the cloud with his sword and cut an unlucky bat clean in half.

Fire Inside ended, and the crawl of my Spirit regen returned to its normal pace. The cloud disappeared, and the dazed bats struggled to get back in the air. Two fireballs and another devastating blow from Otto's sword, and the pack was down.

"That's getting pretty easy." Otto grinned as beads of sweat dripped into his squinted eyes.

"Yeah." I punched his shoulder. "Good thing I'm such a badass."

Otto hefted his sword over his shoulder, and we continued down the corkscrew path of black lava rock.

"You'll have to explain to me why being a bad donkey is a good thing." Otto sounded flustered. Perhaps I was dropping too much slang.

"I'm sure you're getting sick of hearing it, but—"

"It's just *a thing* from your world?"

I shrugged. "Yeah. It means you're really good, or cool."

"That is completely contrary to the actually meaning of the words." Otto's brow knitted in frustration.

"No one really knows the origin of some of these sayings, but we all kept saying them. I'm sure you have some of your own? Like 'sigorsped'?"

Otto frowned. "Where did you hear that?"

"One of the, uh"—I fumbled at the word *housekeeper*—"barmaids said it." I settled on something I knew he would understand.

"Strange."

"Why?"

Flame spurted from the tunnel wall and battered Otto in the face. I stepped in front of the blast, taking seriously reduced damage with the help of Fire Eater, and triggered Shell of Molten Ash. The creature pounced at me, dispelling the shield. A gout of hot embers spit at the [Flametongue Salamander] from the Shell, and it shrieked.

The creature made a mad dash for the opposing wall, skittering up in a flash and hanging from the ceiling before taking a deep inhale for another bout of flame. Before the glow in its open maw could manifest in anything dangerous, I put my hands out and seared the thing with Inferno Blast. My Spirit plummeted by the second as hot destruction burst from the palms of my hands.

It didn't burn, it didn't feel bad at all. The only strange part about Inferno Blast was the sense of *drawing* from me. Like giving blood, when my arm would feel heavier and cold, the life force draining right out. Inferno Blast felt as though it was drawing the life out of me in a blaze of red and gold glory that brought destruction to anyone in its path.

The salamander squealed, dropped to the ground, and writhed about. Otto stomped down on its belly and jabbed the sword through its head. The creature went still, and we sighed together.

"Why's that?" I opened the creature's inventory, just to check. Sure as shit, nothing there but a worthless tattered hide and some talons I could exchange for a single copper. Not worthy of my inventory space.

"Sigorsped is from an old tongue, from mountain-dwelling Wode. It means good tidings in battle. I can't imagine any of the barmaids bidding you so." Otto nudged the salamander with his boot and rolled it over, then frowned. "Nothing good."

Good tidings in battle, so strange. Maybe the old woman was off her rocker.

"So, tell me more about this Jake person." Otto continued on the hot, narrow descent into hell.

"It's Jack," I corrected, and he grumbled. "He's a great guy. We've been friends for many years, despite a lot of distance between us."

"Great, huh? I'll be the judge of that."

"Do I detect a note of *jealousy*?" I grinned.

Otto's lips pulled down so far it seemed forced. "I do not get jealous."

His pace quickened, and I double stepped to keep up. "Anyway, he's really nice, he's a medic, eh"—I snapped my fingers—"a cleric kinda guy. He's always a team player. We've done lots of raids together."

"Raids?" Otto's forehead wrinkled, his voice carrying a note of accusation.

"Like, a dungeon. Like this. Except bigger." I stammered, trying to worm my way through the awkward conversation. "Anyway, like I said, he's a team player. He'll be a great addition to our duo."

Otto grunted in reply, keeping his quick pace. Maybe I broached the subject too quickly. I was starting to realize Otto was not so much like me, but more like a counterpart to me. Yes, he was still awkward, and forward-thinking, but he was great with crowds and talking to people. His automatic distrust and dislike of Jack was not something I ever did, especially if I had no details about the person whatsoever. There were a lot of similarities between us, but even more differences, it seemed.

"So, when is he getting here?" Otto grumbled, his tone betraying his attempt at seeming uninterested.

I pursed my lips. "I don't know. Lemme check."

The character sheet pulled up with ease, and I came to a stop. I'd experienced the disorientation and sometimes danger of walking around with my character sheet open before, and I wasn't about to put the whole quest at risk for something as silly as that. I opened the friend search and typed a few of his names.

Grim Jack, there he was. That was the name he went by in our first MMORPG, where we had founded the Crimson Alliance together. He was just level 2, so he must've started only minutes ago. He was probably just meeting his NPC and figuring out the rules. I wondered where he'd started, what race he'd picked, what he would look like, what class kit he would go for.

Butterflies fluttered in my stomach as I imagined greeting him for the first time in years, giving him a hug, and seeing his toothy smile creasing his cheeks with little dimples. We'd catch up on all the IRL things that happened in the last eight months since crunch started and I went offline. We'd share a pint over good ol' stories of the past and laugh about how he crit-wiped the raid with a misplaced heal.

No, my heart sank, we'd talk about Osmark's conspiracy to rule over all of V.G.O. How he'd sold dungeons with untold wealth to drug lords and corrupt politicians. How we would stop him. I closed my character sheet.

"So?" Otto pulled at the neck of his breastplate, the heat and being stationary obviously getting to him.

I nodded, my voice a touch more solemn than I expected. "Yeah, he made it."

Otto quirked his head to the side. "Are you going to reach out?"

"Maybe. Let's get this done first, then pleasantries." I smiled halfheartedly, and Otto pushed off the wall he rested on.

"Good plan." He moved to give my arm a pat, but with Jinker, I was too quick. I dodged him easily with a smug smile. The quest said I couldn't use any spells, but the passives were in effect all the time without my doing anything. It was great to have the extra Luck, Elemental resistance, Dexterity, Evade Chance, and Stamina. The Frostlock passive, Chilled Bones, was pretty useless down here where it was at least 100 degrees, but the others were unaffected by the stifling heat.

Otto shook his head and smirked. "Let's go."

The way down transitioned from a slow sloping corkscrew to something more like the old hiking trails around Lake Pillsbury. With the added Stamina, it wasn't such a problem for me. I took the loose gravel and four-foot drops just as well as Otto did.

I opened the quest log to check the distance for what seemed like the hundredth time when a chittering cry, something reminiscent of velociraptors from Jurassic Park, jerked me out of the menus.

I pulled up next to Otto and tugged on his arm. "What was that?" I whispered.

He stiffened, then drew his sword at a snail's pace, holding the sheath to reduce the noise. Whatever it was, it wasn't a bat or a salamander. The chittering came again, but farther away, and we continued down the smooth, glassy stone path like ninja assassins. I readied a fireball and followed after Otto. The cast was a crippling three seconds long, but I could hold the spell at the ready in my hand for as long as I liked.

The tiny lava-carved tunnel finally deposited us at the bottom of the cavern, which opened to a massive crater-like landing. I looked up and saw a tiny pinprick of light, the sun, at the top of the mountain opening.

The corkscrew path was visible from the center, and it looked as though a giant drill bit had ripped through the top of the mountain, leaving just the small, winding path untouched by its destruction.

Otto stopped short, then crouched on his haunches. I'd never seen him make himself smaller, and I immediately followed his lead. Frantic thoughts of ambush permeated my mind as my eyes searched the cavern walls. Outcropping here, strange divots there, but overall, a fairly flat and empty space with a pit of lava at the center.

I moved close to his ear and whispered, "Otto, what is it?"

His free hand rose and pointed toward a cave opening bathed in red and gold. It didn't look beyond the ordinary, but I kept watching. I trusted Otto not to call false alarm on something like this after the Septillian encounter.

Time ticked on and I waited, watching, impatience and fear nagging at the center of my chest. Then, it happened. A dark spot moved on the wall, and the chittering echoed through the open space. The shadow reared up, spreading large, translucent wings as it howled into the void. The sound shook the floor, burbled the lava, and rattled my insides. This wasn't a Flametongue Salamander nor some kind of higher level Leatherwing Heatleach.

Otto stole forward, his body rotating with every step in his crouched position. I followed, keeping my gaze above and around as I watched for any other threat that might try to creep in on us. Otto stopped at the corner of the cave opening where we saw the shadow, taking each I step more carefully than I'd ever seen. I stopped ten feet back, watching the corkscrew spiral exit as well as the dark corners of the lava pit for signs of movement.

"Tsst." The sound was hardly audible over the ambient groaning of hot air moving up through the tunnel. I glanced back, and Otto waved his hand for me to come nearer. I moved within range. He held my shoulder as he pushed me slowly, carefully, around the gold, luminous corner.

Damn Naitee straight to a ball-blistering freezer. There were the golden eggs, four of them, right at the center of a massive nest patrolled by a red, SUV-sized [Hoardling Drake].

EIGHTEEN

GOLDEN EGG

"WHAT THE HELL DO WE DO NOW?" I whispered to Otto, my voice holding an edge of frantic fury. His eyes roved back and forth over the floor, then he poked his head around the corner again. I did the same, just below him.

The creature turned away from the opening, pacing about its den. The four golden eggs shimmered in the glow of a lava pit and something else. I strained my neck and squinted to get a better look at the pool beside the nest. I couldn't be sure, but it looked like a bubbling hot tub of liquid gold.

The Hoardling Drake's outcropping was high ceilinged, but apparently untouched by whatever damage befell the main shaft down into the mountain. Massive, glittering stalactites dripped water into another pool of unknown depth next to the nest. There was a twenty-foot-tall mound at the far end of the cave, with what looked like another passage right behind it.

Otto pulled me back around the corner and returned to a crouch. "Here's the plan. I'll get it to chase me, you grab an egg and hightail it out. The drake will not fit in the passage. I'll be right behind you."

The image of Otto trouncing around, getting the drake to follow him while I ran away from such a potentially awesome fight, filled my head. We'd seen absolutely no loot this whole trip, and a Hoardling Drake was sure to have some goodies hidden away.

I shook my head. "That drake is bound to have some drops, and the XP alone would be worth it, we should take it down."

Otto's face scrunched up in worry. "Does the quest say you need to kill it?"

I quirked an eyebrow. "That's not the point."

"We don't need unnecessary risk." He planted his hands on his hips.

I scoffed. "Unnecessary risk is letting you run around with a fifteen-foot drake chomping at your heels while I sneak out."

We were at odds.

I wanted to take this beast on. We'd gotten really good with the bats and the salamanders, and true they were small fries, level 6-10 mobs, but we could do this, I was sure of it.

"I'll grab the egg, and we'll try to take it down. If it's not going well, we'll bail." I gave him a pleading smile, and I could tell by the growing frown on his face he wanted to take out the drake, too, but was fighting himself.

"Get your points in, we'll need everything we can get. I'm still going to kite the drake—you take shots at the stalactites and pin it down. Once it's pinned, it'll be easy pickings."

I grinned and opened my character sheet. I'd leveled twice more from the brutal trek down and wanted to slap some of the hard-earned points in where they could make a difference. 5 for Spirit, putting me at 50, and 5 more for Intelligence, kicking me up to 41.

Even with my spell strength improved by a little over 60 points from all the stat points I'd been dropping into Intelligence, the drake would have 25% resistance to my fire spells. I'd be hamstrung against it if the stalactite idea didn't work and we had to go blow for blow, but I knew we could do it.

Smokescreen had been a huge win for us, but if Otto was going to kite the beast, that would be next to useless. I could try to get in range and cast Flame of Holding. I hadn't used it yet, the brutal cast time and distance restrictions were holding me back, but *maybe* it would work long enough to shake a few stalactites free and get it pinned without putting Otto at risk.

Without putting Otto at risk… I closed out of the menus and looked back to him. He wanted to do this, but if he died, I surely would too. Firebrand would be lost to me forever, and I'd be down my only friend and eight hours behind Osmark.

"How many potions do you have?" I asked in a hushed voice as the Hoardling Drake cried out. Its floor-shaking stomps shook the loose stones on the floor as it turned to patrol farther in.

Otto's eyes went vacant for a second, and then he looked to me. "Six."

I pulled two healing potions from my inventory and handed them over. "Take these, too. You're going to need them."

He accepted the potions without a word, and they disappeared from his hand as he stuffed them in his inventory.

"Kite it in a clockwise circle, and do one loop at the nest." I recalled there was a particularly nasty looking stalactite above the pit of liquid gold. "I'll stand on the raised mound and shoot at the spikes just ahead of you. If it's not going well, we bail out.

"Hold up," I whispered, recalling the spell Magnus Armor. I didn't know what that drake was capable of, but it might be able to cast spells. I hit Otto and myself with the buff and waited a moment as my Spirit refreshed. Once the bar filled, I conjured a fireball. "Are you ready?"

Otto gave me a cocky smile. "I was born ready."

"Go get your two hits, then." I grinned back, but worry tugged at my navel. I didn't want to lose Otto, he was too important.

My NPC stood and poked his head around the corner. A second later, he disappeared around it. I crept to the edge and watched as the Risi I thought was huge shrank in the presence of the Hoardling Drake. The closer he got, the more my anxiety peaked.

"It's okay, it'll be okay," I mumbled to myself and ran through what I would do. Otto would get in two hits, he would start the clockwise run for the left wall, and I would dash in for the egg. Put that sucker in my inventory, and then drop fire on the ceiling. Easy. It'd be easy.

I watched with trepidation as Otto inched closer and closer to the spiked tail of the drake. He raised the sword over his head, and I dug my nails into the fire in my palm. The sword came down, followed by a harsh sound of steel on plated scales, and the drake bellowed in fury.

The Health bar on the miniature dragon flashed, 1% down. The red, scaly beast bent at the center, twisting its snakelike body in half to get a good look at who just smacked its butt. It shrieked, raising its back leg and kicking straight at Otto's chest.

Otto rolled left and slashed at the lifted leg as he moved, landing the second hit and earning an even louder, more pissed-off shout from the drake. Damn, he was pretty good! He hopped up to his feet and ran faster than I could've imagined someone that big with that much plate mail could run.

The drake took off after him, the thumping of its massive feet drumming in the deep as it charged. With it well out of the way, I ran toward the nest. My heart battered my rib cage as I watched the chase. Otto was staying well out of range, good.

I reached the nest and leaned down to grab an egg.

Unable to inventory item: Golden Egg! This item, [Golden Egg], is too large to fit in your inventory. You may carry it by hand, reducing your movement speed by 20% and evade chance by 50%, and inhibiting you from casting spells requiring both hands or engaging in melee combat with a two-handed weapon.

No. Freaking. Way.

"Otto, we have a problem!" I screamed, pulling the egg under my right arm and clipping my staff to the back of my bandolier.

"What?" he screamed back as they rounded the far right corner, heading back toward me. The drake's gaze locked on the nest, then the egg under my arm, then me. Its eyes narrowed to slits, and it turned, wings lifting in a powerful pump to pivot.

Oh shit. I loosed the fireball in my left hand directly at its face, but it kept coming. I brought up the Smokescreen spell and got a nasty beep blaring through my ears.

Unable to cast spell: Smokescreen! You are currently carrying an item that prevents the casting of spells requiring two hands. Put the item down, or free up your second hand to cast two-handed spells.

Double shit!

"Abby, *run!*" Otto screamed as he charged the backside of the drake.

It pumped its wings again, lifting its front legs into the air with sickening speed. The drake narrowed on me as it came down with a hard swipe. I dove forward on the strip of stone between the nest and the gold pit and came up into a run. My Stamina bar hit midway depleted as I charged up to the mound at the back of the room. I could still cast Fireball and activate Fire Inside and Shell of Molten Ash.

The monster's shrill roar pierced the air, deafening me. Fear pounded through my neck and up to my temples, but I turned on my heel and brought up my shield. It was there one second, then immediately gone.

The air around me shuddered, and ashes poofed in a gout of liquid fire that splattered against the drake's eye.

It reared, crying out as its Health dropped by 7%. Otto swung at the drake's back leg, scoring a critical hit and slicing through the tendon. The drake thrashed and turned to face Otto again. With the aggro back on my tank, I scurried up the mound and readied another Fireball.

Otto had to change directions, running counterclockwise with the drake in tow, but it was *in tow*. Otto swung his arms like a relay racer, pushing himself forwards as he just barely stayed out of range of the drake. I had to get some of those stalactites down on it.

I aimed a few seconds ahead of Otto and laid into the base of a smaller rock. It fell away with a single hit and crashed to the stone floor just behind Otto, kicking shrapnel up into the drake's face. It staggered and shook its head as smoke billowed from its snout, then charged on with renewed strength. The drake's Health was just below 92%, but it looked as though it was about to unleash the first wave of boss-mob-bullshit on Otto.

I called up Smokescreen again, and the same negative sound blared in my mind as the spell couldn't be cast. This freaking egg! I set it down and pulled up my inventory. *There!* An old set of level 1 cloth pantaloons. I scooped the egg up into the waistband and wrapped the legs over my right shoulder and around my left hip, then tied them at my chest. It was heavy, but bearable. I triggered the Smokescreen spell and was surprised to find there was no angry, negative sound and my hands moved in the wrist-flicking, finger-twitching motions to cast the spell.

The gray cloud puffed into existence just at Otto's backside. The drake wheezed, stumbled, and plowed into the wall. Down to 83%! I pumped my fist and gave a "Woo-hoo!" but Otto was too busy running for his life to notice.

I triggered Fireball and took aim at a large stalactite at the other end of the cavern. The cast took long enough that I could watch for two seconds and aim at the last possible moment. Otto rounded the nest, skirted past the gold pit, and sprinted toward the wall farthest from the entrance.

I looked back to my target and unleashed the spell. Immediately, I started the cast for another. The first fireball hit with a sizzling crack, but the spear of rock held tight to the ceiling. The second fireball was away when the drake gave a new kind of roar. I turned my head just as the drake opened its mouth wide and forced a column of flame out toward Otto.

The fire licked his back, and Otto's Health dropped by 10%, leaving him at 60%. Otto ripped a red potion from his bandolier, popped the cork, and sucked it dry, all while keeping the same pace.

I dropped one more fireball on the stalactite just ahead of him, but it seemed unfazed. This wasn't working… at least not on the chunks that would make a difference. I found a smaller rocksicle and tossed another spell at it, loosing it from the ceiling and dropping it on the drake's head. Another 2% of its Health, but that didn't slow it down.

Otto's Stamina had to be running low by now, and my Spirit was nearly depleted. I drained one of the blue vials on my belt and sighed as my spell currency refreshed to 450. The vial hit the ground, and I was halfway through another Fireball cast, aiming at the larger rock I'd already hit.

"Guh!" Otto grunted, and I whirled. Smokescreen was still on a thirty-second cooldown, and Otto was on his back, crawling away from the drake toward the far end of the mound.

The monster padded forward with a limp, its back leg still rended from the Achilles attack. It wasn't human, but I could see the leer in its cheeks, the glee in its eyes. It wanted Otto's blood in its mouth, on its claws, and spread across the den floor. The drake was poised to kill.

Ice Lance! My mind thought of the spell, and my hand glowed blue.

I gasped. I cut off the spellcast just before the Ice Lance launched from my outstretched palm. If I used that spell, I would fail. Firebrand would be locked forever.

We could do this, I just needed to get aggro.

I started the cast for Fireball and popped off Fire Inside. The invigorating rush of heat filled my chest and spread down my arms. The fireball growing in my hand glowed a bright orange, pulsing with the buff of the semi-passive ability. I lobbed the boosted shot toward the drake's head. The bolt landed with a puff, and the drake's jaw jerked, taking its Health from 81% to 78%, but its eyes stayed locked on its prey. Otto was going to die.

NINETEEN

TRIAL BY FIRE

"I'VE GOT YOUR BABY, YOU STUPID LIZARD!" I screamed, throwing another fireball down to the Hoardling Drake. The flame landed with a weak smack, and the creature's gaze snapped to my body. I turned and pulled on the waistband of the pants turned knapsack to reveal the golden egg.

"Yeah!" I taunted. "That's right! You're a bad mom, or dad, whatever you are!" I started another cast, and the long, slender monster stalked up the side of the mound, its head bobbing like a cobra's as it stared me down.

"Abby, what are you doing?" Otto's voice was a comfort. He was okay, alive, and I knew he still had a few potions.

"Saving your ass!" I threw the fireball.

The drake opened its maw at the incoming spell, then swallowed it.

The hairs on my arm stood on end. It *swallowed* my fireball, purposefully taking 3% of its Health in damage doing so. I may have hecked up.

The drake stopped ten feet from me and opened its wings. It was *huge*, the leathery wingspan at least thirty feet wide. Lavalight shimmered off the creature's red scales and twinkled in its murderous golden eyes.

It puffed up its chest, delaying my agony to revel in victory. I didn't see why it was trying to intimidate me if it was so confident it would kill me. The drake whipped back its right paw in a flash and brought it down, but I was faster. Shell of Molten Ash melted in around me, then dispelled in a brilliant flash of red as the drake ripped it apart with a single hit.

Pain radiated from my left side, and I soared through the air. I landed on my right arm, went ass over teakettle, and rolled to a stop at the bottom of the mound. The drake roared in victory as I noticed my flashing Health bar.

Debuff Added

Fractured Hip: You have suffered a crushing blow that fractured your pelvic bone! You cannot walk, stand, or use your left leg. Suffer 2 points of damage per sec for every attempt to move your left leg. Duration, 1 minute.

<<<>>>

Oh holy shit. It went *through* my shield! I snapped a Health potion from my belt and sucked it dry, shooting my Health back up to 70%. The drake slithered down the mound, its red scales shimmering with the golden light of the burbling pond of liquid metal behind me. A scene from an old classic, *Alien 3*, flashed through my mind. If I could get the drake into that pool and then lure it into the water, the temperature change could turn the liquid gold solid.

I pulled myself backwards, keeping my left leg still as the right dug into the dirt and pushed. The drake stalked toward me, a sense of victory in its swagger. It was the cat, and I, the injured mouse clinging to life. I scooted again. Beads of sweat rolled down my temples and tickled my neck.

"Yeah, you big, ugly gecko, come get me. You're not even a dragon. You're a fraud." My taunts were getting weak and my voice shaky. I imagined the pain of being bitten in half or bitten partially in half and shaken like a squirrel caught by a dog. The muscles in my stomach tightened, and I gritted my teeth, pulling myself backwards once more.

My hand slipped at the edge of the pool, and I felt the inferno of molten gold searing my back as I jerked my arm back to my chest. Of course, I could only hope it would try to bite me in half, overcommit to the bite, and thrust its face into the hot gold. Then, get the drake to follow me into the water next to the bubbling gold pit. I hoped the water wasn't acidic or boiling. Shit, my plan sucked.

I sat upright and checked my debuff timer: 35 more seconds. I leaned to the side and stood up on my right leg. The drake watched, smoke rising from its nostrils as its throat glowed. It pulled itself up to its full height, straining its powerful neck and flexing its jaw. This was it. Please, Jinker, don't fail me now.

I blinked, and in the darkness, time slowed. My eyes eased open as everything except the drake crawled. While the rest of the world sauntered along, the drake seemed to move uninhibited. An icy fire burned in my chest, freezing my muscles in place. Then, a notification flashed in the corner of my vision.

Debuff Added

Paralyzing Gaze: You have locked eyes with a huntress out for blood, and you are trapped in her stare. You cannot move, speak, or cast spells until eye contact is broken!

The drake's tongue shot out and tasted the air. "Sss'now, you h'are my'ine."

I wanted to scream, breath, move, do *something!* But I had completely lost control of my body. The drake reared her head back and shot forward. I watched, helpless, as five-inch fangs surged toward me. Her mouth eclipsed my vision, and my mind wandered to another place. It was like watching my life flash before my eyes: I was born in Kamloops, grew up in Vancouver, emigrated to the U.S. in my teens, graduated magna cum laude from Stanford, got my job at Osmark Tech, cried when my father was diagnosed with pancreatic cancer, laughed when Jack wiped the whole raid, raged when Osmark charged criminals millions of dollars for in-game favors.

When the drake's eyes disappeared behind its jaw, I was set free. I dove hard to the left, and my hip screamed in agony. My Health flashed an angry red at me, and I cried out at the sharp pain running from my ribs into my neck. I missed the drake plunging her face into the pond, but the aftermath was beautiful.

The scaled monster shrieked and pulled back, her snout covered in golden lava. She whipped her head from side to side, splattering the liquid metal over the den floor, and across my dress. I tried, but couldn't escape the heavy heat on my legs.

The sound of metal on flesh sliced through the cavern, and I looked up to catch Otto cutting the drake's other Achilles. She tried to open her mouth, but the cooling gold held her jaw shut with only a small hole up front and one on the right of her jaw. Instead of chomping down on him, the drake used her solid mandible as a bat. She barreled into Otto and sent him sailing across the room. Otto landed in a heap at the entrance of the den and didn't move.

I popped another healing potion and stood, the broken hip debuff finally ending. "Otto!" I screamed, and the game responded by showing me his Health bar. Just above 20%, and his skin pulsed red with the light of the lava pits.

The drake whirled on me, her eyes ablaze with pain and indignation. She padded forward, and dust floated down from above in a waterfall. The drake parted the curtain of gravel, and my eyes shot up to the ceiling. The stalactite I'd been working on—there was a massive crack building at the base and sediment falling down from it. I readied another fireball and the drake grinned.

She struggled to speak with her jaw held shut, but managed as her tongue licked out through the small hole. "Fire iss-s in my sssoul. You h'ave no powersss h'ere."

The cast finished, and I thrust my hand overhead, aiming for the fracture. The drake cocked her head at the sound of *crack, crack, crumble!* The stalactite dropped down on the drake's right shoulder and pierced through to the ground. She bellowed, and her Health dropped to 35%.

I rushed around the bubbling lava pond and dropped to Otto's side. "Get up!"

Otto dug his sword into the earth for support and wrenched himself to a kneeling position. "Let's finish this beast."

The drake cried out, and I turned to catch her last tug to free herself from the stake in the ground. Her wing tore at the first joint, and her transparent, leathery skin split down the middle. The drake's gold-coated maw turned toward us. She limped, determined to get her egg back and see me slaughtered. The drake's Health bar flashed over her head at 25%. She'd inflicted 10% of her total Health in damage just to get off the stake and come kill me.

I wouldn't be sorry to disappoint her. I needed this egg, I needed my class kit, I needed to see what was in that dungeon, and I needed to stop Osmark before he took over all of Eldgard.

The drake closed in and reared her head back once more. Sounds like a jet engine spooling up accompanied a bright white glow in the red scaly flesh of her esophagus.

"Move!" I shoved Otto, putting myself directly between him and the drake. The hyper-focused beam of fire from the tiny hole in the drake's golden muzzle slapped against my body, and though the heat was painful, it was not what I imagined *actually* being on fire was like. The flames licked at my skin and hair, stinging like hundreds of pinpricks, but nothing I couldn't bear. Fire Inside likely had something to do with that.

I tried to conjure Shell of Molten Ash, but it was still on cooldown. I rolled back to get away, but she turned with me, her flame breath getting wider and less painful as her golden jaw-clamp melted away.

The fire cut out, and I didn't wait to see what happened next. I ran for the mound between the inferno pools and popped my final Health potion, getting me back up to 85%. The tromping of the following drake was punctuated with stumbles as her ruined back legs gave out with each step.

Sounds of fast wind in a narrow tunnel alerted me to the intro of the drake's fire breath. There wasn't time to turn and block, nor did I have the Health or potions to take another hit from her front paw, so I turned to the next best option. A narrow crack on the west side of the mound looked like it could give me cover, at least for a second.

I dashed between the rocks and shimmied my way into the constricted cave, the golden egg scraping and scratching as I wiggled through. Flames licked the edge of the rock beside me, then died out as the drake roared. Her gold-speckled snout came into view, and her teeth glimmered a brilliant white as she wound up for another blast of fire.

"Die, winged snake!" Otto bellowed, and the drake's face pulled away from the narrow crevasse.

"Otto, no!" I turned to scoot my way out, but the egg caught, wedged between me and the rocks. I slipped out of my harness and wrenched myself free of my hideout, watching as the 15% Health drake slapped Otto into the ground. He bounced and flipped back onto his feet, his skin a luminescent red, and charged into the drake's guard.

The drake would resist my fire damage, but I would take as much attention away from Otto as I could. I popped the cork on a Spirit potion and held it between my teeth.

"Huck oo!" I shouted and unleashed Inferno Blast. My Spirit trickled away, and the drake ignored the fire slapping against her backside. Not for long she wouldn't. I tilted my head back and sucked down the potion, then spit the bottle to the ground as my unending flames splashed against her shiny red hide.

12%.

10%.

She raised her paw to slash at Otto, but he dodged.

8%.

6%.

Finally, she turned with a deep bellow of injustice. We'd invaded her home and stolen her unborn baby. I questioned my actions for a fraction of a second, but as her claws surged toward me, I knew I only had one choice.

I popped Shell of Molten Ash and begged for Jinker's grace one more time. The shield dispelled as the drake whacked it, and I flipped back onto my hands to get away. I hadn't done a back handspring since I was eight, but muscle memory copied over to V.G.O. characters just fine.

The taloned paw swiped where my body had been, and the drake shrieked with rage at my trickery as the hot ashes spit into her watery eyes. She thought I was going to make the same mistake twice, how wrong she'd been.

2%.

My Spirit was down to 30, and I opened up my palms for Inferno Blast. I wanted to say something cool, have a great killing blow, but honestly, all I felt like saying was "Sorry."

Fire seared against the drake's skin, stealing the last few hit points of her life as my Spirit bar hit zero. She stumbled to the side, her eyes distant and glazed as she tried to lock on me. Then, she crumpled, shaking the cavern as she went down.

TWENTY

CLASS KIT

OTTO AND I STOOD ON OPPOSITE SIDES OF THE downed drake and stared at one another. We'd done it. Against all odds, especially the 25% resistance to all my damage, we'd still killed the Hoardling Drake. I looked down at her ruined body: snout scales singed from the liquid gold, left wing mangled at the first joint, back legs ripped at the ankle… and for what?

I looked at the pile of three eggs, eggs that would never hatch, and my egg still wedged in the crevasse. Guilt. That was all I felt. This was the second time I'd killed a parent and its babies, all for the sake of progressing myself.

Stop. Stop it, Abby. These are lines of code. This is a game. They were put here for you to kill.

Otto stepped up next to me and put his hand out. "Up five!" He grinned.

I tried on my best smile and gave his hand a slap.

"What is it?" he asked, reading me.

I chewed my lip. "We killed a mother, and her other babies will die."

227

Otto stroked his chin. "We could put them closer to the lava. I'm sure they'll still hatch."

"Yeah, but who will teach them to hunt? Who will show them how to catch the Flametongue Salamanders?" I imagined the little drakes working together to catch a salamander or a few bats and slowly starving to death. It was just as bad as not being born at all.

Otto shuffled his feet. "What do you want to do?"

"Naitee is pretty fond of fire. Maybe she can help them?" I shrugged.

He nodded. "If that'll make you feel better."

Feel better. I damned myself for feeling anything. These little eggs weren't real, nor were they even alive yet! I gritted my teeth and cursed myself again.

"Yeah, let's loot her, grab the eggs, and head back."

It was becoming a trend that wherever Naitee sent us held no gains. There were a few chunks of gold lying around the den that we could take with us, but the molten gold pit couldn't be collected, and the drake was devoid of anything of value. Some crafting materials that might sell on the player market alright, but otherwise, nothing.

I unwedged my egg from the crevasse and stepped up to the nest. "Ready to go?" I looked at Otto.

"Anytime."

I pulled the Scroll of Return from my inventory and popped the seal. I watched Otto go first, then reached out and touched the portal. White light enveloped me, and the typical nausea that came with porting crept through my guts. I swallowed hard and took a deep breath through my nose as the light dissipated, and the Boar's Head filled my vision.

"Back again! At least you don't reek this time, but what's that?" The barmaid pointed at me and the eggs I had under each arm.

"Bounty," Otto said matter-of-factly, and the barmaid scurried away without another word. My mind turned at her behavior. She'd been boisterous and unabashed before, but now, she ran to the back without a single quip or protest.

Sigorsped, the old woman said: good fortune in battle. It was a quiet inn at the center of action in a large city. High prices on *everything*. The Boar's Head had another reputation I was starting to get a picture of: a safehouse for headhunters.

The eggs were slipping free in my sweaty-palmed grasp, so I bumped my hips and jumped to keep hold of them. I looked down at each and watched as my Stamina bar in the corner of my vision dropped by the second. There was no way I'd make it to Naitee with them.

"Otto," I whined, propping one of the eggs on a nearby table and the other on my knee, "how are we going to get these back to Naitee? Walking through town with two big golden drake eggs under each arm is going to attract a lot of attention."

"Wheelbarrow," Otto declared.

He plopped his eggs down next to mine on the table and disappeared into the back. The eggs rolled precariously close to the edge, rocking like little boats as they tried to escape. I pinned one down with my chin and clamped the one balanced on my knee between my thighs to free up my hand. I nudged the others into a stationary position, earning awkward glances from the two sitting across the room. Stupid, not even real eggs, why did I care?

These eggs weren't real. Their mother wasn't real. But the guilt was real. Otto was right, the quest didn't say anything about killing the drake, and I did it anyway for experience and loot. But… that's what the game was about, right?

Otto opened the front door a moment later and returned to grab his eggs, then motioned for me to follow. I heaved the unbearably heavy unhatched babies under my arms, sumo squatting down to also balance them on my legs. I pivoted and stomped my way out the door like a cowboy who'd been riding for six years straight.

The wheelbarrow was a sight for sore eyes, but nothing special. I slowly eased my eggs into the one-wheeled wooden baby carriage and sighed. Holy heck, my arms were tired. I knew I couldn't afford it, but I wanted to drop a few points into Strength.

Once all four eggs were securely in the basin, Otto fluffed out a cloth tarp and covered them. He tied the cloth in strange positions, making the content of the wheelbarrow look less giant eggish.

"All right, let's make a delivery!" Otto motioned for me to pick up the wheelbarrow, and my brow pulled down in a scowl. He chuckled, grabbed the handles, and led the way through the streets.

It was just past 10 AM, and the city was in full morning routine swing. Bakers, florists, butchers, and tailors stood outside their shops hawking goods. Ironworks bellowed away with the pounding of hammers. The fall sun was warm, but a cool breeze stole away any of the discomfort brought on by the heat. Birds chirped on light posts and building roofs, waiting for some of that fresh bread to fall in a more accessible place. It was a beautiful day.

It was a beautifully designed day. The Overminds could make the weather do whatever they pleased—have the sun boil our skin or the winds whip the soft canvas covers of the shop stalls right off. They had so much power over the world I now called home. A home ruled by servers donated by Chinese diplomats, AI created on gold from drug lords, and code generated from thousands of hours of slave labor.

Otto and I turned down the alley to Naitee's shop, and I snapped back from thought. I'd have to stop going on autopilot.

I barked with laughter as realization dawned on me, and Otto shot a glare over his shoulder.

"What now?" my NPC demanded.

"Autopilot. Otto, pilot! Get it?" I laughed again.

He quirked an eyebrow. "No, I don't."

"Okay, well never mind. It's funny, though." I offered him a shrug, and Otto rolled his eyes.

Otto dropped the wheelbarrow and wiped sweat from his brow. "Are you going to knock?" He pointed to the door with a bit of a pant, and I chuckled. I didn't know why he was so afraid of her. Other than being a little creepy sometimes, she was mostly sweet—except when sending us on quests with literally no loot.

I rapped on the door, then remembered we had an open invitation and turned the hot knob. The inside of Naitee's shop was still a smoldering wreck, but the shards of glass from the display cases were gone.

"Naitee?" I asked, but only silence answered.

Otto poked his head in. "I think I hear her out back."

I didn't know there was an *out back* to this place. I closed the door behind me and walked around the side of her gnarled, crooked, blacked-out building. Heat met me first as I came around the corner, then I saw the fire.

Naitee stood, both palms open, Inferno Blasting a large pot. I didn't want to get any closer and get a face full of her spell—who knew what level it was—so I waved my arms over my head. She cut the cast off and grinned, her blond hair falling back to perfectly straight as the fiery wind died down.

"Ah, you're not dead!" she exclaimed.

I put one hand on my hip. "What else would you expect from Eldgard's greatest Sorceress?"

She smirked. "But what about my egg?"

I turned and motioned for Otto to bring the wheelbarrow. He set it down, and I unveiled our bounty. "How about four eggs?"

Naitee's face shifted from amused to concerned. Her voice held a tone of accusation. "You killed her, then?"

I bit my lip, the unwanted guilt returning. "Yes."

Naitee moved to the eggs, placing a loving hand against a shell and stroking it. "Kak'rana was the last female drake in a thousand miles. The shells of her eggs created many Firebrand potions. This is most unfortunate."

She pulled the top egg up into her arms and cradled it. Otto shuffled his feet and rubbed the back of his neck. I wondered if there was another way to become a Firebrand, or if we'd just totally screwed over the game economy. Maybe she would respawn, or maybe there were other ways to make the potion. Or maybe we were jerks. No, I was a jerk. Otto didn't want to kill her.

"Can you help them hatch?" I put my hand on the egg she held and felt a tiny shudder.

Her gaze snapped from the unborn drake to my face. "Is that why you brought them all?"

I nodded.

She sucked a deep breath through her nose and set the egg back down. "I've only ever raised a single drake at a time, but I suppose this is doable. I owe it to Kak'rana."

"So, you were friends with her?" I asked, and Naitee screamed with laughter.

When she was collected enough, she spoke. "Friends? No, child." She wiped a tear from her eye. "We were business partners, whether she knew it or not. I sent her delicious treats, she gave me eggs for potions, I helped repopulate the drakes in Eldgard. Honestly, I feel like I'm doing more work here."

I mulled over her statement. She was helping to repopulate the drakes so their eggs could be stolen for potion ingredients. Really, she just raised the things for inevitable slaughter. My stomach tightened with the feeling of being wronged.

"You're upset?" Naitee crossed her arms.

I shook the creases of worry off my face. "No. It's just—"

"This is how they survive. The Hoardling Drakes would've gone extinct ages ago if I had not rescued them." She tapped a finger on her crossed forearm.

I nodded. "It's good that you do that. I'm sure they appreciate living." *Living*, I reminded myself, was not what they were doing. Putting on hold the idea that they were just code, having their population boosted by external means and surviving in deep tunnels under impassable mountain terrain was not my idea of living.

"Well, you are an overachiever, I suppose it's time you accept your fate." Naitee's foreboding words prompted the quest pop-up.

Quest Complete: The Path of a Sorceress

You've returned to Naitee with not 1, but 4 golden eggs! She's impressed by your tenacity, increasing your reward XP by 2x. You've unlocked the Sorceress: Firebrand Class Kit.

"Come inside, I have something for you." She beckoned to a small stairway leading to a second-floor patio on the back of her shop. Otto waited with the wheelbarrow of eggs as I ascended the rickety staircase with her. I held tightly to the railing, though I was sure it was more likely to send me over the edge if I leaned on it. At the top, I looked back to Otto, who was doing his best to not be concerned.

She opened the burnt wood door and motioned for me to go first. I really wanted whatever the scalable item was, so I ducked under the low doorway and stepped inside. I blinked a few times in the darkness, then cast Fireball.

Naitee closed the door behind her and cast her own Fireball. It was a bedroom. No, it was a laboratory with a bed in it. My eyes roamed the shelves of ingredients: huge jars filled with dark fluid, tiny vials of shimmering lights, glass boxes of swirling sandstorms, and so much more.

"Here." Naitee moved to the wall and placed her hand against it. Firelight spread through a small clay valley filled with oil that wrapped around the walls of the room at shoulder height like a scene out of an old temple movie. I extinguished my fireball and stepped farther in.

Next to a large work desk covered in books and in-progress concoctions was a pot of bubbling gold liquid. I pointed to it. "Is that the Firebrand potion?"

"No, it's just the drake shell ingredient, a post-hatching product that does indeed go into the Firebrand potion. I conserve the shell as much as I can, as it's not every day I get it replenished. Those four shells will last me quite a while…" She snapped her fingers and said, "But that's not what we're here for." She looped her arm in mine, and we walked to a wardrobe next to the bed. Her fingers fiddled with the latch, and she tugged on the handle, pulling the wardrobe open just a hair. The tightness of injustice in my gut had been washed away by excitement. I bounced on my toes, salivating at what could possibly be in there.

The door slammed shut. "Do not squander this lovely gift." Naitee wagged a finger at me.

"I won't," I urged, desperate to know what was behind that door.

She pulled it open all the way, revealing a long, blood red gown with jewels studding the chest and waist. *Her* gown. My head snapped to Naitee, and I realized she was wearing a black garment adorned at the chest with small gold beads in the pattern of the Firebrand symbol.

My eyes turned back to the red robe in front of me. Why would she give me the clothing off her own back?

"The greatest Sorceress in Eldgard needs the greatest gear." She answered my silent question and reached for the robe, then held it out to me. "It's yours."

TWENTY-ONE

Duplicate Scrolls

MY VOICE CAUGHT IN MY THROAT AS I TOOK THE garment into my hands. It was warm, like it had just come off her body. I rolled it over, inspecting it visually inch by inch. It was beautiful, soft, and radiated power.

"Don't be such a dolt, put it on." Naitee snapped me from the trance.

I popped open my inventory screen and was bombarded by a level up pop-up.

x3 Level Up!

You have (15) undistributed stat points

You have (15) unassigned proficiency points

There was something else, a red blinking on my messages tab. Hmm, maybe Jack found me first? I'd have to save it for later, I needed to get this robe on!

I popped to my gear and selected to wear [Wildfire]. A negative buzzing rang in my ear and a new pop-up appeared.

Item Incompatibility: Wildfire! You are not able to wear the item [Wildfire] until you meet the minimum Intelligence requirement!

I inspected the robes.

Wildfire

Armor Type: Light, Mixed Cloth/Gold Thread

Class: Ancient Artifact

Base Defense: 50

Primary Effects:

- +30 Intelligence

- +25 Spirit

- +20 Vitality

- +10 Constitution

- +3 Luck

- +22% resistance to Fire damage

- +12% chance of critical hit with Fire spells

- +5% chance to trigger Burning Affliction with all relevant Fire spells

- Increase Spirit regeneration by 5.5 Spirit/sec

- Increase XP gained from monster kills and completed quests by 8%

- *Item Restrictions*: You must have a minimum base Intelligence of 40 and a minimum base Spirit of 30 before you are able to don this item.

- *Item Boons:* This item scales with your level. The Item Restrictions and all stats except Luck will increase by 2.5% with each increased character level. This item has a 2% chance to add a new bonus or stat with each character level earned while wearing it.

The unstoppable destruction and immeasurable beauty of the raging inferno will capture your heart, then burn it alive.

Dear. Gods. I needed this on me, *now*. I needed a base Intelligence of 40 and Spirit of 30. I checked my stats and saw I only had 28 base Intelligence, but for base Spirit I was at 32. Getting up to 40 Intelligence would be nearly all of my unused stat points, but so, *so* worth it.

Without a second thought I dropped 13 points into Intelligence and the remaining 2 into Spirit, just to keep it high enough for my next level. I realized that I'd nearly always have to place my stat points in Spirit and Intelligence to keep the robes on, but with a 2% chance to *add* a new stat and with all other stats increasing by 2.5% each level I earned with it… That seemed like a steal, honestly.

With my stat situation squared away, I popped back to the item and selected to wear it. Power unlike any other boost I'd felt rushed through my limbs and tickled the back of my neck. My heart pounded in my ears, and my stomach fluttered like being kissed by a crush for the first time. The warmth from the robes stifled the chill that threatened to make me shiver, and then, it was over. I felt stronger than ever before, like nothing could stop me, and *that* feeling lingered.

I looked like a certified badass, and now the red shoulder pads from Hasan matched! The robe hugged me from chest to hips, then flowed and billowed outward before stopping at the top of my boots. The cloth of the arms was tight, but not restrictive. I closed my character sheet and did a few warm-up stretch movements to test the flexibility of the dress. It was completely unrestrictive!

"Now you're starting to look like the greatest Sorceress in Eldgard." Naitee grinned, and I beamed.

I sucked in a breath to say something, but there was nothing to say. I flung my arms around her neck and held her tightly. Naitee wrapped her arms around my back and returned the gesture. A *hug!* I hadn't been hugged since Tristen back in the capsule room. Before that, I hadn't been hugged since I last saw my mother, months and months ago.

My eyes watered, and my throat constricted. It felt good to be hugged, especially by someone who cared enough about me to literally give me the robe off her back. More importantly, it was an ultra-rare item that probably took her years to find!

But… it didn't take her years. She didn't exist more than a few months ago. My enthusiasm, which felt so real seconds ago, deflated, and I pulled back from the embrace.

"It's amazing. I love it. Thank you," I said, my voice still shaking from the rush of power and the threat of tears.

Naitee wiped at my cheek as a tiny, salty drop escaped my eye. "You're very welcome, Abby Hollander. Don't let me down."

I bit down to stop more tears and nodded once.

"Now, off you get."

My mind sparked at the next step in my rare quest. I needed to look into that dungeon, but I likely couldn't do it alone… I needed Jack.

"Naitee, could you copy a scroll for me?"

She tutted. "Of course I could, but will I?"

"I brought you four drakes." My eyes narrowed on her, our moment of bonding now over.

"Something I didn't ask for, but you are correct. You brought me quite a lot of crafting materials, and the four precious little babes. Show me the scroll." She held out her hand, and I fished the Ca_Co_Ca.Scroll from my inventory and passed it to her.

She turned it over and over, then closed her eyes and ran her fingers along the ribbon. She gasped, "This is unlike anything I've ever felt. Where did you get it?"

"The bottom of a chest when we were collecting the Lumalgae." I shrugged.

Her eyes moved back and forth behind her lids, like she was reading the parchment in her mind.

"It's very complex, but yes, I can duplicate this."

"Great, can you make two copies?"

Naitee's eyes snapped open, wild and frustrated. "Four drakes is not enough payment for two copies."

I opened my inventory. I had a few gold chunks from the Hoardling Drake's den, and eight gold pieces. "Okay, how much?"

She paused, then said softly, "A promise."

I closed the character screen and looked her dead in the eyes. "What promise?"

"That I may call on you, and you will answer that call, no matter the circumstances."

My nerves tingled with adrenaline. That was a terrifying request. She could ask *anything* of me, and I would have to say yes.

She smiled. "Don't look so worried, child. I'd never ask you to do anything too terrible. Do you want the copies, or not?"

I gritted my teeth. Scrolls were one-time uses, so without the copies, I couldn't get Jack to come with me, and I couldn't investigate it beforehand to see what we were up against. One favor for two scrolls.

"Yes." I swallowed hard, wishing I could take back the word. Why couldn't she have asked for anything else or told me what she needed? Maybe she didn't trust me enough, or maybe she didn't know yet. The gleam in her eyes told me she did know, but it wasn't time.

"Good!" With a flourish, the scroll in her hand disappeared into her inventory. "It will take me about an hour to complete both scrolls, so run along and be back here just before noon to collect them."

I turned to the door, then spun on my heel, pointing at Naitee. "Don't. Lose. That."

She put her hand to her heart and bowed her head. "I would never. Now get out, I need to focus." She shooed me to the door, and I left with a smirk.

The sunlight blinded me, and I blinked a few times to adjust. A low whistle brought my attention to Otto. He was standing, hands on his hips, a huge grin on his face.

"Well, don't you look fancy," he catcalled.

"I will burn your face off," I threatened playfully, my palm pointed at his head as I descended the stairs.

He laughed. "I'm starving, and you owe me. Let's go, Firebrand."

"So, should we just leave the eggs right here?" I shrugged as I reached the wheelbarrow.

Otto rolled it over to where Naitee had been flame-blasting the large pot and covered them again. "They'll be fine right there. Everyone knows not to mess with Naitee's work."

We carved our way back through the streets to the Boar's Head, and I went on Otto pilot as I opened my character sheet for a good look at everything that had changed. At some point from the time I turned in the quest to now, the Firebrand and Sorceric Power potions had been forcibly canceled, likely when I accepted the robes to complete the class kit quest. No matter, I was a Firebrand now, no potions necessary!

J.D. Astra

Name:	Abby	Race:	Wode	Gender:	Female
Level:	16	Class:	Firebrand	Alignment:	None
Renown:	1,200	Carry Capacity:	450	Undistributed Attribute Points:	0
Health:	570	Spirit:	930	Stamina:	510
H-Regen/sec:	20.425	S-Regen/sec:	22.1413	Stam-Regen/sec:	8.23
Attributes:		**Offense:**		**Defense:**	
Strength:	10	Base Melee Weapon Damage:	3	Base Armor:	75
Vitality:	41	Base Ranged Weapon Damage:	0	Armor Rating:	83
Constitution:	32	Attack Strength (AS):	45	Block Amount:	2.5
Dexterity:	10	Ranged Attack Strength (RAS):	42	Block Chance (%):	9.76
Intelligence:	81	Spell Strength (SS):	121.5	Evade Chance (%):	3.6
Spirit:	77	Critical Hit Chance:	17%	Fire Resist (%):	28.8
Luck:	9	Critical Hit Damage:	5%	Cold Resist (%):	6.8
				Lightning Resist (%):	6.8
				Shadow Resist (%):	6.8
				Holy Resist (%):	6.8
Current XP:	2,720			Poison Resist (%):	6.8
Next Level:	13,280			Disease Resist (%):	6.8

My stats were looking pretty great for level 16, thanks to Wildfire, but my focus now was where to put those ability points! Everything was reset, a clean slate, and I could throw the points where I wanted.

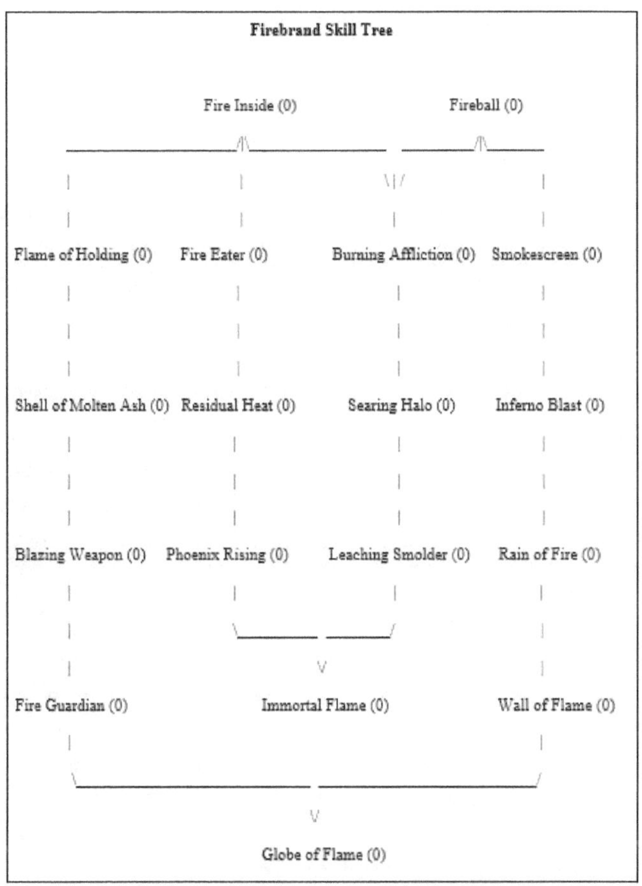

<<◇>>

I knew I wanted to make my way to Blazing Weapon as fast as possible. On more than one occasion I'd tried being a battlemage and failed miserably because I was so weak. Blazing Weapon would swap my Intelligence and Spirit for my Strength and Stamina temporarily and allow me to wield a weapon of fire. Pretty freaking sweet, but unfortunately, it looked like I needed to be at least level 25 before I could even add a point to it. And the same was true for Leaching Smolder, Rain of Fire, and Phoenix Rising.

If I was going to solo, Blazing Weapon would be great… but I wasn't. So, I needed to put my points where a group-style Firebrand would put her points. Support. I sighed, and through the semitranslucent skill tree, I saw Otto glance back before shaking his head and returning to face forward.

I dropped 1 point each into Fire Inside and Fireball. Those were essential. I put one more point in Fire Inside, giving me an 8% bonus to fire spell damage and an extension on the active ability of increasing spell damage by 50% from 30 seconds to 60. It increased the duration of my Spirit regeneration debuff, but that was all right.

Burning Affliction didn't seem *that* useful because I'd have an increased chance of it proccing on most of my fire spells anyway; however, the more I leveled it up, the greater the damage it would do over more time and the more it would increase the chance of my fire spell critically hitting. It was nice to see the next level of the spell for a preview into what goodies it held. So, Burning Affliction got a point.

Eleven points left. Smokescreen had been great for mob clusters, same as Inferno Blast, so they each got a point. Searing Halo was a no-brainer, so it got a point, too. It was a ten-minute-duration self-cast that would debuff anyone who hit me with Burning Affliction, which stacked up to three times… so hitting me would be a pretty big deterrent!

I hadn't used Flame of Holding, but saw its potential. More importantly, I couldn't get to Shell of

Molten Ash without putting a point there, so I did. Another point for the shield spell and I was down to 2 points. I definitely wanted Phoenix Rising, so Fire Eater and Residual Heat each got a point. Well, now I had one of everything… and no points left.

I looked over the skill tree, disappointed there hadn't been just *one* thing I really wanted, but happy I had quite a few spells to choose from in combat.

The flashing of a new message blinked on the *social* tab of the menu, and with my points allocated, I figured it was time to see what Jack was up to. I selected the new menu and scrolled to my inbox.

Everything stopped. The sounds of music and chatter became tinny and far off. My limbs froze in place, my heart lurched to a stop, and my gut clenched into a knot as I stared at the message title and sender.

Sandra: *I knew I recognized you, Abby.*

TWENTY-TWO

EXPOSED

"ABBY, WHAT IS IT?" OTTO'S HAND ON MY shoulder jerked me from the menus. I looked down to see I'd conjured a fireball that I was gripping in my tightly clenched fist. I extinguished the flame and shook out my hand.

"It's nothing." I smiled as my heart restarted, pumping away at a million miles a second.

Otto cocked his head. "Are you sure?"

"Yeah." I gave him a gentle punch to the shoulder. "Just thinking about how much food you're going to eat and how broke I'm about to be. We could probably eat cheaper somewhere else, you know."

My hands trembled as I thought of the message. What did she know? How could she know it, if she did? What would she do with what she knew? I was terrified to discover the answer to any of these questions.

"Yes, but nowhere else we can have a meal and a quiet conversation without eavesdropping." He shrugged.

"Fair enough." I gave him another shaky smile. "Lead on."

He stepped aside, and I saw the sign for the Boar's Head. I'd been walking blind a while, then. He pushed through the door and held it open for me. We walked to his seat, and I scooted into the little booth, my feet tapping on the floor.

I looked around the tavern and spotted three people, two Wode men and a dwarf woman, sitting at the far end in a booth similar to ours. They were talking quietly, until the dwarf noticed me looking, at which they all glared my way. I popped my head back into the booth and drummed my fingers on the table.

"Abby," Otto said, putting his hand on mine to silence the tapping, "what's going on?"

"Back again, so soon. Delivery go well?" the barmaid asked, a pitcher of something strong smelling and three cups balanced on the wooden tray held at her right shoulder.

"We'll have what's hot," Otto grumbled, pulling his hand away from mine, "and a pitcher of that." He pointed to the liquid on her tray. She smirked, nodded, and hurried off to the other customers.

When the others had their drinks and the barmaid returned to the back, he stared me down, silent, waiting. I opened my character sheet and panned to the social tab.

"I have a message from Sandra." My voice cracked, and I cleared my throat. "The title says, 'I knew I recognized you, Abby.'"

I closed the menu, not wanting to read on, and looked to Otto. He had a huge frown on his big green face, his tusk-like canines just barely poking out from behind his pursed lips.

"She could've seen your name when we were in combat, but your face was unrecognizable with the broken nose and swollen eyes. How do you think she's come to discover you?" He laced his fingers together on the table.

I shook my head. "I don't know. I don't know what she knows, either. She could know everything or nothing, but she does know we were in that bar, and she likely knows we talked to Verin."

The barmaid returned with two steaming plates of something gamey with a side of tubers, and then set a pitcher with two glasses down at the center. "Shout if ye need anythin'."

She turned to Otto and held out her hand.

"No, I've got this," I piped up, grabbing some coin from my inventory. Otto had given her five silver the first time and she scoffed, so it must've only just been enough. I dropped ten silver in her palm, and she stared for a moment, then gave me a kind smile.

"Remember, just shout for Meredith and I'll be right over." She hurried away just as quickly as she came, and I turned my attention to the meal.

"Are you going to read it?" Otto asked, pouring the malted drink. It smelled a bit hoppy, with notes of something citrusy. It must've been some kind of beer they started months back when citrus fruit were harvested. No, it was a game. The code called for a citrus beer, and so one was created. I shook my head as I tried to clear the fog. The realism of V.G.O. was starting to get to me.

I jerked forward to grab the glass, all of my movements overstated and hypersensitive. I took a long drink, and then kept drinking and drinking, until the glass was empty. It was *very* hoppy. I was reminded of the beer snobs back IRL who gave me shit for not liking IPAs, and it was probably one of those jerks who programmed this beer. The orange aftertaste wasn't bad, and it wasn't too bitter, either. Otto filled my glass again, and I opened my character screen, then panned to the message.

Personal Message:

Your face was so screwed up after that brawl, it took me a while to put your name to it. You were a senior architect for Osmark Technologies, right? The one whose father died during production? Very sorry to hear about that.

So coincidental to run into you at the Drunken Donkey. Robert certainly will be interested in a status update on how many of his employees are taking the plunge. He made this safe haven for you, and I sincerely hope you understand what that means.

Did you hear everything you needed to out of Verin?

Cheers,

Sandra

I slapped the menu shut, grabbed my full cup, and chugged the hoppy beer.

"That good, eh?" Otto asked.

I stopped, remembering how easily I'd gotten drunk the day before, and set my drink aside. There was fear in my gut, and alcohol, but something else, too. My hands trembled harder, and blood rushed to my cheeks.

Very sorry to hear about your dead father. The sound of her venomous voice swirled in my brain, coupled with the last video chat I had with my father. His gaunt, colorless face, pallid lips, and sunken eyes told me it was the end. I hadn't cried. I smiled through the whole conversation, told him I loved him dearly, told him how sorry I was.

I'd almost broken my wrist after that call when I punched through the drywall. I had to wear a brace for weeks, and my scrum master never let me live down the productivity loss. She was always going on about our burndown charts, reduced velocity, and missing story points. What a prick.

But Osmark did what he did to save us. He could've scaled back on everything and made himself a personal digital island to live out the rest of his days—or millennia—in peaceful solitude. He chose to keep moving forward, to take risks, to make dirty deals, and drive people like slaves so that he could save as many people as possible. My wrist ached with remembered pain, and I rubbed my knuckles at the thought of giving him a good punch for all the shit he put us and our families through.

"So, how much does she know?" Otto broke my fury-filled trance.

I picked up my fork and stabbed into what looked like a parsnip. "Enough to put us at risk. But perhaps not so much that we're in trouble." I popped the salty roasted root in my mouth and chewed. My mind was no longer interested in eating, only revenge. My body needed food so I could perform well. I needed to perform well so I could level up and take him down.

"We've done a lot together. I'm not worried." Otto shrugged it off and started in on his steak.

I put back the meal without much enjoyment, my mind fixated on Sandra and her vile words. *He built this haven for you.*

I helped build this place. Osmark sat back with the grand vision and left all of us to do the work. Sandra did even less. She was always running around settling deals or hovering over the directors' shoulders.

Otto pushed back his empty plate and stood. "We should exchange these gold chunks for coins."

I gave a nod and followed him out to the street. He took us to the local mint, and we exchanged our pieces for ten gold coins, which we split evenly. It was just past 11 AM, and with nothing else to do but wait for Naitee, Otto took us to the Requests Bulletin.

The small castle in the background everywhere we went in Harrowick was finally front and center. It wasn't as small as I'd thought, but it was still only about the size of the White House with tall turrets flanking the center spire.

The Requests Bulletin was just as I'd assumed, a spot for Travelers and NPCs alike to pick up quests. There were several lowbies gathered around the board in a sort of "afk" situation, definitely scanning through their character sheets or looking up information on the wiki. We looked through a few of the quests, but nothing was particularly inspiring, or rewarding for that matter.

It was near enough to noon that I suggested we head back to Naitee, and Otto nodded his agreement. The message from Sandra rattled between my synapses in an unending echo of both fear and fury. I was terrified of what she might do to us, to Jack if he got involved and if we pulled off this dungeon raid, but I also wanted to see her face and Osmark's when they'd had something stolen from them, like me.

It wasn't enough to just take this one dungeon away from them, I needed to take away their plot for the future. Whatever was at the bottom of the dungeon was instrumental to that. I opened the message and read it one more time. The words were already burned into my digital retina, but I wanted to look at it again—I wanted to push down the fear and let the anger through. My gut roiled as I read it over, and again, but the fear remained.

In V.G.O., there were worse fates than death, much worse. They could torture me, bring me to the brink of death, then give me a Health potion. They could camp my bind location and grief kill me over and over. They could torture Otto and Jack the same way and leave me powerless to help.

I bumped into the back of Otto and closed the menu. He smirked and put his hand on my shoulder. "You don't need to dwell on it. We're capable, and if your friend is a *team player* like you said, we will be fine."

My head bobbed in agreement, but I didn't feel any better. Otto lead the way into Naitee's shop, for once, and we were greeted by Naitee's distant voice, yelling, "You're too prompt! I'm almost finished!"

I shuffled around the room, adjusting burnt tapestries and smoothing out singed rugs. Nothing helped. Nothing kept my mind from visions of torture and agony. They were already so much more powerful than us. They were already more numerous than us. What could we do against this?

"Abby." Otto's voice pulled me to the present. I was facing the wall, another fireball clenched in my fist.

I extinguished the flame. "I'm fine."

"I hope you understand," Naitee shouted from the room upstairs, "how difficult this has been! Copying a scroll as complex as this without being able to see it, you're lucky I'm a skilled Scriptologist!

"There!" she declared, and I heard the rolling of parchment. Seconds later, she appeared on the stairs with three rolled scrolls and a huge grin.

When her gaze met my face, her smile faltered. "What is it, child?"

The concern in her creased forehead made her look just like my mother for a moment, and the dread in my stomach gobbled away all the anger I had left.

Otto boomed with confidence, "The road ahead is dangerous for us, but our obstacles are no match for our tenacity. We will prevail." He plopped a heavy hand on my shoulder and shook me gently.

Naitee looked about as convinced as I felt. The scrolls disappeared from her arms back into her inventory, and she stepped to me, grabbing my hands in hers.

"You may be one woman, but you have strength beside you and around you. Your cause is noble, and your heart is in the right place. Don't fret." Her words were gentle and kind, but were they right? Was my cause noble?

Taking down Osmark to save the people had been the line I spouted, but with Sandra's threat, revenge was all I could feel alongside the fear. Nothing noble, nothing that screamed to me I was a good person or doing what was just.

I shook my head and dismissed the doubt. My motives were shit, but the end result would be the same.

If I could stop Osmark from whatever he was plotting, I could save Eldgard from his tyranny. That was what mattered.

I gave my best attempt at a smile and nodded. "Thank you."

"Now"—she pulled the scrolls from her inventory and held them out to me—"you remember our deal, yes?"

"Yes." I reached for the scrolls, and she pulled them away.

"Anything."

I groaned. "Yes."

She passed them into my grasp, and I stowed them away in my inventory.

"Oh." She held out three more scrolls. "For your trip home."

I accepted the Scrolls of Return and ferried them away into my digital safe-storage. I didn't know how much Scrolls of Return cost, but was grateful that Naitee was thinking ahead for me.

"Thank you." I shook Naitee's hand, then turned to Otto. "I need to send a message."

"Take your time." He nodded, wiping a bit of sweat from his forehead. I realized with a skill point in Residual Heat, the warmth of Naitee's shop was *nice* instead of nearly unbearable.

I stepped to the other side of the room and plopped myself down on a burnt rug. Should I get Jack involved? Should I risk someone else's life? *Choice, Abby. Jack can choose to help you. Just give him that chance and see what happens.*

"Okay," I sighed and opened the social tab in my character screen. I selected to write a new personal message.

New Personal Message

Recipient: Grim_Jack

Subject: You made it!

Body:

Jack,

I wasn't sure you were going to take the leap or not, but I'm glad to see you're in here. Look, I've got a sensitive, ultra-rare quest. It's sort of a hidden feature created by some of the Devs at Osmark, but I need someone I can trust on this. I need *you* on this.

It's not without its risks. Sandra, Osmark's right hand, seems to already be onto me. I don't want to pull you into anything...

Ugh, damn it. I deleted the last paragraph. I didn't want to freak him out so badly he wouldn't even show up to check out the dungeon, and plus, if we didn't meet up at the dungeon, it could be days or weeks before we could meet up anywhere else given the lack of fast travel and the probable distance between us.

The countdown timer for the Edge of a Blade quest blinked in the corner of my vision as it dropped down to 27 hours remaining. I gritted my teeth and started back in on the message.

New Personal Message

Recipient: Grim_Jack

Subject: You made it!

Body:

Jack,

I wasn't sure you were going to take the leap or not, but I'm glad to see you're in here. Look, I've got a sensitive, ultra-rare quest. It's sort of a hidden feature created by some of the Devs at Osmark, but I need someone I can trust on this. I need *you* on this.

I don't want to say too much, but this is big. Could be a game changer for us. I've attached a scroll of teleport to this message. Please meet me tomorrow afternoon, 2 PM in-game time. This is a time sensitive mission, so please don't be late.

—Abby

I nabbed one of the copy scrolls from my inventory and attached it to his message, then looked at the "Send" button. *He has a choice, Abby, but only if you give it to him.*

The "Send" text pulsed at me, seeming to know what step I needed to take next. I selected the button, and the message was off to its recipient. I panned to my "Sent" tab and saw the status was "Delivered, Unread." Well, that was it then.

"Otto, are you ready to go?" I brushed crispy rug fibers from my Wildfire gown and approached my NPC.

"Go?" he asked, arms crossed. "Did your friend already reply?"

"No." I grabbed the other copy scroll from my inventory and flipped it once in the air. "But I want to go check this place out, get a feel for it, see what we're really up against."

Otto nodded. "Reasonable. Let's get stocked up."

Naitee walked us to the door and stopped me after Otto stepped out. She pulled me in close, locking her haunting blue eyes on mine, then whispered, "You put on a good show, child, but you're weak inside. Find your strength. Without it you will fail, and he will die."

I gritted my teeth and nodded, internally fuming at her accusation. My strength has always been there, I was strong. The possibility of Otto or Jack being captured and tortured to death, that made me scared, and weak. Otto made me weak… just like Sandra said.

Naitee bid us farewell and good luck as we walked out into the midday sun. The warmth of light on my skin couldn't combat the cold inside, the tightening of my muscles, and the swirling doubt of my actions.

Had I just damned Jack? Would my weakness kill Otto? Even if we could defeat the dungeon, that was just step one. We would be on the run from Osmark and his goons forever, scrambling for survival while piecing together his plans and how to take them down. Would the casualties be worth the reward? What was the price for peace, and who would pay it?

The dreaded questions consumed me as we finished gathering potions and selling our inventory junk to make space. We stepped out to a clearing, and I popped the seal on the scroll, plunging myself into a future of pain and struggle.

TWENTY-THREE

RESTRICTED AREA

THE OTHER SIDE OF THE PORTAL WAS NOT WHAT I was expecting. Honestly, I sort of expected Naitee to get something wrong and send us into the middle of a mountain. But, after a quick glance at the in-game map, which showed us on a tiny island, Eldgard not even visible, it seemed we had indeed arrived at the restricted area my fellow Devs had created.

The area was grassy with little daisies sprouting here and there, surrounded by a lush deciduous forest, with the sound of a rivulet nearby. I bent down, plucked a few blades of grass, and smelled the ends. It reminded me of Vancouver at the edge of fall, the last grass cutting of the season, when the soil had been well watered all year.

A large, leaning stone archway grabbed my attention, and I rotated in my crouched position. Not just one arch, but five or six looking something like Stonehenge, encircling a large pit with a short set of stairs. The clumsily put together landmark was obviously the entrance to the dungeon. The door at the bottom of the stairs was not just some crude wooden barrier. The hinges looked like steel, much stronger than iron or bronze, and the deep, chestnut wood was adorned with gold swirls.

"It's quiet," Otto said with the undertone of suspicion.

I stood and searched the tree line. "Yeah, but if we were going to be ambushed, I think it would've happened as soon as we stepped out of the portal. It doesn't seem like anyone is here yet."

As if to prove me wrong, there was a shuffling just beyond the edge of the forest, where the light was obstructed enough to impair my vision. A fireball readied on command, and I squinted, trying to get a better look. From the corner of my eye I saw Otto unsheathe his sword. The blade glowed blue, the light emanating from his hand and licking up the steel like a soft flame. It must've been a new ability he just unlocked, as I'd never seen it before.

I returned focus to the trees ahead. "Who's there?" I demanded.

A low grumble was the only reply. A shadowy figure, as tall as Otto but even more broad, came into view. I didn't wait to get a closer look and launched my fireball at the thing's chest. The flash of fiery impact illuminated the creature for a brief second, and its name appeared as its Health ticked down 10%, [Corrupt Valdgeist].

Its face was monstrously contorted, held together with some kind of black muck and packed with rotting leaves and twigs. The goopy tree-monster roared, moving faster, but still at a snail's pace. I readied another fireball and popped Fire Inside. I launched the spell and stepped into range for Inferno Blast, then let the thing have it.

The Corrupt Valdgeist's Health dropped sharply as it went up in flames, three Burning Afflictions taking hold within seconds and searing its remaining HP away. The creature dropped to the ground in a smoldering, oozy pile of what looked like forest floor remnants. There were little, half-decomposed mouse corpses, some larger bones like a fox or bobcat, and misshapen masses of unidentifiable matter.

"Not an ambush, but certainly unhappy to see us." I approached the smoking lump and covered my nose with my arm. The smell curled the hairs in my nostrils and turned my stomach. It was something like burning feces and flesh, mixed with three-week-old, hot garbage.

I breathed carefully through my mouth as I backed away and pointed to Otto. "You loot it, it's making me sick."

Otto balled his hands and straightened, then bent down to the steaming stink monster. He stood and backed away, then gave a deep sigh, like he'd been holding his breath. "Five gold."

"Five? Five gold!" I exclaimed. We'd seen little more than a few coppers off the mobs Naitee had us killing, but this new quest was a serious payout. I popped open my character sheet and checked my "XP To Next Level" field.

Holy. Crap. That thing was 1,500 XP all on its own. The first quest I had done was 1,500 XP, and I'd almost *died* completing it.

Otto held his hand out to me, and I opened my palms to receive my share of the loot. I stared at the two gold coins in my palm and had a terrible, gut-wrenching revelation. This place was a power-leveling zone. If Osmark gave this kind of power to every wealthy, corrupt piece of garbage back IRL, they would out-level every other player in the game in a few *hours*. They would be wealthier than every other player in the game for *months*. This was seriously bad news.

Otto retched a bit and swallowed hard. "So, how about you let me do the killing next time."

I chuckled, though the dread made it difficult for me to find amusement in his discomfort. "Yeah, okay. I'll stand back and pop Smokescreens and lob a few Fireballs."

Otto led the way into the forest, and I turned to look at the dungeon entrance one more time. We'd do a little exploring, then come right back. We'd been so broke for so long, having some extra cash and levels would do us good.

Not far into the trees we encountered another two Corrupt Valdgeist. Otto slashed them down easily, and I tried not to proc Burning Affliction on them, though I failed. The rancid smell of fiery crap followed us as we moved deeper and encountered more Valdgeist. Each gave us 1,500XP and five gold like clockwork, and each took about four solid hits to take out.

Whether it was the flaming stench that followed us from corpse to corpse, or there was just nothing else to be found in the forest, it seemed the Corrupt Valdgeist were the only things around. Though, if I knew anything about games, and I did, there was going to be some source of the corruption around here.

After our eighth Valdgeist, I leveled to 17. It was a bit of a grind, but really not too bad. I decided to save my ability point, but of course, had to drop all my stat points into Int and Spirit. I panned over to my character sheet and inspected Wildfire, disappointed to see the 2% chance of adding a new stat or bonus hadn't been in my favor this time.

Despite all the distractions and the joy of now being up twenty gold, the nagging worry of Sandra slashing my gut open and playing with my digital intestines remained. What would they do when they found out we raided their dungeon? More importantly, what would Aleixo Carrera do? It was "his" dungeon after all, which made me think there must be some kind of unique, specific item at the end of it.

"Let's get back to that dungeon entrance. We know what's around here, we need to know what's in there."

Otto grunted in agreement and scraped the last five gold out of the dilapidated corpse. We were surprised to find that the Valdgeist were already respawning behind us and didn't hesitate to earn ourselves another cool five coins each, though we could've easily avoided or outrun them.

Back at the clearing, Otto took a moment to manage something in his inventory, and I popped open my own character screen, checking for a PM from Jack. I sighed with impatience. Nothing yet.

We looked down the sloping stairs to the intricate door with apprehension. I didn't want to open it, honestly. If it closed behind us or if we triggered some sort of quest start, it might set off alarms for Sandra. I had no idea what kind of setup she had for monitoring the secret dungeons, but if I knew anything about Osmark, there certainly would be one. Sandra hadn't pinged me again since our arrival, so I had to assume it was related to the opening of the door. Otto stepped forward and put his hand on the large metal ring that served as a doorknob.

I grabbed his elbow. "Otto, they might be watching the door somehow. I don't think we should go in until we're ready. And even if Jack *does* show up tomorrow, which he hasn't messaged me back, we're not ready."

He nodded thoughtfully. "I'm not sure how they would monitor the door without actually being here, runes perhaps, yes that might be it." Otto stroked his chin. "You're right. If they're keeping an eye on this door, we'll want to be prepared for what's on the other side of it and what might follow us in after. What do you suggest?"

It was interesting having Otto, who had been our battle planner since the beginning, now looking to me for council. I imagined it must be that Otto was starting to really trust me. Dread tugged at my heartstrings. He trusted me, and I might get him killed with this quest.

If he was already bonding with me, it would be a hell of a time getting him to stay behind for this quest. Even if I could convince him, I couldn't afford for him to stay behind. If Jack and I were going to take this thing down, we would need everything we had. But if everything we had wasn't enough, I'd lose Otto.

If I could hit 25, unlock the tier-four abilities like Phoenix Rising and Rain of Fire, maybe, *maybe*, I could duo it with Jack, depending on his class. Twenty-five was a long way off, and it was already 3 PM. Just twenty-four hours to get the dungeon started. I hoped an hour was all we'd need to talk when Jack arrived, if he arrived.

I'd have to figure out how to get Otto to hang back, however I could manage that.

I sucked in a deep breath. "We need to grind."

With a resigned sigh, Otto turned and headed back into the forest of Corrupt Valdgeist. The dread in my gut spread to an aching in my chest. I would have to hurt him, badly, to get him to stay behind. The kind of hurt that friendships don't come back from. The kind of hurt that burrows inside your soul and changes you forever.

I was an only child, but being with Otto gave me a taste of what it was like to have a big brother. A big, ugly, somewhat smelly, green brother, one that I didn't want to watch die, or worse, be the cause of his death.

It seemed this quest was going to force me to lose Otto, one way or another.

TWENTY-FOUR

A Violent Farewell

OTTO GRUNTED AS HIS SWORD CHOPPED DOWN THE last Valdgeist. He leaned against a nearby tree, wiping sweat from his brow.

"Abby," he panted, "it's nearly midnight. Let's head back and get a good rest for tomorrow."

I shook my head, grabbing the expected gold from the corpses. A few of them had some random midlevel gear, mostly for Otto or the vendor, but otherwise, gold. I was level 22, and though the gold drop stayed the same on the Valdgeist, the XP started to drop with every level. The cruel curve I forgot about, but perhaps it was good. The monsters wouldn't get any higher level for when—*if*—Jack showed up, and he'd be able to take some on himself.

He still hadn't messaged me. Still. Eleven hours since my message and no reply. If Jack didn't show, there was *no way* Otto and I could duo it. If Jack or I died, we would respawn. It would suck, but it would be fine. But if I tried to do this with just Otto, I would lose my only friend. Even if Otto stayed behind, if I failed, we could all be stuck under Osmark's boot. But maybe his slavery would be better than my NPC's death.

I checked the social tab on my character sheet again in the sent messages. *Yes!* Its status was "Delivered, Read"! But, still no reply. What the hell, Jack!

"Abby," Otto said, a little louder than he needed to, "let's head back."

"No, Otto." I rounded on him, my finger pointing up at his face as I closed in. "I'm only level 22. There's no way that's high enough for whatever is in that dungeon. I need to hit 25. I need to hit as high as I can before 2 PM tomorrow."

Otto closed his eyes, and I could tell it was more than just the exhaustion that was getting to him. "I'm tired. You're tired. Look at your debuffs."

I ground my teeth from side to side in frustration, but opened my character sheet.

Current Debuffs

Tired (Level 4): Skills improve 20% slower; Carry Capacity -40lbs; Attack Damage -15%; Spell Strength reduced by 40%

Thirsty (Level 4): Health, Stamina, and Spirit regeneration reduced by 50%

Hungry (Level 5): Carry Capacity -100lbs; Health and Stamina regeneration reduced by 50%; Stealth 45% more difficult

Unwashed (Level 3): Goods and services cost 15% more; Merchant-craft skills reduced by (3) levels

<<<>>>

Shit. Not that I needed to buy anything right now, nor was it very important to improve my Two-handed Staves skill. In about 20 points it seemed I would unlock a spellcaster buff, but I did need my spell strength, and I definitely needed my regen rates to be higher than... negative. I didn't realize I'd been popping all my Spirit potions. I was down to three, and two combo potions, which tasted even worse than the Health and Spirit separately.

"So what?" I closed the menu. "We're not ready for this, and there's precious little time left."

He raised both fists and bared his teeth, then took a deep breath. I nearly flinched, but I knew my own NPC wouldn't hit me. At least, not yet.

"I'm tired, and we're getting nowhere. These mobs aren't giving us enough XP anymore, and while the gold is nice, we're loaded down. This stuff is heavy. I need to sell, eat and drink, take a bath, and sleep. And so do you."

This was it. I could push him over the edge.

"Yeah?" I threw my hands up in the air. "You're just going to give up? Loser! Why would I even want to party with you if you surrender this easily?" I stormed around the corpses, stomping my feet to hold back the tears. If I cried, he wouldn't believe me.

His eyes widened, forehead creased. "Why are you being like this? We have time to sleep, Abby, and we need it. Come back to Harrowick. I'll even pay for you," he offered, and the gesture was sweet—a sweetness I could exploit.

"I'm not some child who can't make it on her own. I don't need your money, Otto, and I don't need your weak DPS for that matter, either. You should sit this one out, since you're not in it for the win."

I turned away and crossed my arms, biting down hard on my lip to prevent the sobs that threatened to break through my facade of anger. The muscles around my throat tightened, and my shoulders trembled. I didn't want to say goodbye to him like this, but I didn't want to say goodbye with him on the ground, in a pool of his own blood, dead.

"What has gotten to you? Sandra?" Otto grabbed my shoulder and turned me around. It was all I could do not to break down, but he gave me another easy win.

"She was right," I spat, "you've let me down. You've failed. All that's left is for you to die, so why don't you run along home to Harrowick before you do that."

I hated myself. I hated the way my words stabbed into his digital heart, one I could clearly see he had. He pulled himself upright, a glisten of tears in his eyes, and sniffed.

"If that's how you feel, I'll see myself back to Harrowick."

I bit down on my tongue, unable to say any more without collapsing into hysteria. I hadn't felt the closeness of family in so long, and Otto had given me that. At the end of the world, with all of my blood relatives dead or about to die, my greatest family was a few lines of code. I didn't want him to go, I didn't want to lose him forever, but I didn't want him to die, either.

"All right. See you around, Abby, the *greatest* Sorceress in Eldgard." Otto pulled a red-ribboned return scroll from his inventory and popped the seal. He gave me one last glance and reached into the glowing portal.

White light glowed about his body, and with a crackle, he and the magical doorway were gone.

I dropped to my knees, screaming until my throat burned. A curious Valdgeist stumbled into my vicinity, so with tear-blurred vision I staggered to my feet. I launched a fireball at the form in front of me, then another, then blasted it with the inferno of my desperate fury. Why! Why did it have to be like this?

I smacked down into the flaming, moonlit figure with my staff until it stopped moving and slumped to the ground. I wanted to go home. Not Harrowick. Home to my mother. Home to her couch. Home to die with her when 213 Astraea hit.

I opened my character sheet and stared at the disabled "Log Out" button.

"Damn you! Goddamn you, Robert Osmark! Shit!"

I closed the menu and rolled onto my back, staring at the twinkling stars in the computer-generated sky. It was beauty unfathomable. Blue and pink nebulae shimmered in strange, distant constellations known to the world of Eldgard. An aurora of greens and yellows snaked across the north, over the frost-tipped mountain peaks and into the abyss of uncharted territory.

Find your strength, Naitee's voice echoed in my mind. I felt weaker now than before. But Otto was my weakness. Otto's death would be my downfall. Why now, when he was safe, did I feel worse than ever?

I staggered to my feet, desperate to find something else to kill, to take my anger out on. I stumbled through the trees until I found another Valdgeist, but I didn't cast. My spells were stronger than my staff, true, but beating the thing to death felt better. Taking the scrapes, the hits, felt better. Hurt me. Kill me!

"Damn it!" I stabbed the bottom of my staff through the creature's face, and it went limp. I dropped to my knees, pressing my forehead to the base of my staff.

I wanted to go home.

But this was home now, there was no escape. I swallowed back my emotion and found my feet again. Though my legs trembled with exhaustion, and my grip was loose on my staff, I fought on. Valdgeist after Valdgeist, until I collapsed.

I checked the time; after twelve Otto would've gone to sleep by now, or at least not be in the tavern of the Boar's Head. I would sleep somewhere else, somewhere away from him. It would be easier.

I grabbed the gold off the mangled Valdgeist and popped a return scroll. The glow of the portal enveloped me, and with a pop, I was back in the warm wooden inn of Harrowick. I knelt on the polished floor, holding my staff tightly as I fought back more tears.

"You're back." Meredith's voice snapped me from my stupor.

She looked tired. She'd been working from early that morning, so it seemed appropriate. But why was she *still* working?

"He was here," she remarked after looking me up and down, guessing what it was that left me on my knees and broken.

I tottered as I rose to my feet. "Where is he now?"

"Left, about ten minutes ago." She wrapped the cloth in her hand around and around.

"Did he buy a room for tonight?"

She shook her head, and I bit down on my lip. "Good," I lied. "I'll have a room, whatever's hot, and a bath."

"Take your seat." She gestured to the open tavern.

I looked to Otto's spot and moved as far away from it as I could. I waited as Meredith brought me a plate of what I'd had for lunch, and a glass of something strong.

"Need anything else?" She stuck her hands in her apron pockets, unlike normal when she asked for payment.

I stared down into my plate of food I didn't want to eat and shook my head. She turned to leave, then sat across from me instead.

"It can't be that bad," she cooed. "Tell me what's wrong."

I picked up my fork and stuffed a slice of gamey meat in my mouth, chewed, then swallowed hard to keep the tears from coming back. I picked up the cup and took two gulps, realized it was hard liquor, and took one more.

"I didn't ask for this." I set the cup down and pushed it toward her.

She stood, flattened her apron, and pushed in the chair. "It looked like you needed it."

The barmaid turned without another word and left me alone in the tavern. I bit down my self-hatred, finished the meal and the drink, and dropped ten silver on the table.

There was a hot bath already prepared for me when I got to the back of the inn. I stripped down, placing everything in the repair wardrobe, and stepped in. My frizzy, gore-matted hair straightened, and my skin reveled in the bubbly heat.

But I couldn't drown out the pain in my heart, the sting of my venomous words. Otto trusted me, believed in me and us, but I let him down. *I* failed *him*. And now, all that was left was for me to die.

TWENTY-FIVE

SOLO

RRH ERRH ERRH! I SHOT UPRIGHT AND BEAT MY fist at the nightstand that wasn't there. I fell from the bed and landed hard on the wood floor. My body ached. My head pounded. My gut turned with the fury of an all-night rager.

Errh errh errh!

"Alarm off!" I screamed, holding my ears to no avail until the painful noise ceased.

I opened my character sheet. Nearly 8 AM. I wanted to crawl back into bed and die. It felt as though thousands of tiny needles were poking through my skin, and millions of mosquitos were crawling down them, under my skin, biting, gnawing, and eating me alive. I curled into a ball, forcing my face into my knees as I moaned in agony.

"Ever'thin all right, love?" asked the same old woman from my first morning in V.G.O.

"Yes," I groaned. "Just feel like shit."

"I'll put an elixir out at your table," the granny said. I heard her take a step, and then she spoke again.

"Sigorsped, child. Don't let Otto get into any more trouble."

Otto. My heart ached at the mention of his name. He wouldn't be getting into any more trouble on my account, that was for sure. I idly wondered what all this trouble was he'd been in, but realized, with deep contempt of myself, I didn't need to care anymore.

I rolled onto my back, my insides feeling like they were being stabbed by hot pokers through the whole motion. I rubbed at my face. The only cure for this was food and drink. I had an appointment I needed to keep and a quest that wouldn't wait for me. The countdown timer at the corner of my vision blinked as it ticked over; seven hours left to get into that dungeon.

The silent countdown I was keeping wasn't much longer. Twelve hours until I hit my full seventy-two and either died or transitioned. The way this morning was going, it felt like the former was more likely than the latter. All the more reason for me to get this done and figure out what was going on before there was no one left who knew *anything was* going on.

I crawled to the wardrobe, pulled Wildfire down, and put it on. I instantly felt better, but not nearly enough. The rest of the gear equipped easily, but without much of a benefit, and I used my Obsidian War Staff to prop myself up to my feet.

Though there were no blinking notifications, I checked my social tab one more time. Nothing from Jack. I had to assume he wasn't coming, and I was on my own. That was fine. I'd been on my own most of my life, and I made it okay. V.G.O. was no different.

I hobbled down the stairs and saw a cup sitting on Otto's table, but no Otto. Ah, the elixir the old woman spoke of. I shuffled to the booth and sat in my regular spot, looking up at the wall where Otto would normally tower over me. What had I done?

The right thing. I did the *right* thing. Otto was safe now.

I pulled the cup to my lips and sniffed. It smelled like liquid death, but I trusted the woman enough to take a sip and find out what it was.

Buff Added

*Elixir of Health:*You've consumed the Elixir of Health! Increase Stamina and Spirit regen by 35% for 2 hours. Regenerate 25 HP/sec for the next 5 hours.

Never doubt the powers of an old wise woman.

I slammed the whole shot-sized beverage and sighed as the pounding in my head dimmed to a dull ache. The flavor wasn't as bad as the magic-unlocking potion Naitee had given me, but it still gave me a gross burp I let fly freely without Otto around to blush.

Meredith bustled up and dropped off a plate of eggs, hot bread, pears, and cheese. I stopped her before she could run away again. "Don't you get tired?" I asked.

"Whadja mean?" she asked, blissfully unaware of the exhaustion I was under.

"I mean, you were here past midnight last night, and now it's eight in the morning." I took a sip of the cool water she brought with the hot plate and felt even better. The itchy-burning sensation under my skin subsided, and I was again able to think clearly.

Meredith looked confused. "You must mean my sister, Makenna." She left me without another word, leaving me in silence. I turned back to the food and looked up at the void left in Otto's absence. It was better. I was better off alone. I had my class kit, I was level 22, my gear was decent; I'd be fine. He'd be fine.

Most of my gear was decent, I reminded myself. My little war staff was piddly compared to everything else, but I had enough time to stop off at Hasan's to see what he had for me. With 290 gold, he'd likely have plenty for me.

I stuffed the rest of breakfast down my gullet, hardly enjoying the punch of flavors. The eggs had been a perfect over-medium: no jiggly whites, no solid yolk. I wondered if the game was cheating, looking into my personal profile to find my preferences, or if over-medium was just the standard.

Feeling a little less generous than last night, I dropped a single gold on the table and made my way out into the street. It occurred to me in that moment that I hadn't paid attention most of the times we walked around the town, and I wasn't completely certain where Hasan's was.

I popped open my map, and to my relief, it was marked as one of the places I'd visited. I set a tracking node down and closed out of the menu. A smaller map in the corner of my vision appeared, highlighting the way to Satin and Beech.

The typical affair of the early morning hustle and bustle was more annoying now that I didn't have someone to clear a path. Strangers bumped my shoulders, cried their indignation at my clumsiness, and then checked their coin purse. I did the same, keeping one hand pressing it against my thigh to be sure it couldn't be snatched or rifled through.

Hasan was setting out new wares from the back when I arrived, but he stopped upon seeing me and smiled. "Glad to see you're enjoying the shawl! How can I serve you today?"

"I need a new war staff." I popped the old Obsidian War Staff from the holster on my bandolier and held it out to him.

He took the battleworn wood into his hands and looked closely at the black gem at the top. "Yes, I see this is not going to serve you well for long. I have the perfect thing."

He shoved the staff back to me as if the substandard item tainted his being. With a whoosh, he pumped his huge wings and moved to the back in a single thrust. It seemed all the "perfect things" came from the back of the shop. I wondered if what Hasan put out front was actually any good.

"Here we are. Come, come." Hasan appeared at the opening and beckoned for me to follow him to the back. My thinning patience pinged me with annoyance, but I kept my smile on. I trudged up the few stairs to the back room where Hasan grinned broadly, holding something behind his back. I could see over the top of his head the glint of a ruby.

"Don't peek! Close your eyes!" Hasan scolded, and I smirked, then closed my eyes. I heard the ruffling of his wings as he moved the staff around his body.

"Open!" he declared, and I did as ordered. In his outstretched hands was a gorgeous, sleek staff. I'd had a lot of cool swords and warhammers in past MMOs, but this thing was a work of art.

The black-stained wood was engraved with glowing red runes that snaked up the slender body to the head of the staff, which clutched a deep red gem that was polished into an oval. I placed my hand on the wood, and a jolt of power zapped me like a live wire.

My hand recoiled on instinct, and Hasan chuckled. "It's safe, you will become accustomed to the feeling."

He held it out to me, and I took it in both hands. After a moment, the nerve jumping feeling of being shocked subsided, and I was invigorated with a sense of might. My eyes roved over the solid, smooth wood, watching the runes pulse like hot embers at my touch. This thing was beautiful, without a doubt.

Hasan stroked his hawklike chin. "It is a good match for you, I think. Yes, it is for you."

I opened the item's info card and let out a low whistle as I read.

Embergrave War Staff

Weapon Type: Two-handed Staff

Class: Ultra Rare

Base Damage: 25

Primary Effects:

- +5 Intelligence

- +5 Spirit

- +20 Spell Strength

- +30% Spell Critical Damage

- +3% Spell Critical Chance

Firelight illuminates the darkest time, but Embergrave warms the soul of the world.

The flavor text was puzzling, as though there might be another weapon out there called "Firelight." All the same, I enjoyed the little quips and comments the creators of the weapons left behind.

"So? What do you think?" Hasan asked, though he looked assured I wanted it. Of course I wanted it, but I didn't want to see the price tag associated with it.

"How much?"

I tried to pass it back to Hasan, and he refused. "You can afford it. Just thirty gold. Such a good price for such a perfect weapon."

Otto had scolded me for not bartering better with Hasan, bartering at all for that matter. So, when Hasan said something was a good price, I had to assume he'd be willing to go lower.

"No." I shook my head and sliced my hand through the air, mimicking gestures I'd seen Otto use while bartering. "Twenty gold."

"Deal!" Hasan clapped his hands, then extended one for payment.

Shit... He would've gone lower. I sighed and handed over the twenty gold. It was my staff now, though, and the item became available for equipping. I exchanged the old shaman staff for Embergrave, and the electric shock renewed in strength, radiating up my arms. Within seconds, it subsided to a mild tingle.

I pulled the Obsidian War Staff from my inventory. "What'll you give me for this?"

Hasan grimaced. "Three silver."

I huffed. "You'll sell it for three gold—probably more. How about you trade me for an uncommon ring of my choice?"

He seesawed his head, then nodded agreement. I passed him the old staff, and he led me up front to a glass case of jewelry. There were some cool bracers too, which a quick glance at my own let me know they were now the lowest-value gear on me, but in the end, I picked a [Spellcaster's Rose Gold Band]. It was a pretty thing with +5 Spell Strength, +5% Critical Hit Damage, and +5 Spirit.

"How about the rest of this stuff?" I laid a sample of my junk on the counter, and he raised his brows.

He riffled through what I'd set down. "How many pieces do you have?"

I panned through my inventory and got a rough count. "About twenty-five."

"Hm..." He put his hand to his narrow chin, but Hasan was a businessman, he already knew how much he wanted to offer me and how much he'd accept in the end. "How about four gold?"

"How about eight?" I countered, knowing double was likely not a loss for him.

He tongued his cheek, then slapped eight gold on the counter. I dropped off the random gear from my inventory, thanked Hasan, and stepped out into the street. Just past 9 AM. I needed to grind uninterrupted, but only had one scroll left to get to the restricted area and couldn't afford another one. Quests and local grinding would take too much time, as I'd have to walk and deal with having my kills stolen by random newbs in the area.

No, there was only one option. It was time to head back to the secret dungeon.

I pulled the scroll, the original copy, from my inventory and thumbed the string holding it shut. I could do this without him, without any of them. I would do this. The string came away easily, and the glowing portal opened before me on the street outside Satin and Beech. I took a deep breath and stepped through.

TWENTY-SIX

REUNITED

I WIPED SWEAT FROM MY BROW AND RUBBED MY stinging eyes. The stench of burning Valdgeist was easier to stomach now, but the toxic smoke still burned my eyes and nostrils. I'd worked my way back behind the dungeon entrance in the hopes that there would be different mobs there, but I was disappointed. Corrupt, stinky, slow Valdgeist everywhere.

The area was much larger than I'd thought, and it seemed the farther I went from the entrance to the dungeon, the higher level the Valdgeist became, which meant more XP and more gold. With a few extra levels under my belt, I'd been able to put some additional points in my class tree, getting some great new bonuses.

It was just past 12 PM, and I was a few thousand XP away from hitting 25, so I buckled down and trudged further into the dark forest. I figured it'd taken me an hour to wind my way to where I was, and with the Valdgeist getting easier as I moved my way out, it wouldn't be much of a problem to fight my way back with my new tier-four ability. I opened my skill tree and looked over the abilities one more time.

I wanted Blazing Weapon, *badly*, but knew I needed to get Phoenix Rising first, and then Rain of Fire after that. Inferno Blast was great, but the range was so limited. Rain of Fire would let me hit a swath of targets in a huge radius, from pretty far away. Leaching Flame was also pretty high on my wish list. It would give me that Spirit regen synergy I'd been so desperately needing.

The cracking of undergrowth snapped me out of the menus, and I scanned the dim clearing. Behind me, a distant war cry nothing like the Valdgeist's hair-raising roar rang out. I checked the time again, 12:15. I'd told Jack 2 PM, but maybe he was early. I checked my messages, nothing new. I clicked my tongue on the roof of my mouth in frustration.

There was another option… Aleixo Carrera could be here.

I spun in place at the grumbling of a Valdgeist, and I launched two successive Fireballs at the first thing that moved. The monster cried out as Burning Affliction level 2 took hold, twice. It shambled toward me, but I'd become so in tune with the necessary damage to kill the mud lumps, I knew it would collapse before it got anywhere near me. On cue, the creature melted into a reeking pile of goo and died.

Another shout, closer this time, raised hairs on my arms. I crouched and moved toward the sound, stealing from bush to tree to boulder to conceal myself. It took me a few minutes and several "Stealth Failed" notifications, but I arrived at a clearing littered with three Valdgeist corpses and a huge, dark green Risi bent over the bodies to collect his gold. My heart leapt with joy. I wanted to hop out from behind the trees and give him a hug.

But I remembered why I'd sent him away in the first place and hardened my face. I straightened from my crouch and walked into the dark meadow. "I thought you went home."

Otto's grip tightened on his sword for a flash as he turned at the hips, then he relaxed as his gaze locked on me. He sheathed his weapon and returned to picking gold off the creatures. "I did."

"Why didn't you stay there?" I growled, my pulse pounding in my ears.

He brought himself up to full height. "I haven't failed, and I won't. I do not give up, especially not on my friends."

The last word stabbed into my chest, but I maintained my outward cool. "I don't want you here, Otto."

"I know." He nodded. "But not for the reason you want me to believe. You're *afraid*."

"I am not—"

"Yes, Abby, you are. You're afraid I'll die."

We stared at one another for a long beat as my emotions raged under my calm facade. I wanted to scream, "Yes, I am! I'm afraid I'll lose the only person left I feel I can call family!" But my mouth stayed shut tight. I could still save him. I could still send him back home.

Wait.

"How did you get here?" I asked, my voice laden with the curiosity I felt.

"I made the same deal as you." He took a step toward me, then another, until we were standing face-to-face.

I crossed my arms. "Yeah, what was that?"

"A promise."

I bit down on my cheek. He'd sold himself to Naitee for a scroll so he could come back to help me. It was, in the end, all I asked for: dependability, loyalty. I didn't want to lose that, not now that we'd become friends.

I turned my head away. "I don't want you here."

"Too bad," Otto retorted without missing a beat. I could see from the corner of my eye he was smirking. That jerk. Damn him.

"Fine," I sighed, "but if you die, I won't cry."

"I wouldn't want you to." Otto put his hand out for a high five.

I grabbed his arm and pulled him in for a hug. He was tense at first, then wrapped me up in a tight squeeze.

He whispered above my head, "I won't cry if you die either."

I pushed back and scowled at him. "That's because I'll just respawn at the Boar's Head eight hours later."

He smirked. "Let's get you to 25."

We moved even deeper into the forest where we encountered [Greater Corrupt Valdgeist]. *Significantly* harder, and three times as rewarding, we cranked through the groaning, vaguely human-shaped monsters until the magical moment of leveling.

"Hold up." I grinned. "I've got a point to spend."

I opened my skill tree, looking at the 3 saved skill points I was *so* ready to drop.

```
                          Firebrand Skill Tree

           Fire Inside (2)                    Fireball (3)
    ________________________/|\______    ________/|\________
       |              |            \|/              |
       |              |             |               |
 Flame of Holding (1)  Fire Eater (2)   Burning Affliction (2)  Smokescreen (2)
       |              |             |               |
       |              |             |               |
       |              |             |               |
 Shell of Molten Ash (1)  Residual Heat (1)   Searing Halo (1)   Inferno Blast (2)
       |              |             |               |
       |              |             |               |
       |              |             |               |
 Blazing Weapon (0)   Phoenix Rising (0)   Leaching Smolder (0)   Rain of Fire (0)
       |              |             |               |
       |              \_________  _______/          |
       |                        \/                  |
       |                        V                   |
 Fire Guardian (0)           Immortal Flame (0)          Wall of Flame (0)
       |                                                  |
       \______________________  ______________________/
                              \/
                              V
                      Globe of Flame (0)
```

Without blinking, I dropped a point each into Phoenix Rising, Leaching Smolder, and Rain of Fire. I wanted Blazing Weapon, but if I was going to be a *team* player, I needed to support the team, not go solo.

Skill: Phoenix Rising

You may go down in flames, but you'll rise again! When your Health drops below 10%, the roiling smolder in your chest will come alive, restoring 20% of your HP instantly.

Skill Type/Level: Passive, Level 1

Cost: None

Range: N/A

Cast Time: N/A

Cooldown: 3 hours

Effect 1: When your Health drops below 10%, instantly regain 20%.

I wished the cooldown wasn't so brutal, but this would *definitely* come in handy for what was to come. It didn't make me less squishy, but at least made it harder for me to die.

<<<>>>

Skill: Leaching Smolder

Bend the fire to your command and steal Spirit from your enemy! For each Burning Affliction the enemy is encumbered with, steal .25 x character level in Spirit/sec for 30 seconds, as long as the enemy has Spirit to leach.

Skill Type/Level: Active, Level 1

Cost: 100 Spirit

Range: N/A

Cast Time: Instant

Cooldown: 30 seconds

Effect 1: For each Burning Affliction the enemy has, steal .25 x character level in Spirit per second for 30 seconds.

<<<>>>

Burning Affliction itself only lasted twenty seconds at level 2, but even if I only had one Burning Affliction on the enemy at level 25, Leaching Smolder would earn me 125 Spirit. *But*, if the enemy died early, I'd lose all that Spirit casting the spells for nothing. Leaching Smolder was good for bosses, the long-haul fights, and I knew without a doubt there was one of those in the dungeon.

The cooldown on it was a bit lame, but I supposed it was to prevent me from popping three quick Burning Afflictions on several targets in a row, hitting them all with Leaching Smolder, and going on Spirit regen OP Overdrive.

<<<>>>

Skill: Rain of Fire

There are few things in life more terrifying than being caught in a shower of a thousand tiny fireballs. Bring this terror to your enemies in a 20-meter radius from the target location for 20 seconds with each fireball hit having a 5% chance of setting your enemy ablaze!

Skill Type/Level: Active, Level 1

Cost: 500 Spirit

Range: 50 meters

Radius of Area Effect: 20 meters

Cast Time: 4 seconds

Cooldown: 10 minutes

Effect 1: Rain down fire on your enemies in a 20-meter radius for 20 seconds. Each fireball deals .2 x Spell Strength in fire Damage.

Effect 2: Each fireball has a 5% chance of adding Burning Affliction to the target.

The price was high, but the effect was so cool. Not only that, but with my Spell Strength at 168, I would deal about 33 points of damage with each little fireball, and there were *a thousand* of them. I was stoked to use it, but the cooldown was a bit more punishing than I felt necessary. It did decrease at level 2, so I would just have to spend my next points wisely.

"Ready?" Otto prompted, and I closed out the menus.

"Ready to burn some face off." I nodded.

We wandered a little deeper and realized to our dismay that the Greater Corrupt Valdgeist gave way to [Raving Greater Corrupt Valdgeist], and after tangoing with just one of those, we were ready to head back. The XP off it was insane—5,000—but it was also unnaturally fast, with more HP and armor than the other Valdgeist. This one took us six to seven minutes of dancing around, dodging, and downing potions. Just not worth it.

With the border of the higher-level zone identified, we moved back into the smaller fries that went down in a few hits. It still didn't feel like enough. It was 1:40 PM, and I'd only just hit 26.

"Otto, we need to head back to the clearing." I swiped up the last coins and checked my balance: a very pleasing 612. I was already wealthier in V.G.O. than I'd ever been IRL.

Otto's eyes went vacant for a moment and he became still, probably checking his gold like I had, then he asked, "Has your friend messaged you?"

I popped into the PM screen. Nothing. "No, but it doesn't matter. We're running out of time on the quest. He might still show." I shrugged.

"Let's go find out." He sheathed his sword and marched southwest toward the dungeon marker.

The way back was eerily devoid of Valdgeist, but all the better for us to make good time. Otto held up a hand to stop me at the edge of the clearing, and we both crouched down. I crept up beside him, and he motioned silently to the blond-haired figure lounging in the grass at the center of the meadow. Jack's hair was brown, and if he stuck with his IRL appearance, like me, it definitely wasn't him. Could it be Carrera?

Otto pulled a short dagger from a sheath at his back so quietly, if I hadn't been looking at him I wouldn't have known he'd done it. He motioned for me to stay put, and I was about to protest, but realized having a sneak attack fire ambush would be better than exposing myself, so I nodded.

He circled the tree line until he was positioned behind the apparently sleeping man, then moved in. The sunlight hit the dagger, and he held a hand over the blade to keep it from reflecting.

When Otto was a few feet away, the man tossed, uncrossing his legs and then crossing them again. Otto stopped cold, completely motionless, and I held my breath. Otto moved again, one more step, and then lunged.

TWENTY-SEVEN

JACK

"WHAT IN THE BLOODY 'ELL!" THE BLOND-haired man kicked and tugged on Otto's arm as the hulking Risi pulled the man upright. Otto was definitely stronger and quickly got him under control in a tight headlock, the blade poised at his neck.

"Who are you?" he roared in the man's ear.

The man sputtered. "I'm just a hired thief here with my ward, wherever he ran off to."

I moved to the edge of the tree line, ready to pounce at the first sign of Otto in danger.

Otto's grip tightened, and the man squirmed. "Who are you talking about?"

"Grm J—"

"Who?" Otto loosened his grip, and the man breathed deeply.

"Grim Jack," he panted.

Another man, a Murk Elf, appeared at the south end of the clearing, and I readied a fireball.

"Don't take another step," Otto snarled viciously. "Not unless you'd care to see what the inside of your friend's throat looks like."

The Murk Elf at the tree line froze and muttered something inaudible to me, obviously peeved at the man in Otto's grasp.

"I fell asleep!" the thief replied. "Now please do what the smelly thug says, since I'm a huge fan of not dying. My kind doesn't respawn like you Travelers—death is sort of a big, permanent deal for us."

He really was the Murk Elf's NPC. Was that... Jack? I extinguished my fireball.

"So," I spoke loudly, drawing the Murk Elf's attention, "the thief really is with you?" I stepped from the shadow of the trees, and the fear on the Murk Elf man's face shifted to curious recognition.

"Is that you, Abby?" Jack's voice warmed my chest and smoothed the hackles on the back of my neck. It was him.

I couldn't contain my smile as I gave him a little nod. "It's good to see you, Jack. Otto"—I looked to my loyal NPC holding tight to the threat—"you can let him go."

He didn't seem happy about it, but Otto let the thief go and gave him a shove to let him know how lucky he was.

I wanted to run into Jack's arms and give him a hug, but with the mixed company having just been at each other's throats, I needed to stay composed. So I walked, slowly. "Otto, why don't you and the thief—"

"Name's Cutter, not thief," the blond-haired man pouted, arms crossed.

Wow, this was Jack's NPC? I remembered Jack had been a little young at heart, but he was nothing when compared to Cutter. I withheld my comment about the thief's childishness and gave them my best smile. "Okay. Otto, why don't you and Cutter get to know each other while Jack and I have a word. Just catch up a bit, then we'll all be on our way."

Otto gave me a concerned glance, then said, "Of course."

He grabbed Cutter by the arm, growling, "This way, thief," and pulled him toward the tree line behind us.

I grabbed Jack around the shoulders and pulled him into a hug, whispering, "It's so good to see you."

I released him and held him at arm's length, taking in all the interesting choices he'd made. A Dokkalfar, really? Five-o'clock shadow on his chin, tribal tattoos across his extra-muscly biceps, and taller. I knew he was taller because I'd made myself taller too, and he still towered over me.

"You too, Abby." He smiled, genuinely. "You too. I can't believe this place." His eyes roved around the clearing. "V.G.O. is seriously incredible—I've never seen anything like it."

"Oh," I scoffed, "it's definitely incredible." His gaze snapped back to me, and he looked confused, head cocked, brow ruffled. I guess it was time to explain some shit. "Will you walk with me a bit?"

He bobbed his head with a smirk and offered me his arm. I linked my arm in his and was hit with the fond memories of our college days. He and I would walk to class just like this, nearly every day. We moved toward the dungeon entrance. I didn't want to wander into the forest and accidentally attract a Valdgeist.

What the hell was I going to say to him? All of it? I checked the in-game time, 2 PM, then checked the timer on the quest. We had just under an hour to open that door before I would fail the quest line. Had to get him on board, fast.

"You look good, are you a human?" He stammered a bit, still the Jack I knew from all those years ago. Bashful and sweet.

"A Wode." I nodded. "I wanted to actually look like myself, and the human races were the only ones that offered my natural skin tone. Personally, I'm sort of surprised you went with a Murk Elf. Not that I mind, exactly..." He didn't look bad, but the black eyes were a little creepy. "You just look so different. I sort of expected you to be human, too."

"The Murk Elves had some cool racial bonuses," he said, an excited gleam in his eyes. Then, his chest sort of slumped, and he became quiet. I didn't mind the silence as we walked, but I could tell by the way he kept taking quick inhales, he wanted to say something else.

"So, how's stuff been back IRL? I mean aside from the world ending." He rubbed the back of his neck, and I smirked.

"Good to see you haven't changed too much. Still the same old, awkward Jack I remember." But, the comment brought my attention from the moment at hand to all the shit I needed to tell him. So. Much. Shit.

"Truthfully, I'm tired." I sighed. "It's been a long year for me. A tough year. I lost my dad about six months ago. Large cell lung cancer. Ugly stuff." I saw his gaunt face in my mind's eye, but shook it off. "And with the schedule Osmark had us on, I didn't even get time off for the funeral."

"Wow, Abby, I'm so sorry to hear about your dad." He glanced down at me, but I kept my eyes on the grass and waved the apology away.

"It's the end of the world, Jack, everyone's going to lose loved ones. Everyone. But to really top things off, despite my best efforts, my mom won't make the leap to Viridian. She says she's too old to start over, even though she's only sixty-five. So, I guess it's been a pretty shitty year, all things considered. How 'bout you?"

He bobbed his head. "Yep. Pretty much the same. By the way, I never properly thanked you for the capsule. But, you know, thank you—you saved my life, after all."

"You're welcome." I faltered, remembering the horror of watching the first accidental, permanent death. "But maybe you should wait to thank me until you've fully transitioned. I've seen what happens to people who don't live through the process, and it's worse than watching someone die from cancer. I know from personal experience."

Wow, dumbass. Did you just really? Poor Jack was grimacing, chewing on his lip. Now I was the awkward one.

"So, what's the deal with the tank?" He grasped at anything to get him out of that shit-show I just laid down.

"Otto? Oh, he's my starting NPC." I waved off the question like he'd understand, then realized he might not. "The one who walked me through my intro to the world. A lot of players end up forming pretty strong bonds with their paired NPC. Is Cutter your starting

NPC?" I offered, trying to get the conversation back on a normal track.

"Well, he was in prison with me, if that's what you mean." He stumbled, the cogs in his mind turning in his eyes. "Wait, so are you saying everyone starts with their own NPC?"

I dipped my head. "Every player has a completely unique starting scenario with a custom NPC to lead them into the world of V.G.O. The seven Master AI controllers—the Overminds—analyze each user based on that specific user's internet profile and personal history. Then, the Overminds create a starting NPC guide and a specialized initialization sequence which acts as a sort of hyper-advanced Myers-Briggs Type Indicator."

Jack's eyes were getting larger and larger by the second, but this line would take me closer to where we needed the conversation to go.

I went on. "The way each player reacts during the sequence and interacts with their NPC tells the Overmind what type of character class they'll most likely meld well with." I decided to give him the "how the sausage is made" shortened version.

"Wow," he gasped. "That's incredible. Intense." His brow furrowed. "But it's also kind of creepy. How does Osmark Tech get away with profiling people like that? Seems like a massive invasion of privacy—aren't there laws against that kind of thing?"

"Oh, it's definitely a breach of privacy," I said, glancing up at him, "and yeah, there are totally laws against it, but Osmark Tech gets away with it because players sign an information release in the user agreement. Naturally, the release is written in legalese so dense a team of Harvard lawyers couldn't figure it out, and then it's tucked away in print so fine, you'd need an electron microscope to find it. But it's there, and when you agree to play, you accept Osmark's terms of service, profiling and all."

Jack exhaled, puffing out his lips. "Man, if players found out, they'd be pissed. Why even go through the hassle anyway? Seems like it'd be a lot easier to just let players choose their class like in every other MMO in the world."

I shrugged. "That's not my area of expertise, but if I had to guess, I'd say it's because the VR game play is so intense and personal, that if you played a class outside of your personality tolerance it could have adverse side effects. Or…" I considered Osmark's need for control, for things to all be perfectly in their place. No. It wasn't time for that yet. I quickly came up with another excuse. "It could be a marketing gimmick. I don't know. But then, there's a lot I don't know about V.G.O."

We fell quiet as we approached the stone archways. I didn't want this shit to be going on. I didn't want this quest to be waiting for me. I didn't want people like Carrera and Osmark to exist here, or I wanted someone else to be there to take care of it. There was no one else. Just me and Otto. I needed Jack.

"Hey," he started back up again, trying to avoid the silence he found so awkward. "Out of curiosity, do you know if the NPCs are actually self-aware or not? If I didn't know any better, I'd say my starting NPC's a real person. Sort of a jerk, but a fully fleshed out jerk." I nodded along to that. The thief was definitely rude.

Jack kept going, speaking fast, so I knew he was uncomfortable. "He certainly seems to think he's real—

but it's weird, because from what I've gathered, he also genuinely believes V.G.O. isn't a game. It's really tripping me out, actually."

"Honestly..." I sighed. When I first arrived, I thought they were all executing predetermined code, but Otto reacted to me, and not just like a machine would, not like how the other AI had in the lab. Otto was interpreting me, understanding me.

"Honestly, I'm not sure. No one is." I dropped my head in defeat. "We rushed the testing to get the game online, so I can't give you a straight answer one way or the other. The NPCs are procedurally generated by drawing on information from all over the internet— history, Facebook profiles, fiction novels, movies, games—which gives them their uncanny realism. I've never met an NPC that failed to pass the Turing Test, but whether they're actually aware?" I sucked in a breath and cocked my shoulder. "Time will tell, I guess."

We fell quiet again, my thoughts fixated on Otto, the tears in his eyes, his tenacity, his loyalty.

Jack smiled, his voice shifting to something more chipper. "Well, would you like to tell me about this big secret mission you've got for us?"

We'd reached the point of no return. If I told him and he ran, that would be the end of it. We'd never know what Osmark was up to until it was already too late. But if I told him and he joined us, it could seal his death warrant. I could condemn him to a life of eternal pain and suffering, with no way out. Could I live with myself if he were captured over my hacking, my stealing? Could I even call myself his friend for sending him that damned scroll?

TWENTY-EIGHT

SHITSTORM

I PULLED MY ARM FROM JACK'S, GETTING THE physical distance needed to push him away. We'd only just reunited, and now I wanted him to leave. Even if he didn't come with me, I was going. But just being around me would put him at risk. Sandra would be hot on my tail after this heist, and *anyone* who aided me would be on her hit list.

"Jack," I said as tears crept into my vision, "maybe you should just go. It might've been a mistake to drag you into this mess." The salty drop broke free from my eye and rolled down my cheek. I swiped it away, upset I hadn't been able to hold it together. It had been a rough couple of hours, with not nearly enough sleep.

"Abby." He placed a warm hand on my shoulder, and I melted into it. "What in the hell is going on? You're not a weepy damsel in distress. I've never seen you cry, not in all the years I've known you."

I bit back a sob and swallowed.

He gave me a gentle shake. "So why don't you tell me what's eating at you? Just get it off your chest."

"It's bad, Jack." I sniffled. "Bad for everyone. Maybe as bad as the asteroid. Even telling you could land you in a lot of trouble." I chewed my lip and thought of Sandra with her high Dexterity and quick blades, shredding through Jack's chest and making Murk Elf Swiss cheese out of him.

"Are you sure you want to know?"

He straightened, and his voice went a little deeper and stronger. "Abby, tell me. What could possibly be as bad as the asteroid?"

Oh, what a treat he was in for. I steeled myself for what came next. I paced to a fallen log and sat, patting the spot next to me for Jack to come sit. He definitely didn't want to be standing for this.

"Tell me what's going on."

"It's hard to know where to even begin." I looked to the tree line for inspiration on what step of the messed-up chain of events I should start at.

"Jack, there's just so much crazy shit going on. Like mind-blowing, world shaking, secret conspiracy, Illuminati shit. Tin-foil hat shit. And I haven't shared this with anyone else because I don't know who'd believe me or who I could trust. Most of my 'friends'"—I air quoted the word, since I hadn't had any IRL friends for years— "work for Osmark Tech, and I sure don't trust anyone there. Not anymore."

I took a deep breath after dumping that out. Jack had survived the first wave of madness without batting an eye, so, let's see if he could take some more. "It all started a few months ago. It was a typical day; I was checking a line of code when I ran across an oddity. Someone had added an unauthorized, locked quest, accessible only by special players. There'd been all kinds of other crazy stuff leading up to this, so when this popped up, I decided to take a peek." I tried to justify my actions, but what I had done was wrong, in the strictest sense. "Thought it might offer some clue about what in the hell was going on around the company. That's when I discovered there were hundreds of these locked areas scattered all around V.G.O., inserted by Robert Osmark's inner circle."

Jack interjected, "Are they supposed to be some kind of content for future patches or expansions?"

I clicked my tongue. "At first, I thought so too, but I kept looking. Digging." I paused. It felt dirty not to admit the whole truth. It wasn't just gentle code investigation of the stuff I had access to. I'd been… "Hacking," I finally admitted.

I thought of my last hack, the one where I ripped off the very scroll that got us here. That code was so deep under wraps, so hard to get at, there was no way any of the floor engineers would've ever noticed it.

"These areas were never meant for the general player population," I continued. "These areas were built into the game as rewards for some of the big financial backers of V.G.O."—I thought of Carrera and gritted my teeth—"people with lots of money and lots of power."

That led me right into the dirty deal. "Here's the thing, Osmark Tech knew about the asteroid long before the general public ever did. The government didn't release the info to the masses because they didn't want to cause premature panic, but my boss, Robert Osmark, knew. I'm sure of it." If he hadn't, he was just a horrible, greedy toad, and high-ranking scum across the world really wanted to play V.G.O.

"He didn't tell us peons"—I gestured loosely to myself—"obviously, but in hindsight it's clear. He had us working around the clock, paying out overtime through the nose, rushing through beta trials to get things up and running ahead of schedule." I thought back to that crazy HR associate, Alan Campbell, who'd dropped himself into V.G.O. over a year ago... His trial had prevented the whole project from being shut down and helped us discover better, gentler logout methods, which were totally unnecessary now, but the poor bastard died for it. Made me wonder if he'd really done it against Osmark's will or if Osmark had pressured him.

I snapped myself back into talking at a gentle prompt from Jack. "Then his inner circle started adding in all of these extra features last minute. To top things off, a few weeks before the media started to carry the story about the asteroid, Osmark himself dropped the news on us worker bees—sort of an extra work-your-asses-off incentive." I scoffed. Jack seemed to be taking it okay, maybe. The crease in his forehead was getting pretty deep.

"Based on a series of hacked emails I uncovered, I think he had these special areas installed in order to help certain individuals game the system. I personally believe Osmark realized that V.G.O. wasn't just a video game," I said, pointing up at the sky, "not with that asteroid inbound."

We both glanced up, and I went on. "He realized V.G.O. was the birth of a new world. A new dimension. Initially, the game was set up to put all starting players at the same disadvantages, to level the playing field for everyone. But the mega-wealthy, the politicians, the banksters, people in organized crime, they don't want a level playing field. They want an edge.

"And all of these new areas were expressly added to give those people that edge. In a couple of weeks, after the asteroid hits and it's too late for anyone IRL to do anything about it, V.G.O is going to turn into a new feudal dark age, and everyone is going to be scrambling to carve out a piece of this empire for themselves. And the little guys, people like us, are going to get crushed in the mix. People like us are going to end up being the serfs, Jack. The unwashed masses for uber players to lord over. Unless..." I thought of all the things I'd done to get us here. "Unless we fight dirty."

I let him process this for a while, and I could see the gears cranking away in his head, his lips mumbling gently as he thought it through.

"This zone right here"—I pointed to the dungeon opening—"has already been bought and paid for by a South American dictator named Aleixo Carrera. I don't know what's buried in these ruins, but I know Carrera paid twenty million for it. Twenty million, Jack. That's a lot of money for a few strings of digital code, so I've got to think whatever's here is powerful." I remembered how damn fast and powerful Sandra was at our first encounter. That chest had to have some sweet loot in it. Sweet loot that all the worst people in the world were getting their grubby hands on.

"These entitled assholes are going to have an advantage none of us regular folk get, and in the long run it's going to turn ugly. And all the chaos coming down the pipeline only accounts for the human elements. The AI controllers running this system are cutting-edge beyond belief. None of the Overminds are really conscious, thinking beings." The quest about this very dungeon came to mind. I thought of Sophia, the quest generator, and how she had delivered my rogue code to me, but I waved it away.

"They're more like forces of nature that maintain the world's integrity, spawn creatures, create quests—but they're still dangerous. Really dangerous. I mean, the Overmind responsible for overseeing Serth-Rog and his personal army is run by a repurposed military AI unit. Osmark acquired it from the Chinese military last minute to save time with development. Who knows what that thing might do?"

"Wait," he said, rubbing at his temples. "Okay, I can believe Osmark Tech might have the ethics code of a Banana Republic Dictatorship, but here's what I don't get. Why sell off V.G.O. real estate for IRL money in the first place? The world's going to end in less than nine days. So, what's the point?" He was starting to believe me.

"Well, Carrera didn't actually pay cash." My hands were getting expressive, and I was trying to talk faster, to get it all out. "Nope, maybe six months before news of the asteroid broke, Carrera selflessly 'donated' twenty million worth of essential tech components to help get V.G.O. operational in time." Jack's face was starting to look like he was having an aneurysm, but I had to go on.

"He supplied Osmark Tech with colossal amounts of refined indium, gold, silver, copper, platinum, palladium—all essential components in the physical machinery powering V.G.O. He also supplied cheap labor to help at the NextGenVR capsule facility, churning out capsules at a crazy rate. And Carrera's not the only one, either."

Here came the best—or worst, depending on how you looked at it—part.

"US politicians railroaded laws allowing Osmark Tech to bypass testing requirements, they rubber-stamped the import of dangerous and restricted materials, plus about a hundred other illegal things. Osmark even got help from NASA to launch his satellite into orbit. And that repurposed AI I told you about? Another 'donation' from Chinese military leaders. The amount of supplies and materials to get V.G.O. up and running ahead of schedule were staggering, I'm sure. And I bet my completely worthless life savings there were people lining up around the block, willing to help in return for future kickbacks. I think he's repaying favors to the powerful people who made V.G.O. possible."

I sighed and massaged my temples. This whole spiel was making Osmark out to be a demon, and while he was a robotic prick, I did think he had better intentions than "enslave the remnants of the entire human race." I hoped.

"I want to give my boss the benefit of the doubt and assume he isn't actually a monstrous asshole. I like to believe he was just doing what he needed to do to save a lot of people"—*if we're lucky*, I reminded myself—"but he made some really shady deals to do it. And even if he isn't a monster, I can't imagine people like Carrera or the CIA or the KGB are going to be beneficent masters. They're going to amass power for themselves and be colossal dick heads just like they were in the real world, except there's not going to be a Constitution or police force to keep them in check."

Jack put a hand up, squinting his eyes tightly for a moment. "But why go through the quest system? Why not just turn these players into in-world gods right out of the gate? Just program it into the system?" Jack didn't have the context I did, so it was easy to ask these questions. But the solutions he suggested were just impossible. I had to at least try to explain it.

"It's complicated," I started, then noticed the quest timer ticking down in the corner of my vision. Only thirty-two minutes left, and Carrera could arrive at any second. I needed to get him on my side or get him out of here, fast.

"After we brought all of the Overminds online, they closed the system to major changes—they're calling the shots now. The Devs can only tweak things that're already consistent with the Overmind directives. Hence using the quest system as a back door."

Jack bent forward, his dark face pale, then grabbed his knees and panted. That's just about the reaction I expected, honestly. He was handling it pretty well. I gave him a moment, then placed my hand on his back, rubbing in small circles.

"You okay?"

"Nope." He gulped back what I assumed was bile. "Not even a little. V.G.O. was supposed to be a safe haven, but if this is true, dying back on Earth might actually be the better option."

He possibly still had that option, not being more than twenty-four hours in yet. I did not.

"So..." He pushed himself upright, his breathing steady. "What are you suggesting? We're nobodies,

Abby. We don't have money or connections or powerful friends. What exactly do you think we can do about this?"

I hadn't been through hell and back to be told I was no one. I would be the greatest Sorceress in Eldgard, damn it.

"We aren't nobodies, Jack. We know MMOs better than most of the assholes entering this world, and knowledge is power, too. What I'm suggesting is that we get ahead of this shitstorm while we still can." I turned to face the dungeon entrance. "What I'm suggesting is you and I form our own clan—one that actually has a chance of standing up against the rising powers in this new world, one that can give people like us hope. And we start by stealing whatever's inside this restricted zone."

I eyed the dungeon entrance and thought of what could be hiding in the chest below. "Whatever Carrera paid twenty million to get his hands on."

Jack stood with a "why me" moan and headed to the stone archways. I followed behind, giving him some space. I watched as he mumbled some more, his forehead crease deepening to the point where it might be able to hide a whole peanut butter and jelly sandwich between the folds.

I'd given him enough time to think, and I only had eighteen minutes left. It was now or never, but he still needed to know the dangers, the consequences. How much of them, though? Should I tell him everything? Sandra too? No, there wasn't time for that much, but he had to have the choice.

"Before you say anything, before you answer, I just need to tell you that if we do this, there's no going back." Except Jack could probably still log out, for at least a few more hours. I was in it for the long haul.

"You need to know that we're going to buck the system in a big way and potentially make some very powerful enemies with connections and deep pockets. And they'll come for us. Sooner or later, they'll come."

I took a deep breath, prepared for the worst, with only fifteen minutes to go. "Now, what were you going to say?"

"I want to know, why me? This is my life you're asking me to put on the line," he huffed, "and I don't want to be manipulated into being someone's fall guy. You could've picked anyone, but you came to me with this. So I want to know why."

I bit my lip, considering the truth, or a kind lie. Better go with the truth. "Because I trust you, Jack. And"—I chewed my lip harder, not wanting to admit it—"because I like you."

Color poked into Jack's cheeks for the first time in many minutes, and though I was being honest, I knew I'd struck the cord. We'd had a great friendship that never went anywhere. I was really sad about that, honestly.

"And," I steered the conversation back toward something more relevant, "because you're the kind of guy who plays a Cleric instead of a glory-seeking warrior or a flashy mage."

"Wait. What?" The cute blush I'd worked out of him disappeared with his frown. "You picked me because I usually play a Cleric? I don't understand, not even a little."

I sighed. "Clerics aren't about glitz, glamor, flash, or glory. They're a support class. They end up in the background, and they worry about the success of the team instead of their personal achievement. I thought about reaching out to some of the other guys from the Crimson Alliance." I name-dropped our old MMO gaming group and saw recognition in his face that smoothed out the grimace.

"But in my gut, I wasn't sure I could really trust any of them with something this big. At least, not in the beginning. But you're a good guy, Jack, one who's always wanted to make a difference. That's why I worked my magic to ensure you got a capsule well before the news about the asteroid hit." I remembered begging Osmark to let me ship just the one after our big "town hall" meeting where he clued us in. He finally caved, but not before I had to surrender every waking hour of my life to the cause for the following five weeks.

We locked eyes. Jack's, terrified. Mine, determined. "Because I wanted you on my team even then. So, what do you say?"

He turned away from me, and I was sure this was it. This was the end. Not just of our friendship, but of the quest. There were nine minutes left to open that door, and I needed an answer.

Then, I got one I wasn't expecting.

"Alright." He spun back to me, a gamer's gleam in his eyes. "I'm in."

TWENTY-NINE

SECRET DUNGEON

WE GOT THROUGH THE DOOR WITH ONLY moments to spare, and just as I'd suspected, it was a trap. Within a minute I had a new notification blinking in the corner of my vision, but I didn't have time to let Sandra get up in my business. We were doing this. Together.

Otto took the lead down the slippery stone slope, with Jack in the middle and me in the back. Jack's NPC, Cutter, was actually a decent thief. He was invisible somewhere up ahead and, I assumed, scouting the way for us.

Though I was glad Jack was with us, he didn't have a class, which was extremely concerning. It took me several levels to get Firebrand, but at least I was on the quest. Jack didn't have one yet, or at least, he didn't tell me about it. Then again, we hadn't had much time to catch up before I ushered us through the doors as the quest timer nearly hit 0.

The sloping finally evened out, and seconds later, Cutter, Jack's NPC, materialized in from the shadows with a finger to his lips. "Unfriendlies, up ahead."

He went on once we all gathered around. "I disarmed several very nasty traps on the way in—spring-loaded spikes, a plate-triggered flame wall, a ceiling mounted buzz saw big as a horse. Someone definitely does not want visitors—"

"What about the unfriendlies?" Jack interrupted, obviously having a decent relationship with his NPC already.

"Tough." The thief eyed each of us individually. "Not your typical brainless cave dwellers. These are real guards. Mercs. They're sitting around the fire gabbin' and eatin', but they look dangerous."

Cutter knelt down. "There's a trio of plate-armored warriors, nearest to us"—he began tracing a map of the encounter—"a Ranger with a mean looking bow on the left, plus two spellcasters, one might be a Priest or a Warlock of some kind, here and here."

Cutter paused, then turned directly to me. "What's the plan, flame-lady?"

Flame lady. I ignored the jab and looked to Otto. He was great with battle plans, and I trusted him. Otto locked eyes with me and nodded; he'd take this.

"We're going to play this one straight and simple. You and you will Stealth out." He pointed at Jack and Cutter. "Thief," he said, his pointing digit lingering on Cutter, "you target the sorcerer." He looked back to Jack. "Grim Jack, you take the Ranger. I'll give you both a fifteen count to get into position, then I'll blunder out and draw their focus."

Otto made some small marks in the dirt to represent their positions. "Once the fighting begins, Abby will lay down wholesale suppressive firepower. Straight, simple, easy."

Jack and Cutter stared at Otto, openmouthed, and I could see the color rising in the Risi's cheeks at their noncompliance.

"Well, don't just stand there, move." Otto was great. He snapped them into action, and then the boys were stealthed, and off.

Otto leaned in toward me and whispered, "You think they can do it?"

"Don't cry," I said, elbowing Otto, "but we might die."

We grinned at one another and stood. A tiny pop, and the hawk-like Ranger jerked her head, staring at a spot near the wall. Had to be Jack. He was only level 14, after all, couldn't ask too much of him. Otto marched forward, and I grabbed at his arm, but couldn't catch him.

The hostile tanks all moved toward Otto, hands at the hilts of their weapons, but they didn't attack.

He cocked his head to the side, eyes narrowed. "Who are you? How did you get here?" He seemed truly curious, like it was obvious we shouldn't have been able to be there. But he was expecting a lowbie party, so maybe there was something else I didn't know we needed.

"You don't have the seal of Lord Carrera, yet here you are in an area reserved for him. Explain yourselves or perish."

My mind went back to the lines of code, the ones about a "Loyalty_Seal." I hadn't thought they were related, since there was literally no code linking the two—I'd just happened upon it.

Shit.

Well, it was time to do something. I pulled my shawl up around my head, obscuring my face. Maybe I could word our way out of this with the help of my Leader's Bandolier. I jogged out behind Otto and caught him just before he entered the ring of firelight.

"We are servants of Lord Carrera, the owner of this reserved area." My voice came out much stronger than I felt, and I was relieved for the false confidence. "I wasn't told to expect your party, so"—I ran my sweaty palms along Wildfire—"can you please explain what *you* are doing here? What is the role and function of your group?"

"We're the mercenaries," the Warlocky Priest replied, eyes narrowing to slits. "Mercenaries hired to lead Lord Aleixo Carrera through this dungeon, to help him and his party power-level and claim the treasure at the dungeon's end. That is the nature of our contract." Just like Verin was hired to help Sandra, these guys were assigned to Carrera.

The potato-sack man continued. "If you are Lord Carrera's servants, why aren't you aware of these details?" The tanks drew their weapons at this accusation. This damn belt didn't seem to do shit in the way of actual negotiation.

"Unless, of course, you are schemers and connivers." The caster smirked. "Give me the pass code. Now."

Double shit. Was there a pass code? Was this a trick?

Otto's battle cry answered the question for me, and I popped a quick Searing Halo to protect myself, then slapped the three leading tanks with a Burning Affliction each. Cutter and Jack sprung into action, Jack landing a first good hit and Cutter disorienting his target. Going good, we weren't going to die!

I popped off two more Burning Afflictions on the tank Otto wasn't targeting, then hit him with Leaching Smolder. My Spirit bar climbed like an eager toddler in the kitchen searching for cookies. I smacked the second tank with a fireball, then another, dropping her to 15%. My fire DOT seared into her flesh, taking the remaining HP away.

My heart skipped a beat when I noticed off to the left that Jack was on the ground, his leg and chest slashed, bleeding everywhere. The Health bar above his head flashed, and he scampered back on his elbows, but he was too slow. I wasn't.

I dashed into range as the Accipiter raised a bloodstained dagger, preparing to strike down my friend. Bullshit. Not this time. I skidded to a halt and opened both palms, praying my spell wouldn't hurt Jack, and let Inferno Blast rip.

The column of flame rocketed out of my body with a force I'd never known, and a notification popped up.

Spell Modification: Raging Inferno Blast

You have used Inferno Blast at a time of desperation, modifying the spell with your sheer force of will! When you cast Inferno Blast, you will now use the modified version.

Modification Effect 1: Send a shock wave of hot air out in a dome configuration preceding Inferno Blast. The shock wave will disorient your enemies, interrupt spellcasting, and reduce Stamina regeneration by 20% for 35 seconds.

Modification Effect 2: Raging Inferno Blast has a cooldown of 10 minutes. If you cast Inferno Blast before the cooldown has expired, you will still be able to cast the spell as the unmodified version.

Holy shit. That was *awesome*! I staggered back, catching a glimpse of my handiwork. The Accipiter shrieked, batting at her face as Burning Affliction seared her feathers off. She dropped to the ground and rolled, but the fire couldn't be put out that way.

Her cries of terror chilled me to the bone as I watched her Health plummet. I hadn't fought humanoids with fire spells before, at least not in V.G.O., and the desire to help her left me stupefied. Jack slammed his hammer home and silenced the Accipiter, then stood over her corpse, his slack hands trembling.

"Abby!" Otto ripped me from my horrified trance, and I snapped into action, launching a fireball at his opponent, then another.

Cutter stepped in and started laying down the damage on Otto's target, so I focused on the tank that stalked toward a petrified Jack. I popped off the active component to Fire Inside and launched a fireball at the axe-wielding man, scoring a crit and proccing Burning Affliction.

The tank turned to me as I grabbed aggro, and Jack shook his head, looking around the room. He was still so new to this, and the poor guy had been a medic for the last five years IRL. Watching someone cry out for help and beg for relief probably triggered an instinctual reaction to save them. I couldn't imagine.

"You're messing with the wrong man." The axe slinger whipped his weapon around for a heavy strike. I jumped back, and realized I no longer had Jinker as the tip of the metal sliced into my hand. The shock of the strike made me cry out and recoil, but that bastard got his.

All at once, the tank's long beard and hair went up in flames. I could thank Searing Halo for that. I pulled my damaged arm into my chest and used the other to lob a fireball into the jerk's face.

In a blink, he was down. So was Otto's target, and that just left… Jack! He was straddling the man in the potato sack, whaling on him with his bare fists.

"Jack!" I screamed, but he didn't hear me. He raised his blood-splattered fist for another strike. That was the only merc left, our only informant. Without a guide, we could be *totally* screwed.

"Jack, stop!" I yelled again, but his war cry drowned me out. The man on the ground was near death, his Health bar hardly visible. This was it. The end of the raid.

THIRTY

OF GODS AND MONSTERS

"CUTTER, GRAB HIM!" I POINTED TO THE THIEF, who reacted in a flash, grabbing Jack's upraised fist and wrapping another arm around his chest.

"You're good, Grim Jack," the thief urged.

Jack kicked as he was dragged back. "But he's still breathing!"

"We know." I jogged up beside them, scanning the poor man's battered body. Jack really let him have it. His face looked about as busted as mine felt after I'd been laid into with that single gauntleted punch.

We might not need this guy, but a guide would definitely be better than not having one, and he seemed to be the ringleader of the group we'd just slaughtered. But how could we make him cooperate?

Flame of freaking Holding. I smiled and bent over the man's prone body. I hadn't used it before, but now was the perfect opportunity. I called up the spell in my mind and my hands worked of their own accord, weaving and whooshing over the man's body. When the cast came to the finale, little vines of red-hot embers wrapped up and down the victim's body.

A notification let me know the cast was successful, and my Spirit regeneration had been reduced by 10% indefinitely. That was awesome. I could keep this cast up forever for the price of 10% Spirit regen. I became innately aware of the fact that I could move him, and with a jerk of my hand, I pulled the man from the ground to a hovering position with just my mind.

I recalled Star Wars, and the way it looked when Darth Vader pulled someone from the ground and choked them. I felt that badass in this moment. I saw Jack staring, jaw slack, and smirked at him. "Flame of Holding. This'll keep him immobile while we question him."

I grabbed a Health potion from my bandolier and stared at it. Did I really want to waste one of my potions on this guy? Ugh, yes. We needed his intel. I pulled the stopper, grabbed his jaw, and poured the contents of the bottle into his mouth.

The man inhaled sharply and coughed. I knew what it felt like to come back from the brink—it wasn't pleasant. I saw Jack, a wide-eyed horrified expression on his face, and decided to do some team morale damage control.

"Good work, Jack." I reached out and gave him a pat on the arm. His head turned to me, then his eyes, and he was no less shaken than seconds before.

"Now, we don't have much time." I saw the blinking Personal Message in the corner of my vision and was reminded that Sandra might be sending goons or even coming after us herself. "Aleixo Carrera and his thugs could show up any moment. So, Otto and I are going to interrogate our friend here." I gestured to the shivering, hardly conscious Priest-Warlock thing. "See if we can't get a heads-up about what we're going into. In the meantime, you and Cutter loot these bodies. Sound like a plan?" I smiled kindly, and he didn't respond.

"Oh," I added, "and you can keep whatever you find."

Otto glared at me from the left, but it was fine. We'd got our fair share of gold in the forest and would get whatever was coming to us in the end chest. Cutter nodded, much more enthusiastic than Jack. I took that as good enough and walked with Otto down the hall as we dragged our prisoner along.

Once we were out of earshot, and I heard the pair rifling about the downed enemies' wares, I laid into the potato sack man. "Who are you?"

"Morgan," he coughed.

"What are you doing here, Morgan?" Otto stepped in.

"Just like," he wheezed, "I said. I'm the Warlock here to help Mr. Carrera and his team through the dungeon."

I puffed up my chest. "Well, Mr. Carrera isn't coming, so we're the party now. Got it?"

Morgan laughed.

"What's so funny?" Otto demanded.

The Warlock grinned. Blood smeared his teeth, but the swelling in his face was subsiding. "You haven't," he wheezed again, blood trickling from his lips, "paid me."

Otto grabbed a fistful of his tunic. "You're lucky we haven't killed you. Now answer. Do you understand?"

The man raised his slack head, his eyes gaining clarity for the first time in many long minutes. "Eat your mother's hair pie."

Great.

"Well, you can shut the hell up." I twisted my fingers and conjured a flaming ball gag, then stuffed it in his mouth.

"What now?" I looked to Otto for guidance, then at the blinking notification in the corner of my vision. Sandra's message demanded viewing, but I didn't want to get distracted, not now, when we were already committed.

Otto stroked his chin. "We keep moving forward. Get as far along as we can without him. Then, when we need him, we make it very clear"—Otto paused and glared the man down—"what will happen if he does not cooperate with us."

"And those guys?" I jerked my head toward the clearing where Jack and Cutter were happily looting bodies.

"The thief has been useful so far. Your friend…" Otto said, then cleared his throat, "is very low level, with no class kit."

"Yeah." I sighed, watching as Jack equipped a new chest armor he desperately needed. "I know."

Otto whispered, "Do you think we can do it alone?"

The Warlock chuckled behind his fiery ball gag, and I gritted my teeth. "Apparently not."

We both glared down the prisoner until he stopped, a stupid smile plastered on his swollen cheeks.

"Let's get going then." I turned my head toward the long hallway down. There were no lights, so I'd have to keep a fireball in hand at all times. Not really a problem, but a bit frustrating when I also had to keep up the Spirit-regen-sucking Flame of Holding.

Otto collected the giddy boys, and we started down the long path ahead which was littered with more Valdgeist. Unlike the ones at the surface, though, these ones dished out XP and gold like that was their job. Between us and the apparent end of the dungeon there were a good fifty Valdgeist, and four more levels in it for me, putting me at 29.

I wanted to spend a few more skill points, but knew if I opened my menu I might check that message. This was no time for whatever that bitch had to say… Unless maybe she would let on about when she was going to arrive and how many would arrive with her.

"So this is some kind of quick and easy grind for the uber rich, huh?" Jack pulled me from the thoughts of opening the message.

"Yeah. Doesn't seem fair, does it? Everyone has to start off fresh in a new world, but guys like Carrera still find a way to game the system in their favor. It's incredible." I scoffed and shook my head. "Really pisses me off, you know?"

"But you're benefiting, and you don't seem to be complaining," Morgan piped up. I should've left his ball gag in, but his directions were proving more useful than not.

"If you were really so noble, you'd leave this place untouched. Just turn around and walk away. The fact that you're continuing onward suggests you don't mind the benefit so long as it's directed at you."

Heat rose in my cheeks. I was doing this because I needed to find out what was at the end of the dungeon, in that chest, because it was instrumental in stopping Osmark or at least understanding his plan. I wasn't here for the gear, just the quest. But my reasoning felt like lies. My inner gamer rejoiced at the copious handfuls of gold and the potential for what else might be in the chest at the end.

I looked to Jack, who wore a sheepishly guilty expression. Time for more morale damage control. "It's different with us. We're doing what we need to in order to make it in Eldgard, and we're going to help other people. To benefit the people who couldn't afford to pay to cheat their way to the upper echelons in this new society."

"Ahh," the Warlock sneered, "so you're an ends-justify-the-means kind of lady."

"No," I said through clenched teeth. "You're twisting my words and skewing the situation out of context. All I'm saying is this stuff is here, and that means someone is going to get it. It's definitely better for people like us to get it than some cocaine-financed dictator."

Jack jumped in, defensively. "Yeah. Besides, what's it to you anyway? You're a mercenary who works for the highest bidder; I don't think you're in a position to judge us on issues of ethics."

"No judgement. You're right, I'm a mercenary." Morgan eyed Jack, then me, with a smug smirk. "Personally, I think your logic is flawless, but then I regularly do questionable things for money. I only bring it up because I think there might be an opportunity for us to work together in the very near future, supposing you all can get past your veneer of self-righteous hypocrisy."

Jack scowled. "What are you talking about?"

The Warlock let his head fall back, contempt in his tone. "You'll see soon enough."

I'd had it with his BS, time for another gag. "That's enough out of you." I stuffed the fiery bond in his mouth, and he chuckled. Goddamn bastard thinks he knows me, us, what we're trying to do? Self-righteous hypocrisy… What does he know?

After two more Valdgeist and a hundred or so meters, the crypt-like tunnel gave way to something more like the Wayward Caverns, complete with the stream I'd heard running topside and a spattering of Lumalgae hanging from the ceiling. The Lumalgae provided enough light that I could cut off the fireball, and I was grateful to have a bit of my Spirit regen back.

"I wonder why they didn't give the mobs here even more XP?" Jack just couldn't stand the silence. "Not that eight thousand a pop is bad," he said, shrugging, "but if cheap leveling is the name of the game, it seems like the Devs should've just dumped a bunch of Corrupt Valdgeist with like, I dunno, a hundred thousand points apiece or something crazy like that."

I thought of Sophia and her delicate balance. "I'm sure they would if they could, trust me on that. But the Devs only have so much control. Early on maybe they could've done something like that, but not now. Now, the Overminds are the real power in V.G.O., and once they were up and running, we could only tweak relatively insignificant things. Really, the Overminds do all the heavy lifting—they generate content, creatures, quests, everything," Otto looked at me with a puzzled expression, and I faltered. "They're basically in-game gods."

"Each Overmind has an underpinning of base directives that govern their 'character'—keeps them from going completely rogue, but it's like holding a lion in check with a leash made of bacon. One of those essential directives is to prevent hackers and game modders from tinkering around in unsanctioned ways. Cheating the game, specifically. And this"—I gestured to the dungeon around us—"almost qualifies."

The sound of rushing water and light at the end of the tunnel indicated an upcoming intersection. I wanted to take out Morgan's gag for directions, but then remembered he'd pissed me off. I considered it more carefully as the cave ended at a deep, black, ten-meter-diameter pit, with no way forward but down.

THIRTY-ONE

Boss Room

OTTO WASTED NO TIME FINDING A NARROW PATH off to the left that spiraled into the pit and took the lead—after Cutter of course, who refused to let us proceed ahead without scouting.

Nerves urged me to keep talking as I followed behind him. I returned to the idea of the dungeon being *almost* cheating. "So, to get around the rules and the Overmind screening protocols, I think the Devs probably created these restricted areas with a carefully balanced ratio of XP, loot drops, and mob difficulty. I'll bet a thousand gold the algorithm they came up with skirts just below what the Overminds will flag as unsanctioned modding."

I glanced over my shoulder at Jack, who seemed intently focused on making it to the bottom safely. "It's still cheating, obviously, but it's really smart cheating. The kind of cheating only insiders could come up with."

We slipped and tripped our way down the winding passage, Otto calling out a few "Careful" or "Loose rocks" reminders as we went. I looked up from the bottom, watching the afternoon light stream through the opening of the pit. I wished I could be up there instead of down here, wished Osmark hadn't sold this dungeon to Carrera and I didn't have to steal it just to find out what was going on.

"Come on." Otto nudged me, and we moved away from the spiraling pit to a large, open atrium, more like the first room we'd come to with the mercenaries. There were blazing torches lining the walls and murals of a grand, beautiful forest, leading us deeper. The air tasted moist and earthy, with a hint of something foul. Not like garbage or excrement, but like evil.

Cutter's voice, strikingly absent most of the way down, materialized from thin air up ahead. "We've got something strange up here!"

Otto and I exchanged a glance and, without a word, broke into a jog. We rounded a corner and the hall opened up farther to allow for two gargantuan, rune-etched doors. Brass fastenings secured the hinges, handles, and each massive board on the doors to one another. The planks of wood making up the doors were easily four feet across and twelve feet tall; the trees they came from had to have been enormous.

"Can you ungag him?" Jack pulled me out of slack-jawed awe as he pointed toward Morgan, and I nodded. With a snap of my fingers, the mouthpiece disappeared.

"I've got a question for you." Jack stepped up to the merc held back by tendrils of fire. "What were you and your team doing here?" Morgan was silent, apparently annoyed he'd already been asked that question.

Jack shrugged. "Anybody could work their way through this dungeon without the help of a mercenary team, so why were you put here?"

The merc grinned like we were finally getting his bad joke. "We were specifically contracted to help with the thing beyond that door. Before this mission, my team and I were briefed about this dungeon. And your friend is right," Morgan said, nodding toward me, "this is a very special place. Drastically underpowered mobs scattered throughout, easy kills for weak players, granting significant XP." He paused, his eyes glistening with joy. "But the tradeoff is a dangerously overpowered Guardian. One so powerful it raised the difficulty level of the dungeon as a whole.

"And I happen to know that without me, you don't stand a chance of getting into that room. Even if you do somehow manage to find a way in, you'll never get out alive."

Otto huffed, and I rolled my eyes. Typical, narcissistic merc talk.

"But, as I mentioned earlier, I might be willing to help, assuming of course you can find it in your hearts to work with someone like me. And assuming you're willing to pay my price."

"Which is?" Otto barked. He was of the mind that the merc's life should've been payment enough.

Morgan grinned. "I want half of your gold."

"Half?" I snapped without a second's pause.

His gaze followed me as he stated again, slowly, "Half your gold, and half of what's in that room."

"Oh bollox, no way." Cutter stood and paced to the boss room entrance. "No merc's gettin' half my hard-earned coin for a stupid door."

The thief squatted down in front of the lock and fiddled with it.

Morgan leered maliciously. "I wouldn't if—"

Cutter yelped as a pop like a gunshot and a flash sent him rocketing ass-first away from the doors. He landed in the dirt with a heavy thud, his HP bar down by half.

"—I were you," Morgan finished as Cutter sat up with a groan, holding his gut.

"Y'alright, buddy?" Jack sniggered and tossed Cutter a Health potion.

The thief caught the vial, mumbling, "Shuddup," before tossing it back. Cutter laid into Jack's less-than-spectacular looks and clumsy footing. They were so like children, finding joy in even the darkest place, at a critical time. It was kinda nice having them around, if for nothing more than their silly banter.

I turned to Otto. "Looks like this is our only option."

Otto growled as he eyed the mercenary, then whispered, "I don't trust him."

"You and me both, but this is the hand we were dealt, and honestly, we're pretty lucky this dude's still alive. We can turn back, forget everything, and just go about our merry way." I glanced at Morgan. "Or we can pay him half our gold, see what's in that chest, and finish this quest."

Otto mulled it over, gritted his tusk-like teeth, and nodded. "I'm with you, *flame-lady*."

I turned back to the group and declared loudly, "I'm in."

Cutter's lip curled up in disgust. "You're gonna give this git *half* of your gold to open a door?"

"No." I looked to Morgan. "Anyone who wants to go forward is going to give him half their gold, and he's going to open the door, fight with us, and then"—I pulled up close to the mercenary—"he's not going to tell anyone about this dungeon or who was here, ever. Right?"

Morgan wriggled a bit, trying to pull his arm out for a handshake I guessed, but Flame of Holding didn't budge. He settled for a smile instead. "If that is the deal, I agree to the terms."

"You know I won't let you go alone," Otto grunted, then tossed a satchel of gold at Morgan's bound feet.

Cutter looked to Jack and whine-mumbled something about, "I came here to make money, not lose it."

I dispelled Flame of Holding and dropped a sack of 684 gold down at Morgan's feet. He stretched, took his time making sure each limb was sufficiently worked out, then scooped up the money.

"Jack, are you coming?" I stood next to Morgan and Otto at the door to the boss room.

My old college friend nodded. "Yeah, what the hell. We came this far."

"But Jack," Cutter urged. Jack cut him off with a wave of his hand and tossed his own sack of gold toward the mercenary. Cutter growled, fished a bag out from under his tunic shirt, and threw it at Morgan.

"Ready yourselves," the merc barked in a baritone voice. "What lies beyond this door will likely claim one of our lives, if not more. If you prefer it not be you, make the necessary preparations now."

I had 20 stat points and 4 ability points just *sitting there*. My eyes landed on Otto, then Jack and Cutter. If we were going to have a real fighting chance, I'd need to apply those points. The dread of the little red reminder of a personal message swirled in my gut.

I popped open my character sheet and focused my eyes on the image of my character. Even my avatar's face had little creases of worry in it. I put 6 more points each in Intelligence and Spirit, then 8 in Vitality.

Next, the abilities. I'd avoided the general Sorceress tree for the most part, but now it was time to dig into it. There were other people on the line, and I needed to provide support for them. I dropped 1 point in [Caster's Spark], increasing party members' Spirit regeneration by .2 x my character level/second. Right now, that evened out to about 6 Spirit/second. Not too bad.

One more point for [Magnus Armor], as its benefit to the whole party was clear, and 1 point for [Immunity Aurora], which increased all party members' resistances to elemental, holy, shadow, disease, and poison damage by a flat 5%. Pretty intense.

The blinking red [1] called to me, and I thought maybe it would be best if I checked it, just to see if she had already sent someone after us. Maybe we needed to wait on the boss in case of an ambush. I bit my lip. I didn't want to freak myself out, but if she let on about sending someone to take us out in that message, I needed to know.

I selected the social tab and went to my personal message. My ribs suddenly felt too narrow for my guts, causing my breathing to drop into shallow gasps as I read the title of the message. [Touch ANYTHING and you will regret whatever idiot impulse drove you…] It was cut off. Shit. Shit, damn, balls, hell.

The trembling in my shoulders shook the cowl from my head, and I straightened. *Find your strength.* Naitee's reminder blared in my head. I needed to hold it together. I opened the message.

Personal Message

I don't know how you came to have Mr. Carrera's Scroll of Allegiance, since I delivered it to Osmark myself, but I swear by all the gods, goddesses, devils, and demons, if you touch a single thing in that dungeon, I will spend the rest of eternity delighting in your torture, and anyone who colluded with you. But it could go differently, Abby, and that's your choice.

There's still time to get your mother in the game, and I know how much you *begged* her to join you. We could get her for you if you turn back now and leave the dungeon untouched, or we could do much worse with her if you don't.

Consider it, Abby.

Sandra

My mother.

I reread the message twice more as my breath caught in my chest. Sandra was the kind of person to make good on a threat like that. Sandra could go get her, force her into a pod, make a character for her, and pull her into the game against her will. She *could* do that.

But no. This close to the end, Sandra had few resources on the outside, and I doubted she'd spend them on getting my mother. She would still try to make good on the first threat, capturing all of us and torturing us for eternity. But what if we could save this new world for everyone?

I closed the menu and looked to Otto, who stared blankly at the wall, likely digging around in his own character sheet. He was still code, he was just ones and zeros executing on a server somewhere deep in the earth… but he was my friend. I didn't want him to be tortured for eternity.

Jack and Cutter were play-sparring, and the Warlock summoning his horde of magical skeletons and rock demons. I shimmied closer to Otto, the urge to tell him of the dangers once more driving me forward.

"Otto," I whispered, and his vacant gaze snapped to my face.

His eyes widened. "What is it?"

"Sandra. The door was rigged somehow like we guessed. There's no indication she's sent anyone for us, but… if we take anything she'll want our heads. Ours and Jack's."

Otto's face relaxed. "I've been threatened by the Viridian Empire before, and I'm still here," he smirked, but it was no comfort. He hadn't *really* been threatened before. He hadn't existed before I got here.

"Loosen up, flame-lady. We're going to take down whatever is on the other side of that door. We're going to find out what's in that chest. We're going to stop Osbark."

"Osmark," I corrected, and he grinned, nudging me.

Otto's bunched cheeks flattened as his expression became placid, and he placed both hands on my shoulders. "Eldgard is not a small place. It will be very difficult for her to find us."

I nodded, taking a deep breath, then another, and blowing it out hard. My old tricks from back when I had a body still seemed to work, and my stomach tightness dissipated.

"Okay," I declared to the party, "let's do this thing."

Otto took the lead and pointed us into position. "Cutter, Grim Jack, stealth and drop behind me. Mercenary, bring your minions about me. I want to be able to charge the boss and get aggro, so I don't want any fodder getting in my way. I'll need *two* solid hits. *Two!*" He held up two fingers to Cutter.

"Yeah, alright, I got it." Cutter waved him off.

"Abby." He said my name with a certain kind of relief and fondness. "Stick to the rear with the merc, drop all your Burning Afflictions and keep them up, hold AOEs for swarms."

I nodded along as he laid out the game plan I was already thinking of. We'd grown used to each other's company and accustomed to fighting together. I already knew his rules, why to follow them, and how to combo hit with him. We were a destruction dynamo.

"Everyone ready?" Morgan called as we pulled into our battle formation.

"We are as ready as we will ever be, mercenary," Otto spat the word, then shot a glare over his shoulder. "One thing, though. If you betray us as you betrayed your former master, I will find you. And I will end you. One way or another, I will end you."

Morgan clicked his tongue. "Keep me well supplied with gold, and we won't find ourselves at cross purposes.

"Now," the Warlock said, grinning wickedly, "shall we?"

THIRTY-TWO

DEATH DILEMMA

The Warlock murmured and chanted, his hands glowing with an otherworldly blue light. He swept them open wide, and the door shuddered. *Thump, thump, creeeak.* The once locked door swung open, revealing a massive chamber eerily reminiscent of the chamber the Hoardling Drake had been camped in, except five times as large.

The doors came to a halt with a massive *boom* that shook the dust from the cracks above. We all stared in wonder, our breaths held in collective silence. Then, Otto bowed his head and spoke. "I might see you soon, don't be too mad."

But who was he speaking to? It didn't sound like a prayer, not one I'd utter at least. Was he speaking to someone in the afterlife?

Before I could ask, he stole into the room with sword held at the ready, the conjured minions surging around him. I lost sight of Jack and Cutter as they pulled off to the left and the right, cloaked in stealth.

"After you, *flame-lady*." Morgan grinned.

I filled my lungs with stale cavern air and followed after my faithful NPC. Red appeared in the corner of my vision, and a blinking [1] popped into view. Oh, shit. The boss room door was rigged too, I should've known. I kept a steady pace and opened the menu.

<<<>>>

Personal Message

You should've taken my offer. You're dead, Abigail Hollander. No, better than that. You're mine, *forever.* And your mother? She'll wish you were never born.

Sandra

<<<>>>

I slapped the menu shut, my heart slamming away at a breakneck pace. My mind traced the possibilities of our demise. Die at the hands of whatever boss—who was seemingly absent from the room— lurked here. Die at the hands of Sandra over and over again. Die at the hands of Carrera after weeks of torture.

I scanned the room. These walls were lined with murals of a much different kind from the rooms behind us. Gruesome images of human torture and sacrifice brought a new sense of heightened awareness to the fact that if we opened that chest, Sandra would hunt us for eternity. I didn't want Jack to die, though he would respawn. Otto would be gone forever. And my mother… No, Sandra wouldn't waste the energy getting her.

We could still turn back. We could leave the chest untouched and walk out of here scot-free. Or could we? What if Sandra had already told Osmark? Even if she hadn't, what if Sandra made it her personal quest to destroy me now for defying her?

"Are you with us?" the merc murmured to me.

What was "being with them" truly? Standing beside them and fighting the boss? Maybe. Saving them from eternal torture that could come from looting that chest?

But if we didn't loot it, the entirety of Eldgard would fall under Osmark's control with no one to understand how he got there and no one to know how to remove him from power. The remainder of humanity would be ruled by cocaine dictators and corrupt politicians for however long the servers held out. The possibility of peace, destroyed.

The answer was clear. I couldn't allow it. I would sacrifice everything to ensure the safety of these millions of people and NPCs.

I held a fireball in one hand. "I'm with you."

As we made our way deeper, the room's focal point became clear: another ring of Stonehenge-esque runes, all engraved with green glowing sigils that felt *corrupt*. Just looking at them made my skin crawl. Weak light streamed in from a hole in the cave ceiling, casting a glow on the star of the show: the boss.

At the center of the semicircle sat a hulking, gnarled, pale-white tree, dead as winter. It was scrawny, but intimidating, and though completely placid right now, it was definitely the thing that was about to rip into us. Below, at the base of the unholy arboric beast, was a decadent chest accented in gold and silver.

Otto's head whipped around, and his steely gaze landed on Morgan. "Where's the boss? I told you betrayal would be met with swift violence, sellsword."

"Just because I was hired for this quest doesn't mean I know what we're up against here." The Warlock gave a sheepish shrug. "Not the specifics, anyway."

I'd played way too many games to not know this song and dance. The boss wanted us to get in close, that's why the chest was at the base of the trunk. It wouldn't strike until we got in range.

"The chest, Otto. Open the chest, and I'll bet we flush this thing out." My voice was weaker than I'd wanted it to be.

Otto nodded, the nerves audible in his unusually loud grunt of approval. He was scared to get that close. I was scared for him to get that close.

"Everyone take your positions," he barked to the invisible forces and the Warlock's minions.

I got just within range of the tree; sixty feet out was as far as I could be for all my spells. The summoned minions spread out around the tree, and the Warlock pulled up next to me.

"This is going to be a show," he sniggered, and I gave him a narrow sidelong glance. At the back of my mind, I sort of hoped this tree-monster would whoop his ass. Otto bent down, rubbed his hands together like in the scene from *Indiana Jones*, then reached for the latch of the golden chest.

All at once, the room exploded in a cacophony of moaning wood and movement. My knees buckled as the ground shook like a magnitude 4 earthquake beneath our feet, and the aberrant tree jerked forward, then up, up, and up. The trunk sprouted from the rotted, bone-strewn earth until a ghastly, loose-skinned face, not unlike Grandmother Willow with fangs and a single eye, broke free of the dirt.

Morgan and I stared, mouths open, as the [Greater Corrupt Valdgeist] bared its six-inch fangs and yawned. This was *nothing* like the Greater Valdgeist from above. This thing was a nightmare come to life. The boss bellowed in defiance, strings of vile green saliva whipping from its maw as it rocked the cavern with its war cry.

The nightmare tree-creature snapped a massive branch at Otto's chest, cartwheeling him into the air. I lurched forward, desperate to do anything to help him, but there was nothing I could do except rally in his stead.

"Attack!" I launched my held fireball at the Corrupt Valdgeist, and Morgan's minions responded at my command. Burning Affliction took hold on the first hit, and the tree's lower branches were singed.

Otto landed with an "oof" five feet from me.

"Get up," I called to him, but he lay there, immobile. "Get up, you big lazy oaf! Make your keep, or I'm not paying you for today."

Otto groaned, rolled to his side, and downed a cherry-red potion. My racing heart fluttered with relief, then I returned my focus to the real problem: the boss.

I slammed the massive, evil Grandmother Willow with two more Burning Afflictions, followed quickly by Leaching Smolder, then unleashed hell with Fire Inside and Fireball after Fireball. The boss' Health bar jerked down with each hit, and even Morgan was providing some good DPS with his green bolts of corrupt energy.

I still had twenty seconds on Fire Inside and targeted the boss with Rain of Fire. The red targeting circle appeared on the ground with the monstrous tree right at the center, and I unleashed fury. Some quick math told me if 80% of the spell hit the tree, with the 50% bonus from Fire Inside, I'd deal close to 60k damage. The competitive gamer in me reveled in the thought of dealing more DPS than anyone else in the party. If only we had tracking mods!

Otto finally got to his feet and charged back into the fray, just as Cutter swooped in like a feral feline. The thief growled as he planted his dagger in the tree's single milky eye above the fetid maw, dropping the thing to 60% Health. There was still no sign of Jack, but that was probably a good thing; he was a bit gimp. I didn't want him to die all because of me, anyway.

Another red [1] blinked into the corner of my vision. Not this time, bitch. She could threaten me over PMs all she liked, but this boss was *ours*.

Cutter was bucked free and sent sailing across the clearing. He rolled into one of the stone pillars, and the glowing runes pulsed faster. The boss roared, spreading its branches wide in a menacing stance. A putrid green mist shook free of the outstretched limbs and swept over the clearing as white, gnarled roots sprouted under Cutter and Otto.

<<<◇>>>

Debuffs Added

Rooted: Your party has been rooted and is unable to move; duration, 1 minute.

Toxic Cloud: Your party is poisoned: 10 points of Stamina damage/10 secs; 20 points Health damage/10 secs; duration, 2 minutes.

Death Cloud: Instantly kill all summoned creatures.

<<<◇>>>

Damn it. Morgan and I were just out of reach, but Otto and Cutter, who could *die forever,* were caught in the choking fog. Morgan's summoned creatures dissolved into salty ash that dropped to the floor in tiny, conical piles. Otto slumped to his knees, sucking down potion after potion. The tree whipped him with smaller branches while the larger ones maintained the AOE. Despite the potions, Otto's Health continued to plummet.

No, bullshit. Not today, not on my watch. I was going to get to the bottom of this. I was going to get into that chest. And Otto *absolutely was not* going to die in the process.

I charged into the cloud and popped Fire Inside, then, with my breath held to avoid the wracking coughs brought on by the cloud's effects, opened my palms and let rip Inferno Blast. One, two, three Burning Afflictions piled up on the boss, and I hit it with Leaching Smolder again, my Spirit bar climbing like a mad hiker on a fourteener. I tried to back out of the cloud, but couldn't! The root debuff had taken hold, wrapping tight knots of sickly white wood around my cloth boots.

The burning ache of oxygen deprivation forced my mouth open and a gasp to overtake my determination not to fall prey to the AOE. The poisonous pollen filled my mouth, tasting of rot and bitter acid. I hacked and bent over, then fell to my knees as the debilitating debuff stabbed at my innards. I grabbed a Health potion from my bandolier and slammed it back.

I looked to a gasping Otto and a red-faced Cutter. There was nothing I could do to help them, and while they were just code, I felt sudden and desperate regret. This was all my fault. Not only were we not going to figure out what was in that chest, but Jack and I were going to lose our NPCs in the process. I was such a fool to think the five of us could've taken on the boss.

Movement caught my attention as a batshit-crazy outline of a stealthed Jack flew from the ledge behind the boss. He landed with a heavy thud, sinking his hammer into the boss' skull. The tree branches receded, and the cloud of death dispersed as the boss changed its attention to the serious stealth attack that dropped it to 35%.

No. We'd be all right. We could figure it out or fight our way out. We were going to get to the bottom of this Osmark mystery and put an end to his reign in Eldgard before it could begin.

"Get it, Jack!" I shouted, my confidence in our purpose renewed.

The Greater Corrupt Valdgeist bucked and twisted, trying to shake my friend from its back. Poor Jack slammed against the tree's shoulders over and over, his eyes squinted shut with determination and agony.

Fire Inside was ready again, so I chugged down a Spirit potion and started a Fireball cast. Just before it was ready, I popped my passive spell bonus and laid into the tree creature. Its rampant rodeo bull display quieted, and Jack gained his footing as he climbed the tree's mangled shoulders.

"Die, bastard!" I hurled fireball after fireball into the thing's face. The half-rotted skin shriveled at the touch of my magic, and the boss cried out in fury.

Jack held fast to the Valdgeist boss' head as he drove his hammer home like a baseball player swinging for the fences at a tiny, vile stub at the top of the boss' head. The thing's Health dropped by 5%. Then another 5%. Jack found the *weak spot!*

We could actually do this. Otto staggered to his feet, and Cutter stalked into the tree's guard. Just 8% left. I lobbed one last fireball at the monster. It shuddered, lurched, and keeled forward as its Health bar hit 0. I staggered backward, taking in the sight of the boss flopping clumsily to the ground.

Cutter stepped in the path of the falling tree. "Don't worry, friend, I've got you."

Jack pinwheeled and leapt from the boss' shoulders, just as Cutter stepped aside. Jack face-planted in the dirt, his Health taking a 10% dip from the fall.

Cutter stuck out his hand with a grin. "What I meant is, let me help you up."

Jack slapped his palm against Cutter's and grabbed hold. "Thanks, jerk."

I looked at the boss as Cutter went on about catching damsels and stealing their jewels. We'd really done it. A sense of dread and excitement surged down my limbs and up into my brain stem. That chest was ours now, and whatever was inside it would unlock the key to taking Osmark down for good.

The red, pulsating [1] drew my eyes back to the corner of my HUD. Whatever was inside it could doom us to a life of unending suffering, too. I was torn in half. One side wanted desperately to be the hero who saved humanity from a dictatorship, the other, a friend who wanted desperately to ensure her friends were safe from harm.

A sharp elbow in my ribs brought me back to the moment. I shot a glare at Otto, the source of the offending elbow, and he nodded toward Jack. He was brushing dirt from his pants, clearly uninterested in whatever Cutter was blabbering about.

I rushed toward them and threw my arms open wide. "Wow, Jack!" I pulled him into a tight embrace. "That was incredible. Seriously. How did you ever think of that?"

He wriggled out of my grasp and shrugged. "Lucky guess?"

"Well," I said with a bit over-the-top enthusiasm, "I don't care how you did it, that was a brilliant move. Seriously epic. I knew I picked the right guy for this."

His eyes sparkled with the shower of praise, and in that moment, I worried I might never see him happy again. I leaned in and pecked him on the cheek, the rough stubble of his five-o'clock shadow brushing against my lips. A stupid, silly grin spread over his face.

We were on the right path. Perhaps not a path that would leave us carefree, chasing quests and leveling gleefully, but one that would bring us a sense of duty. One that might get my mother killed repeatedly at the hand of my boss' personal assistant. No, totally unlikely. We did the right thing, and my mom was not going to get murdered for it.

I took a deep breath and blocked out the anxious thoughts. "Now, let's go see what's worth twenty million dollars."

THIRTY-THREE

PARTING WAYS

THOUGH THE DEATH CLOUD WAS GONE AND THE battle over, I felt like I'd been run over by a thousand angry bulls. My muscles ached, and stomach burned with an acidic fury. I bent down and inspected the Greater Corrupt Valdgeist boss.

One single key.

That was all it had. Fine by me, because I knew what it went to. I wondered if the chest was also rigged to set off alarms with Sandra or whoever was on the lookout. I wondered a lot of things as I held the large, gold answer in my hand. This would not just unlock the dungeon chest, but the *truth*.

Jack looked on the key with a greedy gamer's glee, one that I just didn't have. I wanted to be excited, I wanted to be freakin' stoked for whatever might be in the chest, but the dread of what came after was weighing me down.

I held the key out to Jack. "Why don't you do the honors?"

"You sure?" His eyes widened with worry and excitement.

I wrinkled my nose as I thought of opening the boss chest. No, I'd already opened one of those, and this was Jack's first. "I think it's for the best. Besides, you deserve first crack at the goodies—you did save the day this time around."

Jack shook his head in disbelief, then took the key gingerly into his grasp. He looked down on it with reverence, then turned 180 degrees and hurried to the chest, eyes still locked on the contents of his palms. We all followed, our movements jittery with the anticipation of a good heist. The chest popped open, and its inventory menu projected onto my vision.

Oh. Holy. Shit.

Why had I bought a new staff? Damn it, why had I bought a new staff for twenty gold! There, right in the chest, lay a [Staff of the Enchantress], definitely for me, and it was Ancient Artifact gear, just like Wildfire.

A round of whistles went by as I just cursed myself, looking at the chest contents. Alongside the new staff was also a new ring, [Ring of Insight]. Jack grabbed the two pieces of gear obviously intended for me and passed them into my hands.

The staff was smooth, old wood. Older than the realm of Eldgard, it seemed. When I touched it, ancient knowledge leaked down the shaft into my arm and tickled my brain. This thing was *wicked*. Just like Embergrave, this staff had a physical power to it.

The staff's wood twisted, with little knots here and there that emanated a soft white glow, like the very core of the weapon was light itself. The chestnut grooves all led up to a gorgeous, shimmering opal nestled in the grasp of the staff. This also glowed gently, like a disco ball surrounded by heavy fog machines.

J.D. Astra

I equipped it and the new ring in an instant, shivering at the rush of strength as power surged through my limbs.

Staff of the Enchantress

Weapon Type: Two-handed Staff

Class: Ancient Artifact

Base Damage: 50

Primary Effects:

- +20 Intelligence

- +20 Spirit

- +10 Vitality

- +5% Potency to Sorceress Spells

- +45 Spell Strength

- +50% Spell Critical Damage

- +10% Spell Critical Chance

All is right when the greatest Sorceress in Eldgard holds an equally great weapon.

Ring of Insight

Armor Type: Jewelry, Metalware

Class: Ancient Artifact

Base Defense: 20

Primary Effects:

- +5 Intelligence

- +3% Spell Critical Chance

- +10 Spell Strength

- +5% additional chance to detect all Illusionist spells

- Immunity to low-level Charm and Suggestion spells

When unseen powers are at work, your vision is second to none.

It was too tempting not to pan over to my stats for a quick look-see.

Name:	Abby	Race:	Wode	Gender:	Female
Level:	29	Class:	Firebrand	Alignment:	None
Renown:	1,200	Carry Capacity:	520	Undistributed Attribute Points:	0
Health:	870	Spirit:	1620	Stamina:	650
H-Regen/sec:	31.5	S-Regen/sec:	31.6288	Stam-Regen/sec:	10.495
Attributes:		Offense:		Defense:	
Strength:	10	Base Melee Weapon Damage:	25	Base Armor:	75
Vitality:	58	Base Ranged Weapon Damage:	0	Armor Rating:	83
Constitution:	33	Attack Strength (AS):	93	Block Amount:	2.5
Dexterity:	10	Ranged Attack Strength (RAS):	68	Block Chance (%):	17.69
Intelligence:	150	Spell Strength (SS):	280	Evade Chance (%):	4.9
Spirit:	133	Critical Hit Chance:	40%	Fire Resist (%):	33.9
Luck:	10	Critical Hit Damage:	60%	Cold Resist (%):	9.9
				Lightning Resist (%):	9.9
				Shadow Resist (%):	9.9
				Holy Resist (%):	9.9
Current XP:	8,900			Poison Resist (%):	9.9
Next Level:	35,180			Disease Resist (%):	9.9

Hells to the yeah, I was looking mighty fine.

"There's one more thing," Jack called, and I closed out the menu. Indeed, there was one more thing at the bottom of the chest that was neither gear nor money. A gold, flat disc the size of my hand lay at the bottom of the chest. True, the gear had been nice, and the gold from the chest was no chump change, but this strange object had to be the true prize.

Jack held it up to the light and read aloud the text lining the top and bottom: *Imperatorius Factio Signum* and *Domini est Terra*.

Otto stepped closer to him for a better look. "The top reads 'Imperial Faction Seal' and the bottom 'Lord of the Land.'"

"What does it mean?" Jack handed him the object, and Otto's face scrunched into frustration.

Otto's voice carried a tone of fear. "I don't know."

"Give it here." I put out my hand, certain that once I touched it my quest would update.

Sure enough, as soon as the heavy plate brushed my fingertips, the quest update popped into view.

Quest Update: On the Edge of a Blade Hangs Balance

You have traversed the secret dungeon and opened the fabled chest to discover an Imperial Faction Seal. You have earned 30,000 XP! The item will not reveal its purpose to you, and your local companions have never encountered such an item, so you will need to do some digging. But be wary in your dangerous travels, the Imperial Faction Seal can be stolen off your person both when you're alive… or dead.

Quest Class: Unique, Personal

Quest Difficulty: Infernal

Success: Gather your resources and discover the purpose of the Imperial Faction Seal.

Failure: Fail to identify the Imperial Faction Seal's purpose, or lose the item.

Reward: 50,000 XP, +20 to all base stats, not including Luck, and Sophia's Favor.

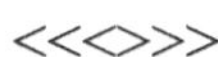

What the actual hell? *Sophia's favor?* The Overmind was beginning to scare me with her behavior. It was her purpose to keep balance in Eldgard, but this was just beyond what I'd expected to encounter.

"Let me take a look." Cutter put out his hand.

I shook myself from the trance, accepted the quest, and passed the medallion to him.

Jack shimmied up next to me. "Any ideas?"

"None." I sighed, though I did have a new, infuriatingly vague step to the quest that led to nowhere.

"Welp, I've never seen this thing in my life, but it looks important." Cutter passed it to Jack one more time.

My stomach roiled and tightened, the hot acid fury changing to something more like a tornado. Sweat beads formed at the sides of my neck, and my hands trembled with the feeling of low blood sugar. I checked the in-game time: 6 PM. Shit, I was coming up on seventy-two hours *fast*. I needed to get back to safety.

Jack bounded up the stairs to the hall he'd found at the back of the room, the hall I knew would magically lead us back to the surface. He grinned like a kid finding a secret passage behind the bookshelf in his grandfather's study, and I smiled at him.

The trudge through the tunnel was more taxing than it ought to have been, and I noticed my Stamina bar refused to refill. I huffed and fell to the back of the line next to Otto.

"You okay?" he whispered as Cutter popped out of stealth and surprised Jack, who punched him in the shoulder.

I shook my head. "I… don't feel great."

Otto put a comforting hand between my shoulders. "I've heard of this, Travelers having trouble transitioning into the world, something about a *dimensional shift*. You'll be alright, I'll be right here."

The gesture was a welcome comfort. If this transition was going to take me out, Otto would be there to watch over me as it happened. And if I came out the other end alive, he'd be there to get me back to health. Three days, that was all the time I'd spent with him. Yet in those hours I'd grown closer to Otto than most of my friends, maybe even my mother. Guess the Devs really did their homework with the companion pairing.

Evening light shimmered at the opening of the exit tunnel, and we all picked up the pace. It was good to feel the sunshine again, even if it was dying light. The orange and pinks cast across the sky like soft beach sand washed by rippling waves. I wanted to make it. I wanted Leon to make it, and Tristen.

Jack was basking in the sun, sucking a deep breath of fresh forest air. He looked so happy, so peaceful. I wished I hadn't brought him into this shitstorm, but maybe I could keep him safe yet. I could keep the quest a secret, follow it with just Otto, and we'd get to the bottom of it while Jack got his damn class kit. What a slacker.

I walked toward him with my best smile on, despite the pain and clammy heat in my chest. "Well, I think it might be time for us to part ways for a bit."

Jack's face wrinkled from serene to confusion in an instant. "Wait. What? Why would we do that? We worked great together as a team. Jack and Abby all the way." He chuckled and threw out a fist for a bump I didn't return. "We rocked it down there."

"I know. And this isn't over." I pushed a bit of sweaty hair behind my ear. "But right now, I think it's best if we divide and conquer. Otto and I, we need to go see some people. Ask around about that weird disk we found. See if we can find out what its purpose is."

I wasn't sure if Jack had his bind spell, but fortunately, I'd asked Naitee to give me a few scrolls for that, too. I searched through my inventory and grabbed a scroll of return off the stack of five I had and held it out to Jack. "A portal scroll to get you home. This'll take you to your bind point, wherever that happens to be."

His lip pulled to the side in a classic-Jack uncertain grimace as he grabbed the parchment. He was so damn cute and kind. I wished I hadn't dragged him into this crap. Jack pulled the Imperial Faction Seal from his inventory and held it out to me.

I remembered the part of the quest that said the seal could be stolen off my dead body by anyone and knew that any *good* thief could steal it right out of my inventory. Sandra was coming for me, but she didn't know who Jack was. It was definitely safer with him. Hopefully the quest would recognize that Jack was in my party, and the seal being in his inventory wouldn't mean it was "lost" to me. I shook my head and held my palm up to reject the item.

"Better not. I think it's safer with you for the time being. I stumbled on this info by snooping around in company records that, strictly speaking, I wasn't supposed to have access to. By which I totally mean I hacked them. So, when Aleixo Carrera shows up here and finds this place empty, he's going to start asking questions over at Osmark Technologies, and those questions will likely point to me. It'll take a while before they find out about you, though." If ever, unless they captured me and Otto or Morgan.

Jack's face squished even more, his dark cheeks getting round and frustrated. "I hear what you're saying, Abby, and I believe you. I do. But there's something you're not telling me. Some piece of the puzzle you're purposely leaving out."

The sweat on my neck and the fire in my chest swelled at his mention of "something else." Yes, there was more. There were three PMs from Sandra about how I shouldn't be digging around or she'd tell Osmark. But there was also my seventy-two hours. Something simple, easy. Something I could give him to put his mind at ease, not in panic mode.

"I'm coming up on my third day, Jack. Just a few hours away now. That's why I needed you here so quickly. Statistically, one in six die during the transition, which means in another five or six hours, I could be dead. Gone." I snapped my fingers, and he jumped. "Just like that."

His eyes softened, and my heart melted. "I don't want to put you through that, Jack. I know it probably doesn't make much sense, but if it's my time to go, I want to be alone." Otto shifted at the word *alone*, and I gave him a kind glance.

"So," I went on as Jack's heart visibly sank, "I'm going to head back to Harrowick, get a good, hot meal, and go to sleep. If I wake up, then I guess I survived and I'll PM you. If not…" I shrugged. "Well, know that I wish the absolute best for you."

He licked his lips, brow scrunched and eyes fixed on the ground, then stuffed the Imperial Faction Seal back in his inventory. "What should I do now?" He shrugged helplessly.

I sucked in a breath. "You need to get a little rest, and then you need to acquire a class, Jack." I scolded him like an old maid. "As is, if you weren't reasonably smart and passably good-looking, you'd be entirely useless to the party. So, while I do the legwork and turn up leads about what that trinket does, you find out what kind of character you're going to be and start maximizing your stats."

He nodded along with me. Jack seemed to be in it for the long haul, seemed to be on board with what I pitched at him, saving all of humanity as it was. I was scared to depend on him, but it was time that the lone wolf died and a new Abby embraced the pack.

"I have a feeling things will get really intense around here before long." I offered him a smile, some bit of kindness to warm his dreary disposition. His eyes glistened, and I saw past the dark skin, hair, and eyes, to the Jack I knew from school.

The Jack who held my hand or locked arms with me on the way to class. The Jack who moved from server to server with me until we found a good PvE spot and we formed Crimson Alliance. The Jack who was there for me, all the time.

I turned toward the clearing, the ache in my chest threatening to bring tears to my eyes. I wished I hadn't let that slip away. I wished I hadn't let that school fondness get snuffed out without a single kiss, but it was too late now.

Or was it? What if I died? What if I didn't make it? I wanted to live at least a single moment like it could've been. And what if I lived through the transition? What if he lived? We could have a fresh start on a thing that could've been great?

I spun back and threw my arms around his neck, pulling him in tightly. He wrapped his arms over my back and held me just as tight. Like when Naitee had held me, it felt like the best thing, the kindest thing, I'd ever felt. I missed hugs so much.

"I know we didn't work out in college, but if we both live through this, survive the next few days, maybe we can do things differently this time around." I pushed my face into his chest and sniffed deep, keeping the wall of tears behind the facade of calm.

One in six wasn't terrible odds, but maybe I'd never get another chance like this. I turned my head up and pushed onto my toes, planting a single, warm kiss on his dark lips.

"In case this is our final goodbye."

His tranquil expression dissolved back to worry, and I gave him a gentle pat on the cheek, then turned to leave. Otto's heavy footfalls followed behind me, and I popped the seal on one of the scrolls of return.

My fingers touched the shimmering portal, and gravity left me as I departed the clearing.

THIRTY-FOUR

Death Sickness, The Other Side

Vertigo struck when I landed on the oaken wood floor of the Boar's Head. No one was there to greet us except… Meredith? I wasn't sure if it was her or her sister. Still, the sight of only her brought me comfort. Sandra didn't know where we were bound and didn't know we'd finished the dungeon yet. I hoped.

"Sit where ya'd like!" the bartender called to Otto, and the Risi tromped to his usual booth along the far wall. I followed, the queasiness canting me to the left and right as I made my way to the seat.

"So," Otto started in, all business, "did you get a quest update?"

I nodded, my throat feeling weak and narrow. Uncomfortable heat swelled in my chest, and I pulled at the neckline of Wildfire.

"Do you need to go?" Otto asked, his words distant and garbled.

"No." I snatched the water cup as it went down in front of me and swallowed in big gulps until the glass was emptied.

"She a'right?" a woman queried as the room spun into oblivion.

I struggled to keep my head up, propping my elbows against the table for support.

"Otto..." The word barely left my lips before my face slammed down, and I lost track of the world.

"Hold on, just hold onto me. You're going to be okay."

My mother's wicked, beautiful, bile-puking face appeared in my mind. "You never even came to say goodbye."

Her face warped into Osmark's as he pushed his glasses up his pompous nose. "You leave now and I'll make sure you never get paid to write another line of code in your life."

Pain swelled in my head and surged down my limbs. I stiffened and cried out, grasping at the cool hand that held mine.

"Don't do this to me, Abby. Don't die, not like her. Don't die."

Tristen's hopeful smile popped to the forefront of my mind. "It was nice being your manager. I hope you make it!"

My fifth-grade teacher handed me an aptitude tablet. "What do you want to be when you grow up?"

Jack's downtrodden, puppy-dog eyes came full view. His face lingered, hanging in a black ether before he spoke. "I guess this is goodbye, then."

He'd wanted me to ask him to stay, to stay with me, be my boyfriend. I'd gotten the internship with

Osmark Technologies, and though he had no prospects in California, he wanted to stay for me. I knew now what I didn't understand then.

I never prioritized Jack. I never made him the thing I woke up for, got out of bed for—it was always the code. I never treated him as important as he really was to me, and that's why it didn't work. That's why he left. That's why they all always left.

I gasped, clutching my chest as I lurched forward. The room was dark and smelled of onions. The bed below me felt like straw with a blanket cast over it and lumpy rocks below that.

"You're awake." Otto's voice was close, just to my left. "I didn't think you were going to pull through with the way you'd been screaming."

His voice cracked with the telltale tone of tears. Candlelight flickered behind me as Otto struck a wick to life with something sharp. I pushed my knuckles into my eyes and rubbed at the agony. My head was splitting, my mouth dry, and my throat raw. The nerves in my skin itched with the heat of an open bonfire two feet in front of me.

"Where are we?" I rasped. "What time is it?"

His gentle hand pulled my fists from my eyes. "It's 5:13 AM, and we're in the secondary pantry of the Boar's Head."

"Why?" I moaned the *y* out much too long and flopped back down on my straw mattress.

"Sandra." The mention of her name set my hairs on end and snapped my eyes open. "She found us. Luckily we'd paid Meredith well enough to warn and help move us before Sandra and a brigade of Imperials stormed the inn."

"Is everyone okay?" I grabbed Otto's arm as he set the candle down on a small desk. Dark circles ringed his eyes.

He nodded. "They got us down here just in time. I had to pay Patel a bit more than I wanted, but we're safe, and they're safe."

I inhaled the oniony musk and relaxed. I'd transitioned. I'd freaking made it! A message from Osmark Technologies Customer Service blinked in the corner of my vision, and I deleted it outright. I didn't have time for that shit.

"Otto, we need to find out what this Imperial Faction Seal is all about. Osmark and at least twenty of his goons all have one. These could be game enders for anyone not siding with the Imperials."

He placed a hand on my shoulder and lowered me back to the bed I hadn't realized I'd left. "We have time."

"No," I prompted, "we don't."

I checked the countdown timer for the new leg of the quest: 9 days, 2 hours, 4 minutes, 6 seconds. Just when Astraea was scheduled to hit. Something was going to happen, something big, and we needed to get ahead of it.

He didn't seem convinced, so I pressed it. "This quest has an expiration date. Just over a week. And by then, my world will be destroyed."

My world, my mother, my everything will be destroyed, and I'm trapped in here with my boss hell-bent on ruling over us like some kind of rightful king. Angry tears formed at the creases of my eyes, and Otto's face melted from frustration to sympathy.

"I'm sorry you had to come here," he started, and I held up a hand to cut him off.

I chose to come here, I wanted this. And honestly, the idea that I could live out my life in a fantasy game was sort of the awesome silver lining to everything on Earth being incinerated. And now I would, because I'd made it. I'd transitioned. Now, I was just the same as Otto: a series of code running on a server.

"I'm not sorry I'm here, and I'm glad that you are too."

He smirked and placed his hand against my forehead. "Fever must've messed with something."

I slapped his hand away with playful indignance. "Don't start, I'm not getting all mushy on you. I need a strong doofus to take all the aggro from the bad guys for me, that's all."

We chuckled, and I held my ribs as spikes of pain shot up into my stomach and throat. Otto passed me a glass of water, and I chugged it down. The cool liquid didn't lessen the pain or the fire, but it felt satisfying.

"Tell me more about the quest." Otto went back to business, taking the deadline seriously.

"It just says 'the item will not reveal its purpose to you, you will need to do some digging.' I assume that means more investigation, but unlike the first leg of the quest, it's not giving us any sort of direction on *where* to dig."

Otto nodded thoughtfully. "Alaunhylles has a Grand Archive, one of three in Eldgard. It holds all of the knowledge of the world. If we're going to find something, it'll probably be there."

My splitting head ripped through my train of thought as I laid out the plan for the next steps on our journey. Get to the archive, find the information. No, get to Naitee first, get a teleport scroll, get to the archive, find information, report back to Jack, take down Osmark. Okay, we could do this.

I looked to Otto in the flickering orange of the candlelight. He'd stayed by my side through my death sickness, carried me to safety, and paid off the bartender of a bounty hunting club. It was obvious he wasn't going to leave my side, and for once, I didn't want him to.

"I need to send a message, and then"—I leaned close to the candle and puffed it out with a single breath—"we're going dark."

Books, Mailing List, and Reviews

If you loved VGO: Firebrand and would like stay in the loop about the latest book releases, promotional deals, and upcoming book giveaways be sure to subscribe to the Shadow Alley Press mailing list and get a free copy of our bestselling anthology, Viridian Gate Online: Side Quests! Your email address will never be shared and you can unsubscribe at any time.

www.ShadowAlleyPress.com

Word-of-mouth and book reviews are crazy helpful for the success of any writer—or in, in our case, Publishing Company. So, if you *really* enjoyed reading about Abby and Otto (or VGO in general), please consider leaving a short, honest review—just a couple of lines about your overall reading experience. Thank you in advance!

Looking for more Viridian Gate Online? Continue the adventure right this minute and get the book that started it all—Viridian Gate Online: Cataclysm!

Already a fan of the original series? Well, then check out the next book in the VGO Expanded Universe, Viridian Gate Online: Vindication (The Alchemic Weaponeer Book 1). Or keep reading to take a sneak peek!

Vlad Nardoir is a Russian weapons engineer who has learned to live with compromise. A prototype can be attractive or functional. A man can work or have his legs broken. A husband can watch his wife die in a state hospital or borrow money from the mob. A soul can be chained or it can be crushed into dust. Freedom is never a choice.

After forty-three years of being a tool in the hands of the oligarchs, Vlad's life has reached critical mass. His wife is dead, he owes a debt he can never repay, and there's an extinction-level asteroid hurtling towards Earth. In a wild twist of fate, he has found a way out. Uploaded to a virtual online world called Viridian Gate Online, he's got the knowledge and the grit to prove the old adage: in Soviet Russia, the tool fixes *you*.

ONE

TIMES OF CRISIS...

Timeline - 4 days before Astraea, 09:45

"INA, IT HAS BEEN TOO LONG." I SAT WITH MY legs crossed at the grave of my beloved. The grass, what little remained of my small backyard, was overgrown and dying. There had once been flower beds under the windows of our home, they were a riot of colors, all shapes and sizes. Flowers I could never keep, but Ina was different. Plants thrived under her eyes, they flourished under her care. Sadly, those were also dead. I had a friend who worked in the Stone Masonry carve Ina's headstone, made of a dark black marble. It was truly gorgeous. He had done a fine job, it looked like her, even down to the way her auburn hair flowed in the wind. He had captured every detail I could remember, everything she was in the picture I had given him to recreate. It was a simple scene, we were at a festival in the Saint Petersburg Plaza, she was looking at the statue of Catherine the Great, the wind blew, her hair bellowed in the wind, and the picture was perfect. She was my own personal Catherine.

"I regret that we cannot be together any longer." I choked back a tear, no, I did not have time to cry. There was much work to be done yet. Time for crying would come later. I stood from the grass and laid a small bundle of flowers at the grave. She wasn't buried here, of course. She was buried in the National Cemetery, for her work to advance the science of Chemistry in Russia. It was the one thing that Mother Russia had given her. The flowers were purchased from one of the small flower stalls nearby, one of the last bundles they had. I was late leaving work again, and it was shameful for me. Bah, regrets are a powerful thing. I needed to get my mind off of her. It had been six months since she passed away, and the pain was still too fresh. Perhaps having her memorial in the backyard was not such a smart thing after all, but I wanted to keep her close, and the grave yard where they buried her was too far away for frequent visits.

I went back inside, and shook my head at all I saw. The house was a mess, I hated cleaning. Ina was always so good at keeping after that. I would make a mess, she would clean it up. We had an understanding. We also had grumbling. But we made it work. I took a sip from the coffee I had made earlier, and forgotten about.

"Shit, tastes like week old engine oil. And not even high test." I tossed the coffee cup into the sink harder than I intended. It shattered on impact, little chips flying in every direction.

"Ina, your coffee was always perfect." I looked down and clenched my fists, caked with years of work, grime and oil. "This was not what was in my head. It is not what I intended." The smell of multi-part oil and degreaser invaded my nostrils, and I was taken back to another time.

Ina had just started working for the National Laboratory's Saint Petersburg branch shortly after attaining her doctorate in Chemistry. She started as a basic research assistant, working on a new type of oil that would last a near limitless time. She quickly advanced through the ranks, working harder and faster than anyone else, until she had taken a position as a Head Chemist in the Chemical Manipulation Department. Ina had always told me that working in the Chemical Plant would kill her; I had thought she was talking about it being the end of her career path, though I often said her genius would last forever. She once clarified that it would be due to the vials that were left open absent-mindedly, or the frequent spills due to careless laboratory technicians. I had not expected her to be so right.

The cancer took her within a year's time. I watched my beloved Ina devolve from a gorgeous, intelligent woman into a bed-ridden husk of what she once was. There was nothing I could do. All of my knowledge and expertise, my absolute genius, was useless. Russia had withheld treatment towards the end, as a result of some perceived debt to society. After all, Socialized Medicine paid for Ina's expensive chemo treatments - well, some of them. The medicine was too expensive for the insurance to pay for, and about halfway through, the medication was not covered at all. There were some situations where we had to seek alternative funding, and Ina no longer could work to cover the costs. Wasn't the cost of having Ina for just a little longer in my life worth absolutely anything I could pay? Mother

Russia, in her "Infinite Wisdom," had taken Ina from me. One day, I knew I would get back at her. Perhaps not in this lifetime, and perhaps not The Motherland herself, but I would fight back.

At the end, she held my hand, gave me the best smile she could afford, and told me she would see me in paradise. When Ina was pronounced dead, it wasn't an hour before Osmark technologies , a virtual world where people would be able to find a new place to exist after the Astraea asteroid struck. It's not as though we could have put her into the game before she died, the system wasn't around yet, and the framework wasn't stable. As luck would have it, or fate, or whatever you want to call the fickle bitch, Almez-Antev, the weapons developers I worked for, had connections and ins with Osmark Technologies. I pulled a few strings, made a few promises that I knew I would never be able to keep, and suddenly Ina and I were admitted to the program.

I regretted making those promises, especially since I was expected to contribute to any future war effort within VGO, on behalf of the big wigs. It felt like a waste, all of the work I had done to renovate the basement to admit a pair of VGO capsules, and I had spent days and weeks working on it. I ran electrical, I adjusted network propensities, and I improved the layout. I even did some off the books excavation to expand our room. I looked at the watch on my wrist, the hands moving with flawless precision. One of my own designs, a small twinge of pride hit my heart, but bounced off the cold exterior. I still had a few hours before I needed to meet the deadline for my transition into VGO, and there was still that project for Almaz-Antev that needed finalizing. Namely the nuclear automata that would usher in the new age of people on Earth; tasked with cleaning, demolishing and rebuilding after the impact.

At one time, Almaz-Antev was the premier weapons manufacturing company for all of Russia. They had colluded with other nations, of course. There was nothing to be done for that. My weapons killed a lot of people, and there are regrets I will never be able to put aside. But now is not the time for regrets. Now is the time for action. "There is still time," I said absentmindedly. "I will fix some of the mistakes I've made. First though, I must wash this mountain of dishes."

I set about to working on the broken coffee cup, gently placing the pieces in the waste bin. The noise from the city street outside my small house filtered through the cracked window, stuck open from the years of Saint Petersburg winters. I had promised Ina I would fix it, but always there was another important thing to be done. It got pushed back further and further, until there was no time left to fix the small things. "Ina, I am so sorry. I will fix the things that I can soon." I pushed the anger and the pain back into its space and finished the dishes.

The six months since Ina had passed had been very challenging, and there was more than one time where I had completely fallen apart. I had lost considerable weight, simply from forgetting to eat, forgetting to sleep. I threw myself into my work, and Almaz-Antev was happy to see the improved work ethic. While Ina was sick, I was almost fired. That would have endangered everything Ina and I had worked so hard for. It would have voided our passes into VGO. Now hers was gone, and so was she. "No, I cannot fall back to this, the anger, the sadness. Always, it comes back to her being gone. I cannot focus on that now, there is so much to do before the morning." I needed to work, I needed to get my mind off her.

Timeline - 4 days before Astraea, 16:52

In the evening, I retired to my basement workspace. I neglected to eat dinner, and as a result, found myself getting easily irritated. "Two more screws here," I said. Talking to myself while working helped me to focus. It allowed me to make sure I didn't miss any steps while making things. And this project was important. The radiation shielding needed to be perfect, both from inside and outside. "Will check the Geiger counter later, I don't have time for this shit." I set the machine core to the side, and changed my focus to another portion of the machinery: the converter. "This will need sturdier wiring. Perhaps dioxymethylene coating will suffice? No, too caustic. That definitely will eat through cables in a few decades. Something stronger, a polycarbon wrap?"

I leaned against the table, both palms flat against it. "Ina would know what was best. She was the best chemical engineer in all of Russia." I slapped my hands down hard, harder than I had thought, rattling the pieces all over the table. The machine core bounced off the table and smacked against the ground. The sound of crunching metal greeted my ears with a toothy smile. "God Dammit! Everything is going wrong!" I picked it up from the floor and cradled the broken core in my hands. "Well, it clearly isn't strong enough yet." I chuckled as I stared at the cracked and broken core. "Back to the drawing board." I shrugged as I tossed the prototype core into a pile of other garbage.

Several hours later, I ended up with a much improved core. It had significant resistance, and I was working on the last bolts. They needed to be sealed with a specific corrosion-resistant material, which I also had manufactured with Ina's help. "Only last bolts, now. Then I can scan and send the schematics to Almaz-Antev, easy as cake. Is that how that goes? No, no, that is not the adage. English is ignorant." I rolled my eyes as I picked up my wrench, hefting it in my hand. The weight felt good, it felt real. It kept my mind focused as I worked. Halfway through fastening the last bolt, which required a considerable amount of force, my hand slipped off the spanner, and raked my palm across the now-stripped bolt head.

"Ahhh!" I shouted in agony as blood poured from my hand, my tool falling to the floor. "You stupid piece of shit!" I picked up the machine core and hurled it as hard as possible against one of the block walls in the basement. It smacked against the wall and fell to the floor. The clang of heavy metal resounded around the small room. "God dammit all!". I stepped over to the medkit I kept in the basement and wrapped up my hand. "Another setback." I headed over to the core on the ground, and picked it up. I turned it about in my hands and noticed that everything was still intact. "Huh, is much stronger. Eh, bolt is not in perfect position, but Almaz-Antev will not care, I am thinking. Project complete."

I spent a few moments scanning the project blueprint into my computer, using my 3D scanner, and emailed it off to Almaz-Antev. Within seconds, I received a confirmation email. Along with a short commision at the end. "Godspeed, Vlad Nardoir." That was it, then. Well, that and to see the grave of my lost beloved one last time.

TWO

BREAKING BONE AND SHATTERING BOND

I HEADED BACK UP TO THE HOUSE AND FOUND A GUEST in my kitchen. The man stood a head and shoulders above me, with a slightly bulging belly that strained against the buttons of his well-tailored black suit. The rest of him was nearly all muscle. I recognized him immediately as my old childhood friend, Bruno. He was standing in the kitchen, looking through some of the cupboards, making himself at home. "Well, this is unexpected, to say the least." I raised my hands to show no hostility towards him. I had not expected to see a member of the Russian Mafia in my home.

"Vlad, it is good to see you have not fled." Bruno was imposing, as he always was. Today, though, he was even more so, easily outweighing me by a solid fifty kilos. "It would not do Almaz-Antev, or my fine employers, any good if you were to disappear before your debts were paid."

"Ah, Bruno." I backed myself up a little bit, and found myself against a wall. "I do not know of what debt you speak. I have paid off what I owed." I wrinkled my forehead, trying to think of what I still owed, but nothing came to mind.

"You see, Vlad, Viktor is looking for the blood price you owe. We spent a lot of money getting medication for your Ina, and now we are owed a debt. The Motherland is more forgiving than we are." Bruno sat heavily into a chair at the kitchen table. He shrugged his shoulders as though it wasn't a big deal. "But you see, there is not much time left, and Viktor, he does not like to wait. He said something about you moving to some kind of different world, the same place he is going. Vermillion Glands, or something?"

Bruno pulled a pair of brass knuckles from his pocket, slipping them onto his fists. My heart was pounding like it would leap out of my chest and scamper across the floor. I looked around for any kind of exit from this situation. I remembered the VGO pod in the basement. I remembered the smell of Ina's hair. I remembered that I wasn't going to die, not today.

"Bruno, let us talk, I will make coffee, we can share Vodka, yes?" It was a ploy to get him to relax, I was hopeful it would work out.

"Ah, so hospitable. You know Vlad," Bruno laid a heavy arm on the table, the wood groaned under the weight. My heart skipped a beat as I heard the chair shifting, expecting him to get up, but he didn't. "I don't remember you ever making coffee. That was always Ina's thing." He plastered a hard smirk on his face, I knew he was being an ass.

"She was always better at it," I said, hiding my anger at his comment. "But I can make it just fine. Might taste like mud, or engine oil, but it works." I set about making said coffee, I also pulled a bottle of my finest Vodka from the shelf. I wasn't going to need it where I was going, or if I was going to die tonight.

"How long have we known each other?" Bruno sighed as he slipped the brass knuckles off his hand and set them on the table. He was letting his guard down, good. Sometimes Bruno asked stupid questions, sometimes he just forgot. He had received a nasty blow to the head shortly after he started working for that Mobster, Viktor, as a bouncer at a Mafia-run club. It was 43 years ago that our parents had given birth in the same hospital, and until he joined Viktor's crew, we were close friends. Sometimes I liked to think we still were. He was present for Ina's funeral, he was there for me when we found out she was sick. He was actually the one who reached out to me when the chemo wasn't covered any longer. He was still a good man inside somewhere, but he was better at following orders than he was at keeping his friends and jobs straight.

"You know well enough," I said as I lit the gas burner on the stove and set the coffee percolator on the flame. I needed to make a plan, and I had one in the works. I just didn't want to have to follow through with it. I used an unnecessarily large amount of room to get everything ready, making sure I could reach my goal. I needed to reach the knife block.

"It seems like yesterday we were going to University together. You were promising and intellectual. I was a mass of raw muscle." He poked at the flab that had started to show over his gut. "Some things have changed, others have not." He raised an eyebrow at the equipment I had strewn about the kitchen and dining room. Nearly all of it was my own design, some of it was from various jobs I had handled throughout the years. "You know, I was almost hired by Almaz-Antev as well. Well," he laughed as he looked away. "I guess I technically still work for them. Hired muscle through their connections." He tilted his head to the side and a loud pop issued from the bones and muscles in his neck. I nearly knocked the coffee kettle over from being startled. I also almost knocked the knife I had acquired from the cabinet onto the floor, which would have given away my intentions. I didn't want to have to use it, but it was a likely conclusion that I would have to. I turned around and carefully slid the knife into the back of my pants, blousing my shirt a bit to cover the handle.

"We don't have to fight, Bruno. Take whatever you want, I have money saved, you can take that too." The coffee was done, I poured a pair of cups, and spiked them both with Vodka. Heavily. I was going to need all the courage I could muster for this next act.

"No, see, Viktor was clear. I bring you back broken, or I don't come back at all. He is beyond wanting money now. You made him mad, he thinks you stiffed him on the bill." Bruno took his cup with a small smile and took a large drink. "Ah, that is good. And the Vodka was a good touch. You were always heavy-handed." He set the cup down and looked at me with remorse. "I am sorry, old friend, but this is where friendship ends, and work begins." He stood and replaced his brass knuckles, smacking his fists together as he wound up to take a swing. I reached around behind my back to grab the knife. The blade felt clumsy in my hands. I hated bladed weapons. He stopped for a moment, then a sly smile rolled over his features. "You were not going to go down easy, always the hard way my friend." He took a heavy swing from the side, and I scrambled out of the way. His fist slammed into the countertop where I was standing just a second before. Cups rattled and bounced, my freshly washed dishes shook in the drying rack. The blow was so strong that it knocked Ina's favorite coffee mug off of the spindle it hung on. It shattered on the floor. The sound of it breaking hurt, like years of memories shattering against cold, uncaring stone. I knew I couldn't get hit by the force of Bruno's swing, I simply wouldn't survive.

"Damnit, Bruno, you're better than this." I was already shaking from fear and anxiety, I didn't need to fight for my life. This was a problem. "I don't want to hurt you, we can still leave this place as friends. I will give you everything I have."

"You, hurt me? You're a brain, Vlad, and I'm a muscle. There will be only one person with pain tonight." He took another swing, and I backpedaled into the large grandfather clock against the wall. It rang as the chimes within bounced around. I dug my blade into the wood behind the clock and pushed with all I was worth. The massive clock creaked and groaned as it fell towards Bruno. He put his shoulder into it, and shrugged it off. The man was a beast, for all that age. The cacaphony of the metal inside the clock's body was painful to hear as the wood splintered and smashed against the floorboards.

"I'm warning you, Bruno. Stop this and we can be friends again. I'll forget it all." I didn't want to end up beaten and battered. I lunged forward and swiped at him with my knife. It left me terribly open, and he punished me for it. I received a quick jab to the ribs for my effort, knocking the air completely out of me. I doubled over on the floor in pain, the knife slipping out of my hands as I wrapped myself in my arms. I gasped for air as Bruno stepped forward, rolling his hands together, cracking his knuckles.

"Only one punch, Vlad?" Bruno sighed heavily as he loomed over my breathless body. Wracking coughs had started to pull air back into my lungs. "You used to be so much more resilient. This is what working with tools and technology all your life gets you." He went to stomp on my head, but I rolled out of the way just in time. His foot hit the ground heavily enough to rattle the dishware and the coffee cup he left on the table. I scampered up to my hands and knees, grabbed the knife, and was almost clear of him until I felt the collar on my shirt stiffen.

"Hurk," I spouted as I was pulled backwards. He had the grip of a rabid bear. I struggled against the clothing restraining me, but it was no use. Before I knew it, he had lifted me into the air with a bear hug. My lungs were beginning to burn as he crushed my torso between his massive arms. "Bruno…" I coughed and choked as I squirmed, my vision starting to darken. Right before my sight left me completely, I had a moment of clarity. The knife was still in my hand! I swung for all I was worth with it, trying desperately to get a cut, a knick, anything that would cause him to release me. After what felt like an eternity, the blade found purchase. It sunk deep into his right thigh, and I was rewarded with him dropping me. The bellow he let out was enough to nearly deafen me. Everything was going to hurt in the morning, for sure. I collapsed to the floor as my body was basically dead weight. I sucked in hard lungfuls of air, doing everything I could to make my body respond to simple commands. Look around, get up, move, get away from him. Nothing was working.

"You put a knife in my leg, you dirty shit!" Bruno continued to howl as he sunk to the floor. I was hoping the blade would simply get him to release me so I could get away, but it seemed as though I had hit a nerve. As I watched the blood spurt from his leg, I realized I had hit something much more important. I had driven the knife into his femoral artery. He was going to bleed out without medical attention. My brain went through a million potential outcomes, but only one mattered. I stretched out and reached for the towels that hung from the handle on the stove. I grabbed both of them, and managed to crawl over to where Bruno was gasping.

His skin tone was already changing to ashen grey mixed with blue. He was losing blood fast. I wrapped the towels around his upper thigh, above the wound, and tied them tight. Then I ripped a large piece of my shirt off, removed the knife from his leg, and stuffed the clothing into the wound. It was immediately soaked in blood, a bad sign. I hadn't meant for the blade to bite so deep, I hadn't meant for him to be bleeding out! My tourniquet wasn't working as well as I had hoped, probably because my dexterity and strength were still reduced from nearly being crushed to death. His eyes started to glaze over as he stared at me. "Vlad, Vlad, please…" His words were gentle and full of fear, and for just a moment I saw that child I had grown up with. My heart shattered.

"Bruno, I am so sorry." I hadn't meant for him to die, I had intended to talk him down, to find a common ground. Maybe even to part as friends. "I didn't mean for this to happen," I said to him, holding his hand which I had gripped without thinking. His hand was so much larger than mine, but his grasp was gentle.

"I...I know I didn't do right. By either of you." His words were slipping now. They were coming slower, his gasps were shallow. "I am sorry, friend." The last words from the one person I had known my entire life were an apology, as he died. I sat there with him for some time before I was able to come to grips with what had happened. I had killed a man, I had killed my best friend.

Timeline - 3 days before Astraea, 00:21

I buried Bruno in the backyard under the dark of the night. I had cleaned up the floor of the dining room as best as I could, but I was still covered in blood. I hadn't thought to take the time to clean myself up. I didn't care, I was exhausted and needed rest. I looked at my watch, which was spattered with dried, flaking blood. I was almost out of time, I needed 72 hours inside VGO to be able to fully transition, and that time was almost up. I kneeled at the shared grave site of my most beloved wife, and my best friend. The shovel fell from my grasp and I sobbed deeply. I could no longer hold it back, and I didn't even try to stop it. There was literally nothing left for me here. I had killed the only person I still cared about, I should have let Bruno take me back to Viktor. I was broken, I was shattered like a glass that was carelessly tossed away. Everything I had in this life was gone. The emotional trauma was almost too much, I would have rather been tortured by the Mafia. At least that pain would subside, either in my death, or when it was over. This pain, though? I expected it to last forever.

Timeline - 3 days before Astraea, 05:19

I don't remember how long I laid there, but I remember waking to the rising sun on my skin, the cold of Russia's morning greeting me with its teeth. I remember panicking, because now I had almost no time left. It would be a near thing, for sure. I brushed myself off, and rushed inside. My pain from the fight last night was screaming at me, everything was agony. My body was nearly in spasms from the effort.

The dew from the morning had made the blood on my hands and clothes fresh again. I left smears on the walls as I stumbled from room to room, heading to the basement. I placed my bloodied palm onto the biometric reader that unlocked the steel blast door I had installed. It beeped and slid open. I trudged in and fell to my knees before I reached the capsule. I dragged myself up the face of it, leaving a trail of blood on the pristine chrome. I punched in a series of numbers on the locking mechanism.

There was a *whoosh* of air as the capsule unsealed. I heard the blast door behind me slam shut, and the three-step locking mechanism kick in. Everything was moving at a feverish pace as I pushed the door to the pod up, so I could get into it. I grabbed the assist handrail and pulled with everything I had. My muscles complained, my lungs burned and ached, and my head felt like it was on fire. I finally worked my way into the pod and watched the pod door close slowly, pressurizing.

"Goodbye, Ina. I will see you in the next life." It was all I could say before the pod sealed, and the processes within the capsule initiated.

The pitch black surrounded me like a blanket, consuming the last glimpse I had of the light of my workshop, until a "loading…" notice came on-screen. I was being logged into Viridian Gate Online.

An intense realization swept over me, I was starting a new life. It had nearly cost me everything. No, it *had* cost me everything. But I was still alive, and that was something worth fighting for.

My last memory of Earth was pain in my chest, not from the fight the night before, but from never seeing my home, my wife, my friend, my house, ever again.

Quest Alert: Continue Reading Vindication

Continue with Vlad to find out what happens next!

Quest Class: Rare, Class-Based

Quest Difficulty: Easy

Success: Read on to continue the adventure!

Reward: 15,000 EXP; Title: Experimental Engineer

Accept: Yes / No?

ABOUT THE AUTHOR

About me... I'm a baller. Keyboard crawler. 20 inch display, on my ink scrawler. Holler. Getting flayed tonight, all my characters getting splayed tonight!

In my spare time I love to cook, hike, play video games, and spend quality time with my people.

Three questions people never ask me are; how do I look at myself in the mirror, what's in the box, and what does it take to build a story with likable characters in an interesting setting with important goals?

The answer to the last is determination, dedication, and sacrifice. I've been working at being a writer since before I could string more than two sentences together, and it never gets easier, but it does get better.

I'm surrounded by people who love and support me, which is the most amazing gift the universe could ever give. I will never give up, never surrender, and hopefully, keep on entertaining for the rest of my life.

VIRIDIAN GATE ONLINE: EXPANDED UNIVERSE

Viridian Gate Online: Cataclysm (Book 1)

Viridian Gate Online: Crimson Alliance (Book 2)

Viridian Gate Online: The Jade Lord (Book 3)

Viridian Gate Online: Imperial Legion (Book 4)

Viridian Gate Online: The Lich Priest (Book 5)

Viridian Gate Online: Doom Forge (Book 6)

⏚

Viridian Gate Online: Side Quests (Anthology)

Viridian Gate Online: The Artificer

Viridian Gate Online: Nomad Soul (The Illusionist 1)

Viridian Gate Online: Firebrand (Firebrand Series 1)

Viridian Gate Online: Vindication (The Alchemic
Weaponeer Book 1)